Also by Lucy Atkins

The Missing One
The Other Child

the
night
visitor

the night visitor

LUCY ATKINS

Quercus

First published in Great Britain in 2017 by

Quercus Editions Ltd
Carmelite House
50 Victoria Embankment
London EC4Y 0DZ

An Hachette UK company

A CIP catalogue record for this book is available
from the British Library

HB ISBN 9781786482044
TPB ISBN 9781786482181
EBOOK ISBN 9781784293239

10 9 8 7 6 5 4 3 2 1

Typeset by Jouve (UK), Milton Keynes

Printed and bound in Great Britain by Clays Ltd, St Ives plc

For Sam and Ted, my boys.
And for John, always.

'The Creator, if He exists, must have an inordinate fondness for beetles'

J.B.S. Haldane

'But what will not ambition and revenge
Descend to?'

John Milton, *Paradise Lost*, Book Nine

Prologue

Olivia

The Hunterian Museum, Royal College of Surgeons, London

Olivia huddled behind Arteries, Heart and Veins. Through the gaps between the tall specimen jars in the cabinet she could see the faces on the ground floor, looking up at Joy on the balcony. It was such a long way down.

The room was packed: all two hundred guests must have come. She couldn't see their faces properly because the jars of hardened arteries and diseased heart tissue were acting as a screen and she didn't want to look as if she was peering through them. She watched Joy's animated profile instead. Joy was saying very kind things. Olivia felt sick.

'Straight in at number two! That's what we consider a triumph!' Joy's scarlet and gold earrings caught the light as she raised her champagne flute and cried, 'A bestseller in its very first week. So, how about it? Shall we take it to number one?'

A cheer rang out through the museum; raucous voices lifted, echoed off the high ceilings and shivered through the glass display cabinets and medical oddities – faces torn by bullets and

bombs, dissected limbs, diseased and malformed organs suspended in cloudy fluid. Bones, so gigantic that they must surely
be from whales or mammoths, were displayed between the
ground floor and this, the mezzanine. Under the clever, bleached
lights they looked so curved and smooth-lined that they seemed
more like sculptures than fragments of anatomy.

'In case you missed it, there's a table by the entrance where
you can get the book for Olivia to sign,' Joy said. 'But that's enough
of a sales pitch from me. Let me hand you over to the woman of
the hour, Britain's favourite history professor, Olivia Sweetman!'

There was nowhere to put her glass so she held on to it as she
stepped forwards. Joy squeezed her arm and moved out of the
way. Olivia walked up to the Perspex-covered railings and looked
down.

It really was too high – ridiculously so. What were the publicists thinking, putting her all the way up here for the speech?
She would have been better off standing on the stairs or even on
the ground floor with the guests gathered round her. But it was
too late, all their faces were turned up, flushed with champagne
and the energy of the night and this spectacle – her – standing
alone in a yellow dress, glowing and supposedly triumphant.
They were all waiting for her to speak.

She took a deep breath. She longed to unfurl wings and soar
off this edge, over their heads and away to somewhere remote
and hidden where none of them would ever find her, but she
forced herself to speak. 'Thank you so much, Joy, what a kind
introduction. And thank you, all of you, for coming tonight to
celebrate the launch of my book.' Her voice came out clear and
calm even though the glass in her hand was trembling. She
rested that on the barrier too. She was used to public speaking,
to facing a crowd and being listened to, but it was different to

be looking down at friends, family, colleagues, journalists, TV people, bloggers and critics with this awful, sickening secret pressing in her gut like a tumour.

'I hope you can all hear me? It's an awfully long way down and as some of you will know I'm not that good with heights.'

There was a ripple of laughter, voices called up in encouragement. 'We'll catch you!' someone – a man – yelled from the back. She wondered if the people directly below her could see up her full-skirted dress. She crossed her legs.

'OK! Well, it's amazing to be here with you tonight in this wonderful Hunterian Museum to celebrate the launch of *Annabel*.' She noticed David standing at the front. His face was a mask of neutrality. Jess was at his side, her bobbed hair held back by a hairband. She was holding his hand. There was no sign of the boys. Olivia smiled directly down at her daughter but Jess didn't react; perhaps she was more interested in the grisly objects in the cabinets that framed the balcony.

'It seemed fitting to have the launch at the Royal College of Surgeons.' She gestured at the cabinets. 'Isn't this an extraordinary museum?' She knew she was stalling, unable to bring herself to talk about the book. She scanned the crowd for Dom and Paul but she couldn't see either of them. She had to control this sick panic inside her – she had to sound relaxed. She'd prepared the speech about *Annabel* and they were all expecting it. She could, she would, deliver it.

'I didn't just choose to write about Annabel because of her diary, though her personal story is certainly sensational . . .' She heard her voice waver and took another deep breath, forcing herself to continue. 'I wanted to do something bigger. I wanted to acknowledge the debt that we owe Annabel Burley and all her brave Victorian contemporaries at the London School of

Medicine for Women. These women had to fight for their calling in a way that few of us today can possibly comprehend . . .'

When she came to the end of her speech, there was enthusiastic applause, whoops, cheers. 'I have so many people to thank,' she said. 'I honestly don't know where to start. *Annabel*'s a collaboration, really.'

She noticed *The Sunday Times*' literary editor standing directly below her. Their eyes met and she saw something – a glint, perhaps, a certain chill – that made her wonder whether he could possibly have discovered, or somehow intuited, the truth about what she had done.

She felt cold, suddenly, as if someone had cracked a hole in the ceiling to let the October night in. She forced herself to smile. 'So – thank yous! Right. I hope I don't forget anyone . . . First of all, I'm so grateful to my editor, Joy, who has given me unstinting support and direction. And my agent, Carol, I don't know where I'd be . . .' She ran through the list she had prepared, thanking people one by one.

'I also need to acknowledge that without the meticulous and detailed research help I got, *Annabel* would have taken years to write and would have been a far worse biography. I'm truly grateful for all the help I had putting this together.' She knew that it was bizarre not to mention Vivian by name. She hoped nobody would notice this omission. She was banking on the fact that, for most of the people in the room, research was a process, not a person. If they thought about it at all, they would envisage postgrads in public record offices – not a dogged and blank-faced sixty-year-old housekeeper.

But she must not think about Vivian. Not here, not tonight, not now. She tightened her grip on the balcony. If she was going to get through this she had to erase Vivian from her mind completely.

'Finally – and I'm going to try really hard not to get too emotional – I want to thank my beautiful children, Jess, Paul and Dom. They're all here somewhere. Thank you for putting up with all my distractions, absences and grumpiness.' Jess was beaming, but she still couldn't see her boys. Dom was probably smoking on a bench out in Lincoln's Inn Fields and the last time she saw Paul he had been Snapchatting a necrotic skull. 'You're so patient and remarkable. I love you three so much.' She felt her voice break. 'You're . . . my whole world.' She cleared her throat and straightened her shoulders. She couldn't let herself disintegrate. The attention in the room had tightened; everyone was suddenly too still, too quiet, the pack sensing weakness.

She hardened herself. She had rehearsed this final part while standing in the toilet cubicle an hour before. 'So, last of all, my husband, David Linder.' She leaned over a little and lowered her glass in his direction. Their eyes met; she didn't blink or look away, she kept her voice low, steady and powerful. 'What can I say? A brilliant writer – no stranger to the bestseller list himself – popular psychologist, columnist and devoted father. How can I possibly quantify what you've done for me, for this book and for us, as a family? You are . . . well, quite simply, you're extraordinary.'

David's face flushed deeply. His body remained motionless but he forced his mouth into a twisted smile while everyone around him cheered and lifted their glasses in his direction. Jess was looking up at her dad, perhaps perturbed by his stillness. She noticed Emma standing behind them, in a pallid shift dress, and Khalil was there, too, next to Emma. Neither friend was smiling. So they must know, Chloe must have told them. She scanned the room, but she couldn't see Chloe any more. Perhaps it had been too much for her and she'd slipped away.

'OK!' she said. 'I'm going to have to stop before I embarrass myself. There are some gruesome medical-themed canapés floating around – has anyone dared to try a quail's egg eyeball? Please help yourself to those and please drink lots of the fizz! Thank you, again, for your extraordinary love and support. I'm just so grateful to you all for coming. I feel really lucky to have you. Thank you!' She raised her own glass and took a swig.

The museum erupted into enthusiastic applause, cheers, more whoops, even a piercing whistle, which she felt sure was Dom, somewhere at the very back.

As she was scanning the edge of the room for her eldest son she glimpsed a figure disappearing through Curiosities – not Dom – a bulky shape, face obscured, wearing a long dark overcoat, and she felt the guests, in their glittering clothes, all their noise and body heat, pause and recede. She narrowed her eyes and strained to see but the figure had vanished into the gloom. It couldn't be. She was imagining it again. The party was invite only. A stranger would never have been let in.

And then Joy's arms were around her and she smelled her familiar musky perfume. 'Well done! ' Joy said. 'That was perfect!'

She hugged Joy back, then clung to her and for a moment she felt as if Joy was holding her up, and were the other woman to step back and release her, she would fall to the floor.

'Are you OK?' Joy hissed in her ear. Then Carol was there, squeezing her shoulder – 'Well done!' – and both agent and editor were steering her away from the balcony towards the broad curve of the stairs.

'You were just great!' Carol said.

'And now there are books to be signed.' Joy guided her to the top step. 'Two hundred of them.'

She felt her ankle weaken and flip on the too-high heel; her knee buckled and she lurched forwards, but Joy grabbed her arm just in time, yanking her back before she could plummet headlong down the staircase. 'Whoopsie! Don't fall – we need you in one piece.'

But Olivia didn't reply because, as they rounded the corner on the stairwell, she was already scanning the shadowy margins of the room, searching not for the figure in the overcoat, but for the one person she dreaded seeing even more than him, the one person who knew the truth and might tell it. Vivian.

Vivian

Ileford Manor, East Sussex, two months previously

Summer has not come to Sussex this year. It has rained incessantly since early July and now in mid-August it shows no sign of abating. Sometimes fat balls roll from the clouds and bounce off the well cover and courtyard, filling all the dips and runnels, but mostly it is just a mindless grey drizzle that scribbles everything out.

I have taken to writing things down while I have my elevenses in the library every morning. I have bought a special notebook and I do it most days now. I need to make sense of how I come to be in this uncertain position. Writing things down seems to ease the chaos in my mind a little and, of course, it occupies my brain. After all, I cannot just sit here and wait for her. Not again.

My thoughts are as hectic as ants disturbed from a nest, they cannot be corralled. This is partly a result of sleep deprivation. Sleep has been problematic since I lost Bertie, but since *Annabel* came to an end the problem has worsened considerably. Last night I didn't drop off until very late. I slept fitfully for an hour or so but then, as I knew she would, my visitor woke me, just before dawn.

When Bertie was with me she almost never came. He protected me from her as he did from so many of life's painful troubles. He was also a great comfort on the rare occasions that she did come. He would calm and reassure me; we would go and sit together in the kitchen, wrapped in a blanket, until my breathing and heart rate were steady. But now that Bertie is no longer with me, now that I'm alone again, she is back and it is as bad now as it was when I was an adolescent – perhaps even worse. For the past nine days she has appeared in my room nightly.

Perhaps the tension of waiting for Olivia has something to do with this. My mind has certainly become overactive. While there is always the cleaning and upkeep of the house – leaks to fix, dampness to treat, roof tiles to pin – these tasks do not occupy my brain. I did not realize how dependent I had become on working with Olivia, what purpose it gave me, until it was over. For eighteen months my mind has been engaged. I had almost forgotten what it felt like to be stimulated by work. I was *interested* again, I was developing new skills and learning about the past.

I also, and perhaps this is the greatest surprise of all, miss the contact I had with Olivia. I have developed a great fondness – yes, even admiration – for Olivia, and I never for a moment believed that would be possible.

My email inbox is eerily silent now. The manuscript has been edited, though I have not seen the finished product. It is two months until publication and my services, it seems, are no longer required. It is hard to adjust to this. I have become accustomed to opening my computer every morning after breakfast to find my inbox full of Olivia's messages: responses to my queries, instructions on a new line of enquiry, discussion about how to approach a particular issue or section. Now all this is over, my inbox is a wasteland. This morning I had four emails: one from a company offering knockdown deals on remedies for malaise or pitfall traps, another selling beating trays, a third, walking boots and a fourth announcing the Marks & Spencer summer sale. I long for the words '*Dear Vivian*' . . .

My coffee is getting cold though I seem to have eaten my two biscuits without realizing it. I know I should not have the digestives every morning but this has been my habit for decades now and habits are very hard to change. The mere sight of the oriental ladies on the biscuit tin seems to calm and reassure me. They are almost the only thing, now, that connect me to my old life and routines. I have always found it hard to let routines go, even when they no longer serve me well.

The library door is open and the faint sound of the leak in the gunroom ceiling echoes across the great hall. Drops of rain burrow through the plaster, pause, then clang into the bucket. Ileford is in a permanent state of disintegration, it spits water from every joint, swells and groans and leaks around me. I seem to be constantly calling out roofers and plumbers and damp specialists. Increasingly I feel as if my body is mimicking the house. The joints of my fingers are swampy and tender, my ankles are swollen and pockets of gas explode between my vertebrae when I twist or turn. My left knee is particularly troublesome. Sometimes it is reluctant to bend at all.

I have to get away from this place. I am impatient to get started on the new book. For the first time since my retirement I can see a future for myself, but Olivia has gone silent. She has not even responded properly to my last email. I fleshed out the

Chocolate Cream Poisoner idea for her in the hope of a more specific response or even instructions to start on the background work (which, of course, I already have). I sent it to her exactly nine days ago now, six full days before her departure, so she has had plenty of time to think about it.

Of course, I know that Olivia's life is very different to mine. She is terribly busy, there are a great many demands on her time. But she could, at least, have given me an indication of her intentions. Instead, all I got was, *'Thank you for this, I'll certainly take a look when I get back from my holiday.'*

It never occurred to me, when I began this, that I might end up working with Olivia, or even that there would be a book. My plan was simply to allow her to write an academic paper on the diary.

I had a strategy worked out for piquing her interest. I knew she was likely to come to the Farmhouse at half-term, so I managed to persuade Maureen to visit her sister in Jersey while I filled in for her at the museum. I knew it would be better if Olivia came to me rather than the other way around.

If that hadn't worked – if she hadn't responded to the flyer – then the next step would have been to write to her explaining that I had a sensational and unseen Victorian source, and offering to bring it to her Bloomsbury office. I would have said I had seen her BBC documentary about insane Victorian women and felt sure that Annabel's diary would be of interest to her. She would not have been able to resist a document that Annabel called *'my sole confidant'* and which contained a startling confession – what historian would? Fortunately, I did not have to go to her because the flyer brought her to me. I don't think I really believed it would until she burst through the museum door with her wet child that February day. I was very shocked. I froze behind the desk, unable to look at her, braced, as if for a blow. For a few moments I could not even speak.

And now here I am eighteen months later waiting for Olivia again, albeit in a very different frame of mind this time. This time I am full of such hope, impatience and agitation that I almost cannot bear it.

That's why, late last night, I decided to take matters into my own hands. I decided to take a holiday. To the south of France.

I leave the day after tomorrow, which will give me time to clean and shut up the house. I have booked the ferry and a modest bed & breakfast – they call it a *chambres d'hôte* – and I plan to spend a week walking in the low altitude Provençal hills looking for harlequin ladybirds. The harlequin is a worrying, devious, mimicking species, a most destructive invader and so charismatic. I have always had a soft spot for ladybirds.

The library shutters are open today but layers of rain blot out the view and I can barely see as far as the wych elms at the edge of the lawn. Rain is a brutal jailer, it cuts one off from the world, seals all the edges. It is probably not healthy to be alone so much, even if you are by nature a solitary person, as I am. When Lady Burley and Bertie were here the rain did not bother me at all. Bertie and I would bring the coffee and biscuits into the library on a tray every morning and the three of us would sit together and discuss whatever needed to be done that day. It felt reassuring and calming to hear rain lashing at the windows. When Lady Burley went to the care home it was just Bertie and me, but we did not lose the elevenses habit. Rain rarely troubled us. I would just put on my Barbour and get on with it. Now it is only me, though, I find myself preoccupied by weather. There is no cosiness any more, just the aching damp and the leaks.

I still miss Bertie, intensely, daily. Every day as I pass beneath the minstrel's gallery with my tray I feel as if he is by my side. It can be a jolt to settle into the wing-backed chair, reach for my coffee and find that I'm alone. Perhaps writing things down is also a form of companionship. If so, it is a poor one, because when I lay down my pen I often feel more alone than ever.

The problem, of course, is that I have allowed myself to become tied up in another person's life. Other people are messy; they have a tendency to let you down. It is my great hope that Olivia will turn out to be different. We share a passion, after all, and we are a team now – she said it herself – so she surely will not disappoint me.

But as I put away my notebook each day, I ask myself the same question: What on earth will I do if she does?

Olivia

South of France, Day One

The front doorstep of *Mas Saint Pierre* was an actual tombstone. Olivia dropped her bags and crouched to look at the faded lettering. The word 'sacré' was etched into the stone beneath her plimsolls but the rest of the inscription – a life packaged between two dates – had been erased by generations of feet crossing the threshold. The pocked stone made her think how insignificant it all was, really, their stresses and worries, hopes and fears, how quickly erased and forgotten all this would be. She must keep things in perspective. She could fix this. She had to. Nobody had died.

She heard David stomping across the gravel courtyard below and she straightened, sucking in the hot, herb-scented air.

It had been an interminable drive down through France, but of course the ferry was cheaper than five of them flying. They were three hours later than planned. There was no sign of the others so they were probably lost too. The sat nav didn't work and the sign at the property gate was so decrepit, so snugly cradled in rock, that they'd had to circle back several times before they spotted it. By then Paul and Jess had been fighting, savagely, over a packet of dry French biscuits that neither of them liked while Dominic, plugged into headphones, had let out intermittent snarls and thrown an occasional slap.

When she'd eventually noticed the sign, Olivia had wrenched the steering wheel so hard that they'd almost slammed into the rock face. The children yelled, the car bumped up onto the roadside, wheels hurling up gravel and dust. 'Jesus Christ!' David had clutched at the dashboard, theatrically. She'd said nothing, but when he'd got out to open the tall iron gates she'd put her foot down and driven up and around the corner, leaving him to follow on foot.

She'd pulled up in the shady courtyard beneath the house and next to a crumbling limestone tower. The tower was just a couple of storeys tall with a single slit window. It was in the shade of the hillside, surrounded by silvery olive trees. She had a feeling the owners had mentioned it – a connection to a priest, perhaps – or maybe the ecclesiastical house name had implanted this idea in her mind. She wasn't sure. She had, in fact, only a very hazy memory of booking the place back in January. Work had been so intense at the time.

The house was up some stairs. It was pale, low and wreathed in vines, with lavender bushes lined up along the front like patient purple hedgehogs. It looked beautiful, and expensive. She'd never have booked it if she'd known then what she knew now but she had to put that out of her head – they were here, it had all been paid for months ago. She had to try to push everything aside and enjoy what she could of this holiday.

The August heat was intense even this late in the day, the heavy air busy with the high, tinnitus whirr of cicadas. She knew that she should go back down and help David to bring up the remaining bags, but she didn't want to help him. Jess and Paul were out of the car and over by the tower now, shoving at its peeling front door. Dom was still in the back seat, as if the long drive had softened his fifteen-year-old bones. If they brought him regular food and water he'd probably choose to spend the entire fortnight right there.

David had the boot open and she watched him lift out the bags. His shoulders were solid from his daily swims, his linen shirt crumpled, hair dishevelled, his jaw shadowed by stubble and his skin, always olive-hued, now lightly tanned from a recent week in the States. He looked a little tired, admittedly, but also robust, as if he was stubbornly oblivious to the chaos he'd created. It was unreasonable to resent him for his good health and his optimistic, handsome face, but at that moment she just couldn't help herself.

The tower behind him seemed to tilt slightly, as if wearied by all the comings and goings, all the petty family dramas it had seen. She remembered then that the owners had called it a 'cabanon'. They'd said something about an unsafe upper floor.

'The tower's locked,' Jess yelled over the courtyard. Paul had flopped onto its front step, his pale and gangly legs spread out. The poor boy looked so limp and dejected, like an unwatered plant. He needed feeding. He always needed feeding. At thirteen, he was growing about an inch a day.

'Come on,' she called down. 'Help Dad with the bags. And tell your brother to get out of the car!'

The Parisian owners had extended the place but it didn't look as if it could accommodate three couples and six children. She must have checked this at some point, but she'd been so stressed when she was booking that she couldn't remember the details.

She'd just transferred the vast sum of euros and forgotten about it. David was coming up the stairs now but Jess and Paul had vanished behind the tower. She heard Jess scream, 'Lizard!'

'Christ,' David dropped the bags and pointed at the doorstep. 'Is that a *gravestone*?'

She shrugged and tucked her hair behind her ears. 'The door's locked.'

He held up an old-fashioned key with an ornate handle. 'It was in an open box at the gate,' he said. 'I assume it's for the front door.'

She took it from him.

'Didn't they leave you any instructions?' he said, as if it was all her responsibility.

She looked back at him, blinked, and then she replied, quite slowly, 'They said they'd leave the key in the box.'

The entrance hall was dim and cool. They dumped the bags by an armoire that smelled of beeswax. Jess shot past them. Her long golden hair undulated and her new sandals slapped on the flagstones as she vanished down the hall and through a doorway.

They followed her into a cool living room. Olivia felt a wash of relief as she took in the open-plan kitchen, a pale-hued living area and a wall of French windows through which she could make out a vine-shaded terrace, wooden sun loungers, a long trestle table, a generous swimming pool and a view of dusky hills. Jess started wrestling with the locks.

'Well, not bad.' David went into the kitchen. 'Not bad at all.' If he felt that they shouldn't be here then he wasn't going to let it show.

He was obviously planning to behave as if nothing had changed. Perhaps he was right to take this approach. Nothing

would be gained by ruining the next two weeks with recriminations, guilt and apologies. And yet the effort of maintaining this
pretence already felt immense to Olivia. She felt as if they were
balancing an unexploded bomb between them and if one of
them dropped their end it would detonate, taking out the whole
family.

Dom slouched past her into the kitchen and straight to the
fridge. 'The doorstep to this house is a gravestone,' he growled as
he passed her. 'Is it just me, or is that fucking creepy?'

Paul opened the French windows and he and Jess burst onto
the terrace. Behind her, she heard David say to Dominic, 'There's
nothing in the fridge, buddy, we need to unpack the food first.'
Dom did not reply. He walked past his father without looking at
him, onto the terrace. How much, she wondered, did Dom know
about his father's recent actions? Was that what this was about?

But Dom's refusal to speak to David predated all this. She'd
read about the teenage boy's need to separate from his father in
order to define his own personality, but Dom seemed particularly vehement about this, particularly incensed, as if David had
committed a heinous and unforgivable crime.

He was standing, feet apart, looking at the view. He was
almost as tall as David and good-looking, like him – even-featured
with intense dark eyes and a dimple on his square chin. His
shoulders were broad, too. From behind he looked more like a
man than a boy, a stranger discovered on this foreign terrace. He
felt like a stranger these days. She wished that she could find a
way to talk to him, but every time she tried he shut her down.

'Can I go in the pool?' Jess was by her side, tugging at her
T-shirt. 'I want to go swimming.'

'Do you want to look round the house first? You could help
me sort out who sleeps where?' Olivia held out a hand.

'OK.' Jess ignored the outstretched hand and ran off down the hall.

Jess had firm opinions on where they should all sleep. At eight, she was relentlessly forceful and independent. Olivia wanted to kick off her shoes and lie in a darkened room but she followed her daughter through the house, agreeing with everything she said.

She was fundamentally shattered. She had been up till two or three every morning for weeks now, finishing the *Annabel* proofs, trying to clear her desk, writing student references, ploughing through submitted papers for September's interdisciplinary Language of Insanity conference. She would weep from exhaustion as she brushed her teeth, then she'd fall into bed, before getting up at seven again to have breakfast with the children and to walk Jess to school.

On top of the academic work there had been a last-minute article for the *Telegraph,* an overdue *History Today* piece and a BBC History blog about corsets. In the past week alone she'd made an early morning visit to Sky News to review the papers and had been into the *Today* studio to talk about anachronisms in the latest ITV Edwardian drama series. Somehow, on top of all that, she'd also spent several hours going through the script for a new Channel 4 series. It had been to the producers, executive producers and the channel and had now come back to her riddled with factual errors.

There had been a mid-week lunch, too, with Carol, to talk about TV offers. She'd committed to an appearance on *Pointless Celebrities* – though she'd never watched it and didn't understand the rules – but she still had to decide about the BBC prime-time offer. Carol was trying not to put the pressure on, but it was obvious that she desperately wanted this to happen.

'It's a big commitment but just think of the exposure,' she had said. 'Think how many more books you'll sell and how many more offers you'll get if you do this. It'll open up so much to you.' The thought of dancing on prime-time TV – the degree of exposure and possible humiliation – filled Olivia with dread, but the one thing Carol hadn't said, and of course meant, was 'Think of the money'.

What Carol didn't understand was that, apart from anything else, she'd lose all academic credibility if she accepted the BBC offer. She'd probably have to take a sabbatical to do it but it was more than that, she was already battling with other people's misconceptions. Some historians were openly condescending about her now. David dismissed all this as envy but it could be upsetting nonetheless. At a recent conference she'd overheard an Oxford history professor, an older woman who she'd always looked up to, saying, 'Oh, Olivia Sweetman, the telly-don? I've got no time for eye-candy TV academics. She isn't a serious historian.' She'd wanted to take this woman aside and remind her that she'd spent twenty-five years in serious academia, that she'd published two well-regarded, complex and highly academic books and that there was nothing wrong with inspiring the general public. She wanted to point out that she was still a professor at a leading university and that there were academic advantages to making TV shows too: she got to pick up and touch precious documents she'd normally only be allowed to see in microfilm; she had access to experts, manuscripts and places that she would never normally encounter.

There was also an undercurrent of misogyny in some of the academic sniffiness. One influential male historian, on hearing of her book deal, wrote in a column that she was *'the latest photogenic historian to secure a lucrative deal for yet another historical Mills*

& *Boon*'. She'd submitted a furious piece in response but it still astonished her that such knee-jerk reactions were given airtime. Others felt as if they were free to discuss her appearance and judge her on it. It was true that she'd worked with stylists for one or two of the shows; she now knew how to dress better and her appearance had changed because of it. She knew she was more attractive in her forties, and better dressed, than she ever had been. But this didn't mean she wanted people judging her on her clothes and hair, feeling that they could comment freely on them, or dismissing her mind because of how she looked. Recently, at a photo-shoot for an American magazine, she'd actually been asked to put on a tutu. She'd asked herself, 'Would Simon Schama put on a tutu?' When she refused to do it, she overheard the journalist on the phone, presumably to his editor, saying 'She's a difficult woman'. If she put on sequined dresses and started dancing on prime-time TV she'd destroy what credibility she still had among her colleagues. Worse than that, she'd lose respect for herself. She just couldn't do it, no matter how much they paid her.

Sometimes, juggling these identities felt exhausting. She was driving herself insane trying to do it all, something had to give, but she loved her work, all of it. She belonged in the lecture hall and the archives, but she'd found a freedom in front of the camera; there was a genuine joy in bringing history to a wider audience. She also loved being part of a team, the glass of wine in the pub with the production crew at the end of a long day's filming, the feeling of collaboration. The idea that her TV shows could ignite an interest in someone who might never have picked up a book also made her feel that it was worthwhile.

But writing *Annabel* to such a tight deadline, and dealing with Vivian, had almost pushed her over the edge. She badly needed a break. Her thoughts were scattered, her stomach felt perpetually clenched. But with the *Annabel* launch less than two months away, there was a huge list of publicity tasks to do. Her suitcase was full of work.

The only consolation – and this was a colossal relief – was that she no longer had to manage Vivian. Every time she remembered this she felt a weight lifting from her chest. She could put Vivian behind her now. They could both move on.

She had responded in the vaguest possible terms to Vivian's first three emails, in which she'd outlined an idea for a new book. Eventually, after the sixth message, she had replied, rather more firmly, that she would get to it when she got back from holiday. At some point she was going to have to sit down and break it to Vivian that they would not be writing another book together. But she didn't need to think about that now. Vivian, at least, could wait.

The upstairs rooms smelled musty, corridors twisted off corridors like the branches of an old tree and she saw that, although the layout was more complex than it seemed from the outside, there weren't enough bedrooms. Some of the children were going to have to sleep in the old priest's tower.

As she and Jess came back into the living room she heard a splash: Paul was in the pool. Dom was still dressed, standing on the side. He called something in a deep voice to Paul, who ducked, displaying his boxers and very white feet. David was still in the kitchen, unloading a box of beer that he'd bought at Carrefour.

The master suite was palatial, with floor-to-ceiling windows, a pitched ceiling, pale walls and an ornate dove-grey French bed. Under different circumstances she would have looked forward to falling into it with David, but right now the thought of him touching her filled her with cold, chemical fury.

She cranked the shutters open and looked at the bruised hills and the valley below, with pale village rooftops clustered around a church tower. At that moment, its bell tolled, a forlorn sound that echoed off the hills and grew louder and louder until she felt as if it had entered her brain and would never stop.

Dom had stripped off and was in the water with Paul, then Jess burst out of the house in a polka-dot bikini. Currents of light spiralled to the ends of her hair as she ran to the edge and leaped.

She heard the floorboards creak behind her. David was at the doorway. They stared at each other across the room for a second and neither of them spoke. Then he stepped in. 'Well,' he said, jovially, 'this is very nice.'

He came over and they looked down at their children. Paul bombed into the deep end, almost hitting Dom, who cuffed him, spraying water; Jess was waist deep, roaring at her big brothers, wading through the shallows, the ends of her hair released of their tension and spread across the water's surface.

'They're happy.' She folded her arms and managed to swallow the 'at least'.

He looked at her. 'We aren't?'

It was such a preposterous question that she couldn't even reply.

'Let's not let it spoil the holiday, Liv,' he said, gently. 'I don't want to keep apologizing. We're here now, let's make the best of it.'

She moved away, went over to the bed and tested the mattress. It was hard, but she longed to crawl onto it anyway and blot everything out with sleep. She sat on the edge and yanked at the heels of her sweaty plimsolls.

'Do you think it's bad if we take the master suite?' David threw himself on the bed behind her. He folded his arms behind his head and let the air out of his lungs. His linen shirt was half unbuttoned; dark chest hairs fanned out.

'We should probably ask the others.' She hated the strangled, uptight sound of her own voice. She wished that she could parcel up the past fortnight and pretend that everything was still fundamentally working between them.

The dust from David's trainers had scraped a long grey shadow on the bedspread. 'You know best thing about this room?' he said.

'What?'

'It's about as far away from the children as we can possibly get. They could be murdered in their beds and we'd still get a good night's sleep.'

She wanted to accept this lame attempt at humour, lean across the awful gap and take the offering, lie down next to him, rest her head on his chest, but she couldn't do it. She wasn't ready to laugh. She wasn't ready to forgive him – though she wished that she were. She didn't want to feel like this, she didn't even like herself like this. She got up and walked into the marble en suite, which smelled of bleach, bolted the door and went over to the window. She could see the roof of the car and, behind it, the priest's tower, surrounded by scratchy-looking olive trees.

It wasn't far across the courtyard. The three older boys could sleep there. This place was perfectly safe – they were in the middle of nowhere. Buried in shadows, the tower's slit eye watched her back.

As she cranked on the shower and peeled off her clothes she felt a small but insistent voice calling from the folds of her subconscious, warning her about something in a whisper so faint that she couldn't make sense of it. It wasn't just exhaustion or anger at David; it wasn't the gravestone at the front door, which had set the mood all wrong. It was deeper than that, more fundamental. Something inside her was off-kilter and fearful. As she stepped under the jets of water she had the feeling that the spinning disc of her life was dipping on each turn and she could neither correct it nor anticipate its crash.

Vivian

Ileford Manor, August

A wind has sprung up and violent gusts of rain spray the kitchen windowpanes as I eat my lunch: four slightly slimy slices of ham, a hard-boiled egg and lettuce that is definitely past its best. Yesterday, I cleaned the upper floors and my shoulders ache from reaching up to do all the spiders' webs, but I cannot rest. There is still so much to do to secure the house before I leave tomorrow morning. There are nineteen items unchecked on my list, including tackling the fridge. It does not feel right to leave the house anything other than shipshape. If something were to happen to me, I would not want people to think I neglected the place now that Lady Burley is no longer here.

Since I came to Ileford five years ago I have not left the house for more than the occasional night. It is a relief to be going away for a whole week but also a great responsibility. So many things could get out of control – roof tiles falling, leaks springing, intruders slicing through glass – without me here, watching.

When I first arrived at Ileford, the place was in great

disrepair. There was so much to do and, of course, I had to look after Lady Burley, so I could not have gone away even if I had wanted to. She was frailer than she had led me to believe but I did not mind that. In fact, it helped to know that I was so useful. I had accepted her job offer because I had nothing else to do and nowhere else to go. I had lost my home, my job, my future – everything I cared about in the world. It is no exaggeration to say that my early retirement felt like a death sentence. The routines of more than thirty years were taken from me; everything I had worked for – my security, my identity – was wiped out, more or less overnight. They simply erased me.

Lady Burley offered me a lifeline, though she did not know it. But even that was not enough for me. I was in a very dark place indeed. The repetitive tasks of sorting out Ileford and looking after Lady Burley kept me going, though internally I was in disarray. I really do not know where I would be now, had it not been for Olivia and *Annabel*.

I never believed that I could possibly be interested and engaged by anything again. But *Annabel* did that for me. Indeed, towards the end of the project I almost felt that I had been reborn. This is not to say that working with Olivia for eighteen months was an unmitigated joy – far from it. Olivia can be extremely frustrating to work with. She is always so distracted. Her life is so full, overfull: she constantly juggles people and projects, she is overstretched, preoccupied and can occasionally be narcissistic, high-handed and thoughtless. But she can be kind, too, and her intellectual energy – the sheer joy she finds in her subject – is infectious. We are not so different, really. We both have obsessive natures and a deep thirst for facts. Her mind is also very sharp. Of course, her ability to present herself to the world is far superior to mine. And, unlike me, she is a natural teacher. She has the ability to communicate not just information but her intensity and zeal to the public. It is no wonder the TV cameras love her; when she talks about history her photogenic face comes alive and her eyes gleam. It is impossible not to get swept up in that enthusiasm.

Perhaps this is what happened to me. As the months went by, Olivia's passion for her subject – the hopes and dreams she has for *Annabel* – became mine. Soon, the book was all I could think about and I did not want to stop. I do not want to stop now.

But of course, there is another side to this. The more I came to know, then admire, and then even to like Olivia, the more I wished I had never met her. The scale of the project changed, radically. It never occurred to me that she would want to write a book about the diary or that I would become involved in the process. At times, the reality of what we were doing would hit me and I would feel quite panicky.

At several points I even made the decision that I could not go on with it. Once, I got as far as sending Olivia an email telling her that I was pulling out, that it was over.

Olivia treated this as a crisis. It was not long after Bertie went, so I imagine she assumed my behaviour was a result of a generally overwrought state of mind.

She left her children and husband with the au pair and drove immediately down to Sussex where, breaking all her own rules, she invited me to the Farmhouse.

Over a lasagna she'd bought en route – and was possibly trying to pass off as her own – she focused on getting me back on side. She needed me, of course, as much as I needed her.

She made me feel that she was genuinely concerned about my state of mind. We talked about Bertie for most of the evening, in fact, and not about the book at all.

Only at the end, very late, did she move on to the question of our collaboration. 'I hope you won't pull out, Vivian, I really do. I think we both believe Annabel's story should be told, don't we? That's why we're doing this, really, isn't it? It's not about money or me writing a bestseller. It's about telling this amazing story. It's so important to tell it. She really was a pioneer – think of all the disapproval and obstacles she faced. She smashed a massive barrier, she – and women like her – changed the world. These women should have plinths in Trafalgar Square. It's almost our moral duty to tell her story, do you know what I mean? I always feel like, as a historian, it's my job to fill in gaps. Women have been written out of history, Vivian, and it's our duty to write them back in. Did you know that only about 0.5 per cent of recorded history is about women?'

I was not sure about the accuracy of this last statistic, but she was so persuasive, so earnest and passionate, that I let it go.

'And the thing is, I couldn't do this book without you, Vivian,' she said. 'You're completely indispensable. You're the equivalent of about ten graduate students, you know that, don't you?'

She was right about that. I was far more efficient and productive than the majority of graduate students, though ten might be overstating it.

'Your eye for detail, your doggedness, you're just remarkable,' she said, looking into my eyes. Hers really are a striking colour. At that moment they reminded me of a beetle called *Necrophila formosa*, whose iridescent carapace is somewhere between violet and royal blue and which feeds on beautiful flowers that reek powerfully of rotting fish.

'I know I can rely on you completely, Vivian,' she was saying. 'The truth is I just couldn't write this book without you.'

I did not point out that this was literally true. Without my approval she could not use the diary. And without the diary there was no biography. She knew that too, of course. That was the subtext of the whole conversation. That, in fact, was almost certainly why I was sitting in her Farmhouse at eleven o'clock on a Tuesday night.

I thought, with longing, of the work we had done together. Our work was the reason I got out of bed every morning. It was the one thing that could temporarily distract me from the distress of losing Bertie. But increasingly it was a torment. I dreaded stopping; I feared to continue.

'You should have been a historian,' she said, generously. 'And you know, the thing is, I'd really miss you, Vivian, if we stopped working together.'

I was being charmed, flattered, but it worked. I did not have the strength to walk away. I could not face going back to long empty days spent dealing with Ileford's leaks and problems with nothing else to occupy me, nothing look forward to, and no Bertie by my side.

She invited me over to the Farmhouse more frequently after that. Perhaps she felt that in order to keep me on side, she had to befriend me. She never invited me when she had London friends there, of course, nor when she had her family down. I had no desire to join her lofty social circle but I might have been interested in her family life.

Other than bringing Jessica that first day to the museum, Olivia only introduced me to her children on one other occasion. It was the night she left me alone in the Farmhouse with Jessica and Paul, just after Christmas, a few months before Bertie went. It was unavoidable and not her fault at all. David was away and she had left her eldest boy at home in London with the au pair. I have no idea where the au pair was that night – if

I were Olivia I would have sacked her for it – but the boy, Dominic, decided to throw a party.

After the police rang her at almost midnight, she woke me up to ask if I could possibly drive over and sleep at the Farmhouse with the two younger children while she went back to London. She sounded very upset, very shaken. She did not want to wake them up or, I suppose, expose them to the chaos of police stations or drunken teenagers. She told me the next day, when she reappeared with her sheepish son, that there had been about two hundred gatecrashers. He had apparently advertised the party on the Internet.

That was an interesting night. I found it impossible to sleep, of course, and so I paced the house. At one point I found myself at her desk. It was quite chaotic with stacks of papers, manuscripts, files and books, pen pots and trinkets. I had to restrain myself from tidying it up. The wall above it was covered in pictures of her children as fresh-faced innocents on beaches and swings. Her laptop was still switched on and buzzing.

It was a fascinating night.

Otherwise, I only ever saw the Farmhouse empty. There was a sense of calm, just the two of us together at her oak table. It might have been a deliberate tactic but she let down her guard on those evenings. She talked about her personal life.

The conversation that really stands out for me, of course, took place last November, almost nine months after our first meeting in the museum. The wind was thumping against the Farmhouse chimney, sucking at it, making the woodstove roar. Olivia had consumed three large glasses of cheap Cabernet. It was getting late. All I had to do was nod and listen.

Her father, she told me, bought the Farmhouse as a gift for her when she was born. It was a wreck, she said, he got it for

£500 and she loved it more than any place in the world. I found this revelation staggering – not the price, but the idea of a father buying a house for his newborn. It seemed like a theatrical and rather controlling thing to do. Perhaps this should not have come as a surprise.

I could think of nothing to say so I pretended to cough. Bertie was curled on my lap. I put him on the floor and got up to fetch a glass of water. He followed me, anxiously, his claws tapping on the flagstones. When I had recovered myself, I returned to the table, picked him up and settled him back on my lap.

'My father wasn't rich, if that's what you're thinking,' she said. 'He was an academic too, a coleopterist. He bought the house with some money his own father left him.'

My face, I hope, remained blank.

'A coleopterist is a beetle expert?' she said. 'He was a bit of a legend in the world of beetles actually.'

Fortunately, an impassive expression comes naturally to me.

'He was a member of the Royal Society – that's second only to winning a Nobel Prize.' She looked at me, sideways, with a smile, aware perhaps that she was being something of a school-girl, boasting about her father. 'But, hang on – you're a scientist, aren't you? Perhaps you've heard of him? Professor Ron Sweet-man? Sussex University?' I spotted a silvery challenge in her eye then and realized she was playing with me. She did not, for a moment, believe I had ever been a professor. I maintained the blank look.

'What was your field again, Vivian, at Oxford?'

I cleared my throat. 'Biology.'

'Ah, biology.'

There was a pause.

'Did you know that only seven per cent of Royal Society Fellows are women?' I offered up this fact in order to save us both the embarrassment of her continuing to tease me. 'It's worse than the Royal College of Surgeons.'

She drained her glass. 'You were never given the nod then?'

I imagined her going back to London and telling her husband and smart friends about my 'big lie' about being a professor. She can use Google and her instinct is, in a way, correct, but I decided that it was the wine talking rather than any true mean-spiritedness on her part. Her voice, I thought, might be teasing rather than mocking. People might not guess this from her somewhat intimidating public persona but Olivia is actually a rather kind and sensitive person. She is much less confident than her public image might suggest. In fact, at times she can be positively insecure.

I eased the subject back to her family. 'You followed your father into academia then?'

'God, I know.' She refilled her wine. 'I'm a bit of a cliché, aren't I? I'm the Daddy's girl, always trying to please him. Sadly, I had zero interest in beetles though.'

'I'm sure he was proud of you anyway.'

'Well, I hope he was, though when I decided to do history he told me arts subjects were useless. He used to say 'You'll be clean-ing toilets with that degree'. Still, he came round to it eventually. And he'd have loved to see me on TV. It's such a shame he didn't live to see that. He was a bit of a performer himself actually – students used to say his lectures were like theatre. He was quite magnetic. But most of all I wish he'd met his grandchildren . . .' She picked at the crisped edge of the lasagna dish, peeling off some crusted cheese with a fingernail and popping it into her mouth. 'He'd have loved them so much.'

I had no desire to enter into a dull conversation about

parenthood so I eased her back to her father again. 'What did he do to get his Royal Society fellowship?'

'He made this massive discovery about dung beetles – don't laugh.'

I wasn't going to.

'He found this amber fossil in Poland that contained a dung beetle with its own tiny ball of dung. This probably sounds arcane to you, but that fossil turned out to have vast implications. Not to get too technical but there are basically two main types of dung beetle – 'rollers' and 'tunnellers'. They split into these two types millions of years ago, scientists call it "divergence". My father's discovery gave rise to a whole new evolutionary theory about divergence. Basically, he proved that dung-rolling beetles were around millions of years earlier than people previously thought. He named it after me, *Archaeocopris olivia*. I have the photograph of it on my bedroom wall in London.'

'*Archaeocopris olivia.*' The words rolled across my tongue like two boiled sweets. 'Well. Isn't that something?'

Bertie looked up and gave a plaintive whine. Olivia glanced at him. 'Is he OK? Does he need to pee?'

I pressed the top of his wiry black head back down. 'He's fine.' He was so tense on my lap that I felt he might explode if I moved.

She laughed, then, and tucked her hair behind her ear. 'Sorry, I'm going on and on.' Her mascara had smudged a bit and she looked slightly dishevelled. She always looked so polished on TV, so it was nice to see her this way, without vanity or artifice. 'I used to be mortified by it actually.'

'By what?'

'By *olivia*, the fossil.'

'But not many people can say they have a beetle named after them.'

'Yes, I know, but a *dung* beetle!' she said, in mock exasperation. 'I mean, I was fine with it as a child. I was nine when he discovered it and I thought it was incredibly cool, but as a teenager I was so embarrassed. I mean, no fifteen-year-old girl wants a dung beetle named after her, does she? My father used to take great delight in telling my boyfriends *all* about it, getting out the photo, pointing out her little fossilised dung ball, you know, just winding me up. But, of course, it means the world to me now. That fossil is really precious to me now he's gone.'

I said nothing. She must have thought that I was uncomfortable about the death of her father because she started to reassure me. 'Oh, it's OK. He died a long time ago – I was an undergraduate, in my final year at Cambridge. That's why his fossil is so important to me, I suppose. It isn't just his academic legacy, I've always felt that fossil is a sort of talisman, you know, a piece of my dad that'll always be with me even though he isn't here.' Her voice wavered. 'God, sorry.' She cleared her throat. 'Too much wine, I'm getting all emotional now.'

'Do you have it?'

'The fossil itself? No, no, it's in the Museum of Natural History in Oxford, where it's safe – now, anyway.'

I tilted my head.

'Oh God, that's a whole other story . . .' She twirled the stem of her glass. 'Don't even get me started.'

I raised my eyebrows.

'Well, there was this thing, a few years ago. It was awful, actually. Someone wrote a paper in *Nature* arguing that my father had made a colossal mistake, that *olivia* was wrongly identified. What he thought was a dung ball was just a contaminant and his evolutionary theory was therefore all wrong. His legacy was almost destroyed. It's too complicated to get into, it turned out

the whole paper was a fraud and thankfully his theory was totally reinstated in the end but it was a horrible business at the
time. It's quite painful to think about actually . . .' Her eyes glistened. 'Even now.'

Bertie lifted his head again and watched me, nervously. His
bushy eyebrows twitched and he let out a small, nervy whine.

'Crikey,' Olivia said. 'I haven't talked about all that in ages
and it still gets to me. Let's talk about something else, OK?'

I decided that it would probably be normal, at this point, to
offer up reciprocal personal information. 'My father died when
I was an undergraduate too,' I said. 'Though unlike yours he
went very slowly. Dementia – it took six years.'

Her eyes widened.

'He was an alcoholic.'

'Oh dear, I'm so sorry.'

We sat in silence for a moment or two.

'You grew up around here, didn't you, Vivian?'

I stroked Bertie's ears. 'My father was an estate manager.' I
named the place, but she didn't know it, even though it is not
far away.

'And your mother?'

I definitely wasn't prepared for this question. I whisked Bertie to the floor and stood up. Pain jolted through my knee. 'My
mother died when I was a child.'

'I'm so sorry, Vivian. I didn't mean to – that's really tough,
losing a parent when you're little . . .'

'I'm going up to the lavatory now.'

'Right. OK. Yes. Sorry. I'll get us some pudding.' Olivia reached
to clear our plates. 'I got you a sticky toffee from M&S, your
favourite!'

As I climbed the stairs I thought about why she would say

such a thing. M&S treacle tart is my favourite pudding. I am not a fan of a sticky toffee and I have no idea where she got the idea that I was. Sticky toffee pudding always makes me think of cow dung, with its warm, viscous interior. I almost expect dung beetles to scramble out as I dig in the spoon.

In the bathroom Bertie sniffed hysterically at the airing cupboard, perhaps catching the scent of a rodent, while I looked out the window and took some deep breaths. My legs felt shaky and my knee pulsed. I am really not good on stairs these days.

I did not need the lavatory so I stayed where I was. The hefty moon hung above the fields. Grey streaks of cloud travelled over her face and below her the flank of the Downs hunched like a smooth-haired hound. I could almost see it breathing. I was reminded how isolated the Farmhouse is, set all alone down a hobbling track, the nearest house well out of sight and sound. With the moon staring in and all the cows chewing and watching with their big, opaque eyes, even I felt exposed.

I snapped the curtains shut and washed my hands. I have often wondered why Olivia would feel safe in a place like this when she claims she once had a stalker. But she says she feels safer here than she does in London. 'Sometimes,' she said to me once, 'this is the only place I *do* feel safe.'

She says that she only ever saw her stalker in London, usually Bloomsbury, outside her office or at the end of the street near the cafe where she goes each afternoon for a cappuccino. There were also a few times when she thought she saw him on tube platforms or disappearing round the stacks at the British Library. She told the police – it was over a year ago now – but they could do nothing since she has never been approached or threatened and has never even seen her stalker's face. She admits that it might have all been in her imagination. The stalker tended to 'appear' when she was overwrought. But even that, she says, does not stop her from being afraid. I should like to reassure her that this is not unreasonable. One's imagination is often more fearsome than reality. My night visitor is the product of my mind, but she is more real to me than most people, and certainly more frightening.

The stairs are uncarpeted and slippery and while Bertie waddled back down ahead of me, his white-tipped tail swinging, I had to grip the banister tightly for fear that my unreliable knee would give out, plunging me head first onto the flagstones.

Olivia had cleared the table and was heating the sticky toffee pudding in a microwave. I sat back down and Bertie hopped onto my lap. There was a bunch of pale pink peonies in a tin jug on the table. Peonies are her favourite flower. They stand for 'shame' in the Victorian language of flowers and I am surprised that she does not know this since it is her period. Bertie sniffed at the table and found a morsel of lasagna. I pushed his nose away. Olivia would not like him eating off the table. She is not a dog person, though she pretends, for my sake, to find him endearing.

She came back over to the table. 'Is that your mother?' I pointed to a photo frame on the shelf above the fireplace in order to take the focus off Bertie, who was licking his lips rather ostentatiously.

'That? Yes, it is.'

The woman did not have Olivia's almost black hair, but she had a similar bone structure and the same intense, bright, half-moon shaped eyes. The photo was black and white so I could not tell whether they were the same deep blue as Olivia's.

'She was very beautiful,' she said. 'She was Danish. She met my father on a scholarship to London. She was a brilliant child psychiatrist.'

People always say their mothers were beautiful, I have noticed. Often brilliant too. It is a form of stealth vanity. My mother was not beautiful and even if she was a genius, nobody would have known, as she spent her days washing and cooking and cleaning other peoples' messes. She was, I believe, a kind and warm person. I have a clear memory of her patting my back and singing a lullaby to me when I was feverish in bed. I must have been very small.

Olivia got two bowls down off the open shelves. 'You know,' she turned to me with one in each hand, 'my mother and I had a tricky relationship but now I'm an orphan I really miss her. I think that's why I wanted a Danish au pair.'

It always irritates when adults call themselves 'orphans'. 'Well, you have your own family now,' I said, perhaps a little brusquely.

She glanced at me and set down the pudding bowls, 'Oh, yes, I know, I'm very lucky, I know that, so lucky.'

I understood, then, that Olivia is quite a lonely person, despite her full and apparently perfect life, with her three children, her handsome husband and all those friends and fans. I wanted to let her know that I recognized that loneliness in her but unfortunately I could not think how to convey this in words.

As she showed me to the door that night I noticed that the flagstones in the hall were damp. She said it happened every winter and when I asked why she didn't damp-proof or lay a nice warm carpet, she grimaced. 'They're so much part of the integrity of the house, I felt I couldn't cover them up. It's daft really, they're probably a health hazard.'

Bertie and I drove back to Ileford very late and as we slid between tight hawthorn hedgerows under the platinum moonlight I thought about that word: 'integrity'. She meant it in the less common sense, of something being whole and undivided from its true self.

Perhaps she's right that some authentic spirit still lurks in the dampness beneath her cowhide rugs. Perhaps our essential nature never really changes, even when we dress it up as something else. I thought, then, of the harlequin ladybird, which can mimic a harmless ladybird so closely that it sometimes even fools the experts.

Still, she should damp-proof that hall. It's not as if she can't afford it. They must be awash with money. David presumably made a fortune from his *Intuition* book, which was on the best-seller lists on both sides of the Atlantic for months on end, thanks to appearances on American TV programmes. Even I had heard of it, though I would never have chosen to read a work of popular psychology or watch an Oprah Winfrey show. And Olivia herself must earn a very comfortable salary, with her media career on top of that. This, presumably, is how they afford two houses.

But I have little interest in Olivia's finances. I do not want or need her money. Even my weekly researcher's fee wasn't necessary, I only accepted it because it would have looked bizarre to refuse. She kept offering me more money as the project went on. She wanted to give me a cut of royalties too. She was obviously uncomfortable about how much I was doing but I insisted that I would not take a penny more.

My knee is aching from sitting too long in the library. When I try to straighten it a white pain zaps up my leg. But I must get up, I really must get on. There is so much to do before I leave for France. I have decided not to tell Lady Burley that I am going. It would only distress her to know that Ileford is standing empty for a week and of course I cannot explain my reasons. That would involve telling her that that *Annabel* is finished, which would confuse and probably panic her.

When all this began I had no idea that she could possibly live for another eighteen months. The doctors said she only had a few months left. I assumed that I would never have to deal with the issue of *Annabel*'s actual publication and so had decided not to worry her with the details.

Though it makes me uncomfortable, I still think it is better for her not to know that the book is done, even if she is still with us in October when it is launched. She sleeps a lot these days and is losing her grip on time so maybe she will not notice that I am away for a week.

'Back so soon?' she asked yesterday when I appeared by her chair.

'It's been two days,' I said, reaching for a Tunnock's as she finds the foil wrapping hard to peel away. 'I always come on alternate days. I haven't ever missed a visit in fact.'

'Why are you always so formal with me, Vivi?' Her tiny, rheumy eyes filled up with tears. 'Is it because you still can't forgive me for what happened to your mother? Is that it? I can't die unforgiven, Vivi, please . . .'

I don't know why she keeps saying such things. I forgave her a long time ago for what she did to my mother and she knows it. Why else would I have moved to Ileford to care for her?

I like to think that I have been a comfort to her. Before I came back, Lady Burley was a lost soul. She couldn't find reliable help and would write me distraught letters about Polish housekeepers drinking the contents of the wine cellar, or her fears that the driveway trees had contracted Dutch elm disease.

She is right to worry about that, actually. The elm bark beetle is a vicious beast that feasts on the inner bark of the tree, introducing fungal spores that swell and block its water vessels, causing total devastation. Vigilance is the only weapon against *Scolytus multistriatus* and Lady Burley was far too old to be peering at leaves and twigs.

She was pitifully relieved when I accepted her offer. She had no idea, of course, that she was rescuing me, too. 'I just need someone I can trust,' she said. 'You'd be doing me such a favour, Vivi, you can't imagine. I can't bear the thought of strangers in Ileford.'

Like me, Lady Burley is quite alone in the world. Almost all of her friends are dead, dying, incapacitated or abroad. Her only brother was killed in murky circumstances in Kenya in the sixties and she never had children. Her infertility, she believes, somewhat irrationally, was 'karma'. When this cancer finally takes her there will be nobody left who knows who I really am.

But I must not feel guilty for leaving Ileford. Everyone needs a holiday once in a while. I wish I were a better traveller but I will try to focus on the more pleasant things that lie at the end of the journey: a warm, dry room, no housework, days spent looking for harlequins.

And, of course, Olivia.

I hope we bump into each other by chance. I do not want to have to go to her – to intrude on her holiday. She will be surprised to see me, but also, I hope, pleased. She can never resist talking about work. We will go somewhere together, a little cafe perhaps, just the two of us, and in those warm and relaxed surroundings, I will put my new idea to her. This awful waiting will be over. I will pin her down at last.

Olivia

South of France, Day One

Olivia emerged from the bathroom in one of the soft bath sheets. David was still on the bed. There was something tense about the way he was lying, with a tanned forearm thrown across his face. His breathing was slightly too shallow and she knew he wasn't asleep. She turned away and dug for her phone in her jeans on the back of the chair.

'There's no mobile signal.' His voice rose from the bed. 'Does this place have Wifi?'

'It'd better. I'm going to need it, I've got a load of publicity stuff to do for the book.'

'Can't you just take a break, Liv?' he said. 'Just for these two weeks? Just stop?'

She looked over her shoulder. He'd taken his hand away and the muscles of his jaw were tight, his eyes combative.

'How,' she said, as calmly as possible, 'can you even ask me that?'

He lurched up, swung his feet off the bed and turned his back on her.

This was a spectacular act of compartmentalization, even for him. Was he really was going to behave as if it didn't matter whether *Annabel* was a success or not? Even if he had somehow managed to dissociate himself from the reality of the situation, he still owed it to her to care about her book. Ten years ago, when he was writing *Intuition*, they'd discussed every chapter, debated the most minuscule points. Without her, *Intuition* would have been a far less readable and significantly less comprehensible work. It was she who had suggested a more conversational writing style, urged him to put aside jargon, the legacy of his abandoned psychology PhD, and write as if to a friend. She'd never said this to him directly but she was convinced that without her input, *Intuition* would never have been the international best-seller it was.

She began to pull on clothes from her suitcase: a clean T-shirt, a pair of linen trousers. Of course, when David was writing *Intuition* their lives had been a lot simpler. They only had the boys, for a start, Jess wasn't even born then. And they were still in their thirties, motivated by a huge mortgage, swimming energetically and confidently, side by side, towards their golden future of professorships, book deals and newspaper columns.

She sat on the chair by the desk, put her head upside down and rubbed her hair with the towel. The irony was that she fell in love with his intellect and charm, his good heart, but perhaps above all with his refusal to worry. He had great ambition and drive but he never took anything too seriously. His favourite phrase was 'It'll all work out'. She had a tendency to be earnest and solemn, and to agonize about everything, but David just seized opportunities as they arose and didn't fret about the future. He never looked back, like she did; he never worried about choices he could have made but hadn't.

His confidence and optimism had helped her to take herself less seriously too. Without David, she probably never would have responded to the TV company's email asking if she'd be interested in screen testing for a documentary about historic houses. David had made her feel there were no limits. But now the opposite felt true. She felt increasingly imprisoned and curtailed by him, more free alone. And of course it was his refusal to worry, his ludicrous overconfidence, that had led to this appalling mess.

She dragged a comb through her damp hair, tugging aggressively at the tangles. What bothered her most was that he had hidden this from her. They were both overworked and distracted but they must have become profoundly distanced for him to lie like this. Things had become difficult between them, she knew, when she'd started *Annabel*. She was just too busy and stressed all the time and he was consumed by his writer's block, his stalling career. Perhaps he also felt threatened that suddenly she was the one writing. Perhaps, deep down, David was afraid that her book might be as successful as his once was. Whatever silent threat or resentment or rivalry was beneath all this, it had certainly stopped them from communicating.

She lifted her head and stared at herself in the mirror. She looked totally washed out. She got out her make-up bag. The only way forward, she knew, was to grow up, forgive him and move on. Everyone makes mistakes. They just needed to work hard and fix this. At some point her anger would fade but right now she wasn't sure that she wanted it to. She had a feeling that beneath her fury lay something worse, something very close to pity.

'I can't keep saying sorry to you,' he said from the bed behind her, as if he'd read her mind.

She didn't look around. She kept putting on her mascara. 'I don't want you to.'

'OK.' He got up abruptly. 'I'm going to put the wine in the fridge. The others'll be here any minute.'

She straightened, put away her make-up bag and went back to the window. The boys were both out of the pool now, sitting on sun loungers, jabbing desperately at their phones. Jess was alone in the water, ducking somersaults; the knots of her spine flickered as the water swallowed them, one by one.

A movement caught her eye beyond the terrace, a shape standing at the end of a scraggy line of olive trees. She blinked and squinted but as her eyes adjusted to the sunlight she could see that, of course, there was nobody there.

It was a stress thing, she knew, this tendency to feel watched. She always used to see him at times of stress.

In fact, it had happened again, for the first time in over a year, just before they left London. She had looked out of her study window at two in the morning and, through the condensation, glimpsed a figure in an overcoat, standing beneath a tree. He had ducked his head, turned and vanished round the corner. Something about the shape, the bulk, made her freeze. For moment she couldn't quite breathe.

She'd never seen him near her home before. If he was real and standing in her street at two in the morning, then this was serious. He must have followed her home, or found their address even though it was not supposed to be in the public domain. She remembered the female TV presenter murdered years ago near her house in a west London residential street just like hers.

She rubbed away the condensation and pressed her face on the glass but the street was empty. She went up and woke David.

Her fear pushed aside his recent betrayal; she just needed to know he was there, that she was safe. He sat up, rubbing his hair, and made her repeat herself. Then he was logical and reassuring, as she knew he would be. He pointed out that the street was poorly lit and she was not necessarily at her most calm right now. He reminded her, gently, that she'd never really established whether she was, or wasn't, being stalked in the first place and that even the GP had suggested it could be a stress thing.

Most stalkers, he said, again not for the first time, made direct contact with their victim either via social media, by phone, or in person. They didn't lurk at a distance, never showing their face, or vanish for a whole year. It was probably a late-night dog walker, he said. She should just come to bed and get some sleep. She found him both irritating and reassuring when he talked to her like this. She spent so much of her time coping, being in charge, being looked up to and relied on that it was a relief, sometimes, to be told what to do.

She rested one hand on the shutter and felt the warmth of the sun on her face, smelled wild thyme and lavender wafting off the hills. The movement was just a rag, fluttering on a pole, perhaps the lost bandana of an olive farmer. Nobody was out there, nobody was watching her. She didn't want to lean on David now. She actually wanted to kill him.

When she turned, he was gone.

She heard Chloe's laugh rising from the terrace, straightened her shoulders and went downstairs to greet their friends.

Al was with David in the kitchen, holding a box of beer. He looked sweaty and slightly bewildered, more portly than he had last time they met. He kissed her on both cheeks and she smelled his aftershave and perspiration and felt a great fondness for him.

She realized that it was at least nine months since they had all got together. There was no sign of Al and Chloe's boys but Chloe was out on the terrace.

She was wearing a cream halter-neck dress with her hair knotted at the nape of her neck. Her posture was always elegant – she'd almost become a yoga teacher once – and she looked particularly luminous in her own patch of sunlight. But then as she turned, Olivia caught something troubled in her expression, something like dread, and she suddenly felt sure that Chloe didn't want to be here at all.

They hugged, then, and Olivia's heart felt full. She hadn't told Chloe what David had done. The only way to cope since she found out had been to keep going. Chloe had texted a few times, asking to meet for lunch or a drink before they left, but there had been no time.

David had begged her not to tell Chloe or Emma what he'd done. He couldn't face the shame. It was unreasonable of him to expect her not to talk to her best friends, but even so, a thread of loyalty to him had remained and she'd decided not to. She was angry but she didn't want to hurt or embarrass him or make the holiday any more tense than it would already be.

But now she realized there was no way that she could spend two weeks with Chloe and not tell her. And if she told Chloe, she'd have to tell Emma too.

They swapped stories of their journeys and the heat, the baffling road signs, the lack of mobile signal, the near impossibility of finding the track up to the house. But Chloe was not her usual laid-back, yogic self. She was jittery and her enthusiasm felt forced as she exclaimed over the view, the village rooftops and the hills on the other side. 'It's paradise!' she cried. 'Amazing!' Olivia had the urge to sit her down and soothe her but she was off again, striding past the pool to peer down at the olive grove beneath the terrace. 'Olives!' She threw up her hands. 'Wow!'

'Where's Paul?' Miles, Chloe and Al's eldest son, and Olivia's godchild, came out onto the terrace, followed by his brother, Ben, skinny and knock-kneed, small for eight. Olivia liked Ben more than she liked Miles, though of course she could never admit this. Miles was overconfident and a bit brash, while Ben was sweet and vulnerable. She told them about the games room and suggested they go and look for the others there.

Chloe fanned herself with both hands when her boys had gone. A fine silver bracelet slid down her forearm, 'My God. It's *boiling* here! Are you hot? God, it's hot!' Something was definitely wrong.

She thought about Chloe's attempts to meet up before they left England. Maybe she had needed to talk about something important. Maybe her marriage was in trouble, too, or something else was amiss. Olivia really been a poor friend lately, swallowed up by her own concerns, too overworked to see anyone.

'What do you two want to drink?' David called out.

'Anything as long as it's alcoholic.' Chloe looked at Olivia as she said this, as if it was her who'd asked the question and not David. Then she looked away again. 'God, it's stunning here, it really is. Where should we all sleep?'

'Well, most of the bedrooms are in that side of the house and there's a lovely big double with a view . . .' Olivia gestured behind. 'Or there's the master suite, up those stairs, that way.'

'Don't listen to her, Chlo.' David came out and handed them each a glass of slightly warm rosé. 'She's already unpacked our bags up there.'

'I have not!' She felt her face heat up at David's pocket-sized betrayal. 'I really haven't.'

'Oh for God's sake.' Chloe touched her arm. 'Don't be silly. You should have the master suite. You found this place, you did all the legwork and I really don't mind what room we're in.' She turned away again, smiling wildly. 'This whole place is paradise!'

Khalil and Emma didn't arrive until much later, hovering in the hallway looking shaken, talking about their delayed easyJet flight, a malfunctioning sat nav, the hidden track to the house – impossible in the dark. They had had to go back and knock on doors further down the hill until they found a local man willing to come out and show them the way. Em, pale and freckled and petite in jeans and a plain white shirt, clutched Nura as if she were a baby and not a girl of almost nine who still sucked her thumb. Nura gazed at them all with anxious spaniel eyes.

'Poor thing, she's shattered.' Olivia stroked Nura's pretty cheek.

'She's been so, so good,' Emma said.

'The sat nav coordinates are out,' said Khalil, again.

Olivia laughed. 'I know, the same thing happened to all of us. Come on, come and have a drink, we're out on the terrace and the kids are all watching a DVD . . . Look, there's Jess – Jess? Nuri's here.' Jess glanced up, drowsily, then went back to the TV. 'Jess! Say hello properly to Nura.'

'Don't worry,' said Em, 'They're all tired, aren't they? It's so late.'

Bedroom negotiations somehow culminated in all of the children, except for Dominic, dragging their mattresses and pillows across the courtyard through the dust and packing them onto the ground floor of the priest's tower.

The day ended with most of the adults out on the terrace, hollow-eyed, opening more bottles of wine and swatting mosquitos. Chloe really was behaving quite oddly. She talked too fast, for too long, gesturing too much, telling them all about a recent commission she'd had to restore a shattered Toby Jug. When she started talking about rivets, re-bonding and epoxy resin Al put an arm round her and she took a deep breath in and fell silent.

Then Al asked Olivia what she was working on next. He meant television, of course, it was all anyone was interested in when they asked about her work these days, but she couldn't face talking about that so she made an excuse and went into the kitchen for a jug of water. As she left the terrace, she heard Al say to David, 'Oops. Sore subject?'

She stood at the sink and stared down at the smeared plates. She couldn't think about work or what she might have to do in the coming year. She turned on the tap and sponged dark red clots of jam from a plate. David was months, perhaps even years, away from finishing *Trust*, and there was no guarantee that it would sell as well as *Intuition* had. Plenty of writers failed to replicate the sales of their big hit debut.

So much, she realized, was now resting on *Annabel*. Joy certainly believed in the book's potential sales. 'It's completely compelling,' she had said, on the phone, after reading the final draft. 'I was up all night with it. My God, that murder confession! You've timed that perfectly now. And then her making it to medical school after all she's been through, and the chapter on her First World War women's hospital work. It's fascinating, it really is. She's coming across now as completely heroic and wonderful. I was rooting for her all the way through. I've got a few small final notes, but it's unputdownable, Olivia. It's going to be huge. You're the new Amanda Foreman, the new Simon Schama!'

It was to be the publisher's lead non-fiction title in the

lucrative pre-Christmas publication slot, with an enviable publicity budget, posters in the Tube, a huge social media campaign, TV appearances, magazine features, serializations. If *Annabel* were to flop after this it would, apart from anything else, be a humiliating public failure.

She heard movement behind her and span round. Emma and Khalil were hovering on the other side of the kitchen. They must have come in from the living room. She pressed a wet hand over her heart. 'Jesus! You made me jump – I didn't see you there. Everyone's outside.'

Emma's strawberry-blonde hair was middle-parted and her kind, freckled face looked drawn. 'Actually, Liv, we were wondering if it might not be so safe for the children to be sleeping all the way across the courtyard in that tower.' She looked as if she might implode with the strain of worrying about Nura.

'Oh? I think they'll be fine, Em, really. The door to the faulty staircase is locked and the owners did say it's OK to use the downstairs room, it's part of the rental.'

'It's just that it's so far from the house.' Emma's frown deepened and her hand fluttered to her neck. 'We wouldn't be able to hear if anything happened.'

'Hmm, I know it feels a bit odd . . . But we'll all have our windows open, won't we, so I'm sure we'd hear? And if anything did happen, one of them could easily just run over and wake us up, or even just shout.' She looked at Khalil for back-up. There was nowhere else to put the children. She wasn't sure if Em had appreciated this.

Khalil fixed his dark, long-lashed eyes on his wife. 'You know what? I think we need to let Nuri have an adventure with the others. Miles is twelve, Paul's thirteen, they'll look after her.' They looked meaningfully at one another for a second and Olivia sensed that this was an issue they had covered before, probably in therapy.

'OK,' Emma sighed, at last. 'Fine.'

'Honestly, Em,' Olivia went over and squeezed her thin arm. 'They'll all be safe, I promise. Paul and Miles are sensible boys, really, and they're only a stone's throw from the house. We'd definitely hear them if anything went wrong.' She felt Emma stiffen. 'Not that anything's going to go wrong. It's totally safe here, Em, it really is.'

Vivian

Newhaven–Dieppe Ferry

I am doing my utmost to blot out the appalling racket and stench but it is not easy.

I have found myself a single seat, unfortunately near the toilets and behind a loud family, but at least I can sit on my own. I am glad to be en route at last – the waiting is over. It is important to distract myself from the mewling infant, the toddler stabbing at his baby iPad, the bickering couple popping Coke cans and fussing with clingfilm, the stink of their clammy cheddar sandwiches.

I am glad to be out of Ileford though. I had begun to feel as if I were living in the carcass of a beached whale – as if the house was collapsing in on itself and I was drowning with it. As I lay in bed this morning in the half-light, waiting for my booming and sickened heart to subside, I noticed that the shadow on the moist lung of my bedroom ceiling is getting bigger and it occurred to me that the damp area of plaster might loosen and drop onto me. If Bertie were here I would have to do something about it urgently. But of course, he is not, and perhaps a swift sharp ending – a crack of Victorian plaster to the forehead – would not be such a bad way to go.

When I tried to sit up this morning I still felt dizzy. The after-effects of my night visitor are more prolonged than ever these days. Even after half an hour or so, my heart was still lurching and I could still feel the warm liquid trickling from her forehead onto mine. The worst thing of all is being unable to move when it happens. I am paralysed and have to watch as she reaches out to fold her slow hands over my mouth and nose.

Eventually, I regained control of myself by listing the common names of ladybirds: water, larch, cream spot, eleven-spot, five-spot, seven-spot, scarce seven-spot, striped, kidney, eye. I was able to get up after that and go downstairs.

I rub my neck. I hope that my night visitor does not come to me in France. It is possible that I cry out in panic sometimes in the moments after the paralysis – I know I did this as a child and it would infuriate my father to be woken. I do not want to disturb other guests at the *chambres d'hôte* or call attention to myself. I do know, of course, that my night visitor is not real, that she exists only in my brain, a by-product of a sleep disorder that has plagued me since childhood. She is a hallucination born of the transitional and shadowy phase that lies between wakefulness and sleep, the result of muscle atonia and post-dormital awareness, an incomplete REM cycle, hyper-vigilance in the mid-brain. I am not the only person to have experienced this sleep problem, it is documented throughout history and across all cultures. My visitor is the Newfoundland hag, the ancient Greek choker, the Norse *mara*, the incubus crouched on the sleeper's chest in Fuseli's famous painting. None of this helps when I wake, paralysed to find her sitting on my chest, dripping blood onto my face before smothering me with her cold hands.

I think perhaps it was particularly bad last night because I was leaving Ileford and therefore, in a sense, Bertie. It is irrational, I know – after all, it is five months and ten days since he went – but I feel as if I am abandoning him all over again.

It is the not knowing that takes its toll. A vanishing can be more cruel than death. But Bertie is dead, I know that, although even now I sometimes hear his claws tap-tapping in the hall and joy rockets me to my feet. The hall is always empty, of course. I feel that the house judges me at these moments, and finds me wanting.

I do torment myself by imagining how he met his end. The word 'terrier' comes from the French '*terre*', meaning earth, and in my sleepless hours I picture him down a badger sett with his gullet torn, or wedged in a rabbit burrow, his muzzle and eyes clogged with soil. I picture him in great pain, struggling to free himself, hearing my voice fade as I walk away.

I have searched for him – of course I have – tracing ever-wider circles around Ileford, day after day, shouting until I lost my voice. I still look for him in the woods and fields even though I know, rationally, that he is dead.

Nobody would have taken him, that's for sure. He was of no value to anyone but me. He was a sooty mutt with a hoary muzzle and bushy eyebrows, a genetic mishmash; fast-moving, suspicious of strangers. I had longed for a dog all my adult life but you cannot bring a dog into a lab, a college or a museum. Nor could I countenance leaving a dog home alone during the day, since I frequently did not return from work until nine or ten at night. Coming to Ileford, at least, allowed me to realize my long-held dream of companionship. Until, on that horrible March day, I was alone again.

I must not blame Olivia for this. It was not her fault, at least not wholly. We must share the blame for his vanishing.

I have finally taken his basket down to the cellar. I cannot bear to look at it, sitting empty, but I also cannot bear to throw it away. I remember when I bought it for him I paid extra for the thickest fleece because he deserved the best. It took him over a year to even lie in it. He would push himself under the table instead and watch me with his nose on his paws. His instinct was to find somewhere dark and sheltered where he might not be noticed.

The rescue centre filled me in on his past. He needed a quiet house, they said, no other pets, definitely no children. He was half-starved and dehydrated when the RSPCA officers got him. He'd been discovered by a bunch of teenage boys who had broken into an abandoned house in Moulsecoomb. He was sleeping in his own excrement, consumed by mange and fleas, very close to death. When the rescue people explained that he limped as a result of multiple fractures in his hind legs, most likely from kicks, I knew that he was for me. He maintained a hearty dislike of men with beards and would cower or snap at them in the street.

I brought him back to Ileford four years ago on a warm September afternoon and nursed him with fresh cuts of meat – pigeon breast, pheasant, chicken or venison from the estate. Every night at bedtime I cracked an organic egg into warm milk for him.

He only ever bit me once. We had been dozing by the fire and my elbow knocked a dictionary from the table. It landed on his head, rousing him from a deep and vulnerable sleep. It was self-defence to bite, pure reflex. When I drew back, clutching my shin, a peculiar terror saturated his eyes, a mixture of guilt at what he had done to me and dread at what I might do in return. As I wrapped my trouser round my leg to stem the blood I felt my eyes fill with tears, not from pain but from pity.

I tried to smile and coax him to me. 'It's OK, it's OK, I scared you, you poor lad. I won't hurt you, Bertie boy, I'll never hurt you.' But he drew himself low on the carpet and quaked.

Someone had done awful things to that dog, but I never would. I still have the pale crescent tattoo of his teeth on my skin. It is a valuable reminder that nobody is beyond redemption, nobody unworthy of love.

I decided, after this incident, that I must make Bertie understand that I would never abandon, reject or hurt him. I kept him with me every hour of the day, I even took him into the lavatory. It took a year and a half, but one cold March evening he crawled up next to me on my bed, ears flat, curled tight at my feet and stayed there all night. I have never slept better.

After that he was my devoted friend. When I scratched the tender spot behind his ears he would gaze at me with pure gratitude in his dear brown eyes. He would never have run away from me, I do know that. So I let him down. I should never have left him with Olivia when he was sick and weak and confused. It was a mistake to allow her to persuade me to leave him.

She keeps telling me that I should replace him. I should get a wolfhound, she says, the sort of proud creature that belongs in a seven-bedroom Victorian Gothic manor. Apart from the obvious lunacy of suggesting that I could ever replace Bertie, I did find it unsettling that she should suggest a wolfhound. I questioned her thoroughly but she insisted that it was just a random breed, plucked from nowhere.

She wanted to know why I was so bothered about wolfhounds so I told her the myth of Violet's ghost. Lady Burley always insists that, if you look out of her bedroom window early on a misty October morning, you can see Violet on the driveway in a long grey dress, corseted and hatted, walking her wolfhound, vanishing between the elms.

Lady Burley has another Violet story, too, which is even sillier. I heard it as a child, on one of my visits to Ileford, and I told Olivia about it, though I did not tell her I had the story directly from Uncle Quentin himself. It was the only time, as a child, that I met him and I don't remember his face, even, just a big tweedy presence and the fear that his words inspired in me. If I pushed back the cover of the well, he said, I would see his mother's face staring back up at me and I would be cursed forever. His mother, Violet Burley, drowned herself in the well after his two elder siblings died.

This was probably a story Uncle Quentin invented to keep children away from a dangerous well, or perhaps just because he liked inventing stories. He was, by all accounts, an unhinged fantasist. He famously brought a dancing bear back from India in the 1930s and kept it in the cellar. He used to wander round the manor stark naked, ringing a cowbell to alert the maids, who would flee when they heard it. He once rode into one of his dinner parties on the back of his dancing bear, which became very distressed and bit part of his leg off. As his eyesight faded, later in life, he got the gamekeeper to clip the wings of all the pigeons and partridges so he could walk right up to them and shoot them. Among his papers I found a set of homosexual pornographic stories he'd written (very badly). They were all set, rather oddly, in Arthurian times.

When I started the preliminary research for *Annabel*, I was able to prove that Uncle Quentin's story about his mother was nonsense. Quentin's two older siblings did die, but she did not kill herself because of it. She in fact died of puerperal fever six days after producing Uncle Quentin. Perhaps he preferred to heap the blame on his siblings. I understand this impulse. A child takes on such guilt for a mother's death.

I have never seen an Ileford ghost, though once or twice I have stepped out of my study very late at night and known, just for a moment, that someone was standing quietly in the shadows by the stairs to the servant's quarters. Of course, the human brain is biologically wired for trickery; we must be alert to the unseen threat. Our capacity for visitations, chimeras and frights is a perfectly sensible evolutionary by-product.

My legs catch my eye. They look very large and pale, poking out of my Bermuda shorts, their lumpy terrain mapped by blue veins and blotches. They look as if they have sucked up the moisture from the Ileford air and brought it with them onto the ferry. I hope the dry heat of southern France will help my joints, my knee in particular. I am beginning to feel seasick now. I am very bad at transitions and departures, even when I have chosen them.

I find myself suddenly filled with trepidation that Olivia might not want to pursue the Chocolate Cream Poisoner idea. If she says no, I actually do not know what I will do. I could resume my own small research studies, of course, but I will never be able to publish them and my days will be taken up, once again, with the Sisyphean task of managing a Victorian structure that is hell-bent on collapse. I cannot bear to go back to that. I cannot live like that again.

Ileford without Bertie, without *Annabel* – and, yes, without Olivia – has nothing to offer me. When Lady Burley goes – if the will passes probate – it will still not be enough for me. I should be glad to own such a place, but I do not want it. All I really want is my own home, with its narrow galley kitchen looking onto the lovely, overgrown garden with my apple and pear trees, my straggling gooseberry bushes. I want my Edwardian windows and the smell of my books. I even miss the faint sound of traffic at rush hour. But that is the one thing I cannot have because, although

it was my home for thirty-three years, it was never mine. Someone else, presumably, is living there now. I wonder if they have
ripped out the bathroom, built a side-return kitchen extension,
laid hardwood floors, brought in a garden designer with gravel
and ferns.

My sudden dark mood, I know, is down to the anxiety of tran-
sit, the judder of the ferry beneath my feet, the smells of vomit
and bleach and sun cream and other peoples' food, the intrusive-
ness of all these bodies, the nesting mess and stink of families.
When I feel this sort of hypersensitivity to my surroundings, one
thing that can help is to distract myself by thinking about work.

The Chocolate Cream Poisoner file is in my bag right now. Perhaps I will get it out in a minute. I must be optimistic. This will
fascinate Olivia too if only she will listen. The subject marries all
of her professional interests, after all: Victorian women, insanity, asylums, criminality. It even took place in Brighton, her
hometown. The desire to discuss my idea, to get my teeth into
the research again, is almost physical. I have the urge to get up
and walk but there is nowhere to go on this container of bodies;
people are pushing and lurching up and down the aisles, bumping into one other while the sea sways beneath.

In just an hour the ferry will dock in Dieppe and this, the
worst part of the journey, will be over. There is a long drive ahead
but I will be alone in my car, which will be infinitely preferable
to this floating hell. I just have to focus on the goal. I am sure
that when I finally get to the village and find her we will talk
about my idea in great detail and – without all the distractions
and tensions of home – Olivia will love it as much as I do. I know
she will. She has to.

Olivia

South of France, Day Three

It was the fifth year running that the three families had been away together and they soon slipped into their usual roles. Em fussed around with the younger children, taking the girls for nature walks or helping them to construct fiddly fairy towns out of twigs. Chloe, always good at relaxation, spent hours on a sun lounger with *The Goldfinch*, wearing a kaftan over her white bathing suit and a wide-brimmed straw hat, her long limbs slowly turning golden. Khalil and Al chucked balls with the boys or drank small bottles of beer in the shade and talked about sport. David either joined them or devoted himself to planning, shopping for and cooking all the meals.

Everyone understood that this was David's way of relaxing on holiday, he loved nothing more than to cook for his friends, so they allowed him free rein and took turns to wash up. But there was something more obsessive about his activity this time. Olivia could see that the pleasure had drained from the process, leaving only a relentless drive to source and prepare food.

He would disappear after breakfast, sometimes taking Jess or Paul, though never Dom, or occasionally with one of the adults, in search of a particular kind of olive oil or a vineyard he had read about, returning early afternoon to a house full of starving, bickering children, bringing bags full of tapenade and olives and bitter leaves, fleshy tomatoes and crisp baguettes, soft-pelted peaches and cheeses that oozed and reeked, even when layered in waxed paper and striped plastic bags.

This feverish catering was, Olivia knew, a reflection of his guilt. She was almost relieved that he could not maintain the pretence of relaxation.

'Is David OK?' Emma said on the third morning, as the two of them drank coffee under an umbrella on the terrace while Jess and Nura played in the pool. Emma's freckled skin was covered in a thick vernix of sunscreen and she was wearing a shapeless linen dress and Birkenstocks. Olivia wished that Emma would just relax, like Chloe, and stop fussing around and worrying about everyone, stop noticing everything. It made things harder.

'It's just that David seems a bit, I don't know, frenetic,' Emma said earnestly.

Olivia made a non-committal noise and stretched out her legs, crossing them at the ankles. David had left early that day in search of a particular kind of cured meat only to be found an hour's drive over the hills. He could have taken Dominic, actually spent some time with him, but, as far as she knew, Dom was still in bed. At the last minute, Chloe had leaped off the sunbed, thrown down *The Goldfinch*, grabbed her straw bag and sunglasses and run after him to the car, shouting, 'Wait! I'm coming!'

Olivia considered explaining to Emma what was really going

on with David, but she knew that Emma's shock, or worse, her kindness and sympathy, wouldn't help.

'So, *is* everything OK?' Emma pressed. 'Is he really stressed out? How's his book coming along?'

'Well, it's not, really. That's part of the problem.'

'But wasn't it supposed to be published this autumn, around the same time as yours?'

'His publication date's been moved. It turns out he still has quite a few revisions, so it's not going to be published probably till next autumn now, at the earliest.'

It was a fortnight since she had seen the email from David's editor with the subject line '*Trust – further notes*'. The attachment contained twenty or more pages of detailed corrections and comments, most of them major and distinctly tetchy.

That was the first thing he had lied to her about. Over the past six months, whenever she'd asked about *Trust*, or wanted to know when she'd be able to read it, he'd said it was almost done. But his editor's email had been overshadowed by what she discovered next in his inbox.

'It might be for the best,' said Emma. 'I mean, you two can be quite competitive, can't you? I was a bit worried you'd be warring over your sales figures.'

Olivia laughed. 'If we did I'm sure he'd win.'

'Really? I don't know, Liv. Would he?' Emma knitted her brows. 'I read an article the other day saying the market for popular history books is booming. And your *Annabel* sounds brilliant – I can't wait to read it – and you've also got a really strong public profile now. Last time you and I went for coffee three people asked for selfies and we were only in the cafe for half an hour. I actually think your book is likely to be huge, bigger than you'd think.'

'Well, there's no way of predicting that.'

'To be honest, though, I don't know how you've written a book on top of everything else you've got going on.' Emma sighed. 'You're just amazing, Liv. Your workload must be horrendous. I know I couldn't work like that any more, not with Nura.'

'You could, you'd just get an au pair. I mean, there's no way I could do this without Marta.'

'Oh no. Marta seems great, and it works for you, but I don't miss the law one bit, I feel nothing but relief to be out of it. And I could never get an au pair anyway. I couldn't bear to miss out on Nura's childhood.'

Olivia tried not to react. Emma didn't mean it as a criticism. After twelve years trying to conceive, it was only natural that she should want to focus on her child. Emma always approached everything with complete commitment and diligence. She'd got herself a City law career straight out of university while Chloe had discovered yoga, travelled to India, then come back and taken waitressing jobs, and Olivia – not really knowing what else to do – had started her PhD. Emma had been the first to settle down too. She moved into Khalil's flat at the hospital only a year after college and married him at twenty-four. It was probably not surprising that she had taken the same approach to motherhood.

Olivia knew that the stab of irritation she had just felt was not really anything to do with Emma's comment about the au pair. Its prickly roots were clamped around her own maternal guilt. She desperately needed more time with her children and they needed more from her too. Dom was troubled and angry and she knew that she wasn't helping him – she didn't know how to help him. Paul was unhealthily obsessed with screens, Marta seemed to give him free rein, and Jess definitely needed more attention than she was getting. All this was only going to worsen if she had to accept the BBC offer. The thought of dancing on TV made her feel ill. She was used to some exposure but not at that level and not of that sort. She didn't want it.

It was certainly true that her life would not function without an au pair. Marta had been with them for almost a year now, and while Olivia had not exactly warmed to her, she was competent, intelligent and responsible. It had been a good decision to have someone older – Marta was twenty-four – and although David complained initially about having someone in the house, he didn't really mind Marta too much. He treated her a bit like a grown-up daughter; Olivia had even come home a couple of times to find them in the kitchen discussing Marta's applications for her Master's degree in economics.

She fanned herself. She was in a black T-shirt and cut-offs and it was too hot for black. There was no breeze at all. Perhaps she should go and get her swimsuit on and join the girls in the pool, but she knew she shouldn't, she needed to go upstairs and get some of the work out of the way. Jess was harassing Nura to do a somersault. She demonstrated without effort, her body lithe and slippery while Nura stood and watched, nervous and static, her skin slick caramel against her pink goggles. Jess always seemed to dominate Nura. Perhaps this stemmed from being the youngest, with two big brothers to control. There was something of David in her, a confidence that Olivia herself lacked. But she did need to learn about kindness and tolerance too.

Emma was right. It had been mad to embark on a book, but at the time everyone was telling her she must capitalize on her public profile. She'd also been intrigued by the challenge of writing a popular book – she instinctively felt she could do it well. It would be fun just to tell a story, rather than produce a rigorous critical analysis. And, in truth, a part of her, that she wasn't particularly proud of, was ambitious and driven, always reaching for the higher rung, always looking for acclaim, praise, recognition.

Still, she could easily have ignored the leaflet that day. If she had, she might still be trawling around looking for a book idea even now. It was the foul weather that did it. It was February half-term, eighteen months ago now, and the rain was relentless. David was away as usual and Marta had mild flu so Olivia had taken the children down to Sussex for a few days. Stuck inside the Farmhouse, the rooms seemed to shrink. Dom was fuming because he had wanted to stay in London with the friends who were, even then, becoming problematic; Paul was glued to the Xbox and Jess either fought with Paul or whined that she was bored. When the leaflet flopped onto the doormat Olivia seized on it.

The Real Diary of a Victorian Lady!

Come and see a most exciting local discovery! A sensational Victorian diary, handed down through one family. On short-term loan by Lady Catherine Burley of Ileford Manor.

The museum was only a twenty-minute drive away. She forced Jess into the car with the bribe of a hot chocolate in town on the way home.

She felt Vivian's curious presence the moment they came through the door. There was an odd tension, as if there had been an intake of breath. Olivia's first thought was that she had been recognized. She waited for a comment, and wished she had remembered to brush her hair, but there was silence.

As she paid for the ticket, she noticed the sticker: '*My name is Vivian Tester. Ask me anything.*' Vivian did not look like a person who could be asked anything. Her square face was blank, framed by coarse, cropped, iron-flecked hair. She looked dense and forbidding. As she handed over the tickets, her small eyes cast down, a low growl rose from behind the desk.

'Bertie, stop it, you fool.' Her voice – loud, quite deep, almost a bark itself – made both Olivia and Jess jump.

'Is that a dog?' Jess peered round the counter edge, her hair curtaining to the floor. She had been campaigning for a dog for years. 'Oh! He's sooo cuuute. What's his name?' She vanished behind the counter before Olivia could stop her.

'Don't touch him!' Vivian's head whipped around. 'He's nervous with strangers.'

Jess backed off and returned to Olivia's side. It seemed a bit irresponsible to keep an animal that was afraid of strangers at the front desk. Vivian fixed her bright eyes on Olivia, as if challenging her to object. 'He only growls if he feels threatened.'

Olivia did not ask where the diary was, then, she just wanted to get Jess away from the disturbed dog.

The museum was only the front few rooms of a seventeenth-century house. Jess gazed glumly at a Victorian wedding dress and a bust of Milton. Not surprisingly, given the weather and the limited scope of the place, not to mention its gatekeeper, they were the only visitors. Olivia felt Vivian's eyes on her.

Jess spotted an exhibit that was constructed to look like a hole in a wooden floor. They went and peered into it together, counting eleven separate, very small, adult shoes, none of them a pair, a leather hat, a child's frothy lace dress and a dismembered doll's arm. It was an early twentieth-century cache.

Jess was curious. 'Why's all this stuff in a hole?'

'People used to hide things under the floorboards to distract the evil spirits, so they wouldn't hurt the family. A sort of decoy.'

'What's a decoy?'

'A stand-in, a trap.' They both jumped. Vivian was right behind them. Neither of them had even heard her cross the room. 'Childhood mortality rates were very high, they were anxious that evil spirits would come for their children.'

'My mum knows all about this, she's a historian,' Jess said. 'She's on the TV. She's famous.'

'Oh. I'm really not.' Olivia shook her head and laughed. 'Don't listen to her.'

'You're not on TV?'

'No, I mean, I am on TV. A bit.'

'What have you done?'

'Oh, well, the most recent thing was a BBC 2 series called *The Incurables,* about Victorian women and asylums?'

'I don't watch much television.'

Olivia felt uncomfortable, as if she had been caught boasting. Perhaps she had.

'She was on *Would I Lie to You?*' Jess said. 'And the news and breakfast telly. And she's on the radio all the time.'

'*Would I Lie to You?*' Vivian raised her eyebrows. Her button eyes gleamed.

'It's a gameshow where people have to decide whether you're lying or telling the truth. My mum's a brilliant liar. They all believed her.'

'Did they?' Vivian smiled, with her lips tight shut.

'She's going to be on *Pointless Celebrities* too.'

Olivia put a hand on Jess's head. 'Vivian's got more interesting things to think about than TV shows, love, she's a museum curator.'

'Actually, I'm not,' Vivian corrected her. 'I'm filling in for the curator, who's visiting her sister in Jersey.'

'Oh, are you? Well, maybe you can help us? We got a flyer – we came to see the Victorian diary?'

There was a pause as if Vivian was struggling to decide whether to show it to them. Then she said, 'Yes. I suppose with your Victorian interests, you'd want to see that, wouldn't you?'

She turned and beetled across the room on crepe-soled shoes.

Olivia and Jess looked at each other, wide-eyed with the urge to laugh. Olivia took Jess by the hand, squeezed it hard, and they followed.

Vivian was standing by a glass cabinet. It contained a notebook, hardbound in black cloth and leather. It was closed, as if the contents were secret. Olivia felt the light, bright thrill of a potential find. In her deepest heart she loved nothing more than to touch an amazing manuscript, to smell an old book. The feeling she got when she held something that had been written a hundred years ago was like nothing else. It was the reason she had become a historian.

'There's a little damage from age, fading and such, and some pages have been torn out, but it's perfectly legible,' Vivian said.

Olivia dropped Jess's hand and bent to look at the book more closely. The lights were bouncing off the glass but Vivian still didn't open the cabinet. 'There are only eight entries in the diary,' she was saying. 'They were all written in 1898 by Lady Annabel Burley, the second wife of Lord Charles Burley. He built Ileford Manor, not far from here. It's very interesting. It's actually a murder confession.'

'A *murder confession*? My God. Really? Who did she murder?'

'Her husband, Lord Burley.'

Olivia stepped closer to the cabinet. 'That's incredible –
seriously? She writes about killing him in this diary? How did
she do it?'

'She pushed him over the minstrel's gallery at Ileford Manor.'

'Did she go to prison for it?'

'Nobody ever knew she did it. His death was recorded as accidental. He was drunk.'

'So this diary's a *secret* confession?'

Vivian nodded. 'She concealed it till she died, then left it to
her stepson.'

Olivia physically needed to get the diary out, now. She needed
to touch it, sniff it, stroke the old leather, prise it open to see the
handwriting, read Annabel's thoughts. But Vivian still did not
budge. She looked tense and excitable, if contained. She tapped
her fingers against her navy slacks.

'Are you a local historian?' Olivia decided that she needed to
put Vivian at ease a bit, before she asked outright to pick up the
diary.

'No. I'm not a historian at all. I'm a scientist. Retired.'

'Oh, a school teacher?' She didn't know why she said this. Perhaps it was because Vivian had the bossy, clipped air of the
teacher that everyone obeyed but nobody liked.

'I was an Oxford professor!' Vivian's face had turned scarlet.

'Oh, were you? I . . .'

Vivian straightened her cardigan by tugging on its hem and
stared hard at the diary with clenched teeth. Olivia had the
impression that she had just been subjected to an outrageous
and impulsive lie, but the subject was clearly closed.

She had Googled Vivian afterwards, of course, and her instinct
had turned out to be right. There were no Professor Testers in
any science department of Oxford University. There never had

been. Presumably Vivian had lied because she wanted to be taken seriously. She did not want some professor, some London TV presenter, dismissing her as a country school teacher. It was quite spirited of her, in a way, to react with such an extravagant lie.

Vivian took a key from her cardigan pocket, then bent down and unlocked the case. She stood back with a brief, permissive hand gesture.

The book was quite heavy, with quarter binding and seven bands of gold foil across its spine, more of a notebook than a lady's diary, with the faintest scent of birch bark. Well preserved. Olivia turned it over, catching a whiff of aged paper. The leather felt stiff. It creaked as she eased the spine open. She had seen and held similar late nineteenth-century notebooks. This one certainly felt authentic.

Inside there were knotty edges close to the spine where pages, quite a few by the look of it, had been torn out. The first page was stiffened with age, crammed with fine-nibbed handwriting. It was tight and controlled, not particularly feminine or elegant. People always assumed Victorian penmanship meant a neat copperplate but it could just as well be untidy and idiosyncratic, like this, and surprisingly modern.

The ink was a faded brown but perfectly legible. Olivia's heart quickened as she began to read the words that had been set down by this woman over a century before.

9th day of June, 1898

I have only two companions in this world – my pen and Thoby, who snores at my feet as I write. They are my only solace in this cold, damp house, where I live in solitude, in a world of my own that scarcely anybody ever enters.

She looked up. The room swayed. She must have been holding her breath. The voice was so recognizable, so modern. She longed to sit down and read the whole thing, right now, but she knew Jess would lose patience. She had wandered off somewhere already. Vivian's eyes were fixed on her.

'This is wonderful, Vivian,' she half-whispered.

Vivian smiled, then, showing small, blunt teeth. She looked like a child who had been praised, unexpectedly.

'Who owns this diary? Who do I have to ask for permission to examine this properly?'

'Well, me, actually.'

'You?'

Vivian cleared her throat. 'I work at Ileford. I look after everything for the current Lady Burley. I'm not planning to leave the diary here. I've been talking to people at Southampton University—'

'Mum!' Jess called, from across the room. 'Can we go now?'

Olivia closed the book. 'Look, I don't know who you've been in touch with at Southampton, but I know people at the British Museum and at the British Library, experts in Victorian documents. They'd *really* want to see this. They could verify it for you, you know, confirm that it's definitely Victorian.'

'Why wouldn't it be?' Vivian looked at it, anxiously. 'Annabel left it to her stepson, Quentin, who left it to his second cousin, the current Lady Burley.'

'Great. That's a really solid provenance.' Olivia felt her own excitement swell. 'Look, Vivian, is there any chance I could examine this, properly, before you take it anywhere? The fact that it contains a murder confession makes it exceedingly intriguing and probably quite valuable.'

A vicious snarling came across the museum followed by a high-pitched scream.

'Stop that!' Vivian bellowed.

'Jess!' Olivia looked at the book in her hands and bundled it back into the cabinet.

Jess ran through, face alight. 'That dog tried to bite me!'

Vivian vanished into the lobby.

Jess was trembling, but more from excitement than fear. She was otherwise unhurt.

Vivian reappeared a moment later, her face dark. 'I told you he was nervous,' she said to Jess. 'I specifically told you not to touch him.'

'I didn't touch him!'

'You are a silly girl.'

Olivia began to object, but then she stopped herself. She could not afford to alienate Vivian. This was suddenly all going in the wrong direction. 'Look – sorry, I'm sorry about this, I should probably take Jess home, but could I possibly come back this week? Could I have a closer look at it?'

Vivian's brass buttons caught the overhead lights.

'Or should I ask permission from Lady Burley?'

'No!' Vivian folded her arms across her cardigan. 'Lady Burley's terminally ill. She's in a care home. She can't be approached. It would worry and upset her.'

'Of course, I wouldn't want that. Is there another family member who might give permission?'

'There's just me.'

'So it's up to you to make decisions on Lady Burley's behalf?' Olivia felt as if she had just chased a slippery dog round in a circle.

'Yes.'

'And would you consider it?'

The corners of Vivian's mouth twitched. 'I suppose I would.'

'Nura, sweetie, have you got enough sunscreen on?' Emma called. 'Your shoulder looks a little bit pink.'

Olivia shaded her eyes and sat up. Her thighs were sticking to the chair and she was boiling hot. She had to stop thinking about Vivian. Thinking about Vivian always made her feel tense and guilty. But she had treated Vivian well. She had paid her generously, offered her more money several times. She had really been very patient with her. But it was the dog, of course. Every time she thought about Vivian's dog, even now, she felt panicky.

Perhaps it was a wider discomfort, too. She had never really grown to understand Vivian, though she had had glimpses of the private, awkward, nervy person behind the static mask. In a way, that professor lie said a lot about Vivian's personality. She was far too clever for a life as a housekeeper, or whatever she was at Ileford, and she did not like to be made to feel inferior. She had a rigorous academic mind but there was something flamboyant about her imagination, too. Pretending to have been an Oxford professor was unhinged, but also faintly plausible.

Of course, to lie like that suggested a certain abnormality. Vivian was almost certainly on some spectrum somewhere. She should have set more limits on Vivian's involvement. But, without realizing it, she had come to rely on her for almost all the research. Vivian had an apparently unlimited capacity to obsess over details and facts. It did not take long before she was as fascinated by the subject as Olivia was. And as the months went by Vivian's confidence as a researcher grew. She was certainly

demanding and unstable, opinionated and touchy, very difficult to manage, but the work she produced was magnificent.
Whatever Olivia asked for would appear in full and on time:
ordered, digestible and always verifiable. Soon, she was following leads on her own, producing new areas for research that
Olivia might never have thought to pursue. Without Vivian,
Annabel would have taken years to pull together and would have
been an inferior book. Vivian had made herself irreplaceable.

Not that Olivia could have replaced her even if she had wanted
to because Vivian controlled the diary. Without Vivian there
was no *Annabel*.

But what a relief that this association could finally end.

Well, almost. She still had to deal with Vivian's hopes for the
future, this new book idea. She had never suggested that they
could continue to work together after *Annabel*. She had no idea
where Vivian had got that idea. The last thing on earth she
wanted was to keep Vivian on. It was far too exhausting.

But a complicated to-and-fro email exchange about this was a
bad idea. She didn't want any misunderstandings and she didn't
want to be unkind. Vivian was on her own in the world. She had
so little in her life and Olivia had the feeling that she had
received harsh blows in the past. She deserved to be let down
gently and tactfully. That would have to wait until she got back.

'I feel like you're very distracted right now,' said Emma in a
prickly voice. Her freckled face was pink beneath the sunscreen
and she was standing up now, her hands bunching her linen
dress on her hips.

'Oh God, Em, I'm sorry, you're right, I am. I totally am, I'm
being awful. I just . . . I've got a few things on my mind, work
and . . .'

Emma nodded but turned away and fixed her gaze on their

girls in the pool. From behind she looked as small and stiff as a huffy child.

Olivia took a deep breath. She really did have to stop thinking about Vivian all the time. Except for that one awful thing – and she could not bear to think about that, even now – she had not done anything bad. In fact, she'd been extraordinarily tolerant, most of the time. Vivian really wasn't her responsibility any more. It was time to let go of the guilt, slough off the discomfort it had left on her and move on.

She turned to Emma. 'I can't sit and stare at this water any more – let's have a swim!'

Vivian

South of France

It is unreasonably hot, sweltering already, down in the village.

The thermometer outside the *hôtel de ville* says thirty degrees and it is only ten in the morning. I had forgotten what real heat actually means and I am not comfortable, not at all. My thighs rub, the waistband of my shorts digs, sweat prickles beneath my hat and I feel light-headed as I walk through the village, carrying all my equipment and my daypack. I look carefully at the tables outside the cafe as I pass it, and pause at the *boulangerie* door. Just in case.

I somehow managed to sleep in this morning, though I never usually do that. I am cursing myself for it now. It is the time difference, of course, and also tiredness from the interminable journey down through France. Mercifully, my visitor did not come in the night and I woke feeling quite rested – and famished. I could not resist the *chambre d'hôte* breakfast that had been laid out in a fussy dining room: slices of ham, glutinous cheeses, hunks of baguette with jam and salty butter and milky coffee, served, somewhat pretentiously, in a bowl. I restrained myself from asking for a cup even though I was sure that the owner herself takes her coffee in a cup. She is steel-haired, goat-faced and does not look particularly amenable to suggestions or requests.

As I pass the fountain at the centre of the village a pigeon defecates from above. Its paintball of excrement splatters just centimetres from my foot. I am reminded of the incident, a few weeks ago now, when I was walking from my car to the scullery door and a roof slate hurtled down. It missed my skull by millimetres and exploded into shards by my foot. For the first time I was genuinely glad that Bertie is not here because the slate hit the exact spot, by my side, where he used to trot.

The roofers have diagnosed 'nail sickness', which is no trivial matter. The repairs to Ileford's corroded roof nails will apparently cost thousands. I tried to discuss this with Lady Burley but she became confused by the notion that nails could become sick. I am thankful that she offered me power of attorney as there is still a considerable sum in the Jersey investment account, and some in a Panamanian fund, too, which she had completely forgotten. She really would not cope without me, her mind is no longer reliable.

I glance at the map and turn into a slightly cooler, narrow street that inclines steeply from the village towards the hill path. I think about roof tiles and pigeon shit. Life can be very circular. A fortune started over a hundred years ago from the import of bird excrement is now paying for the roof it constructed.

Olivia found the Burley guano business amusing, I remember. She liked us to meet in a dreadful artisan bakery in town, with ruinously expensive coffee and tables populated by young men in bushy Victorian beards – a minefield for poor Bertie. It was there that I first told her how Burley had made his fortune in the 1860s. She laughed a lot at that. I remember how her deep blue irises, enhanced by make-up that day, looked almost iridescent.

'I love it,' she cried. 'Ileford's built on *bird shit*!'

'Well, not *on*,' I corrected. '*From the profits of.* Guano's the excrement of Peruvian sea birds. It was used as an agricultural fertilizer; it's rich in nitrates – nitrogen, potassium and phosphate. But the Peruvian supplies went into steep decline . . .'

'No,' she interrupts me, 'I know about the guano boom and bust – the sensible businessmen stayed in nitrates and started getting supplies from the South American desert and selling them as explosives. They got very rich out of the First World War – but I guess Burley didn't do that? I just meant . . . It's quite poetic isn't it, that he built his fortune on bird shit? You know, given that he was such a shit himself.'

I wasn't quite following her and so I found myself retreating to a subject that made me feel safer. 'There's actually a complex and extensive relationship between excrement and the economy. Take your father's favourite, the dung beetle. They create enormous ecological and economic benefits by clearing and fertilizing the land. They save the British cattle industry about £367 million a year.'

'That's right, I read that somewhere too . . . Where was that? The *Guardian*? They're in decline because of the toxic worming chemicals that farmers are shoving down the throats of cattle, aren't they? My father would be really upset by that.'

'Well, yes, it *is* upsetting, very upsetting. Dung beetles are remarkable creatures.' I couldn't seem to stop myself, then; it is a failing of mine. When I start to talk about something that interests me greatly I cannot stop, even if my audience might not share my fascination, even though I may want to stop and know that I am embarrassing myself. 'Dung beetles are the only creatures on earth to navigate using the Milky Way.' I felt panic unfolding inside me. 'Ancient cultures recognized how special they are, even if we can't. The ancient Egyptians had the sacred scarab – they envisaged the God of the rising sun as Khepri, the dung beetle, pushing his ball up from the ground, across the heavens, then burying it again. For the Egyptians the scarab is the cycle of life, rebirth and reinvention – in hieroglyphics it even means "transformation". Of course, you're in good company with your own named dung beetle. Scientists on a Natural History Museum project a few years ago discovered a new dung beetle in Costa Rica and named it after Charles Darwin.' I finally forced myself to stop talking by drinking some tea, even though I badly wanted to tell her its full Latin name.

Her eyes were very wide and fixed on me. 'Wow, Vivian, you sound just like my father.' She put her head on one side. 'You've been reading up on dung beetles then.'

I felt my face grow very hot and looked at my wristwatch and then down at Bertie. I felt very flustered indeed then and quite sweaty. 'It's five to four.'

'Oh, right, yes, of course, nearly four o'clock.' She smiled at me, rather gently. 'Bertie needs his walk, doesn't he? We can talk more about this another time, can't we?' Her voice was suddenly maternal and I knew that she had seen my distress and embarrassment and was trying to alleviate it. I was grateful to her for this kindness. She didn't tease me or treat me as an oddity because of what I had said and the way I had said it. She didn't laugh or humiliate me.

Perhaps that moment marked the beginning of my change of

heart. Perhaps that was the moment when I started not just to tolerate, but to quite like her.

Beneath the shade of a crumbling limestone wall, I stop and wipe my forehead on my sleeve. I am puffing and overheated and I am not even at the hillside path. I have been accused of being an emotionless person many times in my life, but I do not feel emotionless. If anything, my emotions sometimes feel far too intense to manage or control. I remember as a little girl, when my father was becoming difficult, I would feel an over- whelming panic rising inside me, a blinding, chaotic sensation. I learned to get out of the cottage when this happened because my father would become even more difficult if he saw me lose control. In winter I would run to the woods to my hollow oak. In the late stages of heart rot, her cavity was cushioned with moist decomposing leaves and fungi and was livid with beetles. I could climb right inside her and curl there, just watching them for as long as I could. But in the winter it was very cold, even though it was sheltered inside the tree, and sometimes I couldn't last long enough and I would have to go home and face him before he had properly calmed down.

In summer, though, I would hide in the long grass of the cow meadow, sometimes for a whole day and once or twice even overnight. I would distract myself by watching the insects up close. I always loved the dung beetles best. They seemed so busy and constructive. I would get a stout stick and poke around in cowpats to find them coming and going, digging their heads down, re-emerging. I used to imagine that, like these lac- quered little beasts, I too had a protective shield, elytra, covering my body.

The elytra are what make a beetle a beetle. They are

extraordinarily clever devices – hardened wings that cover more delicate membranous ones, acting as stabilizers during flight, protection against abrasion, or a clever defence against predators. In some water beetles the elytra even trap air bubbles so that the beetle can breathe beneath the surface. But dung beetles were always my favourites. I used to imagine what it would feel like to tunnel deep into a warm place where nobody could hurt me, where nobody would ever think to look.

Perhaps this was where my strong preference for solitude began. I am more comfortable alone, not least at work. This allows me to focus intensely, and to produce excellence, but it has also counted against me socially. I have always been the odd one out, something of a curiosity; the uncomfortable person with the empty seat next to her, unskilled in charm, allegiances or game playing.

It is therefore doubly surprising that I came to enjoy my regular contact with Olivia. The solitude of Ileford without Lady Burley – and later without Bertie – was probably too much even for me and I began to look forward to our fortnightly meetings in the bakery. In the beginning, I think Olivia felt it would be prudent to monitor me closely, but as the months wore on I began to suspect that coming down to Sussex to meet me and talk about the book was her escape too. I suspect that she rather welcomed the excuse to leave her children with the au pair and spend a night alone in the Farmhouse.

She did not invite me to the Farmhouse in the beginning. She gave a little talk at the start about her policy of keeping her personal and professional worlds separate. The same, apparently, did not apply to me, since she was always trying to come to Ileford.

I did allow her to come in a few times, but these visits were difficult for both of us. Her eyes lit up the first time she entered, when she rushed to the foot of the wide staircase and ran her hands over the barley twist spindles and ornate newel posts. She gazed up at the oak-panelled ceiling, which I've always found oppressive, and then at the minstrel's gallery, and said, in hushed tones, 'My God, Vivian. It's just splendid.'

I kept her to the presentable downstairs rooms, though she would beg to see the whole house. She would walk through the rooms, touching everything – stroking the balloon-back chairs, picking up a brass candlestick, peering at the dark oil paintings, as if she were trying to connect with Annabel's spirit through these objects. I did not have the heart to tell her that most of the furnishings and ornaments are not original. Uncle Quentin sold off the bulk of the family treasures and Lady Burley has been through bouts of fevered updating downstairs. Olivia seemed entranced by the Annabel who was taking shape in her imagination and who was I to spoil this for her? Indeed, it was the whole point.

I watched with interest as Olivia's Annabel emerged on the pages. Her Annabel has an acute mind and decisive taste in everything from furniture to books. People find her attractive and magnetic and a bit glamorous, if somewhat intimidating, though really she is very detail-orientated and obsessive – what Olivia calls a 'nerd'. As one obituary put it, 'her ideals were high and uncompromising'. Whilst essentially a kind person, she has a tendency towards condescension and pretends to be much more tolerant than she really is. In a professional setting she is purposeful and confident – she is highly intelligent and she knows it – but a deeper insecurity lurks beneath this, a tendency towards self-doubt. She sets impossibly high standards for herself and often feels as if she is not good enough. Whilst never submissive, she certainly cares too much what people think of her – a single harsh comment can derail and preoccupy her. She is highly ambitious, though she disguises that well, from herself as much as from others.

Olivia has, of course, produced a self-portrait, more or less. I have refrained from pointing this out to her. Indeed, I have come to admire her Annabel, almost as much as she does.

I am sweating like an old horse now but the village has come to an abrupt end and I am standing at the entrance to the woody hillside path. I turn to survey the salmon-pink rooftops below and the hazy hills beyond, dotted here and there with holiday homes. A bird of prey floats with unhurried grace across the azure sky. I take off my pack, put it down and unzip it. Fortunately I have brought a powerful pair of binoculars. I expect I am going to need them.

Olivia

South of France, Day Four

It wasn't until the fourth afternoon that Olivia managed to talk to Chloe. She spotted her alone beneath the vines, in her swimsuit and white cotton kaftan with her book, and for once nobody else was around. She went over and lay down on the recliner next to Chloe's. Bees fussed around the lavender bushes that bordered the terrace and a gentle breeze ruffled the vine canopy above them.

For a while they talked about how well the younger boys were getting along. Then they talked about Dominic's grumpiness.

'Poor guy, though, fifteen's so hard, and he hasn't got anyone his own age to hang out with here. The younger ones must be driving him mad.' Chloe picked at a thread on her kaftan. Olivia noticed the sheen of sweat on her face as Chloe bent and took a swig from her water bottle.

She tried to describe, then, how worried she was about Dom – how he wasn't speaking to David, though neither of them could work out why. Usually, Chloe would engage in a conversation like this, she'd be sympathetic and helpful, but she seemed distracted. She picked at the thread, shifted, tucked up her golden legs, then straightened them and pulled her straw hat down over her eyes. Olivia began to feel as if Chloe was fighting the urge to get up and run away.

She wanted to admit to Chloe the full extent of her worries about Dom – she really wanted to tell her that he'd been found smoking weed on the school playing field and had been suspended for a week and almost expelled. She wanted to say how concerned she was about the group of friends he'd got in with, and how helpless she felt. Above all, she wanted to tell Chloe what David had done. But she found herself unable to do any of this because Chloe's edginess was so unfamiliar, so unsettling. It felt like a barrier. It felt practically hostile.

She wondered then if Chloe, like Emma, was thinking that Dom's behaviour had something to do with her, that it was her fault for working too much and not being there for him enough. Unlike Emma, who could not possibly be a corporate lawyer and hands-on parent, Chloe had, against the odds really, managed to combine motherhood with a thriving career. She had built up her ceramic restoration business from nothing and she now managed high-profile clients and three employees. She had also achieved a level of flexibility in her working life that Olivia couldn't possibly emulate. Somehow, she always made it to her boys' sports fixtures and school plays and she was there for them, often, after school too. Chloe had probably never missed a parents' evening. And perhaps as a consequence of this – as well as Chloe's essentially Zen approach to living – it was impossible to imagine Ben or Miles taking drugs or not speaking to their father for weeks on end.

Chloe pulled off her hat, flipped her feet onto the ground

and sat up, suddenly, facing her. Her green eyes looked panicky as she leaned her elbows on her knees.

'Oh my God. What? What's wrong?' Olivia swung her legs down too, so she was sitting sideways on the lounger facing Chloe. She reached out and touched Chloe's hot arm. 'What is it, Chlo?'

Chloe flinched, but then grabbed Olivia's hand and squeezed it between her long fingers. 'Liv, I've got to talk to you about something. It's about David . . .'

The barrier was down, Olivia felt a rush of relief. 'Oh! He told you? It's OK. God – I know. He confessed to me two weeks ago.'

'He *did*?'

'Yes, God. I wanted to talk to you about this but he made me promise not to.'

'What did he say to you?'

'Well, strictly speaking he didn't say anything, I found out. I saw some emails from the bank and I made him show me all the accounts. I don't know how much he's told you, Chlo, but he's been monumentally stupid. We went through all the bank stuff together and it's totally disastrous.'

Chloe said nothing. She nodded, rapidly, and blinked.

'He's basically ruined us.'

Chloe covered her mouth with both hands, then. Her brow wrinkled. She suddenly looked older.

So he clearly hadn't told Chloe the whole story. Presumably he'd blurted something out when they went off together the previous day in the car. She had no idea why he'd done this when he'd made her promise not to say anything. It was maddening of him to ban her from talking to Chloe, then do so himself.

'Did he tell you all this yesterday? Did he tell you he's blown all the remaining *Intuition* money and much, much more?'

'No. No. He didn't tell me that.'

'So he didn't admit that he'd ploughed a fortune into a high-risk fund? Did he tell you he had this whole complicated theory worked out and he truly believed it would make us rich, and then when it didn't, he added the rest of our savings, and then when that vanished too, he borrowed to cover the losses? So we're now getting enormous interest charges that we can't possibly pay – we can't even pay the mortgage this month.'

'No.' Chloe's face was as white as her kaftan. 'My God, Liv,' she said. 'What are you going to do?'

'Well, even with the bits of TV I've got coming up I can't begin to cover it. Our combined earnings are basically nothing compared with the debt we're in now. So it looks like I'm going to have to sell the Farmhouse.'

'But you can't – your father . . .'

'I know, but I'm going to have to. I'm lucky to be in such a ridiculously privileged position that I actually have options. If I didn't have the Farmhouse we'd lose our home at this point. Unless *Annabel*'s a massive bestseller and there's some other miracle, I don't think I have a choice, I'm going to have to put it on the market.' She couldn't even tell Chloe about the BBC offer. Chloe would probably advise her to detach herself from the shame, go with the flow and do it.

'But *Annabel* could do really well, couldn't it, isn't that what everyone thinks?' Chloe said. 'And if you got a lucrative TV deal too?'

'I can't bank on either of those . . .'

'But what about David? He got you into this, can't he do something to pay it off?'

'He's trying. He's very ashamed and very guilty right now. He's been calling round looking for editorial jobs, and he's going to take on a lot more speaking engagements, which can pay well, but he really isn't going to solve this on his own. It's just such a massive sum, Chlo, it's unimaginable. I could kill him.'

'What about his book?'

'Oh, come on, he's been writing that for nine years now and as far as I can tell it's in pretty disastrous shape, so I'm not holding my breath. And we need the money now – soon. Every month that goes by it gets worse.'

'Oh, darling.' Chloe squeezed her hand even more tightly. 'I'm so sorry.'

'No, it's OK. Really.' Olivia straightened her back. She hated pity. It made her feel weak. 'I'm lucky I *can* figure out ways to pay it off. I keep telling myself no one died, no one's sick, the children are OK. It's just money at the end of the day, isn't it?'

'But it's much more than that.' Chloe said, vehemently. 'You can't sell the Farmhouse. Oh God, and . . . look . . . I . . .'

Miles burst onto the terrace shouting, 'Mum! You have to come RIGHT NOW!'

'What?' Chloe shaded her eyes. 'I'm talking to Liv.'

'Ben got bit by a scorpion!'

Chloe leaped off the sun lounger. Her kaftan was stuck to the back of her legs, which were striped from the slats. 'Where is he?'

'He's out by the tower. It might not be a scorpion, but he's blubbing anyway.'

Olivia jumped up, shoved her feet into her sandals and ran after Chloe. Chloe's cotton sleeves flapped, her bare feet trod lightly across the hot flagstones. She reminded Olivia of a swan, stretching her wings, about to take off.

Olivia

South of France, Day Four

That night, Olivia lay rigid in bed. The children had failed to calm down after the 'scorpion bite', which turned out to be a humungous splinter, and they grew increasingly unhinged and combative as the day wore on. There were hours of deranged shenanigans at bedtime as they ran between the house and the tower, panicking about gravestone ghosts and snakes and noises in the upper room; Nura was sobbing because Jess put a praying mantis in her hair; Miles thumped his brother over a Ouija board they had constructed. Paul shoved Jess head first into a sleeping bag, then got in on top of her. Then, when the children were finally asleep, she and David had a row in their bedroom about Dominic.

It started when she asked him to take Dom when he went to buy food the next day. He said Dom didn't want to go. She accused him of not trying, of opting out. He accused her of neurosis and interference. They snarled at one another across the French bed for a long time, until he shouted, 'You have to stop trying to control me the whole fucking time! You have to trust me! Just let me do this my way!'

She couldn't even begin to argue with him about the issue of trust. It was too absurd. She went into the bathroom to get away from him. She took a shower, shaved her legs, removed her toe-nail polish – spent as long as she could in there – and when she came out he was sleeping, or pretending to.

She was far too wound up to sleep. She lay twitching and tense for a long time. Next to her, on his back, David let out a satisfied, glottal snore. She got up, furious, shoved her feet into her plimsolls and grabbed a shawl from the back of the chair. She swept up the American proofs of *Annabel* as she passed the desk. If she was going to be awake all night, she might as well get some work done.

In the stuffy kitchen, she opened and closed cupboards, pick-ing out a handful of salty cashews, sloshing cognac into a glass from a bottle she found at the back of the cupboard. As she stepped out into the fragrant night air, she was halted by the sky; stars pulsed out over the blackened hills, and the ghostly wash of the Milky Way swept in a great arc beneath the constel-lations. The stars made her think of the slides her father had liked to show her under the microscope in his lab, specks of life in hectic motion. He had been so disappointed when she'd chosen the arts over science. Perhaps that was why she'd been so driven to succeed. Perhaps she was still, even now, trying to prove to her father that history mattered.

She put the American manuscript down on the table and covered her legs with the shawl. The night air felt close and still. Moths flapped and fluttered against the outside lamp. Some-where below the olive groves a dog barked; another answered, rhythmically, from far across the valley. Cicadas whirred and clicked like the mechanics of a sprinkler system, a sound that seemed to vibrate in the back of her skull. She felt the tickle of a mosquito on her neck, a needle stab; she slapped it away but the spot throbbed and immediately began to itch.

She scratched at it with a fingernail and stared at the American manuscript. She realised that she had never even told Vivian about the American publishing deal, and she was not sure why. She had a feeling Vivian would be anti-American, and make some sort of fuss. If she'd known that Vivian would be so tricky to manage, would she have embarked on this book at all? She really wasn't sure. The appeal of the diary would always have been overwhelming, but it had been obvious, from the very start, that Vivian operated marginally outside the social norm and therefore would be difficult.

She'd seen that even at their first meeting. The bakery was the only neutral place she could think of that would allow dogs and Vivian had told her in an email that Bertie could neither be left in the car, nor stay home alone. As soon as she'd sat down she'd realized this was not the right place for Vivian, it was too trendy, too noisy, but Vivian hadn't invited her to Ileford and instinct told her not to have Vivian at the Farmhouse; she needed to keep her at arm's length.

Vivian entered the bakery exactly on time, her black dog cradled like a baby in her arms. Its wet, wiry coat was flecked with steel, its paws and muzzle tipped with grey, its eyebrows streaked and bushy like an old man's, drooping at the edges, giving it an air of great apprehension. Vivian was cube-shaped in a damp Barbour jacket. She moved bulkily past the other customers, her mouth set and her wind-slapped cheeks raw.

Olivia got up, smiling, and held out a hand, but the dog flinched, so she took it away again. Vivian did not seem perturbed.

'Now, then, Bertie,' she said. 'Don't worry, be nice.' The dog fixed Olivia with its nervy button gaze.

'It's lovely to see you again, Vivian. Thanks so much for coming in this awful weather. I hope you aren't soaked?'

Vivian looked puzzled. 'I have a weatherproof coat.'

'Right, yes. Good. Well, I wish I had a more sensible coat – I got a bit wet. It's pretty awful out there.'

Vivian nodded and sat down on the bench opposite. She looked uncomfortable. Droplets of rain clung to her cropped hair.

'So – what can I get you? Coffee? Cake?'

Vivian looked at the blackboard for a long time, anxiously weighing up her options. Eventually she said, 'A pot of tea for one.'

Olivia had come straight from a meeting at Channel 4 and was wearing heeled boots, her dark blue leather jacket and some make-up. This suddenly felt like a mistake. She should have washed her face and changed into wellies and a jumper – she didn't want to make Vivian feel awkward. 'Look, it's really kind of you to come out to meet me.' She smiled across the table.

Vivian lifted the dog off her lap and onto the floor, then unzipped her Barbour to reveal the same navy blue, brass-buttoned cardigan she'd worn in the museum.

Beneath the table Olivia felt the wet dog brush her leg, moving around, settling himself. She kept her own legs very still, half expecting to feel sharp teeth clamp onto her ankle.

'I also really appreciated you letting me come back last week to study the diary,' she said. 'It's just an amazing source. Annabel's completely captured my imagination now and I can't stop thinking about her.'

Vivian nodded and stared at her hands. She clearly did not do small talk.

'So anyway, as I said in my email, I'd love to write something about Annabel and the diary, if you'd consider letting me do that?' She was not sure whether to tell Vivian that she was envisaging a biography. She didn't want to scare her off. She glanced down at her notebook. 'I was really just hoping, today, to get a fuller picture of who Annabel was, you know, to find out some background, what you already know about her and the Burley family, if that's OK by you?'

'Yes, you said that in your email.' Vivian frowned.

'OK. Great. Good. Well . . . shall I just fire away then?'

Vivian nodded.

'Right then . . . So, let's start with Annabel's medical background, shall we? You said she trained at the Royal Free Hospital School of Medicine for Women?'

'That's right. She enrolled there in 1899, graduated in 1904, then she got her MD from the University of London, in 1910. I have copies of the paperwork. She became a house surgeon at Garrett Anderson's New Hospital for Women.'

'A surgeon! Excellent, God, this is wonderful.' Olivia wrote all the dates down. 'So she enrolled at medical school just a year after her husband, Lord Burley's, death? A year after she wrote the diary? Do you think she'd tried to persuade him to let her become a doctor and he wouldn't let her? My goodness – maybe that's why she killed him!'

'I have no idea.' Vivian's face was blank.

'Right. OK. So, Annabel was, what, in her early forties when she enrolled at medical school?'

'She was thirty-three.'

'Oh! She was quite young, really – though of course she'd

have been considered middle-aged and past it. It was such early days for women doctors, Vivian. I don't know how much you know about the history of women in medicine? Elizabeth Garrett Anderson qualified as a doctor in 1865, but she only managed it by exploiting a loophole, which the authorities then swiftly closed. Garrett Anderson was pretty much on her own until she co-founded the London School of Medicine for Women ten years later—'

'Nine years,' Vivian said, sharply. 'The London School of Medicine for Women opened in 1874.'

'Oh, yes, right, nine . . . So, the point is, it would have taken enormous determination for Annabel to enrol and become a doctor at that time, without family support, without any real status—'

'She had some money.'

'The Burley fortune?'

'What was left of it.'

Vivian's eyes were fixed on a bush-bearded man at the next table. Olivia wondered whether she knew, and didn't like, this person. But he seemed oblivious to Vivian's hostile gaze.

The waitress arrived with their drinks. Vivian reached for the teapot, opened it, and peered in. Her fingers were thick and weathered, her knuckles slightly swollen, nails short with a crescent of dirt, soil from the garden probably, under one thumbnail. No wedding ring. Olivia had not until now thought about Vivian's existence outside the museum. She realized that she didn't particularly want to know about Vivian's private life.

She sipped her cappuccino, then picked up her pen again. 'So shall we talk a bit about Lord Burley, Annabel's husband? He built Ileford Manor in the 1880s for his first wife, didn't he? It must be a lovely house?'

'It's a neo-Gothic monstrosity,' said Vivian. She poured her tea slowly, stopping a few times to check how full the cup was. 'But the architectural style was fashionable at the time. He built it to allow the family an escape from London because their daughter's health was fragile.'

'That's right, Annabel talks about this in the diary, doesn't she? Lord Burley had buried his wife and two children when she married him? That sort of loss is unimaginable, isn't it?' It was fantastic, she thought, that Lord Burley's back story was so heart-wrenching. When Annabel married him he must have been deranged from grief. She could make a lot of that – it gave Lord Burley real depth. The loss of his first wife and two children didn't excuse Lord Burley's brutality to Annabel, but it did make his alcoholism and unhappiness understandable. 'This is quite a back story, Vivian.'

Vivian stared at her tea and said nothing.

'And do we know how Lord Burley's two children died?'

'The daughter, Blanche, had consumption. Burley built the house because he thought the country air would cure her. But it didn't: she died soon after they moved into Ileford.'

Olivia shuddered. She imagined Lord Burley and his first wife, Violet, desperately trying to protect their daughter – going to such lengths to get out of London, constructing their big, modern house as a place of safety, only to lose little Blanche any-way, almost immediately. It was a heartbreaking genesis for a house. She scribbled on her notepad: *Ileford house/tragedy: building – hope – despair and loss.* Then she looked up. 'And what about their other child?'

'Their eldest son, Walter, drowned at Eton a year after Blanche died. He was thirteen years old. '

'Oh my God, Vivian, this is devastating stuff! Those poor

parents. And then Lord Burley's first wife died too – of grief, presumably, for their two children?'

'No. Lord Burley's first wife, Violet Burley, died in childbirth.'

'Oh! They had a third child? Did it survive? Was Annabel a stepmother? There's no mention of any child in her diary . . .'

'He did survive. His name was Quentin. The current Lady Burley always calls him "Uncle Quentin". He died in his seventies.'

'Uncle Quentin. Well. My goodness. So Annabel was a stepmother!'

'Yes. Uncle Quentin was three years old when Annabel married Lord Burley. She sent him to boarding school immediately.'

'At three years old?' Olivia shook her head as she wrote this down. 'It doesn't bear thinking about, does it, a toddler in a Victorian boarding school?'

Vivian blinked, but didn't comment.

Olivia did a quick calculation. If Uncle Quentin died in his seventies that would have been some time in the 1960s. This was brilliant – there might be actual stories passed down from Uncle Quentin to the current Lady Burley. That would be biographical gold dust.

'There's a shrine to Violet and the two dead children in the ornamental garden,' Vivian said.

'Is there? How sad. I'd love to see it some time. I'd really love to come and see Ileford.'

Vivian did not offer an invitation.

'OK, so. Can we go back a bit, for a moment, to Annabel's early life? I think you said she was married before, as a very young woman? Do we know what happened to her first husband?'

'She married a young Cambridge doctor, but he died of an arsenic overdose just two years later. Annabel came from Cambridge originally.'

'He committed suicide?' This was getting better and better. Olivia imagined a chapter on Annabel's first marriage – passionate first love ending in tragedy.

'It was an accidental death,' Vivian said. 'I have a copy of his obituary and death certificate.'

'Oh. Right. Well, Victorian men did sometimes take arsenic as a recreational drug.' Her instinct had been right then – Vivian had already done considerable research into the Burley family and Annabel's early life. She liked Annabel as the tragic young widow forced to remarry a rich older man. Vivian really was going to be useful if she'd unearthed all this background stuff already. 'Arsenic . . .' she said. 'It could have been murder!'

'The death certificate doesn't say that.' Vivian pursed her lips and looked down at her hands. 'It says accidental death.'

'That might mean suicide. Sometimes the family would hide a suicide out of shame. I mean, attempting suicide was actually a crime in Britain until the 1950s. That's why it's "commit" – like you commit a crime?'

Vivian stiffened. 'I don't know why Annabel's first husband died of arsenic poisoning, I'm just giving you the facts.'

'Right. Yes. Of course.' Olivia put down her pen. Vivian, she realized, did not respond to speculation. 'Well, either way, it's extra tragic that Annabel was a widow when she came to Ileford to marry Lord Burley. You've done such a lot of work on this, Vivian. I'm so impressed by how much you've found out about them all already.'

'Yes, well, I'm in charge of the Burley family archives. It's part of my job.'

'Poor Annabel. A young widow, packed off to a remote Sussex manor house to marry an old, violent alcoholic.'

'Lord Burley was not old.' Vivian's cheeks reddened. 'He was only sixty-three when she married him.'

'Oh, no, no, not old, of course – not old! I just meant . . . he was a lot older than Annabel.' Embarrassed by her own tactlessness, she decided it was best to move on. 'So, what happened to Annabel in the end? How did she die?'

'Acute rheumatic fever, January 1919.'

'Ah.' It was a slightly prosaic death. It would have been nice to have something a bit more heroic or dramatic. 'Young then? She was only in her fifties?'

Vivian nodded.

'And did Uncle Quentin inherit Ileford Manor from Annabel?'

'Yes.'

'So. The current Lady Burley, the woman who owns Ileford, your boss? She's Quentin's daughter? Lord Burley's granddaughter?'

'No, no. It's a very sparse family. Uncle Quentin never married. Lady Burley is his second cousin.'

Olivia wrote all this down. The line from Burley and Annabel to the current owner of Ileford really was delightfully short. It made this Victorian story feel even closer and more tangible.

'I'd love to talk to Lady Burley some time, Vivian. Do you think I could arrange to visit her in her care home, maybe?'

'Absolutely not.' Vivian's spine stiffened. 'I told you – I can only allow access to the diary on condition that you don't bother Lady Burley with this. No interview requests or requests for information, she's far too fragile. It would only make her anxious. I don't want this to dominate the short time she has left.'

'Of course, no, please – sorry – we must do whatever you think's best.' This was the first time Vivian had admitted that she was intending to allow access to the diary. Olivia tried not to let her excitement show. She felt as if any display of emotion, at this point, might drive Vivian away. She finished her coffee.

Beneath the table the dog began to whine. 'Bertie needs his

walk.' Vivian bent and hauled him back up onto her lap. He looked around, fretfully.

'But you haven't drunk your tea?'

'It's almost four o'clock. I always walk him at four.' Vivian stroked the triangles of her dog's ears and after a moment he nestled edgily into her arms. The two of them seemed to communicate all the time, silently, and the dog obviously took great comfort in Vivian's presence. It was quite touching to watch.

'Well, OK.' Olivia forced herself to sound relaxed. 'Maybe we could meet again later, after your walk? I'll probably stay here and do a bit of work now. I'm just finishing a paper.'

'On what?'

'Oh, this paper? I'm looking at the language used about Victorian women who were put in asylums by their husbands.'

'Did that happen a lot?'

'Yes, unfortunately it did. It was remarkably easy for a man to get his wife institutionalized, all he needed was a single witness and he could have her locked up.'

Vivian's face suddenly creased into an ungainly smile. 'I can see why you're so interested in Annabel then.'

Olivia leaned forwards, rolled up her sleeves and rested her elbows on the table. 'I really am, Vivian. She's fascinating to me. This is my period, my interests exactly, and to have the diary – an actual murder confession – well, it's just . . . It's incredible.'

Vivian shifted. She was about to leave, Olivia could tell. It was now or never. 'The thing is, I've been looking for a subject for a book, not an academic book but something more popular. A historical biography would be perfect. Annabel is pretty much my ideal subject.'

For the first time, Vivian looked right at Olivia. 'You want to write a *book*? I thought this was for an academic paper?'

'Well, originally that was what I was thinking, but there's just so much here, isn't there? Annabel's backstory is colourful, then there's the complexity of her marriage to the brutish Lord Burley and then of course the murder – that's just sensational. And to have her rise from all this tragedy and make it to medical school then become one of Britain's first women surgeons, well, it's just such a triumphant story, isn't it? So I really would love to write a biography of Annabel, if you'd let me, Vivian? I know this might sound a bit overblown but I kind of feel like I owe it to Annabel – to all the women like her who were such incredible trailblazers really – to tell her story. Would you – do you think – would you consider letting me do this?'

Vivian pressed her lips together and stared back down at her dog. Her face was scarlet. The dog looked a bit panicky too. He was sitting up, panting, his eyes bulging. Olivia knew then that this was it: she had to lock Vivian in now or she'd lose her. Vivian had obviously done a lot of the legwork and she could surely be carefully managed.

She had taken a leap of faith.

Olivia swatted another mosquito on her arm and scratched the spot. A bat swooped overhead, a shadowy shape half-glimpsed. She wondered whether, had she known then what she knew now, she'd have done the same thing. She would always have been fascinated by the diary and Annabel's life, but she'd definitely have been more wary. She'd have set clear limits on Vivian's involvement, from the start. Then again, Vivian would never have taken a back seat, it wasn't in her nature. Vivian would always have been fixated on the details.

She hadn't planned any of this. It had been an impulse to say, 'Listen, I'm going to need an RA – a research assistant. I can get a graduate student for the more complicated areas, but you've obviously done such a lot of research already on the Burley family, Vivian. What's your time like? Do you have any capacity to help me with this?'

Vivian's reply was strangled. 'You want *me* to help *you* write a book?'

'I'm not sure I could do it without you, to be honest.'

Vivian clutched the dog. 'I'll have to get Lady Burley's consent.'

'But you said . . .'

'I said she couldn't be interviewed, but you can't write a book about her family without her consent. That would be morally wrong.'

'No. Of course it would. Yes. Would it help if I wrote to her? I could write a letter right now for you to give to her – would that work?'

'It's four o'clock!'

'I'll email you a letter, right now, to give to her.'

Olivia got up, but Vivian was already moving away. 'Goodbye then.' She squeezed past the other customers, pressing the dog's head against her bosom and turning her back on the man with the beard. But then, as she reached the counter, she stopped. 'Elizabeth Garrett Anderson wasn't the first British woman to get a medical degree you know.' Her voice was slightly too loud.

Olivia felt the room grow quiet, heads turned.

'Margaret Ann Bulkley masqueraded as a man to graduate in medicine from Edinburgh University in 1812. She became an army surgeon, served in the Crimean War, feuded with Florence Nightingale, performed one of the first Caesarean sections . . .'

'God! Of course!' Olivia laughed. 'James Barry!'

'They only discovered her . . . female anatomy when she died of dysentery in 1865 and the nurses laid out her corpse.'

Olivia nodded, vigorously.

'Bulkley lived as James Barry for forty-six years to get the career she wanted. Now *that*' – Vivian gave a nod – 'is determination.'

Olivia gazed out at the twinkling lights of the French village in the valley below. James Barry – Margaret Ann Bulkley – must have lived in constant terror of discovery, of public shame and ridicule, of the end of the career that she'd sacrificed everything to have.

Another mosquito whined past her ear and she swiped it away. She should light a citronella candle. She yawned and rubbed her face. She had to stop thinking about Vivian all the time like this, going back over things again and again. She had to let go of the lingering discomfort, this mixture of irritation and guilt and, on some level, trepidation, that she felt every time she thought about Vivian.

She pulled the American manuscript towards her and leafed through the pages until she found the place where she had stopped proofreading that morning. It was the most sensational, but also the most troubling point in the diary. It was the one aspect of Annabel that she still felt she didn't fully understand.

Why would anyone choose to write down something so incriminating? In the book, of course, she'd produced a whole section on the psychology of written confessions. David had helped her with this part. He'd put her in touch with a Stanford University professor who was an expert on the subject. She'd produced a coherent argument about the psychology of self-expression, the therapeutic benefits of writing things down.

But still, intuitively, Annabel's actions didn't make sense. If you'd murdered your husband the last thing you would do, surely, is confess to it, in writing, at the time.

She re-read Annabel's description of that terrible night.

It is several hours since it happened and I am quite calm now. I am in my bed. The house is silent at last, paralysed by shock. Thoby is lying on my feet. He alone knows what I have done.

It started as a simple dispute. We encountered one another at the top of the great staircase and Burley insisted, again, that I come to the Dalrymples. I objected, most forcefully and he came at me and shoved me against the banister, thumping both fists on my chest. The metal knob of his stick pressed into my collarbone and I smelled fish on his breath, and spirits too. His eyes had the deadened look with which I am now familiar: it is the look that precedes violence. His cheeks had turned a patchy fuchsia colour. As he lifted his stick, I heard a snarling and he let out a bellow of pain. Thoby had him by the ankle.

When he raised his stick to bring it down onto Thoby's spine, I acted without thought. I ducked behind him and shoved his back. He pitched forwards, his chest against the railings. Thoby released his ankle and I saw him sway – his hand slipped. Without thought or hesitation, I bent and seized his lower legs. It was so quick. His body made a loud, slack thud as it landed on the floor of the great hall.

I swept Thoby up and ran to my bedroom. As I closed my door I heard Milly's fearful screams . . .

She pushed the pages aside and finished the brandy. There was a hint of relish in that one word, '*slack*'. It didn't quite fit with the heroic, almost saintly, portrait she'd painted of Dr Annabel Burley.

Annabel would, presumably, have kept this confession hidden in her Bloomsbury house until her death over twenty years later. But even that was a huge risk. If a servant, or Uncle Quentin, had found it, she'd have been hanged.

She did understand why Annabel should want to pass the confession to Quentin after her death. It was clear from several sources that Annabel and her stepson had loathed each other; they fought consistently over money and property. Annabel had wanted him to know that she'd pushed his violent father to his death. She had wanted the last word. This, of course, was another thing she'd rather skirted over in the book. Such a spiteful act didn't make Annabel look particularly sympathetic so she'd downplayed their conflict a bit.

It was a shame there was no mention, by Quentin himself, of the diary, of how he felt when he read about his father. Most of Quentin's surviving papers were financial, documenting his many irresponsible extravagances – Gatsby-esque parties, trips to Algeria, dancing bears.

She felt a light shiver across the back of her neck, as if a hand had trailed over her bare skin. She glanced over her shoulder, into the velvet darkness beyond the terrace, then she pulled the shawl off her legs and wrapped it around her shoulders. Goose-bumps had risen on her arms, even though she wasn't cold. Then she heard something rustle in the undergrowth, over on the other side of the pool, somewhere behind the vine canopy and the sun loungers.

Suddenly she knew that she was being watched. Someone was standing in the darkness just behind the vines, she was sure of it. She felt their presence with complete certainty.

She stared over, but it was too dark to see a shape or move-ment. 'Who's there?' she called. She rose to her feet, spooked by the high sound of her own voice. Her skin felt prickly. She didn't hesitate – she left the brandy glass, scooped up her papers and ran towards the open French windows.

Her hands fumbled as she slammed and locked them behind

her. She couldn't look through the glass because she felt sure
that, if she did, she would see a starlit figure staring at her across
the terrace. She imagined her old friend, the stalker, in his overcoat. She felt dizzy. There was a sweet smell coming from the
kitchen, old honeydew melon and the ooze of dark grapes at the
bottom of the fruit bowl. The house was silent except for a ticking clock and the sound of her rapid breathing.

She walked across the room, past the line of windows, keeping her eyes fixed forwards, certain that if she looked out, even
for a second, she would see a face pressed against the glass.

Vivian

South of France, Day Five

I am rather tired after another sweltering day in the dry hills, examining the leaves of limes and sycamores. Today I found both larvae and a total of forty-eight adult harlequin ladybirds. My back is aching from the weight of my beating tray and the heavy backpack; my nose is beginning to peel and my knee is becoming very sore. Ill-advisedly, I crouched in an olive grove for a while, distracted by the view, and when I got up the joint would not take my weight. I made it back to the village, slowly, and I am now keeping it stretched in the hope that it will recover itself.

It is still intensely hot, though it is five in the afternoon. I am sweating at the cafe table, despite the dappled shade of the plane trees. The air is hot and soft, and there is a whiff of cigar smoke from a table nearby. Small French girls in white dresses are playing round the fountain, puffed up and floaty, like dandelion clocks. I have uploaded all of today's harlequin photos and data onto the European ladybird app, I have planned tomorrow's route and written down my findings in my notebook. But I have not yet bumped into Olivia.

The defiantly named Café de Paris is quite busy but it is the best place to sit because it affords a clear view of the village square. I can see the bandstand and the fountain bounded by plane trees and behind that the main village car park.

That dreary February day, eighteen months ago, when I took Olivia to the cabinet and showed her the diary, I could not possibly have anticipated that I would end up sitting in a French cafe with keen eyes, a sunburned nose and hope inflating my heart.

I was probably not a well person, then. I do remember how grim I felt as I sat behind Maureen's desk, unreasonably infuriated by her '*Smile! It's gin o'clock!*' sticker on the till and her '*Keep Calm, It's Only a Royal Baby*' coaster. I was fighting the urge to rip both objects up and put them in the bin. I have known Maureen since childhood; we were in the same class at primary school and she has always irritated me. She is intrusive, bossy and rather dim. She also now pities me, which is probably why she allowed me to persuade her to visit her sister and let me fill in that week. She imagines I'm lonely and bored at Ileford, without enough to do. When I first returned to Sussex, Maureen tried to get me to go to wine bars with her Zumba friends. I was probably less than tactful in my refusals. She has stopped trying to involve me, but she pities me even more now.

That day in the museum, my whole body felt heavy, weighed down by its onerous contents – my dismal self. I was convinced that this week sitting behind Maureen's desk would be fruitless, and I couldn't even speak to Bertie, who lay, very tense, in his basket at my feet.

And then the shock of arrival: the bedraggled child entered

first like a Victorian urchin with her long hair flying around, a blast of freezing air and raindrops and then – Olivia!

They shook rainwater onto the floor like dogs, trod mud through the entranceway and looked around, as most visitors do, with a mixture of hope and disappointment. I felt the startle of recognition turn to paralysis. Olivia is even more striking close up than she is at a distance, or on TV. Her features are more delicate, her face more expressive, the fine lines around her eyes and mouth more pronounced. She also looks taller on screen, and less scruffy. Her hair was held in a simple black elastic and she wore jeans, motorcycle style boots and a grey cardigan, bobbled cashmere, buttoned over a white T-shirt.

As I handed her the tickets our fingers touched and I felt a physical jolt as both our lives switched to this unexplored path.

I am ashamed of the person I was then, that gloomy rotten experimenter, sitting behind someone else's desk.

The child, Jessica, was sullen and not pretty beneath all that ridiculously long and tangled hair. She looks nothing like her mother. She was pushy, too; she would not leave Bertie alone, even though I told her very nicely that he was not reliable with strangers.

The waiter arrives at my little table with a raised eyebrow. I am hungry and think I will eat, even though I had previously decided that I should eat an evening meal at 6 p.m., which would be five in England so I should not be hungry at all. My routines are shot to pieces, I am hungry at odd times, but I have decided that these are special circumstances. It will take a few days to establish my routines here and then it will be time to leave. This is why I hate foreign travel. I order a demi carafe of red wine and *steak frites* and the waiter melts away between the tables.

I made her wait to hold the diary that day, even though I

knew she wanted it, desperately. I enjoyed seeing her eyes flicker between the glass case and me, like an eager dog, as I went on about the Burley family. But she took me off guard when she asked about my background and the words hurtled from my mouth like daemons before I could stop them. I was furious with myself afterwards. Fortunately, she was so fixated on the diary that she seemed to hardly notice my stupid statement about being a professor.

Her comment about sending Annabel's diary to the British Library was not unexpected. I knew that she would need to be certain of its authenticity and I knew that she had a contact who specialized in Victorian manuscripts. I told her I'd have to get Lady Burley's permission to do this, but that was not, of course, strictly true. I was just keen not to appear too submissive.

She came back to the museum on Wednesday that week and spent two hours poring over the diary. After she left – excited by her find, late for her children, in a rush as always – I went and sat in the back room in the chair where she had been. Her coffee cup was still on the desk, with the imprint of her lipstick on the rim. Her perfume, a musky, assertive scent, not at all floral, hung in the air. I couldn't believe what was happening. I knew, then, that Annabel's diary would be immortalized in print. I was still envisaging an academic paper, but even so I was more excited than I had been in years.

From the very beginning, I enjoyed learning a new discipline. Even before I encountered Olivia in the museum, I'd been discovering that I had an aptitude for history. With the forensic process of going through the Burley family archives, and the complexity of the new skills I was learning, I could feel my mind struggling out of its dark chrysalis, coming back to life.

Perhaps it should not be a surprise that, as a scientist, I have a creative side. People assume that science is all about facts but almost all scientific breakthroughs would never have happened without a great dose of imagination. Science relies on interpretative leaps and sideways moves, acts of faith and inspired guesswork as much as it does hard data.

I survey the village square. A group of old men is playing *pétanque* by the bandstand. I scan a group of tourists in the car park; none have black hair.

I wonder how Ileford is getting on in my absence. I have trepidations about leaving it empty since it has a habit of punishing me when I go away. Bertie and I spent a night in Taunton Holiday Inn Express last spring, after a fruitless meeting with one of Annabel's grandnieces, and upon our return, as we entered the scullery, late in the evening, we heard a faint banging sound, high up in the house. We rushed up the back staircase. The noise was coming from the servants' quarters.

A jackdaw was trapped in the red room. The poor creature had been beating herself against the windowpane and was weakened and disorientated, her glossy black wings heaving in intermittent, frantic attempts at escape. I opened the window but she flew back to the chimney. I leaped at her and seized her with both hands, pinning her wings to her pulsing body. She fixed her unsettling silvery eye on me and clacked her bill, aggressively, and I felt her heart pulsing beneath my fingertips as I crossed the room and shoved her out the casement window. I can only think she'd been nesting in the chimneystack. Jackdaws are bold and inquisitive birds, the narcissists of myth and folklore, capable of devious plotting and devoted to thievery. Their collective noun is a 'clattering'. I have always enjoyed that, and their mimicry, too; it is perfectly possible to teach a jackdaw to mimic the human voice, though I have never tried.

Bertie was unsettled after that. He would not stop yapping so I carried him downstairs and soothed him with bread and warm milk. I, too, was disturbed by the ominous message of the bird, and that night, for the first time since I got Bertie, my night visitor came. As I stared into her foggy eyes I saw reproach and I knew that her visit had something to do with that trapped bird. I felt she had sent it to me. A jackdaw coming down the chimney has long been an omen of death.

The waiter appears at my shoulder; he takes away the empty pastis glass and puts down the wine and a plastic basket containing sliced baguette. I take a piece and bite into its crust. When all this began, I was a desperate beast. I have done unforgivable things. I wish I could turn back the clock but it is too late now – honesty would only cause havoc and chaos. It is much better to put it all behind me and to look forward now. Nobody need ever know what I have done.

I think about Olivia up there on the hillside, in the beautiful rented house, with her family and friends, eating jolly, shared meals on the terrace. She needn't have been so short with me before she left, but I can see now that it was not a good time to discuss future projects.

An element of tension is to be expected with any collaboration. Overall, though, we make an excellent team. She said that to me, herself, more than once. She even had the Christmas Tiffany pen engraved with the words, 'To Vivian, my partner in crime'. Since Lady Burley only ever gives me vouchers, I rather relished unwrapping an actual Christmas present. Nobody has ever engraved anything for me before.

The words on that pen mean a lot to me because working with others has never been my strong point. I was an only child and have always found sharing difficult. My school reports would say, 'Vivian does not work productively with the other children. Vivian must try harder to cooperate. Vivian is not a team player.' This was the sort of thing that would enrage my father. We both knew, of course, that he was punishing me for that other, more heinous, act and that no amount of beatings could ever erase that. I accepted it because I knew I was guilty.

But I do not want to think about all that. I have spent a lifetime learning how to protect myself against those thoughts and memories. I do treasure Olivia's Christmas pen. It is in my bag at my feet even now.

The waiter is coming back. I unfold my napkin and watch him as he places the *steak frites* in front of me. His dignity reminds me of the waiters at Formal Hall who would set down each of the five courses with elegant arm movements. I think about those dark, wood-panelled rooms and how the dons would repair afterwards to the SCR for the second dessert away from the undergraduates. There would be fruit and hand-made chocolate truffles, the ritual of passing the port and Madeira, an inlaid silver box of snuff. I was always on the margins of the group, largely silent. Perhaps it is not that different after all to be sitting unnoticed and anonymous in a French cafe.

One of the great benefits of being unseen, of course, is that one can freely watch.

I cannot blame her for delegating almost all of the *Annabel* research to me. Her life is stressful and I am an excellent researcher. She has the pressures of her family, on top of the academic and media work. There was always some crisis or other going on. I remember one day in the bakery she was very distressed. She had no make-up on and her hair was scraped back and a little greasy. She ordered a double espresso before she even sat down and her fingers trembled as she got out her papers.

'Is everything all right?' I said.

'Yes, yes, it's fine, it's nothing. It's just . . . you know. Teen-agers! Jesus Christ!' She lifted her chin and her eyes glistened. I wondered, with a vague sense of panic, whether she might be close to tears. I hoped not. I never know what to do when people weep. She is really quite fragile when it comes to her children. They seem to have a profound power over her happiness. I sup-pose that is something to do with love.

She started to talk, then, and all her supposed professional boundaries were forgotten. Her eldest son, she admitted, was out of control. She had found cannabis in his bedroom, his GCSE predictions were dire, he was furious all the time and suddenly he wasn't speaking to his father.

I felt rather sorry for her as she talked. She looked exhausted. I did not know what to say so I just nodded. She took this as encouragement, and told me how frustrated she was by David's lack of engagement in family life. She told me that he was always travelling, giving talks or interviewing people, or visiting librar-ies or academics to research the book that, she said, was 'going basically nowhere'. She sometimes wondered whether he was avoiding her, or the family, or both.

Seeing her in public you would never guess that any of this was going on. In fact, you'd think her life was perfect. I caught her on Radio 4 the very next morning, talking about buildings that were once psychiatric institutions. She sounded lively, witty, erudite and charming. Perfectly relaxed. Perhaps her skill as a performer, her ability to beguile, is inherited from her father.

It might also stem, as most things seem to, from childhood. Olivia must have had to work very hard to be noticed by her busy and successful parents. She is very good at managing what she once referred to as her 'public persona'. People stop her in the street or in cafes; sometimes they actually sit down and write to ask her for a signed photograph. She is also, I believe, very active on social media. But even now I cannot bear to go online in order to look for her.

When *Annabel* is published this scrutiny will no doubt escalate. The book is sure to be reviewed in the broadsheets since Olivia and David are friends with many of the editors. She will be on *Start the Week* or *Woman's Hour* and she will be on television, too, perhaps even on that dreadful gameshow again, where the best liars win.

She has also already written articles for the kind of magazines she keeps in the Farmhouse toilet: *Vogue, Harper's Bazaar.* They seem to work months ahead – she was writing them in late spring even though they will not appear in the magazines until the autumn. She had her photograph taken on the front steps at Ileford for one. That was an extremely trying day. A bearded photographer, two assistants, a journalist and some kind of make-up artist descended on the house. I confined them all to the gunroom where they set up clothes rails and fussed around for hours with hair and make-up, trying on ridiculous outfits, drinking pots of coffee and eating all my digestives.

Much to the photographer's dismay I refused to allow pictures to be taken inside the house. I had already told Olivia this, so they did know about the restrictions. Not that this stopped them from haranguing me. But I held firm. I could not have magazine people snooping around Ileford. And I could not have her upstairs.

The upstairs would not have been suitable for photographs anyway. The discrepancy in décor never bothered me before I met Olivia; I only really felt the dissonance when I was forced to look at it through her eyes.

Lady Burley had updated most of the bedrooms in a burst of bad taste in the late 1980s when she briefly lived here full time before decamping to Morocco. She relied on Laura Ashley prints and allowed her fondness for ruffles and festoons free rein. She also went quite mad with a stencil. She has done very little to it since. Before she went into the care home she was talking about redecoration, but that fell by the wayside with her diagnosis and I am not fussy.

I had not even noticed how shabby the kitchen was. I remember the disappointment on Olivia's face as she took in the anorexic brown stove and scarred pine units. She had no doubt been expecting an Aga, flagstones, a scrubbed wooden table, hanging copper pots and jugs of peonies. She said something about how 'cosy' it was. I pointed out that cooking for one requires very little in the way of amenities, something she might have forgotten with her family of five and friends dropping in to discuss films and books and art exhibitions over 'kitchen suppers'.

I saw her eyes travel to my wall calendar; that month it was a rather ugly Airedale Terrier. The only days with writing on them were those on which I was seeing her. Perhaps she realized she had overstepped the mark because she looked away and said something about the trees.

She did admire the grander public spaces, though: the library, the drawing room, the hand-carved Tudor ceiling and decorative panelling in Lady Burley's morning room. She always noticed the details, like the cornices and decorative mouldings, the dado rails and original parquet floors, the Gothic stone fireplaces. The downstairs is preserved in vague Victoriana with flock curtains, walls in hunting green or oxblood, dark mahogany pieces and oil paintings. She loved it all.

When she asked, that day with the photographers, to be allowed upstairs, I was firm. 'Lady Burley has forbidden it.' She had to remember, I said, that Ileford was not my house. Whatever my job title – private secretary, manager, housekeeper, caretaker, trustee – I was merely the employee and it was not my place to show strangers into Lady Burley's private spaces.

'But she'd never know.'

'Are you asking me to lie to a vulnerable eighty-six year old?'

'No, no, God, of course not, no.' I saw her exchange a glance with the photographer, whom I already instinctively disliked.

I said nothing. Olivia was used to getting what she wanted. But not from me.

In the end, the photographer had her standing on the front steps because he liked the mullioned windows and the dressed stone of the arched front door. He seemed to know a little about architecture. The pictures actually turned out rather strikingly. Olivia's dark hair and pale skin looked dramatic against the knapped flint walls. She was wearing a rich yellow silk dress and uncomfortable-looking spiked shoes, with one of her drapey leather jackets over the top. The amount of make-up they layered on her face was quite extraordinary and, in my opinion, rather ghoulish in the flesh, but I concede it looks less odd in the actual photographs.

On a recent day trip to Kent I came across the sulphur beetle in the sand dunes. I spotted a flash of yellow on a wild carrot flower and there she was, *Cteniopus sulphureus*, showy and bright with her little antennae wiggling at the sun. She made me think of Olivia, who also thrives in the spotlight, teetering on the tips of flowers, displaying her colours to all who pass.

When I have finished my steak and counted out the euros, I decide that I must try to walk around a little. I am somewhat unsteady on my feet from the wine and the intense heat and a searing and unpleasant pain shoots through my knee when I put weight on it. The meal feels leaden in my stomach as I limp towards the bandstand.

And that is when I hear the familiar laugh. It floats to me on the warm, scented air. I turn my head, searching, and then I see her on a bench beyond the fountain.

She is in a red dress and is accompanied by her slim, strawberry-haired friend and two small children, neither of them her own. They are all holding ice creams. I wish she were alone but she isn't and it's too late to hide because I am fully exposed, now, standing in the middle of the square. She stops dead. She has seen me.

Olivia

David had driven Miles and Paul down to the coast and they came back late in the afternoon with sunburned faces, lugging a big plastic tub of live lobsters.

The animals glistened like huge, flinty beetles; their taped claws and armoured tails clattered against the plastic and their antennae twitched in panic and confusion. Ben, Nura and Jess were fascinated. They crowded round and watched the lobsters until Dom told them they were to be boiled alive. Nura then burst into tears and Ben turned dangerously pale. Only Jess looked interested still.

'It's OK, guys, it's a totally painless death.' David kneeled, gentle and patient, next to the younger children. 'They don't feel a thing, I promise. It's actually quite nice – they just fall asleep.' The anger Olivia had been nursing abated, slightly, as she watched him. She had always loved him like this: handsome, patient, paternal. He was good with children. While Olivia found parenting stressful and worrying a lot of the time, David always seemed able to simply enjoy the children, moment to moment.

This made him an excellent father. Perhaps the situation with Dom was even more troubling because of that.

'But I don't want you to boil them!' Nura cried.

'I know, darling, but they won't suffer, I promise, they'll just have a lovely warm bath and nod off.' David reached out and stroked Nura's hair out of her eyes. 'And also, they taste really, really good.'

Ben made a choking sound and ran off. They heard the front door slam. Khalil called out to Al, on the terrace. Al looked around for Chloe, but she was nowhere to be seen. After a moment, he heaved himself off the lounger and lumbered after his son.

Nura was looking at Jess for back-up, but Jess was a pragmatist; those lobsters had to die. Nura fled to her mother's open arms.

Olivia raised an eyebrow at David. 'They do just fall asleep,' he grinned.

'You could anaesthetize them in the freezer first.' Khalil walked in from the terrace clutching a small bottle of beer. 'It puts them into a coma. Then you stick a knife through the back of the skull before you put them in the water.'

'Not helpful, Khal.' Emma looked up from their sobbing child.

Al came back then. 'Ben's locked himself in the sodding tower.'

Half an hour later, Ben was still bolted in the priest's tower, Nura remained inconsolable and Emma was beginning to look as distraught as her daughter, so Olivia suggested driving down to the village for ice cream.

The promise of ice cream got Ben out of the tower and stopped Nura's sobbing. Nobody else could be bothered to come, so it was just Olivia, Emma and the two children who sat in drained silence as they drove down the winding road towards the village.

'Can you get scissors?' David called from the kitchen as they left. 'There aren't any – we're going have to gnaw our way through the claw tape.'

The approach to the village was a straight and functional road that passed estate agents, a Crédit Agricole and a basic Tabac. The village centre was more picturesque, though, with small shops and cafes grouped around a grand, pink and white *hôtel de ville* and a square lined with plane trees. In the middle sat a yellow-striped bandstand and a fountain.

As they skirted the square they passed a cafe with tables set out under the trees, a *boulangerie-pâtisserie*, a tiled *fromagerie*, a small Casino supermarket and a Maison de la Presse. They parked beneath speckled trees near some old men playing *boules* in baggy trousers, waists belted high. They paused their game to stare as Olivia and the others got out of the car.

Even at six in the evening the heat was intense. Olivia fanned herself. 'The shop here does the best ice cream in the region,' she said. 'It's famous.'

The children perked up a bit at that.

The ice cream was, in fact, excellent. Olivia chose the fig and ricotta, the children both had strawberry and Em had a speckled vanilla. They found a bench in the shade by the fountain where the heat felt less intense; Emma began to teach Nura how to order ice cream in French and Ben did an impression of Jess trying to kill a lobster, like *Psycho*. They all laughed. It was then that Olivia noticed a bulky figure crossing the square towards them.

The sun was in her eyes so it was hard to make out a face, but there was something all too familiar about the lopsided stride, the swing of the arms.

It could not be. She was hallucinating. She had to be.

But no – it really was.

'Vivian?'

'Olivia! It is you. Goodness gracious!'

For a moment they just stared at one another. Vivian came to a halt, ramrod straight, square on. Olivia caught a whiff of perspiration beneath the familiar washing powder she used on her clothes.

'What are you *doing* here, Vivian?'

Vivian's nose was very sunburned and sore-looking. Sweat glistened at her hairline. 'I'm looking for harlequins,' she said. She was carrying a safari hat and wearing an unflattering pair of Bermuda shorts, rolled-down woollen socks and dusty hiking boots. There were smears of dirt on her linen shirt, as if she had wiped her fingers down it repeatedly. Minuscule bubbles of sweat clung to her upper lip.

Emma held out hand. 'Hello, I'm Liv's friend Emma.'

Olivia gazed at Emma and then at Vivian again. She felt completely helpless. She struggled to speak. 'Vivian is . . . She's been . . . helping me with the research for *Annabel* . . . I've probably mentioned her to you.'

Emma smiled and frowned. 'I'm not sure . . .'

Vivian shot out a hand and Olivia jerked her arm away instinctively; the fig and ricotta ice cream flew off its cone and plopped into the dust.

'Oopsie!' Emma cried.

Vivian looked flustered. 'But I was trying to save it, it was slipping off the cone.'

'It doesn't matter.' Olivia turned away and threw the empty cone into the bin. She stared down for a second at the cigarette packets and sweet wrappers and a single, crushed man's shoe.

'Let me buy you another ice cream.' Vivian was behind her.

Olivia balled her fists. She turned and said, as calmly as she could, 'That's OK, Vivian.'

'But—'

'I really don't want another ice cream. Thank you.'

Ben and Nura were staring up at Vivian. Their smeared faces were both wary and curious. They looked at the floor when Vivian's gaze rested on them. Emma introduced them, explaining that Ben was Chloe's son and Nura was her own daughter.

'That's nice. Three families on holiday together.' Vivian grinned, oddly.

'Yes, it's lovely actually. We do it every year,' Emma smiled. 'Chloe, Olivia and I were at university together.' She gestured in the direction of the hills. 'We're staying in a house a couple of miles out of town. You might even be able to see it from here. It has an amazing view out over the valley. Liv has a knack of finding us gems to stay in. Last year we went to a Greek island.'

'Olivia has excellent taste.'

Olivia could not speak. She was going back over every interaction she'd had with Vivian about this summer and she was positive that she had never once said where, exactly, they were going in France.

'We get to sleep in a priest's tower,' Ben said. 'It's haunted.'

'Really? I live in a haunted house.' Vivian looked at Ben and Nura. 'I have a ghost who walks her dog and another who comes and sits on me at night.'

Ben and Nura's eyes widened.

'Our ghost is buried under the front doorstep,' said Ben. 'It comes out at night and walks around outside the tower.'

Emma gave a nervy laugh. 'The sleeping arrangements here are quite an adventure for the children.'

This was too much. Olivia put her hands on her hips. 'What are you doing here, Vivian? When did you get here?'

'I came a few days ago. I'm here for a week.'

'But how did you—'

Vivian cut her off. 'Jessica, Paul and Dominic! How are they?'

'They're fine,' Olivia said. 'Everyone's totally fine.'

'And David?' Vivian said. 'Is David well?'

'Yes. He's cooking lobster right now. In fact, I'm afraid we're going to have to get going in a minute. '

'Apologies for the way I look!' Vivian shouted. 'I've been in the hills looking for harlequins. I must look a fright.'

'Harlequins?' Emma raised her eyebrows.

'A species of ladybird.'

'Oh, yes,' Emma nodded. 'Aren't they the cannibalistic ones that are causing all sorts of problems? I think I read about them somewhere.'

'The harlequin is the fastest spreading invasive species on record,' said Vivian. 'They're monstrous predators, they—'

'Vivian!' Olivia was not going to allow her to get started on another one of her obsessions. This was just too much. She could not just show up like this. 'We have to go now. We've got to get back up to the house for dinner.'

'Oh yes. Goodness. Listen to me. Of course, you must go.' Vivian waved a hand like a butler and said, with some formality, 'Your lobster awaits.'

The children stared.

'Yes. Yes, it does.' Olivia tucked her hair back. But she could not just go. She could not just walk away without referencing this bizarre intrusion. She made herself stay where she was. 'I really didn't expect to bump into you out here, Vivian, I have to say.'

Vivian blinked. 'What a coincidence, yes! But I must let you go, I don't want to spoil your lobster.' She took a step back.

'Listen, I'm sure there's enough for . . .' Em looked from Olivia to Vivian.

Olivia waved her keys then and started walking away. 'Well! We need to go! Goodbye, Vivian. I hope you find lots of harlequins. Come on, kids. Time to go!'

As they walked back to the car she could feel Vivian rooted beneath the plane trees by the fountain, watching them.

'I don't think finding lots of harlequin ladybirds is a good thing, Liv,' said Emma, hurrying to catch up. 'They're the evil, invasive ones.'

'What?' Olivia felt queasy.

'Never mind. Isn't it a bit rude to just—'

'It's not, really, Em, no.'

'But . . .' Emma sounded confused and slightly upset now. She could never bear rudeness.

'Em, listen, it's fine, I promise.'

'Are you OK?'

'I'm totally fine! I just didn't expect to see Vivian here, that's all. It's unbelievably weird that she's here.'

'Well, it's a small world.'

Olivia beeped the car locks. 'Not that small.'

Olivia was not ready to discuss Vivian with Emma. It was too complicated to even begin to explain why it was so disturbing that Vivian had followed her here.

'She seemed a bit uncomfortable,' said Emma.

'Vivian always looks uncomfortable.'

'I felt kind of sorry for her, Liv. She might be glad of some company. Do you think she's on her own here?'

'I don't know. Probably.'

'You said she helped you with your book?'

'She gave me permission to study the diary in the first place.'

'Vivian's *Lady of the Manor*?'

'No! God no. Ileford's owner, Lady Burley, is in a care home.

Vivian's . . . Well, I think she was originally hired as a sort of companion, private secretary type thing, then Lady Burley got sick and I suppose she took over more and more responsibilities. Now she's kind of in charge of everything.'

She opened the car door and a wave of heat rose from the driver's seat. Her eyes felt strained. How could Vivian possibly be here? The encounter was beginning to feel chimeric. She could feel the sun burning into her face.

'What is she do you think, early sixties?' Emma opened the car door for Nura.

'I have no idea. I've never asked her how old she is. We mainly talked about Annabel.'

Olivia's hands trembled on the steering wheel as she started the car. This was just so intrusive, aggressively so. She was never going to be able to relax now, knowing that Vivian was lurking around in the village. The air conditioning puffed hot air at their faces. Olivia slapped at the vents.

'It'll cool down in a moment,' Em said, as if reassuring a child.

They pulled out of the car park onto the square and drove past the *hôtel de ville,* round the bandstand and back down the main shopping street.

'It wouldn't hurt to invite her up for dinner, though, would it?' Emma sounded earnest. 'David has a lot of lobsters up there.'

Olivia glanced in the rear-view mirror at Ben and Nura. They were both gazing out of their windows. She could not tell if they were listening. 'Look, Em,' she said. 'I've spent a fair amount of time with Vivian over the past year and a half and she's . . . She can be difficult. I have no idea what she's doing here, I really don't, but I can't have her up at the house, I just can't.'

'But it really could be a coincidence, you know. Encounters like this do happen. I once bumped into my brother at the top of the Eiffel Tower and neither of us had any idea the other was even in France. Life's full of odd coincidences like this.' Emma was looking over her shoulder, craning to see the square behind them. 'Where do you think she went? She just vanished.'

Olivia kept her eyes fixed on the road.

'It just feels mean not to ask her up though, Liv.'

'Em, please! Can you just leave it? Please?' It came out harsher than she intended.

Emma knotted her hands on her lap and tucked her chin in.

'Sorry, I'm sorry. Em? I'm sorry. I'm just . . . Vivian is . . . I just need a break from her. That's all. If she comes up to dinner, we'll start talking about the book and . . .'

'Oh. Right. No. Of course.' Em gave a weak, high laugh. 'God, don't worry. I get it. It's totally fine. It doesn't matter. Let's forget about Vivian.'

When they got back to the house, David was chopping parsley and Chloe was whisking eggs at the stove next to him. She was barefoot in the cream halter-necked dress, which was crumpled now and a bit grubby, with her hair damp, knotted loosely at her neck. They looked relaxed and companionable but when they turned their faces were so tense and unhappy that Olivia felt sure that she had just interrupted an argument. Chloe gave a big, perky smile. 'There you all are! How was the famous ice cream?'

'Really good.' Ben went over to his mother and sweetly put his arms around her waist.

'I'm making omelette.' Chloe hugged him with one arm and held up a whisk, which dripped egg onto the tiles. 'For anyone who doesn't want lobster. Do you like omelette, Nuri?'

Nura clung to Em's leg but didn't reply.

'Well, I don't think she's going to want to eat the lobster, are you, sweetie?' Em said.

'If you say things like that she's never going to try anything new.' Olivia dumped her bag on the floor and her keys on the countertop. The fury that she had managed to contain since they met Vivian was knocking at the inside of her skull.

'Come on, Liv,' Chloe said. 'It's fair enough if they don't want to eat the lobster, after seeing them alive. You know?'

'And I don't believe in forcing a child to eat things that upset her,' Emma said in a stiff and rather hurt voice.

David chopped faster, keeping out of it, his tanned forearms tensed. Olivia realized that if she stayed in the kitchen any longer she was going to say something she would later regret. Chloe was still reproachful, but Emma's face had closed tight.

'Dammit. I forgot to buy the scissors in the village,' she said. 'I'll go back.'

'What? Don't worry.' David held up the chef's knife. 'I can use this.'

'No, no, I'll go back down, it's OK. We need scissors anyway, we're here ten more days. I want to get paracetamol, too, I've got a headache.'

'I've got some in my . . .' Chloe began, but Olivia grabbed her bag and keys and sped back through the house, ignoring every-body's protests.

She had to deal with Vivian. She had to go back down there and find out what she was playing at, coming here. If she didn't confront her then Vivian's presence in the village was going to poison this holiday. It could not possibly be a coincidence. This was too much. She paused at the front door and leaped clean over the gravestone. She could not bear her feet to touch it – it felt like a curse.

Vivian

South of France, Day Five

After the encounter with Olivia and her friend I go straight back to the *chambre d'hôte*. I lock the bedroom door and sit on the hard single bed for quite a long time.

I do shed a tear, then, as the feelings rise up inside me: some old hurts, some new. The predominant emotions are shame and confusion. I no longer feel so sure that it was right to come to France. Perhaps I do not, after all, understand what has happened over the past eighteen months. Perhaps I have been deluding myself that we made a good team and even that we had become friends, of sorts.

Our encounter did not follow the pattern I had expected or hoped for. Everything suddenly feels out of control and I am only certain of one thing: I have been brushed off.

I can't blame her for it. I must have looked such a mess in my shorts, sweating. My talk of harlequins and ghosts might also have seemed a little odd.

I try to think logically about what else went wrong. Her red dress and black hair – the colours – made me think of a beautiful seven-spot ladybird, *Coccinella septempunctata*. Perhaps this unconscious association threw me off balance in some way, from the very start. I know I was tense and awkward.

She was also with her friend, which was exactly what I hadn't wanted. I had always pictured her alone when we met and I was not expecting to have to deal with a curious, strawberry-haired friend and two shy children, staring up at me with their big, sheep-like eyes.

My throat felt very dry as I crossed the square towards them, my palms were sticky by the time I got to their bench. They were all staring. Olivia's expression was the most off-putting though. Her eyes were inflated and her mouth was in a sort of spasm. '*Vivian?*'

I tried to sound surprised to see her but it was disconcerting because she did not smile, she just said, 'What *on earth* are you doing here?' The two scarlet spots that appeared on her cheeks matched the colour of her dress almost exactly.

I could tell that I embarrassed her. I had not thought about this before, but she might not have told anyone very much about the work I'd done on *Annabel*. I know she has told David about me but perhaps nobody else even knows that I exist. It might be awkward for her to have to explain me to her friends. They were all staring up at me as if I were a giant curiosity, a biological novelty transplanted to this French square in order to startle and disconcert them.

I saw them take in my grubby shirt and legs, my walking boots and woollen socks. I was afraid that I might smell, too, but fortunately Olivia did not attempt to kiss me. I should have taken a shower before I came down to the cafe, but I was later than planned because of my knee and I'd been keen to go and sit where I had a good view of the square.

This had become my routine. For three afternoons in a row I'd gone to the cafe at 5 p.m. after dumping my things back at the *chambre d'hôte* and taking a shower. I didn't want to miss her if she came to the village in the early evening. But standing in the square I felt myself grow larger, hotter, dustier and more distasteful beneath her gaze. I wondered how she could bear to even look at me, how she could bear the sight.

It is possible that I talked too much about harlequins, though I did try to show an interest in the limp children and their gravestone ghost. At one point the friend – who seemed kind, if rather nervy – was going to invite me up to the house for lobster but Olivia couldn't get away fast enough. It was only 6.30 p.m. I know they won't eat until at least seven thirty or eight o'clock, but Olivia insisted that they must go.

As they crossed the square away from me I was filled with shame, both for myself and perhaps a little bit for Olivia. She surely did not need to be so rude.

It takes a while to get my emotions under control but eventually I manage it. I get up off the bed. It is too early to sleep and I cannot sit alone in this room all evening. I will only torment myself thinking about the things I should have said.

I do shower then, and comb my hair and brush my teeth, put on clean slacks and the new M&S linen shirt, and make my way back down to the Café de Paris. I will have another glass of wine to steady my nerves and perhaps a *petit café*. I will collect myself and work out what to do now.

I am relieved to see that my table is free. I order a glass of *vin rouge* from the same disinterested waiter, who must recognize me but shows no sign of it. A middle-aged couple, probably English, are at the table next to me and they stare as I sit down, as if I am the entertainment and they are sceptical about my value.

There is a raucous extended French family taking up three tables behind them. Small dogs and small children abound.

I clasp my hands in my lap and, to distract myself from the noise and thoughts, I think about the Devil's coach horse, which emits a foul odour as a defence. She is an insignificant-looking black beetle with short elytra, her body is covered in tiny black hairs and she can be vicious. She raises her tail like a scorpion and opens her jaws. I had a nip from a Devil's coach horse once and it was really quite painful. The folklore has it that if she points her tail at you, you are cursed.

I drink the wine almost in one gulp, then call the waiter back and order another. This time his eyebrow does give a twitch. As a habitual teetotaller I probably do not have the tolerance for this much wine but right now I do not care. I have seen the dark side of alcohol, with my father and with one or two colleagues over the years, and I know that I should have a *petit café* instead, but I am not yet fully in control of my emotions.

Olivia was obviously thrown by my sudden and unexpected appearance. She knows, of course, that I have come here to find her; it was ludicrous to pretend that this might be a coincidence.

If I am going to repair this situation I am going to have to find her again and talk to her properly about my idea. I am going to have to make her listen to me now. I need to show her that I'm not trying to muscle in on her holiday, I am merely impatient to get started on our new book. As soon as she gives me the go ahead on that, I will leave.

If I go up to the holiday house she will be even more put out, but I cannot just sit and wait here in the hope that I might see her again. It could take days before she comes back. Or I might miss her entirely. That would be disastrous. I must have looked very odd, limping across the square in my dusty clothes, expecting a fond greeting, expecting to be invited up for a lobster supper. I must have seemed such a pushy and ungainly figure, an embarrassment.

I can see now that the idea that she might be happy to see me, once she got over the surprise, was a fantasy born of too many days alone in Ileford. I should probably have waited in Sussex, then picked the right moment when she got home from holiday and was more relaxed and open to new ideas.

I have, I realize, neglected to see this situation from her perspective. This is a failing of mine. My overwhelming need for certainty – coupled with this anxiety about the future – has blinded me to social niceties.

I have also, somehow, allowed myself to believe that we had become friends. I can see now that this was naive too. I am not, nor ever shall be, Olivia's friend. She has offered me kindness and confidences but only in order to get what she needs out of me: loyalty, devotion, thoroughness and discretion. It was a working relationship, nothing more. As her husband put it so eloquently, I was her 'faithful helper'. She merely did what it took to keep me on track.

I will never be invited to her house in west London or introduced to her circle of friends. She does not want me up on that terrace. Not that I would want to be up there with them all anyway. What would I talk about with those people? Her life is very different from mine and small talk has certainly never been my forte.

I feel as if someone has punched my shell, now, bringing me to my senses. To Olivia I am the hired help. And now that *Annabel* is done, she has no use for me any more.

But of course, she is wrong about that. She does still need me. She needs my silence. She just doesn't know it yet.

I decide that I will not stay here. I will go back to England, I will leave first thing tomorrow. I have been exposed and humiliated. I should never have come.

I imagine her sitting up on that glorious terrace, high in the hills as the sky melts into pinks and rich pigeon greys. She will be nursing a glass of Luberon rosé, surveying the valley and the distant rooftops and saying to her friends, 'What on earth does she think she's *doing* here?'

These dark thoughts run through my head as I finish another glass of harsh *vin rouge*. I can feel it all closing in on me, the bitterness and despair. My old self is rising up again, unstoppable.

And that's when I see her.

She is striding towards me under the plane trees in that same red dress. Her hair looks more dishevelled now, her Greek-style sandals slap on the stones and her jaw is set. She is coming right at me, looking right at me, but there is no sign of greeting this time, not a wave or a hello. Not even the smallest smile.

Olivia

South of France, Day Five

They were all out on the terrace later that evening as the sun lowered itself behind the hills. David was cracking open the lobster shells with the chef's knife, but Olivia wasn't hungry. It was taking all her energy just to look calm. She was still shaken; angry not just with Vivian, now, but with herself. Above all with herself.

It had all got so out of control.

'What sort of town doesn't sell scissors?' Al stretched out his chunky, rugby player's legs, which were already quite tanned, the dense hairs bleached by the sun.

'You took a while down there,' Chloe said. 'Did you go for a sneaky cocktail?'

Olivia tried to look normal and laugh. She shook her head and refilled her wine glass, as she'd downed the first one in just a few gulps. There was no way she was getting into what had happened in the village, why she had taken so long, or why she had come back up to the house without scissors.

'You didn't see Vivian again down there, did you?' Emma reached for the water jug.

Olivia put a black olive in her mouth and felt the gritty flecks of thyme on her teeth and tongue. She thought she might choke if she tried to swallow.

Chloe said, 'Who?'

'The woman who owns Liv's Victorian diary – we bumped into her in the village. Amazingly, she's on holiday here too.'

'What – no – Vivian Tester?' David cracked into a lobster with the back of the chef's knife. 'Your faithful helper? Old Baz? She's *here* – in the village?' He wrenched the lobster shell open, prized out a hunk of pink flesh and put it on Jess's plate.

Olivia spat out the olive stone and glanced at him. 'Yes, I know, it's weird.'

He paused and frowned, the knife suspended. 'Why didn't you ask her up? We've got enough lobster to feed an army.'

A headache was pressing between Olivia's eyes.

'I thought we should have invited her up actually, but Liv said not to.' Em twiddled her fork.

'She wouldn't have wanted to come,' Olivia said. 'She's not a sociable person.'

'That old woman looked upset and lonely,' said Nura.

They all looked at Nura.

'She's not old,' Olivia gripped the stem of her glass. 'Or upset. Or lonely.'

Emma put an arm, protectively, round the back of Nura's chair.

'Sorry, Nuri, sorry.' Olivia took a breath. 'Sorry.' She gazed around the table. Everyone was looking at her. 'I'm sure Vivian is perfectly happy on her own.'

'She's looking for harlequins,' said Emma. 'They're a voracious, cannibalistic type of ladybird.'

Jess said, 'I love ladybirds, they're cute.'

Emma turned to Jess. 'Harlequins might look cute, Jess, but they're actually quite dangerous to the environment. They pretend to be ordinary nice ladybirds but they're very destructive.'

'Oh, this is synchronicity!' Chloe's face lit up. 'I literally just took on an eighteenth-century Meissen harlequin figurine. I was working on it just before we came here, doing some research. They were the trickster servant characters in the *commedia dell'arte*. Their origins are really dark – they were the Devil in medieval passion plays.'

'We're talking about ladybirds, my darling,' said Al. 'Not ceramic figurines or medieval servants.'

'It's just interesting,' Chloe waved a hand, 'how things come together, you know?'

'That lady has a ghost dog that sits on her at night,' Ben said.

'It's not the dog that sits on her, it's another ghost,' Nura corrected him in a quiet but firm voice.

Olivia squeezed her napkin into a small, hard ball.

'So do you think Old Baz came here because of you?' David looked at her across the table. There was puzzlement in his eyes.

'You've got a new stalker!' Dom reached over and took a slug of Olivia's wine. Olivia slapped his hand.

'OK, sorry, I'm confused now. Is this the woman who runs the Sussex museum?' Chloe's eyes were deep green against her glowing skin in the tender evening light.

'No, no, Vivian's the housekeeper at Ileford Manor, where they found the diary.' David looked at Chloe as he said this but she turned away and fixed her eyes on the view.

'Wait. Why is this lady looking for ladybirds?' said Paul.

Olivia's head felt as if it might explode. She needed them all to stop talking about Vivian. She was still reeling from what had happened in the cafe. The last thing she needed was everyone reminding her how slippery Vivian was, how tricky and intrusive. 'It doesn't matter!' Her voice came out high-pitched and wavering. 'She's just not that interesting. I have no idea what she's doing here, OK, so can we *please* talk about something else?'

Everyone stopped talking.

Then Dom chuckled. 'All right, Mother. Calm down!'

'OK . . . So . . .' Chloe put on her soothing yogic voice. 'Tomorrow? What about tomorrow? Maybe we could all have a day at the beach? We haven't done a beach trip yet. What does everyone think? Shall we do it?'

But they did not go to the beach the next day because as the peony dawn light fingered the hillside Olivia woke to the sound of her child's screams.

She sat upright at the same time as David. She threw herself out of bed and he did too. Together they raced down the stairs, propelled by the understanding that something horrifying had happened to Jess in the priest's tower.

Olivia

South of France, Day Six

Jess was standing in the gravel courtyard. She looked ghostly and insubstantial in the pastel dawn light, wearing a sprigged cotton nightdress, with her hands up at her neck. She was not visibly injured, not bleeding, but something about her had hideously altered. It took a second for Olivia to pinpoint what that was, a flicker of delay while her brain caught up with her eyes.

Jess's hands were grasping at the space where her hair had been.

'Sweetheart!' David got to her first, swooped and lifted her off the ground. 'Oh, darling. What happened to your hair?'

'Oh my God,' Olivia touched Jess's ragged head. 'Who cut it?'

Emma was hurrying down the steps from the house behind them in a nightdress. She must have heard Jess's screams. She saw Jess, stopped and covered her mouth. 'Oh my God, Jess! Your hair!'

'What happened to you?' David sounded shaken. 'Who did this to you?'

'It's all gone!' Jess wailed and waved her hands.

'We know that, sweetheart.' Olivia touched her face. 'But who did this? Who cut it? Was it you?'

'No! No! No!'

Emma ran past them, then, barefoot over the gravel, shouting 'Nura! Nura!' The narrow door swallowed her cries.

The boys wavered out of the tower like drunkards.

'Who did this to Jess?' Olivia shouted to them.

They rubbed their faces, dazed. 'What?'

Over the boys' heads, Olivia saw Emma emerge from the tower carrying her limp child and everything stopped, as if a pause button had been pressed. The birdsong, the rising sun, the scent of herbs, the boys' confused faces – it all hung suspended.

But then she saw Nura's eyes open, and she blinked; she looked stunned, wrenched from an oceanic sleep. Her hair was messy but untouched. She lifted her head and looked at them all.

'Is she OK?' Olivia said to Em. 'Nuri? Are you OK?'

Emma squeezed her daughter against her body, 'She's fine, I think. She's completely fine.'

'Who did this to you, darling?' Olivia leaned into Jess, but she just buried her head in David's neck, sobbing. 'Can't you remember what happened?'

'Just leave her for a minute,' David said. 'Give her a bit of space.'

She opened her mouth to snap at him, then stopped herself because he was right.

Khalil appeared in pyjama bottoms and flip-flops. His white T-shirt looked very bright in the soft morning light, his black hair stood on end. 'What's going on?' He went over to Em and Nura. 'What's happened?'

Emma pointed back at Jess.

It took him a moment, then, 'Whoa!'

Olivia wiped gently at Jess's wet face with her fingers. 'Sweetheart, you have to tell us who did this to you.'

'I – don't – know . . .' Jess hiccupped between each word.

'Nura didn't do it.' Emma carried Nura closer. Khalil was behind them, too.

Nura stared at Jess's head with a look of comical horror, then burst into tears.

Olivia turned to the boys who were lined up, silent, staring at Jess with bulging eyes. 'Did one of you do this?' She looked from Ben to Paul to Miles. 'Was this some kind of joke?'

'It's OK, sweetheart,' she heard Emma say to Nura. 'Olivia's just upset. We know it wasn't you, we know that.'

Ben's eyes were enormous. 'I didn't do it.' He looked at Paul. 'I didn't.'

'Me neither.' Paul and Miles said at the same time.

David smoothed back Jess's serrated locks. 'Baby, are you sure you don't remember anything?'

'I was sleeping!' Trails of silvery saliva linked Jess's jaws as she wailed. 'I was sleeping and when . . . when I woke up . . . my hair . . . was gone . . .'

'The hair . . .' Olivia looked at David. 'The scissors and the hair must be in there – surely?'

David blinked, then handed Jess to her.

She had not held her daughter like this – standing up with Jess's limbs wrapped round her torso – in a long while. Jess felt reassuringly solid and heavy. 'Shhh. It's OK. It's OK.' She stroked Jess's head, trying not to linger on the amputated ends. The gravel dug into her bare soles. All around them ancient herbs sent powerful messages up into the warm dawn air. There was frenzied birdsong. Nobody spoke.

Then Miles and Paul were suddenly sniggering, letting out little snorts like silly, skittish ponies.

'Stop that,' she snapped. 'This isn't funny at all.'

'She looks really weird,' Miles snickered. 'Like some kind of weird cartoon.'

'How about we all go inside?' Em said in a buoyant, Girl Scout voice. 'I'll make some hot chocolate and we can all calm down.'

'They don't need hot chocolate.' Olivia tried not to snap, but didn't quite manage it. 'They need to tell us who did this. No one's going inside until someone tells us what happened to Jess's hair.'

'I really don't think they know, Liv.' Khalil sounded firm and reasonable.

'Could she have done it herself?' Emma suggested, helplessly. 'In her sleep?'

The desire to yell at Emma not to be stupid was almost overwhelming, but at that moment David came out of the priest's tower. He looked bewildered.

'There's nothing in there.'

'Where is it then?'

'I don't know. There's no scissors. No hair. Nothing.'

'Did you check upstairs?'

'I can't. The door's locked and there's no key. You can't get up there.'

So much had been cut off, great handfuls of hair, a lush, golden crop, had just vanished. 'Where the hell is it?' she said, again, and as the words came out of her mouth an unspeakable image entered her head: Vivian holding a pair of scissors.

She suddenly needed to get the children inside. She began to move across the courtyard to the house and heard the others follow. They each stepped over the gravestone and filed down the corridor to the kitchen. Olivia heard David double-lock the front door behind them.

Emma sat Nura, sucking her thumb, on a kitchen stool and began to look for milk and a pan. Olivia carried Jess over to the sofa. The boys started to head for the terrace but David shouted, 'Oh no you don't. You guys aren't going anywhere. Come back and sit on the sofas, we've got to talk about this.'

She saw Khalil go over to Nura on the stool, lean in and begin talking to her in a low voice. Behind them, Emma began to busy herself getting milk from the fridge.

Ben didn't sit down. His legs, sticking out of his pyjama shorts, were bleached twigs. 'I'm going to get my mum.' But before he could move, Chloe appeared in the doorway. Her hair was tangled and she was barefoot in just a T-shirt that showed her long, brown legs. 'What's going on?' She rubbed her face. 'What's happening?'

Olivia pointed at Jess's head; Chloe blinked and then her face shuddered. 'Oh my God, oh – sweetie!' She came over and crouched at Jess's level. 'You cut your hair off?'

'*She* hasn't cut her hair. Someone else did this to her while she was asleep.'

'*Who?*'

'We have no idea. We can't even find the hair.' David rubbed his own hair, which was sticking up.

Chloe looked at her sons, from one to the other. 'Boys?'

Ben wobbled his head and Miles shrugged. He had his phone in his hand. 'Don't even think about Snapchatting this,' Chloe warned.

The best explanation was that this was a practical joke that had got out of hand, and the boys were lying. 'Look,' said Olivia. 'I'm sure it wasn't meant to go this far. Just tell the truth. We won't be angry with you, guys.'

That was a lie and the boys knew it. Whoever had cut Jess's hair was going to be in huge trouble.

'Paul?' David said, firmly. 'You and Jess were fighting yesterday—'

'Don't blame me! I did NOT do this!' Paul's cheeks turned scarlet.

Olivia looked closely at him. He seemed to be telling the truth, she was pretty sure of it. But then she remembered how, recently, he had taken a tenner from her wallet and lied so effectively – went red just like this – that she had believed him until she found the note stuffed into the zip pocket of his school backpack.

'She must have felt *something*.' Miles rolled his eyes to suggest that it was inadequate of Jess to have slept through her own violation.

'This is NOT Jess's fault.' Olivia hugged Jess. 'I don't want to hear any of you blaming her for this, OK?'

'You're all so fucking loud.' Dom came into the room, shirtless, wearing only pyjama shorts, rubbing his hair. 'What the fuck's happening?' Then he spotted his sister. 'Fuck me! If you'd wanted a haircut, you only had to ask.'

'Stop swearing, Dom,' David said. 'It's completely inappropriate.'

'I'd say it's *highly* appropriate,' Dom said. It was the first time he had answered his father directly in months, and under different circumstances, Olivia might have been relieved. But Jess started to cry. Dom suddenly looked younger, less certain. 'It's OK, J.' He turned to Olivia. 'What happened to her hair?'

'I know!' Miles leaped up. 'It was grave-man!'

Paul gave a high laugh.

Ben looked at Chloe with round eyes. 'We heard the grave-man!'

'This is not the time to be silly. This isn't something to laugh about.' David put his hands on his hips.

'No, wait.' Chloe leaned in. 'What exactly did you hear?'

'When we were going to sleep we were all, like, freaked out because we heard him upstairs,' Miles said.

'You heard footsteps? In the tower?' Chloe frowned at her son.

'We didn't hear him!' Jess lifted her head from Olivia's chest. 'I made it up – both times!'

'Wait a minute, darling.' Olivia patted her back. 'What exactly did you hear, boys?'

'Creaking,' Ben said. 'Footsteps.'

'I told you! I made it up!' Jess yelled. 'I wanted to scare them.' She looked at Olivia with bloodshot eyes. 'They were all really scared.'

'I definitely did hear a creaking noise though,' Ben said.

'Yeah,' Miles glanced at Paul. 'Paul and me heard him outside too. We even went out and looked.'

'Last night? You went out of the tower in the middle of the night?'

'Yeah but he wasn't there,' Paul said, and looked at his feet. 'So we came back in.'

'The whole tower creaks all the time, Mum.' Jess's voice was jagged and high. 'It's totally going to fall down at any minute!'

Olivia hugged Jess. 'It's OK, darling. Nothing's falling down. That tower has stood there for hundreds of years. And anyway, you won't be sleeping in there any more so no need to worry about that.'

'Well, what if someone broke in?' said Dom. 'What if they locked the door from the inside and hid up there? They might still be up there now.'

Jess whimpered and Miles and Paul began to laugh, then

Miles, unaccountably, reached out and punched his little brother on the side of the head. Ben howled.

'Boys! Stop it!' David barked, but the room was suddenly chaotic. It was as if it was not just Jess's hair, but the strands that anchored them all to reality that had been severed, and they were now spinning and confused, fearing spirits and intruders, turning against one another; mistrustful, lying, demented.

Olivia looked at David. 'We need to get upstairs in the tower – we need to find a key. There's a bunch in the armoire. Can you try those?'

'Everyone stay here,' David ordered.

But Dom got up and followed his father out and then Miles and Paul ran after them too. Their deranged laughter rang out down the hall. Ben stayed on the sofa next to Chloe.

'You know, it couldn't be the boys because there aren't any scissors in the house,' Chloe pointed out.

'That's right,' Emma called through from the kitchen. 'I remember David was looking for scissors when we got here, on the first day. And we all had a search, yesterday, too, because of the lobster.'

'One of the boys could have taken them?' Khalil stepped out from the kitchen where he'd been sitting with Nura.

'What, on the first day? Before we'd even unpacked?' Emma said.

Olivia looked down at Jess. Her remaining hair was a flat, mousy brown and without its gold-streaked heft her face looked off-kilter; her features seemed to have swollen. Whoever had done this must have taken all her hair in one hand, twisted it, then hacked it off in one go. It would have taken a big pair of scissors – or a very sharp knife. You could not do that with nail scissors.

This was a violent act. The attacker would have had to turn

Jess onto her front or side in order to gather the hair into a trunk that could be severed. But perhaps she was already on her front – she still sometimes slept like that, with her legs tucked under her, her bottom up, as she had done since she was a baby. Olivia felt cold, suddenly, and then nauseous.

After a few minutes, David and the boys came back

'None of the keys work. We can't get up there.' Dom threw himself on the sofa.

'OK, guys,' Khalil said from the doorway. 'Em's made coffee and hot chocolate. Jess is going to be OK. How about we all get some breakfast, sit out on the terrace, calm down and maybe someone will remember something.'

'Do you think we should have a look outside?' said Olivia. 'In case there's still someone out there?'

David nodded and their eyes met. They didn't need to exchange any words; she knew that he wanted her to stay with Jess and he knew she wanted him to be careful. He was present and protective; he loved his family and was there for them. She realized that it had been a very long time since she had felt this from him. It had taken a crisis, an attack, but it was still a relief to feel that it was there.

Chloe got up and stood facing David, with her back to Olivia. 'I'll come with you.' She couldn't see Chloe's face, but David blinked and looked away. He seemed to shrink slightly.

They left the room, Chloe first, David close behind her.

Olivia wasn't sure what she'd just witnessed. Dom got up then. 'Be careful,' she called after him. 'Stay with Dad, OK?' Then she saw Khalil gesturing her into the kitchen. She got up, leaving Jess on the sofa.

Emma was getting out plates now and Nura was still on the stool. Khalil's voice was low, diplomatic and slightly clinical,

'Look, Liv, if someone broke into the tower last night, you probably need to ask Jess if she's in any pain?'

She felt her stomach turn over as his meaning sank in. Khalil squeezed her arm as he left the room.

'Come on, guys, grab a mug and a plate,' Emma was calling to the children. 'Can someone take the baguettes out to the table? They're stale, I'm afraid, but they'll be fine if you put lots of jam on and dip them in your hot chocolate . . .' The children came through and began following Emma's instructions.

Olivia took Jess to one side and asked her if anything in her body hurt.

'My hair,' Jess said. 'The space where my hair should be hurts every time I put my hands up there.' She waved her hands around her shoulders. 'It's like I can feel it, but not feel it, and it makes a sort of noise, like a bad song.'

She decided it was best to be specific. 'What about your vagina?'

'WHAT?'

'I just need to know if you're hurting there, at all. Or anywhere else.'

'No!' Jess screwed her face up in disgust and pushed back her ragged hair. 'Can I go?' She ran out to join the others on the terrace.

'You know, I think we should call the police,' Emma whispered. Even her freckles looked pale.

Nura watched Jess go. Nura and Jess's friendship had no balance, Olivia thought. Nura was slavish while Jess often treated her with indifference. That, surely, must lead to resentment. And Nura might have a complicated relationship with Jess's hair too. They had spent their early lives watching toxic Disney movies involving princesses with long blonde hair.

Olivia bent so that she was eye level with Nura. She felt Em hovering, but didn't care. 'Are you sure you don't know anything about this, Nuri?'

'She doesn't, Liv,' Em said.

Nura's bottom lip wobbled.

'She's upset!' Emma pushed herself between them.

'Can you just let her answer my question?'

Emma recoiled.

'I didn't cut Jess's hair, Mummy.' Nura looked only at her mother. 'I didn't, I promise.'

'OK, sweetie, we know that.' Em's face was puce. 'Olivia's just upset.'

But there was something in Nura's eyes – a flicker of uncertainty – that made Olivia sure that she was holding back. 'You do know *something*,' she said. 'Don't you?'

Nura blinked. 'I don't know what I heard.'

'What, darling?' Em crouched next to her. '*Did* you hear someone?'

'I might've heard the door shutting,' Nura whispered. 'But I was asleep.'

'OK,' Olivia said. 'Did you see anyone come in or out of the room, Nura?'

Nura shook her head. 'I maybe heard the door. I think it woke me up. I thought it was Mummy.' Her eyes grew wider. 'But then I went back to sleep.'

'Do you know what time this was?'

Nura shook her head.

'Was it light outside?'

'I don't know.' Nura reached out her small hands to her mother and Emma swept her into a hug. 'Shhh, it's OK, it's OK. You didn't do anything wrong.'

'OK, Nuri. It's OK. Well done.' Olivia straightened. 'Well done.' She looked at Em over Nura's head. Neither of them spoke.

She imagined a stranger, or perhaps worse, worse even than that, someone who was not a stranger, someone she could not bring herself to think about again, standing in the tower door-way with scissors, watching all the sleeping children.

But of course, it could just have been Paul and Miles sneaking out to look for a ghost.

On the terrace the children were unusually quiet. Jess stared at her plate. She was, Olivia thought, actually quite traumatized. She sat down, put her arm around Jess's shoulders and felt her daughter lean into her.

Paul got up and paced over to the far edge of the terrace, which looked down at the lines of olive trees. 'I can see Al,' he called back. 'But not the others.'

Olivia could see Al walking up towards the house through the olive grove. The bald spot on the top of his head gleamed. Khalil emerged from a line of trees, too, with Dom just behind him. 'Where's David?' Olivia called down. 'And Chloe?'

Khalil looked up and shaded his eyes. 'They're coming. It's all fine. Nothing down here.'

They heard footsteps and David appeared through the French windows. Olivia felt a wash of relief at the sight of his face. 'Well, there's nothing out there.'

He pulled up a chair and poured himself a coffee.

'Where's Chloe?' Emma asked.

Nobody answered. Then Chloe stepped through the French windows, too.

Khalil, Dom and Al came in a moment later and they all sat at the long table together. Em made more coffee, warmed more milk, stirred Banania powder into it. They sat quietly, spreading apricot jam and salted butter onto yesterday's baguettes as the sun lifted itself above the terrace for another perfect day.

'Just a thought, but is it at all possible,' Al said, when the children had finished and, at Chloe's suggestion, gone inside to watch a DVD, 'that Jess cut her own hair?'

'Of course she didn't,' Chloe said.

'No, no, I wondered that, too,' Emma said. 'It does happen.'

Olivia could not speak because inside her head, fear was swelling, leaving no room for anything else, taking up all the space and resources.

'People do strange things in their sleep don't they,' Al went on, 'they make meals, send texts, watch TV, have sex . . . There was this guy who got off a rape charge because supposedly he was asleep at the time. There's some word for it. It's an actual medical condition, a sleep disorder.'

'Jess hasn't got a sleep disorder.' David sounded weary.

'Of course she hasn't.' Chloe looked at David, who stared at her a moment, then looked away. Again, Olivia felt as if the two of them were in the middle of a different, secret conversation.

Al's face darkened. 'Well, presumably no one knows they've got a sleep disorder till something like this happens.' He layered butter on another chunk of baguette. He had a glob of jam on his chin.

'It's possible it wasn't one of the kids,' Khalil said.

'You mean a stranger? What sort of lunatic would come up here and cut a little girl's hair off?' said Al. 'It's hardly likely, is it?'

Olivia looked over across the hills; on the other side of the valley, a far-off hilltop town teetered, blanched, in the distance. Down below, among the familiar flesh-pink roofs of the village, the church bell rang, eight unhurried tenor strikes, circles of sound pushing through the soft air.

'You can sell hair for hair extensions,' Chloe said. 'I read an article about it. It was happening to women in Venezuela, I think, they had their hair hacked off literally as they walked down the street.'

'Jesus fucking Christ.' David's fist, on the table, tightened.

'What if someone spotted Jess when we went for ice cream yesterday?' Emma said, in a tremulous voice.

'Well, the gate was wide open so basically anyone could have just walked into the courtyard,' David said. 'The kids were sitting ducks in there. We're lucky it wasn't something much worse.' He looked at Olivia as he said this and she heard the accusation. And with that, he broke ranks. They were no longer a team. He was the opponent again.

She had been in such a fraught state the evening before when she came back from meeting Vivian in the village. She didn't remember but she knew she could easily have left the gate open. Through the French windows she could see Jess curled in a corner of the sofa with her shaggy head on her knees. The other children lay motionless, not even on their phones, just staring at the TV.

The breeze wafted the scent of lavender and wild thyme across the terrace; it mingled with the smell of chlorine from the unused pool.

'OK. Enough is enough.' David got to his feet. 'I'm going to call the police.'

Vivian

Dieppe–Newhaven Ferry

I left the *chambres d'hôte* before dawn, too early for the breakfast, too early to tell the goat-faced owner that I was going.

As I followed the auto route up through France, paid tolls, filled and refilled the petrol tank; as I queued for the ferry in Dieppe while the sun began to sink; as I left my Fiat in the bowels of the ship and limped up the clanging stairway, down sticky-carpeted corridors that smelled of vomit and out onto the deck, the knowledge of what Olivia did, of what she has hidden from me for all these months, ran through my mind over and over.

The knowledge of what happened to Bertie is unbearable. None of my usual techniques – counting, breathing, listing – will stem my obsessive thoughts. I have found a spot on the deck, now, where nobody else wants to be, next to the guttural engines, below the choking fumes and as I cling to the slimy railings, I relive last night's unspeakable scene.

I got to my feet as she reached my table: she was sorry for the offhand way she had treated me before, with her friend. She had come back to make amends, to listen to my idea.

'Olivia,' I cried. 'I was just thinking about you. I wanted to explain why I'm here . . .'

But her fine features did not soften. 'That'd be good, Vivian,' she said, through almost closed lips. 'I'd really like to know what you're doing here.'

I had never seen this look on her face before. I was not sure exactly what it was, but I knew that it was not warm. I felt the hope stutter and retreat.

'Won't you join me?' As I gestured at the free chair, I knocked the edge of the table with my knuckles and almost sent my wine glass flying. 'I'll get you some wine,' I said. 'Or maybe not? It's dreadful, rough local stuff. How about—'

'Vivian!' she cut me off. 'I don't want a drink.' She pulled out the chair and plonked herself onto it, knees apart, unladylike. 'I want to know what you're doing here.'

'What do you mean?'

She gave a hollow and slightly exhausted laugh. 'You've followed me all the way to the south of France. How did you even know I was here? I don't remember telling you the name of this village. Did I? Because I really don't think I did. I don't remember a single conversation in which I told you the location of my holiday house.'

I felt blood rush to my face. I did not want to tell her about finding her laptop in the Farmhouse the night I stayed over with her children. It was intrusive of me to pry that night, but it was months ago. I'd seen her type in her laptop's password numerous times in the bakery, she had never tried to conceal it. But I felt that if I were to come clean then she would, perhaps rightly, be very angry with me. And I did not want that. I wanted her to listen to me.

I could feel her unblinking eyes fixed on my face.

The bark of the plane tree next to my table was camouflage patterned, as if it had slipped into army fatigues. The waiter appeared, but Olivia dismissed him with a shake of her head. He practically genuflected as he backed off.

I knew I had to give her some kind of explanation, so I said that I had no intention of intruding, but hoped she might be interested in discussing my book idea, now that she was more relaxed, without all the other demands of her life.

'You came all the way to France to talk to me about *a book?*'

I nodded.

She stared at me, then, round-eyed and tight-mouthed and I felt myself coming apart inside, growing ragged, bits flailing around. So I started to make a list. It is a technique I used to use at governing body meetings when they would all turn on me, or in tricky departmental meetings when I was under attack. I developed it as a child for the times when my father had been drinking and would get angry with me for my failings, or when he would lose control of himself – the times when I couldn't get away through the woods to the hollow oak or up to the meadow. Listing is my protective shell. On this occasion I chose tribes of the subfamily *Cetoniinae*: flower chafers, flower beetles, flower scarabs.

'Vivian! Why are you staring at the tree like that? Did you hear me? I asked you a question.'

Fortunately, just those few moments counting *Cetoniinae*

had anchored my panic somewhat and I found that I was even able to look up at her, briefly. Her irises were a dark royal blue at the edges, very striking. She did not blink. She just stared back at me. She was facing me, knees splayed, chin lifted, fists resting on the plastic tabletop. I could not keep the eye contact going. Eye contact, even with someone familiar, can feel like having hot needles inserted into my eyeballs.

I looked over at the pale, ancient stone of the fountain. 'Shall I tell you my idea?' I said. 'It's a book about the Chocolate Cream Poisoner, a Victorian lady from Brighton, Christiana Edmunds. Do you know about her? Her story is rather fascinating.' I glanced at her again. She gave her head a little shake.

I wasn't sure if she was encouraging me, but I decided to continue anyway. 'She lived in Brighton with her elderly mother and fell in love with her neighbour, a married doctor called Charles Beard. When he ended the affair, she injected a box of chocolate creams with strychnine and gave them to his wife, who miraculously survived, though she was very ill indeed. After that, Christiana went a little mad, she started buying chocolates and sweets and injecting them with poison; she killed a four-year-old boy. For a while, the whole town was living in fear, avoiding sweets—'

'Vivian! Stop. Stop this.'

'But this is exactly your sort of subject, Olivia. Just hear me out. Christiana was a bright woman driven insane by loneliness and rejection, lack of prospects, a dismal future caring for her mother. She was almost executed but got off on an insanity plea and was sent to Broadmoor—'

'Oh my God, Vivian! I don't want to talk about the

Chocolate Cream Poisoner. I'm with my family, I'm on *holiday*. I'm with my *friends*. This is . . .'

This was really not going the way I had hoped. There was not even the slightest hint of eagerness. 'I didn't just come here to talk to you about the Chocolate Cream Poisoner.' It was stupid to pretend but I was ashamed and it just came out. 'I needed a holiday. It won't stop raining in Sussex. I'm here to look for harlequins too.'

'No.' She tapped the table, sharply. The words shrivelled in my throat. 'Don't lie to me. This has nothing to do with ladybirds and we both know it. My God, Vivian, you have to stop lying.'

'But it's the truth.' I felt chilly, suddenly, which was odd as the air was still hot.

'I don't think you know the difference between truth and lies, Vivian. You told me you were an Oxford professor, for God's sake! Do you think I haven't Googled you? You don't exist at Oxford University, you never did. You pop up with your Ileford associations, some dispute with the parish council a few years ago over the bin collection, and I've found plenty of other Testers all over East Sussex, in stoolball leagues and in censuses, but as far as a professorial career is concerned . . .' She tailed off, as if it was too much effort to go on.

I was surprised she hadn't confronted me about this before. I certainly never intended to tell her that I had been an Oxford professor. In fact, I had intended not to. It just came out of my mouth that day in the museum. For a long time afterwards I was expecting her to say something and had decided to be evasive, but her delicacy and preoccupation – or pragmatism, she couldn't afford to upset or alienate me, after all – saved me the trouble.

None of this really mattered now anyway. It was suddenly clear to me that coming to France to talk about further collaboration might be construed as unhinged.

And then a sort of crazed defiance settled on me – a compulsion or intense urge to continue even though I knew, rationally, that it was unwise. I just couldn't help myself, I had come here to tell her about Christiana and I had to finish my story. 'Christiana loved to dance,' I said, 'right to the very end, well into her seventies. She'd dress up every day with false hair, false teeth and rouge, and she'd dance. Hence her other nickname, "The Venus of Broadmoor". Now, wouldn't that make a good title for the new book?'

'I have no intention of writing a book about the Chocolate Cream Poisoner, Vivian.'

'But I've already contacted the Broadmoor archivists,' I objected. 'I have copies of newspaper articles from her trial, an account from a Brighton society lady who almost died. I've got a whole file on this, up in the *chambres d'hôte* where I'm staying. It's just up the road behind the square. I'll go and get it, if you like? I'll show you what I have.'

I knew, of course, that this was hopeless, I was only digging myself in deeper, but I continued anyway. It is a failing of mine that when something interests me, I find it extremely difficult to stop talking once I have started. 'She got the strychnine from a chemist friend, she told him she needed it to poison stray cats—'

She slapped her hand on the tabletop. The wine glass rattled against its carafe. 'Stop. Please, Vivian. You have to stop. I don't want to hear about this. You have to listen to me now. I can see I need to be really clear, OK? So, here goes. You've been a superlative RA, you're extremely bright and organized, but I have no intention of doing another book with you, not about the Chocolate Cream Poisoner, the Venus of Broadmoor, or anything else. Ever.'

I must have looked crestfallen because her tone softened. 'You're just not very easy to work with, Vivian. You must know that? I haven't . . . I'm so sorry but the truth is I just haven't got room in my life for . . . for . . .' She waves a hand in my general direction. 'For *this*.'

I could see her mouth opening and closing but all I could hear was a rushing sound – I was at Beachy Head with wind punching my eyes, swaying on the crumbling chalk edge, buffeted by salty air, ready to fall. I started to list tribes of the flower chafer again, scarab, subfamily *Cetoniinae*: *Cetoniini, Goliathini, Schizorhinini* . . . Calmer, just a little calmer, I forced myself back from the edge and tuned in to what she was saying to me. Her voice was softer.

'I really am sorry if I sound harsh, I don't mean to be harsh, I really don't. I do feel for you, I know you don't have much else in your life. You've given me invaluable help, but it's been quite an ordeal to manage you.'

'*Manage* me?' I felt a sort of thunder in my chest, a shuddering sensation, something breaking open.

'Please! It's really not funny,' she said. 'Not to me anyway.' She looked over her shoulder; other customers in the cafe were staring. 'Stop laughing, Vivian.'

'Well!' I bellowed. 'Well, well! I didn't know I needed to be "managed"!'

'Really? Well, yes . . . You did. In so far as it's possible to manage someone like you.'

'Actually, Olivia.' My laughter vanished as fast as it had risen and I adopted a more formal tone. 'It's *me* who has had to manage *you*. I trawled through record offices and archives, I chased down each and every one of Annabel's dull and obstructive descendants, I presented every reference, fact, quote and source to you in simple, usable, narrative-friendly form. I managed *you*. I gave you the data exactly when you were ready for it, in the order you needed it. I maximized your productivity to a very tight schedule. Do you really think you could have done the book in that amount of time if I hadn't? I made you stick to it, even when you were having your own little crises, with that wastrel son and your TV vanity work.'

I was, I suppose, angry, but that last comment was cruel. I wished that I could unsay it.

'My *what*?' Two scarlet spots appeared on her cheeks.

'Let's just be very clear,' I said. 'I managed *you*. If I hadn't, this fanciful tale would not exist.'

She blew out as if extinguishing a big church candle. 'OK. You know what? I can't do this. Think what you like, Vivian, but you have absolutely no idea what it takes to write a readable book.'

'I *made sure* you wrote a readable book.'

'Don't be ridiculous!' She was shouting suddenly. 'Look, I get it, I really do. You're lonely, you're bored, you badly need something to occupy your mind. A person like you should definitely not be a housekeeper—'

'I'm not a—'

She waved her hand. 'I don't care, OK? Just think about this, just for a moment. Why on earth would you want to do another book with me? This can't have been a fun year for you. Surely. Can it?'

'I have loved our work on *Annabel*,' I said, with dignity.

'Seriously?'

I thought about this for a second. 'Except for losing Bertie,' I said. 'That was a very dark time indeed. In fact, it still is very difficult.'

'Oh my God, Vivian, please, not the dog again.'

Very slowly, I reached for my wine glass and drained the last drops. 'If anyone has the right to be aggrieved about Bertie' – I did look her in the eye, then – 'it's me.'

'But you have to get over it! It was six months ago.' She threw up her hands and sat back. 'I've done everything I can, I really have. I've taken endless care of you over that dog.'

'It was only five and a half months ago. He wasn't well. You were supposed to—'

'OK. No. Please. I really can't do this now. You have to get past this. He was just a dog! A neurotic bloody mongrel!'

I felt the anger zip through my veins, tiny, cold ball bearings that shot around my body and rattled behind my eyes.

'Don't look at me like that, Vivian. You see, this is exactly what I mean. *This!* I've lost hours and hours over your dog. I've driven down to Sussex in the middle of the night to comfort you. I've sent you chocolates and bunches of flowers, I've cooked you suppers, I've talked to you about him endlessly, we've gone over and over it. I know you loved Bertie, but he wasn't your child, Vivian, he was just a dog!'

I stared at a red wine stain on the tablecloth. 'He was everything to me,' I said, quietly.

'Yes, yes, I know. I know, I know he was, I'm sorry. But bad things happen, Vivian. Dogs drown. *People* drown. I mean, think of all the refugees stuffed into tiny boats, drowning in the sea, toddlers washed up on beaches. Now *that's* a tragedy.'

'What did you just say?' I looked at her very closely.

'*The refugee situation is a tragedy!*' she cried. Conversations in the Café de Paris stopped abruptly. Then I saw her eyes flicker as she realized what she had just said.

The colour drained from her cheeks.

I wiped my mouth with the back of my hand.

She brushed imaginary crumbs from her *Coccinella* dress. 'I should go.'

I leaned forwards. 'Bertie *drowned*?'

'What?' She blinked and leaned away from me, but I tilted my torso further over the table. 'Bertie,' I said. 'Where did he drown, Olivia?'

'OK. Oh my God. OK. OK.' She pressed her fingers into her eyeballs. Her make-up smudged into moth's wings beneath her eyes. 'Fine. *Fine*. I'm sorry. I didn't tell you the truth because I thought it would upset you even more, but clearly you're never going to get past this if I don't. Bertie fell in the well, at Ileford. I'm so sorry, I'm really so sorry, Vivian. I feel absolutely awful that it happened, believe me, I feel absolutely *dreadful* about it. It was horrendous.'

'The *well*? In the courtyard? Violet's well?'

'Violet's well, yes. It was just a horrible, terrible accident. I got the cover off – I wanted to see if I could see Violet's face in there, remember? I knew you'd never let me, so . . . Anyway, I managed to push the cover half off and Bertie just sort of jumped up onto it, yapping – you know what he was like. He was hysterical, turning circles. It all happened so fast, I couldn't get him to come down. One minute he was there, on the cover, next he was just . . . His hind legs kind of slipped . . . and he was gone.'

I closed my eyes and heard a crackling sound, as if the

feet of a thousand Devil's coach horse beetles were march-
ing through the undergrowth in my brain, tails raised,
spraying poison over everything.

'See?' She sounded desperate. 'See? I knew it would only
be worse for you to know. I just didn't want that image in
your head. Vivian? Are you OK?'

I opened my eyes. I looked right at her then. She is, objec-
tively, a very beautiful woman. Her Danish ancestry is
visible in the bone structure, those extraordinary eyes. But
at that moment I had never seen anything so foul. I saw the
shape of her skull beneath her black hair and I saw her laid
in the earth with her flesh eaten off her bones by blow-fly
maggots, rove, hister, carcass and carrion beetles. 'You left
Bertie to drown in the well?'

'Of course I didn't leave him! I'm not a monster. I tried to
get him out – I tried absolutely everything – but it's very deep.
It must be thirty, forty feet down. Have you ever looked down
there? It's miles down to the water. It was just awful. I ran
around the courtyard looking for something to get him out,
but there was nothing to use. I tried the extendable dog lead, I
thought I might be able to hook his collar somehow, but it
wasn't anywhere near . . . I really tried to save him, Vivian, I
really did.' Her voice caught. 'But in the end I just couldn't.'

'You let him drown?'

'Please, Vivian. Please! Just think about it. What could I
possibly have done? I was about to call the fire brigade, but
then I realized he'd gone. He really didn't last very long, I
think maybe he was weak from his illness, or maybe he hurt
himself on the way down, I just don't know – but it wasn't
protracted, he only splashed for a really short time before
he went quiet.'

I could not speak. I could barely breathe.

'Please don't look at me like that.' She looked hollow-eyed. 'It was just an accident. It was just an awful, unfortunate accident.'

'Unfortunate?'

For five and a half months Olivia had lied to me. She had allowed me to search for him, to go out night after night, calling for him. The night he vanished we even searched for him together – it was all a masquerade. We must have passed the well numerous times that night, and each time she pretended that she did not know he was down there.

Then I realized something. Bertie is still down there. I have passed him day after day for five and a half months. Every time I stand at the sink waiting for the kettle to boil for my breakfast tea, every time I wash up my plate after lunch or afternoon tea, or clear my dinner things, I am looking at Bertie's grave. I cannot even think what five and a half months in well water would do to the body of a small dog.

'I'm so sorry,' she was saying. 'I was trying to protect you. I wasn't sure you'd cope with knowing how he died and I just didn't want to plant that awful image in your head. I didn't think you'd be able to take it, to be honest, I thought you'd fall apart.'

And there we have the nub of it. She couldn't have that. She couldn't have me falling apart. She needed me sharp and loyal and fully functioning, shovelling research her way in regular, reliable quantities.

'It was probably wrong of me, in retrospect. I should have told you the truth.' Her voice is shaky. 'I just . . .'

I raised a hand and pointed at her. 'Mimicking species.'

'OK.' She pushed back her chair and got up, knocking

her hip against the table. 'I'm not sure what that means, but I think we're done.'

'Liar,' I croaked. 'Pretender.'

'You see.' She picked up her floppy bag. 'This is what I'm talking about. I'm sorry, I really am, but I can't do this any more. I couldn't – even if I wanted to – fill this void in your life, Vivian. I can't rescue you from whatever demons are plaguing you. I'm fond of you, but I can't be that person. I'm going to go back now, up to the house, to my children who need me, to my husband and my friends. They have to be my priority now. I'm sorry, Vivian.'

'Yes, Olivia.' I pressed my thumb on the bloody wine stain. 'That's right. You go. You belong up there with your lying husband. You deserve each other.'

She stared down at me. 'What's that supposed to mean?'

'Don't ask me, ask him. Ask him why he and your blonde friend were parked at the viewing point for two hours yesterday.'

'Oh my God, have you been *spying* on us?' she gasped. 'Have you been *watching* us?'

'I have better things to watch. But the view from the hillside is quite comprehensive.'

She shook her head as if I was something to be dislodged and then, without another word, turned and strode away through the tables.

I watched her go, in her red dress and her Greek goddess sandals – other people swivelled to look at her too. Olivia lives in a world that turns its head when she passes, a world that watches her every move with interest and admiration.

Ladybird, Ladybird, fly away home, your house is on fire, your children are gone. The childish rhyme played in my head as her seven-seater car reversed out of its spot, accelerated past the pink-fronted *hôtel de ville*, around the shady square, past my table and off, down the village street – away – to climb the hills, up to her holiday house with its azure pool, its tasteful vine-clad terrace and its ancient tower with all the waiting loved ones inside.

For a second, the image of Bertie scrabbling in the darkness overcame me. Most of the cafe customers had gone back to their conversations. I wanted to go, but my legs were so weak that I could not stand.

People are all the same, really. The one thing you can rely on is that they will behave exactly as you feared they might.

Olivia

South of France, Day Six

Olivia felt sure that the village police weren't taking this seriously enough. Perhaps it was her inadequate French, or perhaps a child's shorn hair just didn't seem like the most important crime, but as the officer took their statements and filled out apparently endless forms, there was something about his body language that suggested scepticism. He clearly thought the boys had done it.

'How many boys are in the house?' he said, in English, shuffling papers.

'Four.' Olivia counted them off. 'Our two sons, our friends' two sons.'

'*Ils ont quel âge?*'

'How old? Our sons are fifteen and thirteen, Miles is twelve, Ben is eight.'

The detective looked at her. '*Il s'agit sans doute d'une mauvaise plaisanterie.*'

'What?' She looked at David.

'A prank.' He glanced at her, nervously. 'He says it's most likely a prank.'

Olivia felt herself grow hot despite the air conditioning. 'The boys did not cut Jess's hair off.'

David reached out and pressed her knee. Though she could understand most of what was being said, she couldn't speak as well as him. This year alone he'd been to Paris twice to interview people or give talks. He said, now, in French, 'One of the children thinks she heard the door closing in the middle of the night as someone left the priest's tower.'

'Priest's tower?' The policeman frowned.

'Isn't that what it is?' David said. 'Across the courtyard, where the priest once lived?'

'There is no priest's tower,' the police officer said in a slow, pedantic voice. 'The *cabanon* is not a religious building, it's simply a small lodging, originally built for a peasant – probably the goat or pig keeper.'

Olivia really wasn't sure why they were talking about this or indeed where the idea that it was a priest's tower had come from in the first place. She suspected she'd invented it and they'd all seized on it as poetic, or somehow fitting, given the gravestone doorstep. She leaned forward. '*C'etait un . . . un estranger qui a entré le tour dans le nuit. It wasn't the boys, okay? Il n'y a pas les ciseaux dans le maison.* There are no scissors in the house!'

'All houses have scissors.' The policeman drew out the vowels in '*ciseaux*' as if it was ludicrous to suggest that a French house might not possess them.

'Not this one,' David said.

Olivia threw up her hands. 'This is . . .' She struggled to find the word. '*Fou. Complètement fou.*'

'Kids do crazy things,' the officer agreed.

'Listen.' David took a deep breath. She noticed that he'd clenched his fists, though his voice remained even, his French smooth. 'We have found no scissors and no hair. I've even checked the inventory – there were no scissors in the house when we arrived. We don't think the boys would do this. We're worried someone broke in and did this to our daughter.'

The officer raised his eyebrows and nodded. 'Hair can be sold. It is possible that this was a theft,' he said in French, 'but very unlikely.'

Olivia felt her face grow hotter.

David was sitting very still. His ability to fabricate calm was impressive. The image of him and Chloe parked at the viewing point popped into her head. They had gone off together to buy food, but what were they doing sitting in the car? What were they talking about? Then again, Vivian might have made the whole thing up.

She thought of Vivian's face the evening before, when she realized what had happened to Bertie. It had been so stupid to blurt it out. She felt dizzy. This situation was becoming surreal. She couldn't think clearly at all. Was Vivian capable of such a deranged act? She could not possibly attempt to discuss, with a French policeman, her row with Vivian; she couldn't try to explain to him who Vivian was, or why she was here. She couldn't even clearly articulate her own feelings about Vivian, let alone communicate them effectively to a stranger.

The police officer looked at Jess, who blinked up at him. With pink-rimmed eyes and her hair jagged at her chin, she looked like a poor Victorian workhouse urchin, so feeble and shaken. Olivia wanted to pick her up and cradle her, like a baby. The policeman became more paternal, suddenly, too. He leaned over and said something to Jess in a sweet voice.

'What?' Olivia leaned in, too. She looked back at David. 'What did he say to her?'

David put a restraining hand on her arm. 'He said, "It's OK, your hair will grow back."'

Olivia felt a surge of outrage. 'For Christ's sake! Someone breaks into a tower full of children in the middle of the night, attacks our daughter and all he can say is "It'll grow back"?'

'Liv, don't.' David pressed his fingers harder into her forearm. 'They're taking this seriously. Losing it isn't going to help.'

They both looked at Jess. Her face was chalky. She was staring at the floor. Olivia reached for her, but David got there first. 'It's OK, sweetie.' He pulled her onto his lap and cuddled her and kissed the top of her head. 'Mummy's just upset, that's all. We're all a bit upset, aren't we, babe?'

When they eventually made it back to the house, it was late afternoon and they'd both given detailed statements. Two police officers were at the house, poking round the tower. Olivia could tell by the way they looked at her with half-closed eyelids that they were wondering what sort of negligent parents would let their children sleep in an unlocked tower, with an open gate, across the courtyard, in a foreign country, in the middle of nowhere. They were fortunate that something far worse had not happened.

And they were right.

Could Vivian have done this? She had certainly been distraught, angry and bitter, but this would be a truly unhinged response to finding out about Bertie. Vivian might be odd, but was she totally insane? The image of Vivian standing over Jess with a pair of scissors made Olivia feel suddenly sick.

It was just so hot, that was the problem. Even in her linen dress she could feel the sweat trickling down her back. Her hair stuck to her skull. She hadn't eaten either; she felt weak, she needed a shower. And a drink. A big drink. David walked ahead up the stairs to the house, holding Jess's hand. He leaned down and said something and she heard Jess actually laugh and then slap him on the biceps, making him reach for her, seize her, tickle her. He was actually at his best at times like this: solid and tender, armed with his annoying Dad jokes, a safety net into which Jess could fall and be gathered up, held above her troubles.

Perhaps the policeman was right that the boys did this. They could have found scissors somewhere, and Jess had been winding them up at bedtime, teasing them about the grave man, keeping them awake. It was possible that they wanted to teach her a lesson. Miles, particularly, had a thuggish streak. But would they go this far? Surely Paul wouldn't have violated his sister in this way. His shocked reaction had seemed authentic. No. It couldn't have been her boy. She was sure of it.

Perhaps it really was a bizarre act of theft by a stranger. She dimly remembered reading about a spate of hair stealing in nineteenth century Paris: women and children violated as they knelt in church. They might feel a tickle on the neck, or nothing at all, and then later they'd find that their long plaits had been sliced clean off. But it seemed so unlikely that this could happen to Jess.

Her limbs felt shaky as she stepped into the cool hallway. David and Jess had vanished down the corridor into the kitchen. She paused and leaned against the armoire, trying to find something to hold on to, trying to think straight. But all she could think was that they could not possibly stay another night in this house. They had to get out. The holiday was ruined.

Olivia

'Listen guys . . . Em's packing.' Khalil came out onto the shady terrace just as Olivia sat down at the table with all the other adults. 'We just don't really feel we can stay here any more after what's happened.'

They had two open bottles of wine in front of them and someone had opened a big bag of greasy, plain crisps. The children were sprawled in the living room, on sofas or floors, staring at screens, eating bread and Nutella.

'We're going to go,' Khalil finished.

Olivia opened her mouth to say they were leaving too, but David struggled to his feet. He bumped the edge of the table and the wine glasses shook. 'What? No! Don't go!'

Olivia stared at him.

'Em just doesn't feel safe here any more,' Khalil said. 'And, I mean, I'm with her, it's not exactly relaxing knowing that someone might've come in and done this.'

'It is horribly unsettling.' Chloe nodded. 'The thought that there's someone out there who could do this . . .'

Olivia looked back at David, but his eyes were fixed on Chloe. Again, she thought of the two of them in the car at the viewing point. With all the trauma of the police and the hair she hadn't even asked him about it. But if she asked him, she'd have to explain that it came from Vivian, and that just felt too difficult. The only way to explain that would be to explain Bertie and the well, and all the mess and complications of Vivian, and she could not begin to go there right now. She just couldn't.

Chloe was the only one who had been for a swim and the kaftan she'd pulled over her bathing suit was patchy and damp and clung to the outline of her breasts as she ran her hands through her wet hair, pulling it back from her face, which looked gaunt and tired.

'I think we're going to go too.' Chloe blinked at Al. 'Aren't we?'

Al nodded and shrugged, then stared glumly at his wine glass, his chin tucked in and resting on the solid folds of his neck.

David began to argue, then, that if it was a one-off act of opportunism then the culprit would be long gone. The online market for human hair was lucrative: beautiful long hair like Jess's could be sold for as much as a thousand euros. Whoever did this would not be coming back.

Olivia watched him as he talked. He was so vehement, so panicky. Perspiration dotted his hairline, his unshaven jaw was tense, his eyes darted from face to face. She could not fathom what was going through his mind right now. How could he possibly consider staying in this place, after what had happened? His denial felt pathological. He flopped back into the chair, spent.

She felt her stomach churn. She was responsible for this. She had failed to book a house with enough bedrooms for all the children, she had persuaded everyone that the tower was safe and she had left the gate unlocked. She had also exposed her family to Vivian – if this had anything to do with Vivian.

She still couldn't work out whether Vivian was capable of this. It could be an insane act of revenge or spite or outrage, or an expression of pain. Or it might just have been a stranger, as the police suggested, an opportunist who saw Jess's beautiful golden hair and knew they could make a lot of money by selling it.

Neither explanation seemed remotely reasonable. Both felt terrifying.

The bottom line was that she had no idea what Vivian was or wasn't capable of. All she knew was that Vivian was odd, obsessive and secretive and had just taken a big blow. The extent of their entanglement was now beginning to sink in. Over the past eighteen months, she had allowed Vivian to cross an invisible boundary; she'd revealed things about her personal life that she would not, had she stopped to think about it for a nanosecond, have wanted Vivian to know.

Vivian already knew more about her struggles with Dominic than Chloe did. She also knew about her career insecurities and her fears that her colleagues did not take her seriously because of her TV work. She knew about the tensions with David, too. She'd shared with Vivian her fears about the stalker, and her anxiety that he might come back. She'd even talked to Vivian about her father, about the *olivia* fossil and the crisis over his reputation, and she almost never talked to anyone about that. Somehow, little by little, Vivian had unearthed things that she would much rather have kept to herself. In return, she knew next to nothing about Vivian.

Khalil was saying something about staying in an Ibis hotel near the airport. Then Chloe and Al were bickering about whether to leave that night or the next day.

'Everyone's knackered; I've just had two glasses of wine. Let's at least go tomorrow, the kids can sleep in our room tonight,' Al said. 'They'll be perfectly safe, I mean, there's still the possibility that they were involved. Got carried away, you know.'

'Carried away? Oh my God! Our boys did not do this to Jess!'

Al shrugged. 'Fine.'

'I'll drive. I've only had one glass of wine,' Chloe said. 'I don't feel safe here. We need to just go, Al.'

Olivia suddenly remembered that she'd left Paul and Jess with Vivian overnight once, on their own. It was about a year ago. David had been travelling and she had brought Jess and Paul down to Sussex for the night. She'd had a row with Dom, who wanted to stay in London; he'd thumped his fist into the wall, making a dent in the plaster and eventually, furious and exhausted by him, she had just left him there. She knew it was stupid. He was fifteen and untrustworthy and Marta had gone away for the weekend.

Her phone had started ringing around 11 p.m., first the neighbours, an intimidating architect couple in their late fifties with impeccable, minimalist taste and no children, and then Dom himself. He sounded more like a little boy than he had in years as he told her that the police were with him and wanted to talk to her.

Paul and Jess had been sleeping upstairs. She knew she would be back first thing in the morning and she didn't want to drag them into the car to face whatever chaos Dom had created back in London. The only person she knew well enough to ask, nearby, at short notice, was Vivian.

Vivian drove over and slept in the spare room. She'd brought Bertie and he clearly slept on the bed as Olivia had later found wiry black dog hairs everywhere and the eiderdown had needed cleaning. When Olivia got back, with Dom, at nine thirty the next morning after about three hours of sleep, everything seemed to be under control. Vivian had made Jess and Paul boiled eggs and they were watching TV while she tidied the kitchen with Bertie at her heels.

It was only after Vivian and Bertie left that Olivia began to get the feeling that everything in the house, every single object, drawer, ornament or book, had been picked up, inspected and put back. In her own bedroom the air felt disturbed, though she could pinpoint nothing except that the succulent she kept on her desk, in a geometric pot Marta had brought them from Copenhagen, was now on the windowsill. She couldn't say for certain that she hadn't moved it there herself.

Her laptop was on, but she'd probably left it that way, and anyway, it was password-protected. The teetering pile of books to be read was in the same place. Her notepads, in which she jotted down thoughts and references, sat as always, behind a pile of papers waiting to be dealt with; student essays needing to be marked, an agenda from an academic meeting, her lecture notes, a public talk on index cards, a manuscript waiting for her endorsement, a folder of archival references. She really couldn't pinpoint anything different; even the pot of pens and her calculator were where they always sat. But instinct told her that her desk had been disturbed.

'So what do you think, Liv?' Chloe said, loudly. 'You've gone very quiet.'

'What? Sorry. I was just . . . What?'

'Are you guys leaving tonight or tomorrow?'

'Tonight.' She straightened. 'We're going to have to find a hotel, I don't know. Or just drive up to Dieppe overnight.'

She suddenly realized how Vivian had known about this place. She'd got into the laptop that night. She must have watched her type her password during their sessions in the bakery many times. It had never occurred to her to hide the password. She felt a chill creep across her hot skin. That was the only way Vivian could have known the location of this holiday house. And if Vivian had got into her laptop then she'd have had access to all of Olivia's private emails, work files, money files.

Among the many administrative university emails, she'd have found caches of personal life: exchanges with Chloe or Emma or other friends, social arrangements – dates, times, places – and confidences. She would have been able to read emails with Carol, about TV offers or next steps in her media career, or with the production company about new programme ideas and script developments. Vivian could have traced every stage of the book deal too. All the details of the publishers' bidding war for *Annabel* were in her inbox: the particulars of the advance, notifications of payments for signing, then for delivery of the first draft, the final draft.

There would also be all her personal communication with David too: fraught exchanges about his travel schedule or the need for him to talk to Dom; her occasional outbursts over something Dom had done or said. There were also the tender messages – the idea of Vivian reading those felt almost worse than the arguments – times when she'd felt vulnerable and reached out to him for reassurance or love. Times when she was missing him, longing for him to come home from whatever work trip he was on.

There would be references to Vivian buried in those emails

too. She hadn't said anything too unkind, she was sure, but she definitely would not have wanted Vivian to see them. There would have been times when she'd complained about how demanding, or odd, Vivian was. And David had called her 'your faithful helper', she remembered that. She'd emailed him after the first meeting in the bakery, commenting that Vivian might be difficult – she'd described how Vivian had shouted across the cafe about James Barry and how embarrassed she'd felt. After that, he had also sometimes referred to Vivian as 'Old Baz'.

Vivian had always been non-committal and tight-lipped about David, and Olivia had had the strong sense that she disapproved of him. In reality, Vivian must despise David.

It was disturbing to think of Vivian sitting in her chair, in her bedroom at the Farmhouse, filleting her life, message by message.

And what did she know about Vivian? Almost nothing. Just that she had lost her mother as a young child and had grown up in rural Sussex with an alcoholic father; that she was very protective of Lady Burley; that she worried a lot about her employer's health and about Ileford's structural issues; that she was extremely intelligent and organized, if socially clueless. That she mourned her dog, profoundly.

Did this mean she would attack Jess? Olivia had no idea. But the fact that she was even asking herself this question meant that nothing about Vivian was safe. This, she realized, included the work Vivian had done on *Annabel*.

Publication was in October, less than two months away. The publicity machine was in full motion. She had been photographed on the Ileford steps; features were scheduled for *Vogue*, *Good Housekeeping*, *Red*, *Woman & Home* and *The Lady*. She could not possibly go back to Joy, admit the extent of Vivian's involvement and demand that they delay publication because she needed another year – maybe more – to double-check every single fact that Vivian had produced for her.

She had to calm down. She took a gulp of wine. She felt sick and sweaty. Chloe and Al were still bickering about the logistics of where and when to go. David was silent, arms folded, legs crossed, staring out at the hills, his profile very still, his dark eyes fixed on a distant point. Khalil had gone, presumably to help Emma pack.

She had to stay rational. Everything felt unstable right now because of Jess's hair, but there was no reason to believe that Vivian did it – or that she had sabotaged *Annabel*.

Olivia had talked her through the research strategy in enormous detail. Vivian had been obsessed with the work and with accuracy. She constantly asked for clarification and guidance, had kept her informed of every find. Olivia might not have been through each archive herself, but she had kept a very close eye on Vivian's work. She'd frequently checked facts just to be sure they were accurate. Without fail, they were.

Vivian was just distraught about Bertie. It was understandable, but that did not mean she would come up here in the middle of the night and hack Jess's hair off.

But Vivian could be dismayingly odd. She knew that she should try to share her fears with the others, but she did not know where to start. She imagined David blaming her for the death of the dog, for antagonizing Vivian by lying about it, for allowing Vivian into their lives. He might even fly into a rage and rush down to the village to confront her. That would only make things worse. If Vivian had done this, she would certainly never admit it, and if she had not done this then she would be doubly wounded. It would be very distressing for her to face angry accusations from David.

Al and Chloe were staring at their empty wine glasses. David cleared his throat, rubbed a hand over his face and said, in a flat voice, 'Well, I suppose that's that then.'

'Yup.' Al nodded. 'Holiday's buggered, I'm afraid, mate.'

'The kids are going to be really upset.' David turned to Olivia, as if she could do something about this.

'I know. But we can't stay.'

'Fucking hell!' He slammed his hands onto the chair arms, making them all jump, pushed the chair back and got to his feet.

Olivia turned to Chloe. 'I'll try and get a refund.'

Chloe dismissed this with a wave of a hand. 'None of us care about the money, Liv.' Olivia realized then that Chloe was crying.

'Chlo . . .' She reached out and squeezed her hand. 'I'm so sorry. This is all my fault, I've totally messed up. I should have checked that there were enough bedrooms, I didn't lock the gate . . . I feel really terrible about this, I'm so sorry. I feel completely responsible for this.'

'No.' Chloe shook her head and wiped her eyes. 'Don't be silly, none of this is your fault, it really isn't.' She covered her face with both hands and began to weep, properly. 'It's not your fault at all – it's just really upsetting and horrible, poor, poor Jess.'

'Come on, Chlo.' Al put his arm around her. 'It doesn't matter that much. It's only a holiday – it's only hair.'

'It's *not* only hair!' Chloe's shoulders shook. 'Jesus Christ! How could you say that?'

'Well, no, OK, it's not just hair, but it's not the end of the world either.'

'I'm going to go and tell the kids we're leaving,' David said. 'Then I'm going to load the car up.'

'I'll come and tell our boys.' Chloe gulped some water, swiped at her wet face with both hands, wiped her nose on her kaftan sleeve and got up. Her face was blotchy. She looked exhausted.

David looked away as he passed Olivia and she understood that he held her fully responsible for the implosion of their holiday. The guilt had shifted and she was now the culprit, the mess-maker.

Everything was in disarray. Emma was obviously bitter that she had been forced to let Nura sleep in the tower, and whatever they said, Chloe and Al must blame her for leaving the front gate unlocked. David clearly resented her for this and for many other less reasonable things: his failure to finish his book, his waning literary star, her own swelling success.

If *Annabel* were a hit, if it paid off some or all of this debt, he would only resent her even more. At a recent party in the ridiculously trendy home of a BBC producer, she had overheard their host introduce David as 'David Linder, who's married to brilliant Olivia Sweetman, the historian and TV presenter.'

She suddenly felt very alone. Their marriage really was in a fragile state. It was not just the money and her fury with him, or the shock of what had happened to Jess. There was a rift between them now, and whilst on the surface it might look manageable, it went deep. Another jolt and they might just break in two.

She watched David and Chloe go through the French windows side by side. He reached out a hand and laid it, lightly, on Chloe's shoulder. Chloe brushed it away with a violent, pent-up gesture.

Everything inside Olivia grew very still. She thought about David confiding in Chloe about the debt, and she remembered Chloe's face, as they talked about this on the sun loungers. There had been a brief look of desperation as she opened her mouth to say something, before they were interrupted by Miles. Chloe, she realized, had looked guilty, as if she was about to make a confession. She remembered Vivian's comment about them parked in the viewing point for two hours.

Since they arrived in France she had felt as if David and Chloe were engaged in a silent debate or unresolved argument. The ferocity with which Chloe shrugged off his hand felt too intimate. As Olivia reached for her wineglass she felt as if a giant's hand was squeezing her torso.

'Right-oh.' Al huffed to his feet next to her. He was red-faced, sweaty. 'I suppose I'd better rally. It's a buggering shame but it's really not your fault, Liv.' He put a hand on her shoulder and gave it a kind pat. 'No one blames you for this.'

Olivia could not answer him; she just nodded and tried to smile. She heard him move away, but she could not get up. She stared at the ripples on the surface of the swimming pool, herding little dead leaves, drowning wasps and whispery bugs towards the edges. She looked out across the valley to the hills beyond, the purple, scrubby hills, and above it the sky so clear and plain and vast and indifferent. A wisp of cloud drifted over the village and she wondered if Vivian was down there somewhere, watching everything unfold.

Olivia

Dieppe–Newhaven ferry

It was a tense and mostly silent drive up through France, with a dismal overnight stop in an Ibis where Jess wailed every time she caught sight of her reflection and nothing felt safe. None of them had the energy to pretend that the holiday was salvageable. They all just wanted to go home.

It was not until Olivia and David were on the ferry deck, with the children inside in the lounge staring at phones and iPads, that she could confront him about Chloe.

'What in God's name are you talking about?'

'The two of you going off together. You confided in her about the money.' She had to raise her voice above the hubbub of the ship's engine, the battering wind.

'What? No I didn't.'

'She told me you did!'

'Wait – what – so *you* were talking to her about our finances?' His expression darkened further. 'I thought we'd agreed not to?'

'Exactly!'

They stood in baffled accusation, the ferry vibrating through their bodies.

'What's going on with us?' She gripped the railing, her hands and face smeared with sea spray. 'I know something's badly wrong between us and it's not just the money – I want to know what's going on.'

There was a long pause before David answered. It was the pause that gave him away. 'What do you mean?'

The sea wind, the engine noise, the glutted oil smells all receded so that all that was left was the two of them, staring into one another's eyes. She hugged herself. Suddenly she was very cold. 'I saw Chloe push your hand away when you touched her shoulder last night.' It sounded wispy and silly.

He looked away, rubbed his stubble, then took the railings in both hands with his elbows braced. The wind shook his sweat-shirt sleeves. 'Do you actually think something's going on between me and Chloe? That's just fucking ridiculous.'

'Why? Why is it ridiculous? Chloe's beautiful, clever, lovely.'

'What do you want from me, Liv?' He didn't look at her. He sounded weary.

'What do I want? The truth!' Suddenly she wanted to grab him and scream into his face, slap him with both hands. 'I just want you to tell me the truth!'

She saw his hands tighten, then he did look at her. His eyes were wide, a fat vein bulged on his temple. 'You want the truth? OK! Fine. The truth is I'm fucking exhausted, Liv. This holiday has gone horribly wrong, the kids are upset, everyone's shattered and you appear to have gone totally nutty. I don't know why – overwork or possibly some kind of celebrity hubris – but I feel like we're now operating from completely different planets.'

'Celebrity hubris?' She gaped at him. Then she almost laughed.

And then the fury returned. 'What the fuck is that supposed to mean?'

'You know what it means! All your TV and radio stuff, all those fawning people, all the magazine photo shoots. You're never here – you're constantly on the phone to Joy or Carol or some sycophantic hack wanting to profile you. It's all about you these days, everything's about you. There's no room for me at all – there's no room for any of us.'

She felt as if he'd punched her.

'That's how it's been for ages,' he shrugged. 'I feel completely irrelevant in your life. You're so full of disdain for me now – you don't even believe I'll finish *Trust*. And now you've got this money thing to hold over me and you can feel even more superior. You can look down on me even more and despise me for fucking up while pretending to be so practical and reasonable, so untouchable.'

'I actually can't believe you're saying all this.'

'Really? I thought you wanted the truth.'

She thought of all the times he had travelled this year, leaving her holding the fort, trying to keep it all going; times she'd stood alone at parents' evenings and ballet shows and primary school pantos or had been forced to leave meetings early to go to Dom's school and deal with the latest crisis. All the lists she'd written for Marta, the meals she'd planned at 2 a.m., juggling and struggling to do it all while David was abroad again, giving his talks, pretending to research his non-existent book, the subject of which was rapidly becoming farcical.

'Don't look at me like that,' he growled. 'I'm just telling you how I feel.'

'I don't despise you but you're right, I'm angry, of course I am. How could I not be angry? I'm either going to have to sell the Farmhouse or spend months learning to dance on TV, messing up my academic career and becoming an object of ridicule to pay off your debts. And as for being away – *you're* the one who's never here! You're away literally all the time, so much that Dom now won't even speak to you. You've opted out of that too – you've done nothing to tackle it, not really. You just leave everything to me. My God, I see more of bloody Marta, who I don't even *like*, than I do of you—'

'Don't be so fucking melodramatic!' He sounded vicious. He'd never spoken to her this way before. It was the first time she'd ever heard that nasty edge in his voice. She felt as if she didn't know him.

And then Jess appeared, pale-faced and shorn, asking for euros, and Paul came out onto the deck after her and lurched over to them on his long legs, saying that he was starving and could he get chips, and then David asked where Dominic was but neither of them knew – and then they were back to being parents again, wrangling their three opinionated offspring, keeping the family moving on. The moment had passed. Neither of them wanted it back.

As they drove back up the M23, she thought about David and Chloe. When she had introduced them, seventeen years ago in a pub, she'd felt a little insecure about the two of them meeting. They were the obviously beautiful ones: magnetic, attractive to others, flirtatious. In those days, Olivia wore her hair in an unflattering short cut and she hadn't learned to dress as well as she did now. She was nervy, too, far less confident or sure of herself. David and Chloe seemed to recognize each other's alpha status, and although they weren't exactly wary, they were definitely polite and even a little formal. She remembered feeling surprised, and quite touched, that they were both so determined not to give her any reason to feel threatened. David had always maintained that Chloe was not his type and that she, Olivia, was his perfect woman. And over the years they'd relaxed with each other. They had little in common, really, and while they were fond and genial, there'd never been anything intense between them. Until now.

But they couldn't be sleeping with each other. It made no sense. David was right, it was a ridiculous thought. It was impossible. They weren't attracted to each other, she felt sure of it. But of course, her instinct might be wrong. Or they might be excellent liars.

Still, she was less sure, now, about what she'd seen pass between them as they walked into the house in France. Everything had been so heightened and unstable at that moment. Perhaps it was nothing – just a moment of kindness rebuffed.

It was Vivian who'd planted this poisonous seed. There was no reason even to believe that Vivian had seen them parked in the viewing point. Vivian was demonstrably capable of audacious lies. She had been in a fragile state when she said it, having just discovered the truth about Bertie. There was no reason to believe a word that came out of Vivian's mouth.

The whole episode in the French cafe had left her feeling both furious and guilty. She knew she'd mistreated Vivian by lying about Bertie, but the impulse behind the lie had been honourable, she'd been trying to do the right thing. The accident was grisly and upsetting but it was still an accident. To lie about it was wrong, but she'd wanted to protect Vivian from the pain of knowing.

She was going to have to resolve this. She couldn't just hurtle towards publication with everything between them feeling so disordered and threatening. She had to straighten things out with Vivian before the book launch. There was no avoiding it: she was going to have to go to Sussex.

Vivian

Ileford Manor

I do not want this image in my head of Bertie down the well, she was right about that. It is torture to have that inside me. It will not go away as I lie in bed, waiting for my visitor to come, which she does without fail each night, pressing her weight on my chest, leaning over and staring at me with hollow eyes and breath that stinks of rotting fish, dripping on me as she reaches her hands to cover my nose and mouth. Nor can I rid myself of the image of Bertie when I get up each morning, shaken, limp downstairs and move through the kitchen making slices of toast and a cup of tea, planning another empty day; nor does it leave me as I go about my business cleaning, fixing, taking care of paperwork, or as I sit in the library, day after day, writing it all down, trying to make sense of what she did, and trying to decide what I should do next.

It has been a month since she told me in that French cafe. The facts of his death have lodged themselves unhealthily in my mind. Bertie's last day has become an obsessional and self-perpetuating thought pattern, but I cannot stop it. The more I think about it the more Olivia's lies assault me – and then the more I think about it. And so on. To the point of insanity.

It was a very cold, grey March day. I had been to Hounslow to see Mrs Sparrow, one of Annabel's many great-nieces, who claimed to have a photograph. She would not put it in the post as it was too precious and she was leaving the country the next day to visit her son in Australia for three months. It was then or never.

Mrs Sparrow, a sharp-faced and not pleasant woman in her seventies, sat me in her overheated flat, gave me custard creams and shoved a silver frame under my nose. It was a black and white picture of a young First World War soldier in shirtsleeves and braces, arms folded. I recognized him.

'Yes. That's Francis Webb, Annabel's nephew.' I probably sounded impatient. 'But you said you had a photograph of Annabel?'

She straightened her cream blouse by tugging on the bottom hem. 'This is the only photograph I have, but I do have important information about Annabel.'

'You brought me here for *information*?'

'It's good. Annabel had a baby.'

'A baby? Yes! Yes, we know she did. It was stillborn in 1898 – she gave birth to it a few months after the death of Lord Burley.' I was fuming – I'd left Bertie, weak and sick, with Olivia, for this.

'He wasn't stillborn. This is that baby. Francis was Annabel's son. She didn't want him. She gave him to her sister, Florence, in Suffolk.'

'She did not!'

'She did. Florence had no children of her own, so they passed him off as hers. Annabel went off to medical school and never bothered to see either of them again, even when Florence was widowed and destitute. I don't know what Professor Sweetman's book says, but my great-aunt was a hard, selfish woman; everyone hated her. Florence died in poverty, from grief probably, just a few months after Francis was killed at the Somme. Annabel didn't even go to her sister's funeral.'

'Do you have documentation for all this?'

'How could I have *documentation*? It was over a century ago! It's oral history – passed down through my family. Annabel Burley was a foul woman.'

'Annabel Burley was selfless and heroic. She was one of Britain's first women surgeons, part of the Endell Street Military Hospital – a hospital run by Suffragettes – in the First World War. She worked with Louisa Garrett Anderson and Flora Murray, she saved hundreds of lives—'

'Well, she also left her sister and child in poverty.'

I was on my way back from Hounslow to the Farmhouse to collect Bertie, Mrs Sparrow's revelations churning in my mind, when my mobile phone rang. I pulled into a lay-by and picked it up. It was Olivia. She said she was at Ileford.

'At Ileford! What are you doing there?'

'I'm waiting for you. Where are you now?' Her voice had none of its usual low assertiveness; it was tremulous, high-pitched and almost childlike. I now understand why, but at the time I thought she was just confused about arrangements, or perhaps chilly.

'I'm only five minutes away from the Farmhouse,' I shouted. 'We agreed that I'd come there to pick Bertie up.' I cannot stand it when people switch plans at the last minute – I was on time, everything was as we'd arranged. She was not supposed to go to Ileford. Now I would have to turn around and drive all the way

back through darkening roads. I didn't know what she was playing at, changing the plan at the last minute, taking Bertie there
without me, but I suspected she was snooping. Poor Bertie. He
would be so confused. I was tired after the drive back from Hounslow. I'd been worrying about Bertie all day.

'Did we say the Farmhouse?' Her voice wavered.

Liar.

'Yes, we did!'

'Sorry. But, look, I'm here now. It's probably easiest for me to
wait for you here.'

As I drove down the straight driveway I saw the familiar tur-
rets and high chimneystacks jutting into the lifeless sky and
marvelled, not for the first time, at the ugliness of its neo-Gothic
architecture. I noticed a dark blob squatting beneath the pointed
stone arch of the front door and realized that it was Olivia.

She was hunched inside a floppy black jumper, hugging her
knees. When she saw my Fiat she leaped to her feet and hurried
down the stairs onto the gravel. She clutched herself and hopped
from foot to foot. I looked past her. I couldn't see Bertie. I hoped
she hadn't left him in the car. I'd specifically told her never to
leave him in the car.

I got out and walked round to her. The air was grimly cold
and she was chalk-skinned, trembling, her dark hair snaggled
and the tip of her nose the colour of grazed flesh. Her eyes were
puffy and pink-rimmed. She looked as if she had been crying. I
knew immediately that something was very wrong.

She held out her arms, wanting to embrace me, but I stiffened
and did not let her. I do not like being touched at the best of
times and certainly not at a moment of such deep uncertainty.

I assumed that she was saying he had got himself lost on a
walk. He did sometimes pursue rabbits – I'd warned her about

that and she'd promised to keep him on the leash. My first reaction was that I should never have left him with her and definitely not when he was poorly. I should never have gone to Hounslow without him. I should have kept him at home, with me, recuperating by the library fire, where he belonged.

I looked around. The light was fading, bony trees swayed. The rooks clung to their branches like fat black ticks. 'Where were you when you lost him? Where?'

'I . . . just . . . round the back. In the back courtyard. Bertie, he just . . . Vivian . . . He was . . .'

Perhaps she would have confessed then, but I moved off before she could finish her sentence. I heard her boots crunching on the gravel, following me round the side of the house.

'Bertie!' I bellowed. 'Bertie, come!' I stood by the scullery door. The sky was ashy. He wouldn't stay in the woods in the dark. He was very afraid of the woods at night.

'He might be in the woodshed,' I said, almost to myself. 'There's a feral cat in there, he's obsessed with it.'

As we passed the well she began to apologize. 'I just didn't see him,' she said. 'You know what he's like, Vivian, he's just so fast. He just . . . He just went – like that.' She clicked her fingers.

I wrenched open the door to the woodshed. 'Bertie!' I whistled. 'Bertie, come! Come on, Bertie. Bertie! Come here, you fool.'

I heard a rustle; my heart leaped as I prepared to fold him in my arms, scold him, feel his licks on my chin and cheeks, but as I clambered over the logs I saw two amber pricks of light glowing in the furthest corner.

'Shoo!' I lunged. 'Shoo, you vile bastard!' The cat peeled back her lips to show her needle fangs, gave a guttural hiss and then I heard mewling, high, thin, tremulous. I grabbed a broom.

'Oh God!' Olivia cried out behind me. 'Don't hurt her, Vivian. Don't! Look – poor thing – look, she has kittens.'

Beneath the cat's scrawny ribs was a tangle of bodies, over-sized maggots.

I knew then that Bertie was not in the shed. If he'd been in the shed he'd have had them, feral mother or no.

I tossed the broom aside and came out again. A meagre crescent moon hung above the bare wych elms; shabby clouds trailed over the sky. 'Bertie!' I bellowed. 'Bertie! Come!' My voice bounced off the flint walls.

Olivia followed, mute, as one by one I tore open the outhouse doors, calling for him, peering behind defunct garden machinery, beneath splintery packing crates and wicker baskets and broken chairs, clambering over galvanized tubs and slabs of plywood, sodden piles of books, a draughtsman's table, soft tubes of wallpaper. He could be stuck, I thought, he could have got himself wedged or crushed in here, pursuing a rat.

Liar.

All that time, she knew and yet she let me search for him. She allowed me hope.

My panic swelled. He would come to me if he could, he would hear my voice. Something was stopping him from responding. He must be hurt.

'Why did you bring him here?' I remember shouting at Olivia. Her head whipped back as if I had struck her.

We were standing by the well.

'He was feeling better. I thought he'd be happier here, you know, he was missing you, whining and things, he wanted to come in the car. He . . . I thought . . .'

'Bertie!' I left her, excuses buzzing around her like blowflies on a corpse.

'Vivian!' she called after me. 'Don't worry. He'll come back.'

She really said those words. I am certain of it.

I heard her running to catch up. I felt her dread, juddering at my back.

'Vivian, please. Please! Listen to me. Try to listen. OK? Can you take a breath? Vivian? Take a few breaths. It's going to be OK.'

I stopped and turned to look at her over my shoulder. At the sight of my face she recoiled, took a few steps back.

I made off again, limping towards the woods, shouting his name. If he was in the woods, then something bad had happened to him, because he would never choose to go in there alone and would certainly never stay there at dusk. I heard her boots throwing up gravel behind me.

We searched for an hour or more but it was too dark by then to see anything, let alone a small black dog. The wind rattled the branches. Night had infiltrated the woods, completely.

'We need a better torch.' Olivia was holding her mobile phone, from which a feeble light was emanating. Her teeth chattered and her hand shook. I ignored her. I imagined Bertie enervated by sickness, unable to lift himself to his feet even though he could hear my voice.

He would not be able to understand why I didn't come and save him.

Beyond the woods were fields, streams, more woodland, the road and then the slope of the Downs. He would not have run away. But perhaps he'd set off looking for me. I'd never left him with anyone before.

I was shaking too. But not from the cold.

'Listen, Vivian, it's freezing out here. I really don't think he's here, why don't we go inside the house and warm up, have a cup of tea and decide what to do next? We'll be no good to him if we freeze to death. Shall we do that? Vivian? Are you hungry? I could make us something to eat. He might come back if he sees the lights on?'

Yes. She really said that, too.

Her face was wan and moon-shaped. I wanted to reach across the space between us and push it away – I didn't want to see it any more. I wanted her to shut her mouth, to leave me alone. Perhaps I had an instinct that she was guilty. But if I did then my conscious mind could not translate this message into anything more coherent than the need to push her face away.

She seemed to sense the change of energy. Without another word she turned and stumbled off through the trees, heading back towards the house. I heard her feet crunching on sticks and leaves and I could tell that she was trying not to run. Darkness swallowed her up.

After a while, I followed.

I found her huddled on the gunroom steps. Her jumper was pulled up to her nose and she was hugging herself, quivering like a shamed puppy. I was surprised that she had stayed. Now I understand why. She couldn't possibly leave. This was damage limitation.

She got up. 'There you are, Vivian. My God it's freezing out here! Come on, let's get you into the house.' There was just a sliver of steel in her cottony tone. I realize now, of course, that she was determined to end this futile search.

I stopped in front of her. 'I know why you brought him here,' I said. 'You wanted to get into the house. You wanted to snoop while I was away. You wanted to poke around the upper floors, didn't you? You didn't care that Bertie was sick and weak, you didn't care that he'd be confused and wouldn't understand

why I wasn't here. You just wanted to *snoop*. That's why you came.
To snoop.'

Her kind expression froze. I stepped closer. I stared at her
mouth. Her lips were the delicate blue of a linnet's egg and her
throat seemed fragile and pale, a stalk growing from the black
soil of her sweater. Tension ticked between us.

Then a high-pitched screech rang out against the flints. We
both jerked, turned, peered out into the darkness. But it was not
a dog's cry, I knew that. It was a vixen's scream.

'OK, look, Vivian, you're worried about Bertie, of course you
are.' She sounded more desperate now. The scream had shaken
her. 'I'm so, so sorry. God, I'm so sorry.' The tears in her eyes
made my anger recede a little bit.

Her remorse may even have been genuine.

I told myself that I must not let panic get the better of me. I
must regain control. I unlocked the gunroom. I let her in.

In truth, I was as guilty as she was. I knew it even then. I
should never have left Bertie with her at the Farmhouse when
my instinct was to stay with him that day. I abandoned him
when he needed me most.

He'd vomited repeatedly the night before. He had probably
eaten a rotting rabbit corpse in the woods. He was still weak
from that, even though he was eating and drinking again in the
morning.

At first Olivia had tried to argue that he'd be OK on his own
in Ileford. She could pop over at lunchtime and check on him, if
I liked? When I said no, that wouldn't do at all, she became quite
bossy. 'Listen, Vivian,' she had said. 'I know you're worried about
Bertie, but you said yourself, he's OK now, and we've got to check
out that photo, we really have. This is basically our only chance
of including a photo of Annabel in the book. I'd go and get it

myself but I have so much work, I can't possibly take a day out to drive to Hounslow and back.'

That was when she offered to have Bertie with her at the Farmhouse. 'Just drop him over on your way to Hounslow. He can have his basket by the wood stove. He'll be perfectly fine, I promise, I'll take very good care of him. I'm a great nurse. I'll treat him like he's one of my own children.'

I wasn't sure that was much of a comfort but somehow I ended up driving to Hounslow for a non-existent photograph.

Olivia said nothing as I led her out of the gunroom and along the corridor to the kitchen. When we were in there, though, she seemed to think she should take charge. 'You sit down,' she said. 'Rest your sore leg, warm up. You'll be no good to any of us if you've caught your death . . . I'll make us some tea. How about an egg? A fried egg? Scrambled on toast? You must be hungry.'

I was not. I could not possibly eat. She plainly had no idea what was going on inside me.

I went out again after she'd driven off. I walked and called for him until the drizzling dawn came through the branches. I called for him until I felt as if sharp stones were rattling around my gullet. I did the same thing the next day and the next, and day after day after that. I covered every inch of Ileford's grounds, the outbuildings, the ornamental garden, the kitchen gardens, the woodland. I peered under hawthorn hedgerows and bushes, into hollow trees, down badger setts and rabbit warrens. I traced circles over the Weald for miles in all directions and went up along the ridge of the Downs. I reported him missing to the police. I put up posters in town. I never saw Bertie again.

Of course I didn't.

The most agonizing thing of all is the knowledge that I let

him down. I left him when he was sick and needed me. The guilt is cancerous. It multiplies and spreads. It has taken me over. I am sickened and disintegrating.

The worst thing of all, you see, is that in his last moments Bertie would have accepted my abandonment. He would have understood that in the end I was no different from the others; I was prepared to let him drown alone in dark, stagnant water, scratching desperately at slimy walls, because I am human, and humans are treacherous creatures.

Olivia

Hammersmith, London

Olivia sat in her study with a glass of red wine, reading through the *Barry* book proposal. Sleep, in the six weeks since France, had been difficult, and she had often found herself working on the proposal in the middle of the night. The irony was that she had Vivian to thank for the idea. James Barry – Margaret Ann Bulkley – the nineteenth-century army surgeon whose true sex was only revealed on her deathbed, was a superb subject. But of course she was not going to allow Vivian anywhere near it this time.

It had been Carol's suggestion to write up the *Barry* proposal. They'd had lunch soon after France to talk about the BBC offer. Olivia broke it to Carol that she was going to turn the show down; she would not dance on TV, even though it meant she was going to have to put the Farmhouse on the market.

Carol was crestfallen. Towards the end of the lunch she asked, in a somewhat forlorn voice, whether Olivia had any ideas for 'the next book' and Olivia found herself talking about James

Barry. Carol perked up a bit as she heard about Barry, the brilliant military surgeon, a teetotaller, dog lover and duel-fighter
who'd famously fallen out with Florence Nightingale. Carol
insisted that if Olivia wrote up a book proposal now it would
sell, potentially for a considerable sum.

The publishing world was already buzzing about *Annabel*,
now that the proof copies were out. Enthusiastic early reviews
were rolling in and editors were already phoning to ask if Olivia
was writing another book and whether she was tied into her current publisher. *Barry* would make the perfect follow-up.

Olivia saved the proposal as '*Barry: The Scandalous Double Life of
Britain's First Female Doctor*' then emailed it to Carol. This was her
final hope. If *Barry* sold and *Annabel* did extremely well then she
might not have to put the Farmhouse up for sale. If either of
those things didn't happen, then she'd have to contact the estate
agent. The interest on the debt was now crippling, staved off
temporarily by a belated payment from the TV company. But
this could not go on.

She sipped her wine and rubbed her eyes with the heels of
her hands. She knew she shouldn't be drinking at midnight, but
before she could go to bed she needed to compose a calm but
assertive note to Vivian, and to do that, she needed the alcohol.
She had chosen a card with a sketch of the South Downs in the
hope that this would establish common ground. She would slip
it into the finished copy of *Annabel* with another plea for a meeting. Nothing else had worked. Since they got back from France
she had sent emails and left numerous voicemails asking if they
could meet. Vivian had ignored them all. The silence felt more
ominous than accusations or anger.

The question of whether Vivian had attacked Jess still dan-
gled, unanswered and unsettling. What happened in France felt

almost more disturbing, rather than less, as the weeks went by. It seemed irresponsible to be getting on with their lives as if nothing had happened. But, as David kept saying, what else could they do?

David had not even seen the finished copies of *Annabel* yet. He was in Edinburgh giving a couple of talks to business leaders and would be away another two days. Things between them had disintegrated further since France. A quiet antagonism played out beneath every interaction and it was cumulatively exhausting. David's response to the tension was avoidance. He worked until two or three in the morning most nights and then slept on the pull-out bed in the study, not getting up before she left the house.

But the night before he went to Edinburgh, they had encountered each other in the kitchen. It was very late and she was making chamomile tea, so she made him one too. As she handed it to him their eyes met and she saw his wariness of her, and his guilt.

'We're in trouble, aren't we?' she heard herself say.

He leaned back against the kitchen counter. After a moment, he nodded.

'We have to do something then,' she said. 'We can't go on like this, can we, we have to move on.' Out of nowhere, the words 'Are you sleeping with someone?' appeared in her mind. Then she saw that he was about to speak.

She waited. But, after a long pause, he looked away, ran his hand through his hair and said, with a sigh, 'OK, I know. We'll talk. But not now – I really need to get some sleep. I'll sleep in the study so I don't wake you up tomorrow. I've got to get up at five for my train.'

When he went upstairs she sat at the table for a long time, letting her tea get cold. The room was chilly, illuminated only by the lights over the sink behind her. The steadily aggressive sound of the ticking clock filled the room. The table was littered with exercise books and newspapers; the children's schedules and letters from school were clumped in ghostly wreaths on the fridge door. She wondered where her unasked question had come from. She thought she'd let go of the fears about Chloe. She didn't know whether David was capable of destroying their family; but after what he'd done with their money, she really could not be sure. The smell of the cooling chamomile tea was sickly. She got up and splashed it down the sink.

Outside, an overgrown buddleia branch scratched at the French window, making her jump. She stared out at the black stain of their garden. Then she stepped back and turned away. This was the same feeling she'd had in France – the feeling that if she looked, she'd see a ghostly face pressed at the glass, staring in at her.

After France, she'd got a locksmith to install new Banham locks on the front and back doors of the house and to check every window fastening. She'd even had the alarm tested. None of this had made her feel more secure. She remembered when she used to see her stalker's long overcoat vanishing round the library stacks, or when she'd catch sight of him standing in the alley across the street from her office and just that glimpse of his coat, his bulky back, would terrify her. She would torment herself wondering what he was capable of, what he might to do her or the children, what he might be planning. And nobody could do anything because she never saw his face, and she never saw him when she was with anyone else. It was as if he had risen from her subconscious – a symptom, rather than a cause, of this insecurity. David had even, once or twice, gently suggested that he might, in fact, not exist at all.

She knew that her mind was capable of playing tricks on her. Since France she'd felt as if Jess's night visitor was with them all the time, breathing unseen behind the door, watching from the corner of the room.

She had a recurring dream, now, where she'd open her eyes and see a shape in the bedroom doorway, a figure holding a silver pair of scissors. Though she never saw a face, she would know, somehow, that it was Vivian. Sometimes, in her sleep, she would manage to tell herself she was dreaming, she'd manage to wake herself up. But then she would get up and go through the house on trembling legs anyway, checking that every door and window was secure.

She'd probably never find out whether Vivian did cut Jess's hair, but one thing was certain: she couldn't go into the hoopla of publication without understanding what this silence meant.

The reality was that Vivian could seriously derail *Annabel*, if she decided to. She could attempt to retrospectively withdraw permission to use the diary and the Burley family archives and if she did this then everything would become very messy very quickly.

Olivia would have to admit to Joy that there might be grey areas around permission. Publication would have to be delayed while they sorted it all out. There would be huge losses if *Annabel* were not released on schedule, complications over advertising, early reviews, extracts that had been scheduled in the Sunday papers. The magazine interviews and features that would already have gone to print would become meaningless; editors would be incensed. In the worst case scenario, which Olivia could barely bring herself to look at, Vivian could withdraw permission for the diary completely. There might have to be a legal battle. Publication could be cancelled. *Annabel* might have to be pulped.

This would destroy her reputation and badly damage her

career. Her integrity would be questioned, both as an academic and as a public figure. The gossip columnists would be feral, it would be appalling, they'd all delight in her downfall: Twitter would explode, the *Mail* would print pictures of her looking hag-gard and distraught, academic colleagues would make snide comments to one another about egotism and selling out. She might lose her professorship. It would be such a total, public shaming. The thought was vertiginous. The consequences were almost unthinkable.

It was extraordinary quite how much power Vivian actually had over her life now. It was an unnerving feeling, both claustro-phobic and terrifying, to know that Vivian could destroy her if she wanted to.

So, she had to establish exactly what state Vivian was in and – whatever it was – neutralize it.

She drained her wine and considered going downstairs to refill her glass. She had to calm down. She might be overreact-ing. This might be a combination of the financial stress, the troubles with David and pre-publication nerves. It was perfectly possible that Vivian had no intention of derailing the book; that she had nothing to do with Jess's hair. It was possible that Vivian was simply, and understandably, upset about her dog.

If so, she might soften when she saw the handsome hardback. It was quite an achievement. Olivia reached out and ran her fin-gertips over the glossy cover. The jacket designer had got it just right: it was eye-catching but not showy. *Annabel* and her own name were in deep yellow letters against the rich blues and blacks of the portrait. Perhaps when Vivian actually held the book she would be proud of what they had achieved together. Perhaps some of her fury and hurt about Bertie would recede a little, then.

It occurred to Olivia that she should also go and see Lady Burley herself. If Lady Burley was demented and close to death – in no fit state to revoke permission – it would be reassuring. And if she was at all compos mentis, perhaps she could get her on side, once and for all.

She opened her calendar. With term about to begin and publication just two weeks away, every day between now and the book launch party was packed with appointments and meetings. The only free time she had was the day before the party, which she'd kept free for last-minute preparations, maybe even for a manicure and to buy a dress. She would just have to shelve all that and go to Sussex.

Olivia put her head in her hands and massaged her scalp. She'd done her best to treat Vivian fairly, she really had. She had supported her as much as she could over the dog. What Vivian needed was something to love, some companionship. Perhaps she could just get her a puppy. She could take it down as a gift. But of course, that would never work. Vivian would never allow someone else to make that choice for her.

It was fair enough if Vivian was struggling to forgive her. She still felt dreadful whenever she thought about Bertie and the lies she'd told. The memory of that horrible afternoon was still very vivid. It had been really traumatic.

It was the stupid story of Violet's ghostly face in the well that had started it. Even though she knew it was nonsense, she couldn't resist trying to get the cover off the well to have a look. It wasn't that hard. She'd just heaved at it a few times and it inched away to reveal the well's dark mouth. A powerful, stagnant pond smell rose up.

Bertie, a few feet away, became outraged. His high-pitched yaps cracked off the flints of the house. 'Shhh!' She'd turned to him and he'd stopped barking, but his eyes bulged and the hairs along his spine stood up, giving him a lurid, cartoonish look. She wondered if he'd sensed a sinister energy in the well. She suddenly felt convinced that if she looked over the rim she really would see Violet's ghostly face staring back at her.

The mouth of the well was a Venn diagram, one part organic blackness, one part wood. She stepped closer and peered over the edge. Bertie burst to life behind her again, barking madly. As she looked into the stinking cavity she felt something uncanny rise up at her – she jerked her head out and jumped backwards, stumbling over her own feet.

The dog went mad then, howling, raging, turning tight circles, snapping at nothing. 'Stop it,' she cried, but he didn't stop, he just got louder. His demented barks ricocheted off the outbuildings and the flints. She walked away from the well, from the mad dog.

But he did not follow. He was filled with a ferocious, desperate energy. Perhaps he had been storing this up all day as he sat forlorn in his basket by the stove. He was deeply distressed without Vivian, but whenever she had tried to approach him he'd trembled and stared her with mournful, dread-filled eyes. Vivian had told her a bit about his background, the poor dog. She had never seen an animal so attached to its owner. Or vice versa.

His distress had worsened all day until she could not concentrate on the paper she was working on, and she felt as if she would go insane if his whining continued. When she eventually picked up his basket, lead and food tin, he'd raced to the front door, eyes victorious, tail up. They had arrived at Ileford at four. A full hour before Vivian was due back.

Bertie had gone behind the well now. 'Bertie!' she called out. 'Stop this! It's OK. Stop now.' But he didn't stop. She looked up at the blank casement windows above her, the knotted flints stretching towards the muddy sky, and for a second she thought there was a face looking down at her from the attic, but it was just the reflection of the clouds.

Ileford really was an ugly, forbidding place. No wonder Vivian didn't like it. She had never been allowed up to those big first-floor bedrooms or the gabled servants' quarters at the very top. She had tried everything – patience, persuasion, pleading, reasoning – but Vivian had been unmovable. She had been allowed once, briefly, up the stairs onto the minstrel's gallery, where Annabel had pushed Lord Burley to his death on the parquet floor of the great hall, but no further. It was infuriating that Vivian had been so controlling about access. It was almost as if she had something to hide.

Olivia hugged herself and went over to the kitchen window. Standing on tiptoes, she peered in. Everything was orderly, as always, the surfaces bare, the dismal tan kitchen units closed. A lonely pheasant mug sat upside down on the draining board.

Her boots crunched on the gravel as she walked behind the house to the scullery door. Trees edged the lawns behind her and the caws of the rooks high in their scrawny branches echoed off the flints. She tested the door handle but of course it was locked. Bertie had stopped barking now at least. He'd come out from behind the well and was standing halfway across the courtyard, watching her with an expression both hyper alert and loaded with trepidation.

'It's locked,' she called over to him. He fixed his eyes on the scullery door as if willing it to fly open and reunite him with his mistress. 'She'll be back soon, OK? Would you stop worrying?'

She walked further along the back of the house and looked through the window of the gunroom. There were no guns any more, thank God. The head of a stag gazed at her with feckless eyes. As she pressed her fingers against the cold windowpane it gave. She pushed again. A fault line ran diagonally across the square of glass. The fissure shifted under her fingers.

She looked back at Bertie. He was on the scullery doorstep now, still watching her, ears in triangles. Vivian would not be back for at least three-quarters of an hour. She remembered there was an old knife in the car that Vivian had given her to cut up Bertie's food. Her leather gloves were in the car too.

It was surprisingly easy. She pressed on the fault line and then, using the knife, worked at the hardened putty along the top to ease the glass away from the lead. She put pressure on the crack and the top half of the pane began to ease out, like a sharp jigsaw piece. She rested it carefully against the wall, grateful for her leather gloves. All she had to do then was reach in and flip the latch. The lower half of the pane stayed put, like a jagged bottom tooth. Vivian should be more careful about security.

She opened the window and climbed in.

The dog began barking again. She put her head back out. 'Shhh! Stop that!' He stopped, but didn't move. His forelegs were splayed, his tail pointing up, an electrified steel rod. 'Go on!' She waved her hands out the window. 'Go away! Go for a walk!' He burst back to life, yapping intensely.

She decided she was making him worse. His outraged barks receded as she passed through the gunroom, down the back corridor and past the scullery, which smelled of Vivian's washing powder. She paused at the kitchen. The chill was numbing. She could feel the empty house stretching above her, all the secret bedrooms, forbidden corridors and shadowy attic rooms within this flinty shell.

Outside, Bertie was distraught now. Maybe it would be better to bring him in too. If Vivian came back early she could use him as her excuse for coming inside. She hurried to the window and looked out at the courtyard. It took her a moment to see him. He was howling and yapping, back over by the well. She leaned over the sink and opened the window.

'Bertie!' she shouted. 'Bertie, come on!' He paused, tail up, ears pricked, head on one side. 'Bertie! Come here, boy!'

He spotted her, then, but far from comforting him, the sight of her in the kitchen jerked him into even deeper hysteria. He stood on his hind legs, springing vertically like a circus creature, then dropping down to turn in a circle. And then, suddenly, he leaped sideways and up onto the open well cover. She saw it wobble beneath him.

'Bertie! Get down!'

He bounced, yapping, turning another circle. The cover wobbled again. His hind legs quivered and slipped – and he was gone.

She slammed the kitchen window, ran down the corridor into the gunroom and scrambled out the window. 'No, no, no, no, no.' She dropped onto the gravel and sprinted across the courtyard.

As she got to the mouth of the well she could hear little splashes and awful, panicked yelps. She leaned over – the smell hit her again – stagnant rainwater and wet mulch. It was impossible to see him, the darkness was complete, but his high, tangled sounds rose up at her.

'Bertie! It's OK, Bertie! It's OK!' His claws scrabbled against the slimy brickwork. 'It's OK, Bertie. I'm going to get you out. It's OK.'

She looked around for something – anything – that she might drop for him to grab with his teeth. The well was narrow – it would be impossible to rest a plank diagonally for him to climb up even if she could find something long enough to reach the bottom. She didn't know how deep it was but his noises seemed to be coming from a long way down. She needed something to hook his collar – a rope and a torch. She could hear his little rapid gasps, his scraping claws, frantic splashes.

'Oh shit, Bertie, SHIT shit shit.' She ran, panicking, around the courtyard in circles, looking for rope, anything, but there was nothing that could hook a small dog out of a deep well.

At her car she wrenched open the boot and dug through wellies, walking boots, children's fleeces, jump leads, a football. Maybe he'd be able to grab the jump leads. She seized them and the lead, tying them together, as she ran back to the well.

'Bertie! Bertie!' she called, dangling them over. 'What's this, Bertie? Take it, boy, take it.'

He was still splashing, still making rapid, desperate wheezing sounds. It was obvious that the jump leads and the leash together were nowhere near long enough. The metal jaws clacked pointlessly against the mossy bricks. It must be thirty feet down, maybe more.

She threw them aside and ran back across the courtyard to the outhouses. She wrenched open the first door – a woodshed – and ran inside, but no rope, nothing suitable, just a rake and a broom and a towering log pile. She came back out, next to it the garage was locked, as were the stables. She didn't have time for this. She sprinted back to the well, out of breath now and shaking. A sickening sensation spread through her stomach as she peered over the edge. She could still hear him, but the splashing was much weaker and his breaths were coming in rapid, faint gasps.

'It's OK, Bertie!' she shouted down. 'I'm going to get you out. I am. It's OK, it's OK. Hold on.' She felt a sense of helplessness. 'Oh FUCK.' How long could a weakened terrier keep afloat?

She remembered the retractable dog lead she'd seen hanging on a hook in the kitchen. She could tie that to the leash and the jump leads – together they might be long enough. She sprinted back to the gunroom window, shoved herself through it.

Back at the well, a few minutes later, she knotted the two dog leads together with shaking hands, gasping for breath, and dropped them down. 'Bertie! It's OK! Bertie, I'm back!'

But there were no more frantic yelps. The splashing was much slower, more faint, with long pauses where nothing happened, then a gasp, presumably as he resurfaced, and his claws scrabbled at the bricks again, but more feebly each time. She leaned further over the edge, shaking the leads. 'Bertie! Bertie!' She called. 'What's this, Bertie? Fetch it! Fetch the lead!'

Nothing. Just little, exhausted splashes. 'Come on, Bertie. Come on! Take it. Take it!' The words caught in her throat. The leads remained slack.

She thought of the fire brigade, they came for kittens in trees – they'd come for a dog, surely. But she knew that by the time the fire brigade got here it would be too late. Vivian would come home to find Bertie dead and a fire engine in her courtyard. Still, she couldn't just do nothing and let him drown. She pulled her phone out. Did people just dial 999 in this situation?

'Bertie!' she yelled over the edge, punching in her password. 'It's OK. It's OK. I'm getting the fire engine, they'll get you out. Just hang on.'

But the well, she realized, was silent. There was no splashing any more. No claws. No whimpers. She leaned further over, bracing herself on the edge with both arms. 'Bertie?' Her voice echoed back at her. 'Bertie?' He was gone.

It was an awful way to go. Vivian's pain was understandable. As was her fury. A pretty thank you card and a book were not going to make this go away. They needed to talk, face to face. She was going to have to go down to Ileford. She had a feeling this wouldn't be ideal – Vivian didn't like surprises – but she had run out of options.

She wrote the card using an apologetic tone, contrite but not overtly guilt-stricken, thanking Vivian again for her invaluable contribution to the book, and asking – with a hint of desperation – for a meeting the day before the launch. She wrote the address on the envelope and licked a stamp. Vivian might not be capable of visiting a child in the middle of the night with scissors, but the book was different. Vivian, she suspected, was more than capable of destroying a book.

Vivian

Ileford Manor

She will not leave me in peace. It must be because it is almost time for the book launch party. First she sent emails, then proof copies, then an embossed invitation to the Hunterian Museum at the Royal College of Surgeons. She left messages on my phone, too, and now she has sent me a finished copy of *Annabel*.

I can hardly bear to look at it. I have put it on a high shelf in the library where it will not catch my eye.

Since France, I have been troubled almost continually by the knowledge of what she did to Bertie and by the many lies she has told me – not just about that, but about other things too. One undesirable side effect of my distress is that my sleep paralysis has intensified: my night visitor's face has taken a more clear shape, the wound on her head is open and messy above her blackened eyes, the greenish-grey pallor of her skin and the fishy stench of her breath are more vivid than ever before.

There is complicated brain science to explain why this is

happening to me. The human threat-vigilance system is biased to interpret any ambivalent stimuli as a danger, to ensure self-protection, but when this system misfires, as it does in my brain, the effects are overwhelmingly convincing. The feelings are as real to me as if a flesh-and-blood murderer were in the room – more frightening, perhaps, since I am paralysed when she comes and therefore unable to protect myself. There is, what's more, nothing ambivalent about my visitor's intentions. She visits in order to do me harm. When she lifts her arms and leans over me with that dead look she is intent on punishment.

It is worse right now because I am in such a shaken state, thanks to Olivia's confession. The only way for me to cope with what I have learned has been to cut off all contact with her. I did consider replying to one of her earlier emails, after France, with a description of the grisly task that awaited me on my return, but in the end I deleted that message. It was too raw to share.

When I got off the ferry at Newhaven I went straight to see Lady Burley. She had noticed my absence, though was a little uncertain about the exact timeframe. She accepted my explanation that I had been poorly, which was not really a lie. 'You do look a little peaky, dear, you shouldn't have come,' she said, with touching, motherly concern, and I realized I was pleased to see her. I felt the urge to lean over and rest my head on her lap, to close my eyes and let go of everything, just for a moment. But I would not have wanted to distress her, and I couldn't stay long anyway because I had to go and get Bertie out of the well.

The grim challenge of how to do this involved driving back to Newhaven the next day to purchase a fishing net with an extending handle. I had to customize it using two more poles wired together. When I finally managed to fish him out he did not look like himself. He was bloated, his hair matted, his poor body half decomposed, an organic, messy thing. His eyes were intact, if glassy, and his inflated tongue poked from his swollen lips like a purple sausage. I noticed that his paws were mutilated from scrabbling at the bricks; several of his claws were torn from their sockets. I had to wrap him in plastic sacks because his smell – a mixture of pond life and sweet, rotting flesh – was overwhelming.

Before I carried him to the hollow oak I heaved a slate through the woods. It did my knee no good but I wanted him to have a headstone. I had engraved his name on it with my screwdriver and the words *'Beloved Friend'*.

I lay him, a tight-wrapped package, surprisingly light, in the grave and I covered him with earth. Then I recited the Shakespeare song. My voice wavered over the words 'Thou art past the tyrant's stroke . . .' but I managed it, until 'Fear not slander, censure rash', when I did have to pause to compose myself. He was my one true friend and he was gone.

Grey summer rain leaked through the oak's branches onto my head. Above me rooks cawed.

I decided not to sully Bertie's memory by sharing these details with Olivia. I am sticking to my decision that there shall be no more contact between us. I have decided what I shall do and I do not want her bothering me any more – inveigling, smiling, talking and persuading and lying in order to get what she wants out of me.

There shall be no more lies, now, from either of us.

Olivia

Hammersmith, London

'Are you sitting down?' It was Carol.

'Yes.' Olivia sat back down on the kitchen chair. There was a piece of baguette by her bare foot. Marta had been sweeping, but had put away the broom and left the room as soon as she entered.

'Are you there, Olivia? Can you talk?'

'Yes, yes, I'm here.'

'So, I'm getting responses to the *Barry* proposal – big responses.'

'And?'

'Brace yourself – we've got a bidding war. I've got five publishers vying for it right now, they've all read *Annabel* and they're all very excited about *Barry*. I've just emailed you a breakdown of the current offers.'

Olivia opened her computer and typed in the password. As she opened Carol's message and stared at the numbers she felt a lightening, a floating sensation. 'My God, these really are serious.'

'I think it's going to go higher. We're not done yet.'

Carol began talking about the next steps, the process of choosing which deal to accept, and then the book launch party, but all Olivia could think about was the fact that with this, and if *Annabel* was also a success, the debt would be covered. She'd be liberated from the dread that had been pressing on her since David confessed, and from the obscene interest charges that were mounting up each month. She wouldn't have to take a sabbatical and dance on prime-time TV, and she wouldn't have to sell the Farmhouse in order to avoid doing those things.

If *Annabel* did well, and if these new offers for *Barry* came to something, then she'd be free to write and research and teach. She realized suddenly that if this worked out, she'd tell the production company that she wasn't going to do any more TV programmes this year. She'd get Carol to pull out of *Pointless Celebrities* and she'd say no to any other TV offers. She'd had enough of being in the public eye, the scrutiny and demands – it was all too much. She wanted to simplify her life from now on. She'd go back to doing what she was good at. *Barry* was an intriguing subject – not quite her period, but that didn't matter. She'd loved what she'd discovered so far about Barry's murky and humble beginnings, and his – or her – life of disguise and adventure.

Perhaps she'd even try to arrange a sabbatical at some point, so she could immerse herself in the research. She might hire a graduate student for some of the duller legwork, but she'd do the bulk of the research herself this time. She said to Carol, 'One thing – and this is really important – I want lots of time to write this. It's going to take me way more than eighteen months this time. You have to build that into the contract, OK?'

When she hung up she felt numb and shaky, probably from

relief. She waited for some kind of elation to kick in, a feeling of triumph, but it didn't. It was huge, a huge help, but it only got her halfway there – to save their finances she still needed *Annabel* to be a hit, or some other miracle to occur. She called David's mobile. He did not pick up. She looked at her watch. It was eight o'clock and she had no idea where he was. She texted him: '*Good news! Call me.*'

The money would vanish the moment it hit their account, but that was OK. She had to move on and leave this anger and resentment behind. It was only money.

But of course, it wasn't only money. The problems with David were much more complicated than that. She got up from the kitchen table and poured herself a large glass of wine. As she shoved the cork back into the bottle, she noticed that her hand was shaking. She felt slightly dizzy, as if she'd turned her head too fast and the room had not quite settled back into place. She could hear the TV in the front room and Marta at the bottom of the stairs calling up in her Americanized Danish voice, 'Jessica! I have to go out now. You need to brush your teeth, OK. Your mum's in the kitchen.' It irritated her that Marta called Jess 'Jessica'. There was something proprietorial and faintly critical about it. And why didn't Marta talk to her, rather than shouting up to Jess like this?

She sipped the wine and watched Marta grab her denim jacket, glance at the hall mirror and run her hand through her short hair. It was still damp from the shower. She was wearing sneakers and a simple grey sweatshirt. At twenty-four, she barely needed to do anything to herself before she went out. The muscles of her thighs looked smooth inside her jeans, her abdomen taut, and as she lifted her arms her breasts lifted too, small and pert beneath the nondescript top. Marta was assured for such a young woman, she knew her own power. The front door slammed.

Olivia was aware, more and more, that Marta did not like her but now the feeling was becoming mutual. Not saying goodbye was just rude.

David hadn't responded to the text. She knew he'd be troubled by the news of these offers for *Barry*, even though it might save their finances. He'd try to disguise it, but he'd feel put out. They always used to be pushing forwards together, side by side, supporting each other, proud of each other. She wasn't sure how things had shifted but nowadays they felt almost like adversaries. She wondered if it was ever going to be possible, now, for David simply to be happy for her.

They were both afraid to open up these discussions because things between them were potentially so rotten. But they couldn't go on like this. This was no way to live. They had to do something, get counselling, deal with whatever this was. She still felt dizzy, as if she was coming down with something. There was a strange, cold pressure inside her body. She got out her phone and texted him one more time. '*Where are you?*'

These absences were beginning to feel systemic. It wasn't just her. He'd withdrawn from Dominic too. It was as if he was afraid of his own son. When they first got back from France – perhaps because of their row on the ferry – he'd tried to tackle Dom, but it hadn't worked well. Dom's fury seemed completely entrenched. There had been a final ferocious row a couple of weeks ago in Dom's bedroom; they'd almost come to blows.

David came downstairs afterwards with ashy-looking skin. 'Fucking hell,' he said. 'They don't tell you this at the NCT classes.' He poured himself a large whisky.

'I couldn't hear what you were saying. Did he tell you why he's so angry?'

David shrugged. 'He's fifteen.'

'Oh, come on. It's more than that.'

'You try asking him then.'

'But I have!'

He looked so weary, his eyes were puffy and his facial muscles limp. Suddenly she could see the disappointed and slightly help-less old man that he might become, and she felt sorry for him. He was a devoted father and this must hurt, not least because he'd always been particularly close to Dom. Since Dom was five they'd gone to watch football matches together at weekends. Paul never wanted to go, he preferred his football on a screen and Jess hated football. But that had stopped now. The two of them used to go to the park some evenings and kick a ball around too. That had also stopped abruptly. She remembered when Dom was nine or ten years old he'd moved his little desk into David's study and would sit at it pretending that he was writing a book too. David indulged him, though Dom would interrupt him every five seconds. David really was a good father, and Dom used to worship him. He didn't deserve this brutal adolescent rejection.

It was disconcerting to see David so upset by Dom, he really seemed lost. Perhaps his failure to finish *Trust* had undermined his confidence in other areas of his life. She'd always imagined that David would grow more powerful as he aged. They'd both assumed that his career would go from strength to strength. Ten years ago, when *Intuition* was an international bestseller and newspaper editors were taking him out to dinner and offering him great sums to be their columnist, it would have seemed inconceivable that he could ever stall and waver like this.

This was probably why he'd made such catastrophic errors with their finances. He wanted to do something spectacular again. He had, perhaps unconsciously, set out to show her – and himself – that he wasn't finished, that he was still capable of magical thinking and inspired acts.

She had realized that night, after his row with Dom, as she watched him drain the whisky and pour another glass, that she was not the innocent one. He was right that she'd been preoccupied with work and with Vivian and with keeping Dom from catastrophe, and she'd failed to appreciate how deep David's crisis was becoming. She'd failed to tune in and support him. Perhaps he was right that she had become self-obsessed and egotistical, perhaps she'd allowed him to push her away because it was easier than facing the problems in their marriage.

She made herself go over and put her arms round him. She felt his familiar, broad shoulder under her cheek, his warm back under the scratchy wool of his jumper. He'd stiffened at first, hesitated, but then buried his face in her hair and she knew that they still loved each other, despite the mess they were in. She told herself she'd help him to dig his way out of this – she'd be there for him. As soon as the book launch was over. He pulled away, downed the whisky and put the empty glass in the sink. 'Right.' He puffed out his cheeks. 'I've got to finish this hunches talk, for Washington.'

They were not going to sort this out before the book launch party, or immediately after it. He'd be home from Washington the day before the party, but then he was to go away again the day after to give a speech at a so-called 'Lifestyle Institute' in Copenhagen. These bookings were lucrative and he was turning nothing down.

She got up from the kitchen table. When their debt was

finally paid, David would be able to be home more. Maybe that would help. She had to stop wasting time now. She still had work to do. Term was about to start, she had her coursework to finalize, as well as a book endorsement to write and an overdue blog for *History Today*. And she needed to check on the final launch party RSVPs. But first she had to get Jess to go to bed, Paul to do his homework and Dom to come home.

'Jess? Did you brush your teeth?' She walked slowly upstairs to Jess's room, picking up a sports sock, a hairbrush and a tattered biology GCSE textbook as she went. 'Jess?'

Since France, Jess had reverted to some of her more babyish habits. She wanted a story every night and was anxious if Olivia or David weren't there to read it to her; Marta would not do. Olivia had tried to factor this into her day and had mostly managed it, but it was clear that what had happened in France had left psychological scars. David had been talking to Jess about managing her anxiety, they had a whole system worked out, with 'Worry Times' and relaxation strategies, but she suspected that Jess needed actual therapy. She had nightmares sometimes where she'd run screaming out of her bedroom. Olivia would lurch out of bed thinking that there was a stalker crawling through the window and she'd find Jess quaking on the landing, only half awake, shocked by the force of her own subconscious.

Jess was lying in a dank nest of stuffed animals. She looked more normal now that her hair had grown a bit. It had been trimmed in a salon and it was now an unremarkable mousy brown bob. Olivia still found it hard to look at sometimes. It felt like a reminder that disturbing and inexplicable things could happen in the blink of an eye.

She noticed that Jess had squeezed herself into an old *Lion King* nightie that had been her favourite when she was about six.

She must have dug it out from the charity bag that Marta had failed to take to Oxfam.

Olivia didn't know why she felt so irritated with Marta these days, but these small gestures of resistance seemed faintly aggressive. The younger woman's physical presence had also begun to feel intrusive. Marta moved through the house soundlessly, on light, bare feet, and would appear, abruptly, in rooms, as if she had been standing listening and waiting for the right moment to enter. But other than Dom, who had gone from teenaged embarrassment to complete avoidance of Marta, no one else seemed to mind her. In fact, David had become oblivious to the au pair, too caught up in his own troubles to notice or care whether she disapproved of them or not. They were never at the table any more with a bottle of wine when Olivia got home, in the evenings; Marta now either went to hot yoga or out with friends. She was due to start her Master's in a year, but a year felt too long to keep her on. Then again, the last thing Olivia needed was to have to find a new au pair.

Of course, it was possible that Marta was just picking up on the family tensions. Jess was not easy at the moment and would have meltdowns over small things. Paul rarely left a screen and when forced to he was passively truculent. And Dom, of course, was either foul or absent. He left the house every morning, hooded and hunched in his headphones, and if she was lucky she'd get a text after school to say he was at a friend's house. When home, he communicated in grunts, or by one-word texts. He also openly despised Marta, which could not be easy for her.

'Mum? Can you even *hear* me?' Jess was propped up on her elbow, looking cross.

'Sorry.' She went over to the bed. 'Sorry, sweetheart, what?'

'I said, did you check my window?'

'Yes, yes. We covered that in Worry Time, didn't we? Nothing bad's going to happen to you, my love. You're in your lovely home, I'm here, everything's safe and sound.' It felt like a lie.

Her eyes fell on *Aesop's Fables*. They were short. 'Oh!' She made herself sound excited. 'We haven't read these for years, have we? I *love Aesop's Fables*.'

'But Dad was reading me this.' Jess held up a thick book by Philip Pullman.

'Then I'd better not read that or he'll be cross with me.' Olivia pulled down the book of fables. 'I used to love these when I was your age.' She remembered the one about a fox carrying the gingerbread man across the river on its back. She'd been fascinated by the idea that helpful people could have malevolent intentions.

She flipped to the contents page and Jess burrowed beneath the covers. A fable or two would not take more than a few minutes, then she could deal with the boys and go and shut herself in the study.

A title caught her eye. 'The Scarab and the Eagle.' 'Hey, look, I'd forgotten there's one about a dung beetle. You remember me telling you about your grandfather, who discovered the dung beetle in an amber fossil and named it after me? We saw it in the Oxford museum that time?'

'I wish he called a beetle after me.'

'You weren't alive, darling. He never even met you. He'd have definitely named a dung beetle after you if he had. *Archaeocopris jess*.'

'I don't want a dung beetle, that's disgusting! I want a nice, pretty beetle.'

'Dung beetles can be really pretty. Some of them are like little jewels. They have magical powers too. Did you know they are the only creatures, except humans, who can navigate using the Milky Way?'

'What else?'

'What else? Well, the Ancient Egyptians loved them, King Tutankhamun was buried with a green stone dung beetle – a scarab – sitting on his heart. It meant he'd rise up again.'

Jess looked unimpressed.

Olivia found the page and began to read the story of the dung beetle who pleaded with the golden eagle to spare the life of a hare. When the eagle ignored the beetle and killed the hare, the beetle was enraged. She found the eagle's nest and destroyed her eggs. In despair, the golden eagle flew to Zeus for protection and this time Zeus let her lay her eggs in his lap. The eagle thought she was unreachable, up there with the gods, but she'd underestimated the dung beetle's grudge. The beetle flew around Zeus's head, making him leap up so that all the eggs rolled off his lap and smashed again.

Jess scowled at that. 'I don't get it. Why did she do that?'

'For revenge. Because the eagle disrespected her. She underestimated the beetle.'

'But the dung beetle was evil, too, wasn't she? She killed the eggs.'

'Well yes, but only because the eagle was being so superior and horrid.'

Jess's eyes narrowed. 'Then they're both as bad as each other.'

'No, I don't think that's . . . The moral of the story is you should never ignore someone just because they seem old or dull or ugly or insignificant or weaker than you. And you should never think you're better than someone because you're more influential, or you've got more important friends.'

'That's a stupid story!' Jess turned away and stared at the wall. 'I hate dung beetles.'

As she put the book away and stroked Jess's head, she thought of Vivian, sitting all alone in gloomy Ileford. As she kissed her daughter goodnight, the same cold and shaky sensation passed through her.

She wondered if she had disrespected Vivian, or underestimated her.

Vivian

Ileford Manor

The trees are flinging leaves around, shaking their jagged limbs at the smeared and murky sky, so today I have decided to stay indoors. I have to make an important decision and to do that I must gather my data. I am trying to recall all the times she has lied.

It is clear as I go back over the past eighteen months that my original hypothesis about Olivia Sweetman was correct: she is a mimicking species. She pretends to be kind, reasonable and morally upstanding, but when it comes to protecting her own interests she is capable of anything. I set out to prove this at the start, but then I allowed myself to be seduced by her charm and by the hope of an interesting collaborative future and I lost sight of my original objective.

When I look back on the past eighteen months with an analytical eye, Olivia's true nature actually never wavered. I just failed to see it.

Take the book jacket. She wanted permission to use the

library portrait. It is certainly a striking image and I can see why
it appealed to her. The woman wears a dress the colour of clotted
cream, her hair masses beneath an extravagant hat of the correct period. She is conventionally beautiful. She has an elegant
neck, big eyes, a full mouth. I think the portrait is something
Lady Burley picked up at an auction in the 1980s, but I have no
paperwork to prove that. I told Olivia this.

She decided to use it anyway. To get around the issue of it not
actually being Annabel, they inserted a disclaimer on the inside
cover, where few readers would notice. 'It doesn't matter too
much if it's Annabel, as long as it makes people want to buy the
book,' Olivia laughed. 'It just gives people something to pin their
imagination to.'

But surely the whole point of imagination is that it doesn't
need to be pinned to anything – least of all to a lie.

Thoughts of pinning always bring me back to beetles, I can't
help it – specifically, the act of removing their genitalia with a
hooked pin to display next to the specimen.

Beetles can be accomplished mimics too and sometimes the
only way to be sure of a species is to dissect and identify the genitalia. Removing a beetle's genitals can be tricky, not least because
some beetles are minuscule; they can be as tiny as a pinhead.
You have to insert the hooked pin through the midline of the
end plates, then find the genitalia, which lie inside the beetle's
abdomen, just to the right. These are then pulled out and secured
to the board next to the specimen like little punctuation marks.
They alone are proof of a beetle's true nature. I have often felt
that it is a shame the same cannot be done for humans. It would
be so useful to know exactly what one is dealing with.

My father was an excellent mimic, not just of people – he
would have made a good impressionist – but of animals too. He

did impressive imitations of a pig, a cockerel, a donkey and a vixen's bark, as well as a whole range of birdcalls. He also liked to play-act. I remember once he took me to the Ashdown Forest. It was rare for him to spend time with me. I must have been very young, perhaps nine or ten. I was, I think, a rather trying child, anxious and self-contained. I remember that day not just because it was unusual, but because he made me taste a boletus fungi and as I swallowed it he let out a blood-curdling scream and covered his mouth with his hands, begging me to spit it out, gabbling that he'd made a mistake, that the mushroom was deadly. 'Say goodbye, Vivian, say goodbye to your old pa!' Real tears sprang into his eyes. I think he even fell to his knees.

At that time, before drink completely ruined him, he was still active in the village amateur dramatic society. With his thin moustache, he looked a little like Clark Gable, if you could ignore the Sussex burr. He had been drinking that day in the woods, I assume, either that or he was under a lot of pressure. I remember, when I'd finished spitting and retching onto the bracken, his laughter would not stop. It was so loud and wild that it made the rooks panic from the trees. He had an idiosyncratic sense of humour.

Perhaps this is, in part, why the mimicking capacity of beetles fascinates me so. I first learned about this natural phenomenon as an undergraduate, how cleverly one species will imitate another. This can have a defensive purpose: the mimicking beetle wants to look more dangerous or impressive than it really is. Or it can be aggressive: a predatory species will pretend to be a harmless one in order to lure its prey.

My father, I think, was the former. But Olivia, I feel, falls into the latter category.

Sometimes she doesn't even realize she's pretending. Take

the first time she showed me the first few chapters of *Annabel*. It was a year ago now, September, six months before Bertie vanished. We were walking up Lewes High Street on an Indian summer's day. Olivia, I remember, was wearing Greek sandals and a grey linen dress, the sort of garment that looks faded and thin but probably cost a fortune in Selfridges. I was sweating in my cardigan but I did not want to remove it for fear of revealing underarm sweat stains.

She asked what I thought of the chapters. I told her that while I was impressed by her prose style, I was troubled by everything she had made up. I suppose this is ironic, coming from me, but I couldn't help myself.

She looked at me in surprise. 'What have I made up?'

'Well, her thoughts, her hand gestures, her outfits and all those decorative descriptions of flowers and table ornaments. They aren't in any of the data I provided. You couldn't know that there was "a look of admiration" from Mrs Beacham because of the "spotless damask tablecloth", or that the hall table had a gold centrepiece with "sprays of Virginia creeper".'

'Well, no – no – those are just sort of imaginative touches, you know, just to bring the book alive. The reader understands what I'm doing – it's a sort of imaginative agreement.'

'But it's not the truth.'

Olivia thought about this for a moment. 'People always think historians are telling some kind of objective truth, Vivian, but at the end of the day history is debate, discussion, conversation; we're storytellers, really, we're always reaching for the truth, but we have to invent the stories that get us there.'

'So trickery and lies are OK?'

'Nobody's tricking anyone, or lying! Look, a famous history professor once said historians "make no greater or lesser truth claims than poets or painters". If you think about it like that it's not possible to be a historian and a liar.'

'Well, I think the reader wants and deserves simple facts.' My position was somewhat ludicrous, even to me.

'But there's no such thing as simple facts. Readers know that. What matters is *integrity*.'

'And there's a difference between integrity and telling the truth?'

'Yes, of course there is.' She thought for a moment. 'Truth's what you say and integrity's the intention behind your words. It's perfectly possible to lie with integrity. Think about people who lied to the Nazis when they were hiding a Jewish family in their attic.'

I waited for Bertie to pee on a lamppost. 'But your readers aren't Nazis, Olivia, they're normal decent people who want to learn something.'

'They will learn something! OK, Vivian, look.' She gave a strained smile and tucked her hair behind her ears. 'How about we agree to disagree on this one? I'm happy to take the rap for my own invent-ive touches, none of this is ever coming back to you. After all, at the end of the day it's my name on the cover, not yours.'

I laughed. 'It certainly is.'

She looked at me for a moment too long, as if trying to gauge my tone of voice, and then gave up and walked off up the hill. She is not keen on conflict but I could see she was annoyed. Ber-tie and I followed.

All her talk of integrity was rubbish of course. When Olivia wants something she is prepared to occupy very shaky moral ground indeed. This was clear from the outset when it came to securing Lady Burley's permission to use the diary and Burley family archives.

Olivia wrote the initial letter and emailed it to me as she sat in the bakery that first day. It was polite and professional. She reassured Lady Burley that I was fully on board and that she would treat her subject with the utmost respect.

She never followed up with Lady Burley herself. She asked, in another email a few days later, whether I'd passed on the letter and whether Lady Burley had given the go-ahead. I replied in the affirmative and she chose to take my word for it. She never checked that Lady Burley was capable of reading and understanding her letter. She never asked for consent in writing from Lady Burley herself.

I suppose she was afraid that if she pushed for it then permission might be denied. She took my affirmation at face value because it was convenient for her to do so, not because she believed me. I'm not sure where the integrity is in that.

I assume she also decided that an email from me confirming Lady Burley's consent would be legally binding. Whether or not that would stand up in a court of law, of course, is anyone's guess.

I do know that when it comes to integrity I myself am hardly blameless, but for most of my life I was an honest person in intention and deed. This did not serve me well. The truth can alienate people. In fact, I have noticed that in a professional setting nobody actually wants to hear it. Groups rely on flattery and charm, tact and encouragement, compromise and grey areas. Ultimately, I am sure that my tendency to see things in black and white and to be blunt about what I see contributed to my downfall as much as my final treacherous act.

That, incidentally, was entirely out of character. A few people even said so at the time. One or two, whom I had known for many years, actually stuck their necks out and said that I had always been a loyal person, though I was – and I use their words – 'socially awkward'. The word 'breakdown' was bandied around by one influential (male) colleague. It made no difference whatsoever to the outcome. I needed to be shot down, publicly. They just wanted me out. I do regret my actions, bitterly, but what is done cannot be undone.

All my life I have found people complicated and baffling, and that now includes myself. When my inner moral compass snapped, I lost a grip on who I was. I did not recognize or understand the person I had become. Perhaps I still don't.

Since I came back to Sussex I have spent a lot of time studying my old friend, the hollow oak. Her red-rotten heartwood teems with invertebrates and I have counted, identified and classified a great many of them: spiders and centipedes, millipedes, woodlice, weevils and ants, earwigs and beetles – oh, so many beautiful beetles. I have identified, among others, the click and false click, the cobweb, longhorn, rove, minotaur, cardinal, stag, darkling and deathwatch. Sometimes I feel that I am a bit like that tree: on the outside I appear static and empty, I am certainly rotten and gnarled in places, but deep inside I am crawling with complicated life that few people notice or understand and even fewer care for or value.

For a short while I thought Olivia might be the exception to this. It turns out that I was wrong.

She can send me copies of the book, she can visit and beg, but she will never erase what she did to Bertie and the lies she told. I will finish my experiment. I must bring it to a close. The question is, how? Will I bring her down in public, at the Hunterian Museum? Or is there a different way?

Olivia

The Farmhouse and Ileford Manor

Olivia felt bleary and deranged as she drove down the M23.

The previous night she'd been forced to drive around west London at one in the morning searching for Dom. Eventually she'd found him, hoodie up, smoking on a bench by the river like a homeless boy. She got out and demanded that he come home. He did get into the car, but then he started shouting: 'You can't fucking tell me what to do any more! I'm not a kid!'

She tried to stay reasonable. 'You're only fifteen. It's a school night, Dom. You told me you'd be home by nine.'

'Yeah, well you tell me all sorts of things that turn out to be bullshit.' His voice wavered.

'What do you mean?'

'You and Dad! You're both full of shit.'

She wondered if he was drunk or stoned. But his enunciation was clear. He was, she thought, just upset. 'Why are you so angry?' she said. 'What have we done? I need you to talk to me, Doms. I really do.'

He jiggled his leg up and down. '*You* haven't done anything.'

'OK, Dad? What has Dad done to you? What's this about?'

'Don't ask me, ask him!' His face went puce, his eyes wide.

'Dad and I are going to talk, OK?' she said. 'I know you've been picking up on some . . . tensions between us. Things haven't been easy, we've had some money issues, but we're going to sort it all out, OK? You don't have to worry. Everything's going to be just fine.'

He grunted and stared out the window. 'Yeah, right.'

Unable to sleep, she'd eventually given up, got out of bed at six, dragged on jeans, a jumper and boots, fuelled herself with espresso and got into the car. She had left a note for Marta to try to get Dominic out of bed and to school.

She felt drained and tremulous as she turned off the motorway. She didn't know how to handle Dom. She needed to know what he knew, or thought he knew, about David, but it was wrong to press him on it, it wasn't fair to put him in the middle of this mess. She also didn't want to explain to her angry fifteen-year-old that deep down she was suspicious of his father too.

Soon she turned onto the narrower country road. It was just beginning to get light, but mist blotted the windscreen, and as she followed the winding hawthorn tunnels along the foot of the Downs she had to keep stamping on the brakes so as not to hit the pheasants that intermittently clattered out in front of the car. She wondered whether Dom might have sensed the tension between David and Chloe in France, but of course it couldn't be that because this anger had rooted in him well before France.

She felt some of her jitteriness ease as she turned into the Farmhouse gateway. As she slammed the car door, rooks launched themselves from the top of a tree somewhere in the semi-dark mist behind the house, cawing madly. She took a breath and the damp sweetness of the autumn air released a bit of the tension inside her. She carried her bag from the car, treading carefully along the slippery terracotta bricks that led along the house front. The path was scattered with fallen leaves and the browning hydrangeas in the overgrown borders balanced droplets of mist in their fading petals. The sight of the Farmhouse door, fringed by wisteria that needed cutting back, and the bare, thorny climbing rose, made her feel a little more stable, as if she'd been out of her depth but had just found the mud with her toes. She felt, again, the hope that she might not have to sell. Selling this place would have broken something inside her.

She'd always imagined that one day, when the children were grown, she'd leave UCL, sell up and come to live down here, writing books, doing her research, walking on the Downs. This was where she belonged, not in London surrounded by noise and people. She realized that now, when she imagined this future for herself, she was alone.

She unlocked the front door and stepped inside. It was very cold and dim and smelled slightly of mildew. She dumped her bag on the tiled floor, turned on the lights, then went straight to the cupboard under the stairs to turn on the heating and hot water. She'd grab some coffee and toast and then go and see Vivian. Vivian always ate breakfast at seven thirty. It was almost eight now. She'd go over to Ileford at eight thirty.

But it took her longer to get out of the house than she'd intended and it was nine by the time she passed through the tall stone gateway of Ileford. The mist-draped manor loomed ahead and the elms threw up tangled limbs as she passed beneath them. She remembered being told that you should never sit beneath an elm tree because they might drop a heavy branch on you; people had been killed that way.

The mist still hung over the fields and woods and blurred the edges of the house, blotting out its tall chimneys. She drove right past the imposing arched front door to park in the back courtyard. Vivian's car wasn't here. She would wait then, she was in no rush. She had the whole day to wait if necessary. She had a bunch of paperwork on the back seat to keep her occupied. Her heart was skittish and her stomach clenched as she got out of the car and walked towards the scullery door. She couldn't look at the well as she passed it, but she felt it sitting behind her like a big eye, watching.

She thumped on the scullery door and shouted, 'Vivian? Vivian? It's me!'

There was no response. So Vivian had ignored her message. Presumably she'd gone out deliberately. This was disappointing. She had been so sure that this time Vivian would be here.

There was nothing left to do for the launch party, the publicists had it all under control. She would wear the saffron-coloured silk dress she had been given after the magazine shoot, which was glamorous enough, even though she wouldn't have chosen the colour herself. She was determined to see Vivian today. She wasn't going to go back to London without looking her in the eye and finding out what she was up to.

It was beginning to drizzle now. The trees swayed and whispered behind the outhouses. She looked up at the windows, then got out her phone and called Vivian's mobile. It went to voicemail, as it had done for weeks. Vivian really was a dangerously stubborn person. She left a message, a little terse. 'Vivian, it's me. It's nine o'clock. I'm at Ileford, as I said I would be. I'm waiting for you here. I'm going to wait till you get back. I need to see you today. I'm not leaving till I've seen you.'

She hung up and walked along the house and banged on the

gunroom door with a fist. 'Vivian?' She didn't know why she was shouting, as clearly Vivian wasn't in. Suddenly, a kind of rebellion overtook her. She'd had enough of being shut out, of being controlled by Vivian.

She marched down to the gunroom window. The pane was smooth, the putty fresh. Of course Vivian would have had it fixed. She was efficient. She noticed the details. That was her job. She looked in at the window catch. It was not shut.

It really was that easy.

She climbed through, then closed the window behind her and trod rapidly down the corridor, past the scullery, which still smelled of Vivian's washing powder, past the silent kitchen, past the door to the cellars with the hatch that Uncle Quentin had installed to feed his Indian dancing bear. She wondered what it must have been like to be a bear trapped in the cellar with servants shoving raw steaks through that hatch. They had never discovered what happened to Quentin's bear. Maybe it died of loneliness. Or maybe they shot it after it savaged its master.

She was standing in the great hall beneath the imposing staircase, the oak-panelled ceiling and the minstrel's gallery, when her phone buzzed. She grabbed it from her jeans pocket. It was Vivian.

She stepped quickly over to the front window and peered out. 'Vivian?' The driveway was empty.

'I got your message.' Vivian's voice was emotionless.

'Good! Well, I'm glad you called me back. I've been trying to get hold of you for ages. Didn't you get my messages – my emails – saying I'd be down here first thing today to see you?' There was an echo on the line. She stepped closer to the window.

'Yes. I'm calling to say that you'll be waiting a very long time as I have to work today.'

'Oh no. Oh. Right. Where? Are you at the museum? Could I come and meet you there?'

'That's out of the question, I'm afraid.'

'Please, Vivian. We have to talk about this, we really do. I know you're upset with me but— '

'Upset?'

'Well. OK. Hurt? Angry?' Olivia stepped back from the window. She hugged herself. 'I don't know what you are! You have to tell me. Can't we talk about this?'

But Vivian said nothing.

'Are you coming to the launch tomorrow? I hope you are.'

There was silence.

'Vivian, please. I'm so sorry you're upset. I just want us to be friends.'

Vivian hung up.

Olivia stuffed her phone back into her pocket. This was too much. She was behaving like a petulant child now. She looked up the staircase. It was her one chance.

Her boots did not make a sound on the worn runner.

She'd always pictured the upstairs as similar to the ground-floor rooms, but the carpet along the corridor was threadbare beige, the walls a grubby magnolia. The musty smell was more pronounced up here and it was very cold indeed, and draughty, too, as if somewhere – perhaps in the servants' floor above – a window was hanging open.

The door to the first room was ajar and she saw faded floral wallpaper. She pushed it open. A huge bay window looked over the front of the house and driveway. The air smelled very faintly of Yardley's lavender, but the room was obviously unused. It must have been Lady Burley's. The double bed had a rather shabby pink eiderdown and old Laura Ashley cushions that matched the curtains. There were almost no possessions here, just a pile of Georgette Heyer paperbacks on the coffee table, a crocheted doily, dried flowers in a Wedgwood vase. It felt like the room of a dead old lady.

She crossed to the window and looked across the front lawns parted by the long drive. She remembered Lady Burley's story of seeing Violet's ghost walking her wolfhound between the elms in the October mist. She stepped away and walked quickly out of the bedroom, closing the door behind her.

The next room was almost unfurnished, just a double bed with an un-sheeted mattress and ox-blood walls, flock curtains, a balding brown carpet. The air had the same forgotten smell. She went back out. It was a shame to see a stunning house like this so shockingly neglected and empty.

As she crossed the corridor to the room opposite, her toe caught on a ridge in the carpet and she stumbled, almost careening into the wall, grabbing the door handle just in time to stop her head smashing into the plaster. She imagined Vivian finding her unconscious in the corridor. That would take some explaining.

She turned the handle and stepped into the room and for a moment she could not work out what she was looking at. Then she knew: beetles. Hundreds of beetles. Wooden display cases propped against the walls, stacked on a big table, each containing pinned beetle corpses lined up in size order.

There was a desk beneath the window and next to it a table with a hefty microscope, specimen tubes and laboratory equipment. The smell – acrid and musty, of mothballs and naphthalene – took her back to her father's lab at the university. She could see his broad, bearded face, his blue eyes, his wide torso packed into his lab coat.

She went and peered into the closest display case at the rows of beetles. Some were hefty, lacquered black with fang-like antlers, others as tiny as fleas. She looked at the labels, the doll-sized writing under each specimen, and the word *Scarabaeidae* caught her eye. She knew that word from her father's work. It was a family – it meant 'dung beetles'.

She felt numb as she moved on to the next case. That, too, contained dung beetles, this time with rich copper-coloured shells. Then there was a case of ladybirds, rows of little bright spotted sweets, each one classified, pinned and labelled.

She walked over to the desk by the window. It was stacked with papers, files and books. There was a tub of tweezers, another containing sharp Stanley knives. Some cardboard boxes, about the size of shoeboxes, sat on the floor by the desk. Each contained tubing or specimen jars. Even the equipment felt the same as her father's. It was like being propelled back thirty years.

There was a shelf by the desk holding rows of small glass jars. She reached out for one and held it up. She was looking at the corpse of an iridescent emerald green beetle, its legs spasmed in a death throe. She put it back on the shelf. A plastic tub by her toes contained brown bottles of chemicals.

This was nonsensical, disorientating. As a child she used to sleepwalk sometimes and wake in the pitch dark somewhere in the house, not knowing what room she was in or how to get out. She remembered the panic of having nothing to navigate by. She felt like that now. All reference points had vanished.

Except from the day in the bakery, ages ago, when Vivian had gone on about scarabs, she had never once mentioned this fascination with beetles.

It could be Lady Burley's collection, of course. But she knew, in her gut, that it was not.

If Vivian was this interested in beetles, particularly in dung beetles, then she must have heard of her father. Yet she'd shown no recognition of the name Ron Sweetman when Olivia talked about him and his work that night in the Farmhouse.

This felt surreal. She felt as if she might actually be hallucinating.

She went back over to the desk. An in tray contained print-outs of papers from scientific journals. She picked the first one up and read the title: 'Lethal and Sublethal Effects of Ivermectin on *Onthophagus landolti* (*Coleoptera: Scarabaeidae*)'. It was just the sort of print-out she'd have found on her father's desk.

She steadied herself with both hands. Her mouth felt very dry, her tongue had gone heavy and swollen. No wonder Vivian had always kept her downstairs.

She needed to get out of here. Vivian might shut up the museum and come back. She could not possibly have Vivian find her in here.

As she was turning to leave she spotted the edge of a maga-zine sticking out of a file, and she recognized her own favourite boots. She pulled the cutting out. It was from the *Telegraph Week-end*, a piece they'd run about four years ago, around the time of her first BBC show, two full years before she even met Vivian.

The picture had been taken near her office and she'd been pleased with it, she remembered. She looked down at herself, at her black jeans and the tight red shirt, buttoned low. She looked younger, and quite pretty. Her hair was glossy, her cheeks more full. The caption read '*Professor Olivia Sweetman in Russell Square*'. Somehow in this article the subject of her father had come up. She scanned it now for the words *Archaeocopris olivia*. The piece had been intelligently written, though she'd been flabbergasted by a quote from a male historian and TV presenter who said,

'Women like Olivia Sweetman are bringing the sexiness back into history'. She'd also objected to the title: 'Sweet History'.

She shoved the article back into the tray. This was Vivian's desk, then, Vivian's room, a coleopterist's den, a container of obsession.

She needed air. Her head felt packed. She needed to get out of this room and away from this icy, baffling house. She stumbled out the door and back down the corridor. As she turned onto the staircase she caught sight of herself in the gilt mirror at the end of the minstrel's gallery, spectre-faced and bruise-eyed – and then behind her, at the far end of the corridor, she saw a shape, just a shadow, a flicker of movement at the corner by the attic staircase.

She felt a jolt of adrenalin; she was not alone. She didn't turn and look, she swung onto the broad staircase, clinging to the banister, and ran down, leaping off the last four stairs onto the wood floor, almost over on her knees, then staggering forwards and off across the great hall, along the back corridor and out through the gunroom window, out into the courtyard, to her car which was waiting by the well.

Olivia

The Farmhouse

It only took a few calls to find out where Lady Burley now lived. Vivian had never mentioned it by name so she Googled local care homes and began phoning round. The friendly woman who answered the phone at Three Elms House put Olivia on hold and tried to transfer the call to Lady Burley's room. There was no reply. 'Can I take a message and have her call you back?'

Olivia left her name and mobile number. Perhaps it was political correctness to make it sound as if Lady Burley might be capable of answering her own phone or returning calls. Or perhaps Lady Burley was not as bad as she'd imagined. If there was any chance at all that the elderly lady was lucid, she needed answers.

She felt both drained and wired, as if her blood were crawling with tiny insects. She could not stop thinking about Vivian's study, not just the study itself, but the fact of it, of Vivian's interest, and of her thunderous silence.

To kill time she read through the Q&A that a woman's weekly

magazine had sent via her publicist: 'How do you juggle home and work life?'; 'Some people have accused you of trading on your looks, is this true?'; 'Your husband is a bestselling writer: are the two of you competitive?'

She slammed her laptop shut and went to get her boots. She had to get outside, just for a bit. The morning drizzle had not cleared but it didn't matter. She sat on the bench in the hall. The damp was coming up through the flagstones again, darkening them a shade or two. She should just forget the integrity of the house and have them pulled up and replaced. She yanked on her boots and grabbed the old fleece that used to belong to her father. It hung off her like a blanket.

She stamped across the field behind the Farmhouse, climbed the stile onto the lane, walked up that and crossed the road, and then began to climb the almost vertical chalky track up to the ridge of the Downs. This walk always made her think of her father. He used to come up the path with his shoulders back, his belly and chest pushed out like the prow of a ship. She would look up at the knotty underside of his beard, whining at him to slow down, but he made no concessions to her smaller legs and puffing.

She remembered him taking her to see a goliath beetle in the British Museum once, when she was nine or ten years old. It was the size of a sparrow. She had not known that beetles could be that huge. A Victorian beetle collector had shot it with a rifle in Africa and you could still see the bullet hole. She felt as if her father was a Goliath; it had been intolerable to watch him fall.

Their relationship was just beginning to shift when it happened. He had come to visit her in Cambridge. As an undergraduate in her final year she had begun to form pockets of knowledge that were new to him and he seemed to relish this. She remembered feeling properly recognized by him, at last. She was becoming an adult with things to offer him, rather than a child to be taught.

Then she remembered something Vivian had said at the Farmhouse when they were talking about their fathers, a give-away, in retrospect, though she had not registered it at the time. Vivian had been talking about her own father's death. She said he died slowly of dementia rather than quickly, as Olivia's father had. But she knew she'd never told Vivian how her father died. She didn't like to talk about that, because even now the memory would shake her.

They had been sitting in the sun outside a pub by the Cam. He'd spilled his pint of beer as he crashed to the floor and it had soaked her dress. As she bent over him all she could smell was hops and even today she couldn't stand the smell of beer. People rushed over to help. A medical student gave CPR as the ambulance screeched over the bridge. The grit from the paving stones stuck to her beer-soaked dress, made small dark dents in her kneecaps.

Vivian could only have known that his death was fast if she'd heard of him. So she did know about Ron Sweetman.

Olivia paused to catch her breath. She was at the ridge now, but the drizzle blotted everything out. As she moved off again she felt as if she was treading forwards with a grey net over her eyes. Seagulls slid overhead, she heard their high, mournful cries and saw their ghostly shapes above her, passing slowly. Close by, a rabbit hopped towards a hillock; light rain pattered onto her face and hair. Her boots were pallid and sticky with chalk mud.

Vivian must have heard of the *Archaeocopris olivia* scandal; she would have read about Ballard's sordid attempt to discredit her father. It was five years ago but Vivian would hardly have missed it; the world of dung-beetle research was hardly riven with scandal and intrigue. It had been all over *Nature*. Someone told her that there had been a huge fuss on social media too, though in those days she had no social media presence. All that had come with her TV career and she did not enjoy it. She only kept her social media accounts going because Carol and the TV people told her she must.

It was not just weird, but aggressive, for Vivian to withhold her interests in this way. Olivia hadn't tried to explain about Ballard's paper that night because she had assumed that it would be too complicated and uninteresting for Vivian. But Vivian had probably even read the original paper, 'A Case of Mistaken Identification of an Amber Fossil', and she would certainly have known what went on. She must have been interested. More than that, she must have been *fascinated*. Yet she'd given nothing away.

It was all about control with Vivian, that was clear. Silence was her weapon of choice and she was using it now, very effectively.

Archaeocopris olivia was more than a scientific discovery. That was why the fraudulent paper had been so distressing. Her father's fossil was supposed to last forever, safe in its tray at the museum in Oxford, and there was something so comforting about that, as if a small piece of him was immortal. *Archaeocopris olivia* had survived for millennia and would go on doing so through all the lifetimes of Sweetman descendants to come. Centuries in the future, their descendants would be able to go into the museum – or whatever replaced museums – and ask to see *olivia*.

The notion that a pathetic, fraudulent academic could try to gain glory by taking that away from them still made her angry. For a while, the episode had shaken her faith in academia. She had written letters to the university and the museum, but she had become so upset by it, so preoccupied and depressed, that David had insisted she cut off from the whole sorry scandal and concentrate instead on getting her own professorship. The last thing she had needed, at that point, was cynicism, distraction or distress.

She had not thought much about this for a couple of years now, but when she did the same fury returned, and the relief that Ballard, that charlatan, had been taken down.

But now Vivian's beetle-filled study had brought it all back. It shouldn't still upset her like this, but it did.

There was almost no visibility across the Weald to her right or over the undulating Downs towards the coast. The effect was vertiginous; she felt as if she might step off the edge at any moment, but of course she wouldn't. She knew exactly where she was going. She'd walked this track all her life and she knew every bump and hillock.

She was climbing over a stile when her mobile rang. The number was local but unfamiliar.

'Hello? Hello?' It was a reedy, elderly and distinctly aristocratic voice. 'Is that Professor Sweetman?'

'Yes, speaking?'

'This is Catherine Burley.'

'Catherine Burley?'

'I believe you rang and left me a message this morning? I'm returning your call.'

'*Lady Burley?*' Olivia swayed on the stile.

'That's right. You're Vivian's Professor Sweetman, I assume?'

'Vivian's . . . Yes – yes. I am, that's me.' Olivia's foot slipped on the damp wood. She steadied herself with her free hand.

'I've been wondering when you'd call,' said Lady Burley. 'I have *so* much to tell you.'

Vivian

Ileford Manor

She came in, then, as I knew she would. More lies, more pretend-ing. She was easy to lure and trap. All I had to do was hide my car in the garage and leave the latch on the gunroom window open.

She crossed the courtyard and went over to the window almost immediately, as I knew she would, and when she climbed in she came straight upstairs. She doesn't actually make a very good intruder, she left the door to Lady Burley's room closed and the door to my study open.

So. At least she has seen it now. I am oddly relieved.

Many people's first response when they hear that you are interested in dung beetles is to laugh. I am not sure why this is funny. I suppose people think that dung beetles are not only unglamorous but comical because of their association with excrement. In actual fact, they are busy and beautiful creatures, not as charismatic as ladybirds, but very varied in appearance and behaviour. I love nothing more, even now, than to put on latex gloves, take a specimen jar and a good stout stick and poke around in a field of cow dung for a couple of hours. The pockmarked sludge offers up such treasures. It calms me like nothing else.

The variety of British dung beetles is extraordinary. Some are small and black, others are oaky-hued, copper or verdigris or even blue-jewelled and iridescent. Some are as tiny as a newborn's fingernail, others as big and black as coat buttons. They are everywhere in Britain, yet few people notice them, let alone understand the crucial role they play in agriculture and our economy; how essential they are to the food we produce and consume, to our ecosystem, to our countryside.

As a child I might not have had many friends, other than my dog, of course, but I did have beetles. I would poke around for hours in the meadow, squatting to observe them at work. Their world always seemed so complete: useful and purposeful. While watching them tunnel and burrow, fetch and carry, I was able to forget how complicated, chaotic and confusing everything else was. They are such neat and efficient little souls.

With beetles to watch and my beloved dog by my side I felt that I was not alone on this planet. Of course, I didn't know until I studied these creatures as an undergraduate that they are so vital in fertilizing and clearing the land. They are immensely thorough; there is even a dung beetle that feeds on the excrement of dung beetles. If they vanish – and they might if we keep poisoning them with worming powders and other chemicals – then our farmland and by extension our economy will be plunged into crisis. We will also be knee-deep in animal excrement. No more picturesque country walks.

It was chance that I happened to grow up in Sussex and that my biology teacher recognized my intellectual capabilities and persuaded my father to let me study the subject at university. It was also chance that one of the world's leading beetle experts should happen to be based at the University of Sussex.

This morning when I heard Olivia's voice on the phone I was almost seduced again by her charm and by that word she used, 'friends'. She really is her father's daughter. But then the memory of Bertie's bloated body crawled back into my head, and her lies. I hung up and waited to see what she would do.

I forced myself to read the finished copy of *Annabel* last night. I actually felt quite numb as I did so. By obligingly breaking into the house and snooping round my study, she has made finishing this whole business much easier for me.

I found a missing hyphen within the first five paragraphs of the introduction. She should have got me to proofread. In my experience most proofreaders are incompetent; they have absolutely no eye for detail. Few people really do. I would dearly like to email her a list of corrections but that would be pointless since this week it enters the bookshelves of the nation.

The diary entries are reproduced in full at strategic intervals throughout the story. There are photographs of the diary too, in the central glossy section. I cannot help re-reading them. The final, and frankly audacious, diary entry is particularly colourful. I do admire our *Annabel*.

Late last night I was roused from my bed by a violent and deranged battering at the front door and a vulpine, high-pitched howling sound. I flung myself out of bed and hurried downstairs with Thoby barking at my heels. Milly and Jane came running, too, whimpering and clinging together in their nightclothes. Thoby threw himself at the door like a brave warrior. Though I could only see a cloaked shape on the front steps, I was convinced that this was a runaway from the lunatic asylum. They are not manacled now and only a month ago a man came through the village half naked.

Belton came down, looking stiff and frail, so I decided that I must act alone. I tore back the bolts and flung open the door, shouting at the top of my voice that they must be gone! The vagabond made off down the driveway and vanished between the elms. Milly insisted on offering a prayer for our deliverance, which I reluctantly permitted. I instructed Belton to escort the girls back up to their room. After a brandy and a slice of bread and butter in the kitchen with Thoby I began to feel positively enlivened by my adventure. I slept like a baby.

I close it and look at the cover. It is quite tasteful, I suppose: the portrait, with the word '*Annabel*' in bright yellow lettering above it, Olivia's name below. I have been sorting through Lady Burley's papers and I now know for sure that she got the portrait at auction in 1989. She paid £180 for it.

The text on the back of the jacket talks about the '*selfless and remarkable journey of one of Britain's unsung feminist heroes*'. This makes me think, somewhat bitterly, of the information I got from Mrs Sparrow in Hounslow on the day Bertie died. Olivia suppressed that, too. Another inconvenient truth.

With all the dreadful business with Bertie, it was a few weeks before I was able to talk to Olivia about Mrs Sparrow's assertions.

We were in the bakery. Olivia looked youthful and relaxed in a blue-checked shirt. Her face was un-made up, her hair pulled back. I, in contrast, had not slept in weeks. My visitor was assailing me almost every night. I was not eating well either. I probably looked quite poorly. She was obviously concerned about me. She fussed around, trying to get me to have cake, asking if I was cold, or hot.

When I'd told her Mrs Sparrow's story I said, 'She says Annabel was a Machiavellian narcissist.'

Olivia gave faint smile. 'It's possible.'

'So can you delay publication?'

'The thing is, Vivian, anything's possible – and she has no proof of this, does she? Nothing written down at all. There are always going to be alternative stories and interpretations, gossip, hearsay, people with grudges. But I've got a good draft now that just needs polishing and tightening. The story works. It's fantastic the way it is. It would only muddy the waters to go down this sort of route.'

I looked at her. 'Are you saying you don't even want me to try to find out about her baby?'

She shrugged and pushed back some loose strands of hair and then she just changed the subject. 'But listen, I've got exciting news!' she said. 'I had dinner with my agent last night and we've had some interest from a Hollywood film company! They think *Annabel* might make a great feature-length drama.'

And that was the end of it. I didn't contact Mrs Sparrow again and nor did Olivia. She shut it down.

And so, I suppose, did I. Perhaps I was spellbound. Perhaps I am particularly susceptible to the Sweetman charisma. Or perhaps I was too upset about Bertie to care.

I still have not decided exactly how I am going to bring this to a close, once and for all, but I do know one thing: I will not use social media. I do not have the stomach for it, after what happened to me.

I am agitated by that memory even now and I have to remind myself that it will not happen to me ever again. It cannot, because my name is nowhere. I have left no trace of myself whatsoever on *Annabel*. I get up, go over and grab the hardback from its shelf and turn to the acknowledgements. I need to reassure myself that I am not there, even though I have already checked it twice.

I remember the discussion we had about the acknowledgements last year as we walked round Hammer Pond. It was a little edgy if I remember correctly. It was not long after Bertie vanished so I was probably quite raw. Even the glorious sight of the bluebells failed to cheer me.

Her initial stance, I seem to remember, was righteous. 'But you've contributed so much, Vivian. I have to thank you publicly. I can't not put you in the acknowledgements, it wouldn't be right.' She pushed strands of loose black hair out of her mouth and fixed her eyes on me in the intense, searching way she has when she wants something.

'It wouldn't be right to mention my name if I don't want it mentioned.' I looked away, at the rusted hunks sticking out of the pond we were passing, lumps of iron ore, known locally as 'bears'. I allowed my mind to massage the word *bear*: to *bear* a hardship, *bear* weight, *bear* the pain, un*bear*able. Without Bertie, I decided, this walk was dismal.

'All I'm saying is we should be honest and open about your contribution to the book.'

I thought about this for a moment. 'If honesty is the issue, then perhaps we should be credited as co-authors.'

Her face turned pink. 'I . . . We . . . Well . . .' she stammered. 'I think . . . that might, um, you know, muddy the water a little bit . . . The publisher . . . My name is . . .' She tailed off.

'That was a joke.' I said. 'I was joking.'

She did not bring up the acknowledgements again.

I read down the list of people she is thanking publicly: Joy, Carol, various contributors, friends, her family members. She has honoured my request and my name is absent. Vivian Tester does not exist.

If I wanted to I could stop this. I could just give it up, fade away, not go to the party, say nothing. Sometimes I want that more than anything.

But then I remember what she did to Bertie.

Olivia

Three Elms Care Home, East Sussex

A Slovakian carer showed Olivia into the communal area, a pleasant and high-ceilinged Georgian living room that looked onto lawns and trees. Lady Burley was in a wing chair facing the garden. Silver faerie hair waved around a crumpled and pretty face that lit up as Olivia came in.

'Professor Sweetman! Well, you're just as attractive as you look on television.' She gave a sweet laugh and held out a tiny crepe-paper hand.

For a second, Olivia was speechless. This bright-eyed person was not what she had been expecting at all. She pulled herself together and stepped forwards. 'Oh, it's lovely to meet you too, Lady Burley.' The hand felt as frail as a kitten's paw; its tiny bones slid beneath downy skin.

'Do sit, sit, please.' Lady Burley waved at the chair next to hers. 'Shall we have some tea?'

'That'd be lovely.'

Lady Burley craned to signal a young woman in a pink uniform. 'I'm so glad you came, Professor Sweetman.'

'Oh, please, it's fine to call me Olivia.' She had been bracing herself for sickness and confusion, possibly distress, but Lady Burley, though obviously frail, seemed perfectly compos mentis.

'I kept telling Vivi she must give you my telephone number, but she didn't seem to think you'd need to talk to me just yet. I'm awfully thrilled that you want to now.'

Olivia nodded and smiled. She knew that people with dementia could have moments of clarity, but surely not like this.

There was some fussing about biscuits and what sort of tea, India or China. The carer went off again to fetch it.

'So, do tell me what you've found out so far about Annabel Burley,' Lady Burley said. 'I'm absolutely fascinated. Vivi hardly tells me a thing. She's very naughty. I told her to give you whatever access you needed to the Burley archives, but I have a few things here you'll be interested in, and I expect you'll want to interview me properly at some point, won't you?'

'Oh . . . But I . . . For . . .?'

'For the book of course.'

'But . . . Gosh. The book . . .' It was possible that Lady Burley was less on top of things than she seemed. 'The book's finished,' Olivia said, softly. 'I've actually brought you a copy, as a thank you gift.' Could someone with dementia appear normal like this, but in fact be losing her mind?

She leaned down, opened up her bag and pulled out the hardback.

Lady Burley looked at it and her face fell. 'But I don't understand. You've written the book already?'

'Yes, look, this is it.' Olivia smoothed her palm across its shining carapace. The portrait gleamed, as did the title: *Annabel: The Shocking Confessions of a Victorian Surgeon.*

Lady Burley reached for the book, but it was too heavy for her and it dipped. Olivia shot out a hand to catch it. She pulled the tray closer and laid it down. Lady Burley stared at it. She seemed baffled.

'Didn't Vivian tell you?' Olivia said.

'This is *it*? You've finished it already?'

'Yes, well, it was quite a rapid process. Vivian's been helping.' She remembered Vivian saying something about Lady Burley having a flexible sense of time. 'She said you were too ill for visitors. I would have come to see you if I'd known you were . . . like this. I need to talk to you about Vivian, actually. That's partly why I came today.'

Olivia stopped. Lady Burley looked so distressed, her bird hand tightened around a lacy handkerchief and she was breathing fast. 'That's not even Annabel.' She pointed at the portrait.

The carer reappeared, then, with the tray of tea things and Tunnock's wafers, and began pouring. Olivia tried to think of a time when Vivian had, specifically, told her that Lady Burley had dementia. She couldn't pinpoint any actual conversation but she was sure that Vivian had said so. Or at least, strongly implied it.

The only thing to do at this point was to tell the truth. Lady Burley needed to know that Vivian had put her off or she would – rightly – want to know why on earth Olivia had not come in person before now, to meet and interview her about her family. She felt queasy. She had to head this one off. What was Vivian playing at?

'I'm so sorry,' Olivia said, when the carer had gone again, 'I think I owe you an explanation. You must think I'm horribly rude – negligent, in fact – to have written a book about a member of your family without coming to see you. But you must know that Vivian told me, very clearly, that you were too ill to have visitors. She expressly forbade me to bother you. I did write to you, I hope you got my letter? Vivian told me you'd given permission for me to write the book but she gave me the impression, the very strong impression, I'm afraid, that you were suffering from dementia. She told me it would distress and confuse you if I tried to speak to you. She's very protective. I honestly had no idea, none whatsoever, that you were so . . . so well.'

'I don't have dementia. I'm perfectly fine.' Lady Burley looked at her over the rim of her teacup. 'Except for the cancer.' She lowered the cup, shakily, into its saucer. 'Did Vivi really tell you that I have *dementia*?'

'Well, I'm not . . . I think so. She definitely strongly implied it.'

Lady Burley looked out at the garden, at the stretch of lawn, the burnished trees and granite sky. Her eyelids flickered. 'The trees are rather spectacular, don't you think?'

'Yes, yes, they're lovely.'

'I'm terribly fond of Vivi, you know. I've known her almost all her life. She's terribly efficient and so good with the administration and the finances. She's a godsend, though she's not what they call a "people person". But underneath it she's a kind, sweet soul. Dear Vivi. She looked after me so well.'

It seemed cruel to leave Lady Burley thinking that she had been betrayed. 'She's obviously very fond of you, too. I'm sure she just wanted to protect you. I'm just so sorry, so very sorry, that I didn't come to see you before. If I'd had any idea you were OK, I would have . . .'

'It's a very big book.' Lady Burley looked at it.

'It's a wonderful story. You mustn't worry, I fell in love with

Annabel. She was such an amazing woman. I've written about your family with the utmost respect.' She thought, then, about her portrait of the drunken Lord Burley and the sections on the wayward Uncle Quentin with his unhinged Ileford parties, his financial eccentricities, his vicious dancing bear.

Lady Burley looked at her. Beneath the folds of skin, her eyes definitely seemed less friendly. 'You didn't even *try* to see me?'

Olivia felt her face grow hot. To her, Lady Burley had been a non-person, disabled by cancer and dementia, close to death. 'I am so, so sorry,' she muttered. 'I really am. Vivian said not to.'

'Do you always do what people tell you?'

Olivia couldn't think how to answer this.

'Well, I wonder what you've left out of this big book of yours. It is rather a shame that you didn't come to see me because I have two photographs of Annabel that you might have liked to include. I didn't give them to Vivi because I wanted to give them to you myself. I had Zuska get them out this morning after I spoke to you on the telephone. I have some family stories you won't have heard from Vivian, too.'

'You do?' She felt weak.

'Uncle Quentin remembered his stepmother quite well, you know and he had some very lively tales to tell. You could have used them in your book, had you thought to come and see me.'

'I don't know what to say . . .' Olivia took a sip of the Earl Grey, swallowing hard to force it down. She had so wanted photos; the lack of photos of Annabel had troubled her all along and Vivian knew that. How could she do this?

'Pass me that . . . the – that – there, would you, please?' Lady Burley pointed to a brown envelope next to the tea things. With shaky hands she lifted onto her nose the large, thick glasses that were around her neck on a gold chain and fumbled with the envelope. Olivia raised a hand to help, but then thought better of it. After what seemed like hours of slippery skin on manila Lady Burley extracted a photograph and handed it to Olivia. With her eyes magnified by the thick lenses, she reminded Olivia of a grasshopper.

She looked down at the photo. 'This is Annabel?' This was not how she had pictured Annabel at all. The woman staring up at her had wide-apart eyes, a small, solemn, cruel mouth and a lot of thick, dark, curly hair. She was not beautiful, in fact she was distinctly odd-looking, with quite a long neck. A scraggly wolf-hound leaned against her leg, looking up at her with comical devotion while she stared directly – challengingly – at the photographer. The name of the photographer was embossed on the mount with the words, '*Lady Annabel Burley with Filcher, Ileford Manor, June 1898.*' It was the very year that Annabel was writing the diary. 'Oh. I wish Vivian had shown me this.'

'I don't believe Vivian's ever seen it. I was keeping a few treasures for when you came.'

Olivia sensed a passive-aggressive engine humming inside Lady Burley's frail exterior. She gazed at the picture. Even the dog looked superior, with its horrid, elongated features. She could barely bring herself to ask, but she had to. 'You said you had another picture?'

'Yes, there's one of Annabel as a doctor.' Lady Burley fumbled around in the envelope again. She laid the second photograph on top of the book and took her glasses off again.

It was recognizably the same face, but changed. She was probably in her fifties, much more thickset, sitting behind a desk in a white coat. Her eyes were hidden by small round glasses and her features had coarsened, her jaw was set, her hair chopped off. She looked mannish, determined and forbidding.

Olivia turned it over, but there was no date. She had longed for a photograph of Annabel as a doctor but had never pictured her like this. Annabel didn't look like someone who had found fulfilment in helping others and she didn't look very heroic. Perhaps they would not have used this photo even if they'd had it. It rather spoiled the romantic image, though it did fit the brutal obituary in which she had been described, by male colleague, as a woman of *'striking intellect'* who *'disapproved of lipstick'* and was unpopular with colleagues, though she always had *'the highest possible standards'*.

'She was unpleasant; quite ruthless,' said Lady Burley. 'You know about Lord Burley's previous wife, Vera, of course, and the poor children?'

'You mean Violet? Violet Burley?'

'Violet. That's right, not Vera. Vera was my own sainted mother, God bless her. You'll have seen the shrine, I suppose, to Violet and the children, in the ornamental garden at Ileford?'

'Yes, I have, it's lovely, very sad.' Vivian had at least taken her to see that. They had included a photograph of it in the book. 'So, did Uncle Quentin tell you about Annabel?'

'Oh yes, Uncle Quentin. He wasn't my uncle, by the way, he was my second cousin, but we all called him that. He was rather a dear actually, totally batty, of course, a raging queer, but such fun – a prankster. Did Vivian tell you about his dancing bear?'

'Yes, the one that bit him? She said he kept it in the cellar.'

'A riot!' Lady Burley gave a brief, girlish laugh. 'He loathed Annabel, of course. She stuck him in boarding school when he was tiny, sometimes didn't even get him out in the holidays. She hated children. Loved dogs, though. Terribly British of her.'

Olivia did not really want to hear any of this. She looked at the first photograph, of the young Annabel and the dog. 'That's quite a hound.' Her eyes rested on the dog's name: '*Filcher.*'

'Would you like to hear another story?' Lady Burley said, sweetly.

Olivia nodded, despair lapping at her heels.

'I have no idea if this is true, Uncle Quentin could be a bit of a fantasist, but he told me that when Filcher died Annabel performed a . . . what do you call it . . . on the dog – on the croquet lawn.'

Olivia shook her head, confused.

'You know, where they cut you up after you die?'

'An *autopsy*?'

'That's right!' Lady Burley's laugh tinkled out. 'Autopsy! Imagine! He came out into the garden one day to find his stepmother kneeling on a blanket in the sun with her sleeves rolled up, drenched in the dog's blood. She'd laid its intestines out on the lawn.'

'Really?'

'Of course, who knows if it's true!' Lady Burley blinked a few times, rapidly. 'Uncle Quentin did love to make things up.'

Suddenly Olivia realized what was bothering her. It was the dog. This was the wrong dog. In the diary, Annabel talked about her beloved little terrier, Thoby. There was no mention of a wolfhound called Filcher. 'Annabel had a terrier, too, didn't she?' she said.

'What, dear?' Lady Burley fiddled with a hearing aid. 'What did you say?'

'In the diary she doesn't mention a wolfhound, but she talks about a terrier.'

Lady Burley's hand fluttered near her head. 'No, no, dear, it's Vivian who had a terrier.'

'That's right, Bertie.'

'No, no, Bertie's her dog now. This was long before Bertie, when she was a child.'

Lady Burley definitely seemed to be mixed up. Perhaps she did have mild dementia. She'd even forgotten that Bertie was dead. Unless Vivian had never told her. Olivia leaned closer and enunciated clearly. 'In the diary, Annabel's dog is a little terrier called Thoby.'

'In what diary?'

'In Annabel's diary, from 1898, her murder confession?'

Lady Burley shook her head. 'I've never seen any diary.'

'You inherited it from Uncle Quentin?'

Lady Burley's hand hovered at her chest. 'I don't know what Vivian's been telling you.'

'But you . . . Vivian has it at Ileford. I've studied it – extensively. It's been verified by a friend of mine at the British Library. It's the entire basis for this book . . .' She pointed at the glossy hardback between them.

'Well, I don't remember any diary.' Lady Burley's hand fluttered to her throat. She looked perturbed and suspicious, as if Olivia might be lying to her.

Olivia felt suddenly very cold. She wanted to reach over and shake Lady Burley, make her remember. It made no sense that she wouldn't know about the diary. She really must have dementia. She remembered how protective Vivian was of the elderly lady's emotional state – perhaps this was why.

'Never mind.' She tried to drink her tea. She couldn't quite work out what had just happened. She put the cup back down. It was fine, this was just forgetfulness, the confusion of the elderly. Lady Burley must be on a lot of medication for the cancer too. Vivian said that affected her. In a moment, she'd remember the diary, of course she would.

'I suppose Vivian's told you about the Ileford ghost?' Lady Burley clearly wanted to change the subject.

'Violet walking her wolfhound in the mist?'

'I've seen her myself, many times, vanishing under the elms on early October mornings. Elms are such sinister trees, I don't know what all the fuss is about with preserving them. If they weren't protected by the council I'd have had them all cut down. They drop their branches, you see. You know the saying, "Elm hateth man, and waiteth."'

But Olivia couldn't just leave it like this. She picked up *Annabel* and opened the middle section, finding an image of a diary entry. 'Look,' she said, gently. 'This is Annabel's diary.'

Lady Burley fumbled with her glasses again, got them onto her nose, squinted at it. Then she sat back. 'My eyes are no good, I'm afraid, even with these.'

'Oh. OK. It's just that the diary, the confession, is definitely real. My friend at the British Library has even dated the ink and paper.'

Lady Burley looked very flustered. She lifted the glasses off again with trembling hands.

Olivia closed the book. It felt cruel to press her like this. 'Actually, Lady Burley, I came here partly to ask you about Vivian.'

'Oh, poor darling Vivi.' Lady Burley gave a wistful smile. 'She has her own ghost, of course.'

'Does she?'

'We call it her night visitor. It's terrifying for her. She wakes up to find the ghost of her badly injured mother sitting on her chest, trying to suffocate her. She's totally paralysed when it happens. It's probably something to do with trauma – what do they call it – PT . . . D?'

'PTSD? Post-traumatic stress disorder?'

'That's right. It all stems, they think, from Vivi's childhood trauma, losing her mother in such a violent fashion. She's had it since childhood. A child can take on such guilt when a parent dies.'

'Really? I knew her mother died, but she's never told me much about it. Do you mind me asking what happened?'

Lady Burley patted her cream blouse. 'Well, it was a car accident. Poor Dottie. Here, pass me that . . . that.' She waved at an ornate wooden box on the side table.

Vivian had been so upset when she'd asked about her mother that night in the Farmhouse. This must be why. Olivia reached for the inlaid walnut box. It was quite heavy. She held it open on her knees and watched Lady Burley fiddle yet again to get her glasses on.

'I had Zuska bring this down today so I could show you some of my Annabel treasures but I think I've also got . . . in here . . . somewhere . . . a picture of Dottie.' Lady Burley rifled through the letters, photographs and scraps of ribbon and extracted a black and white photo. 'We were great chums.' She sounded immensely sad, suddenly, as if the years had concertinaed.

The photo was of two young women, standing side by side. One was slim, tall and pretty, with blonde hair, as long as Jess's used to be, wearing a well-cut 1950s style dress. The other was shorter and square-faced, much less pretty, but with bright, friendly eyes beneath a straight fringe. She was wearing a tweedy, bulky suit. Lady Burley peered at it. 'Yes, that's it. That's me with the long hair. I could sit on it in those days. I was considered quite a beauty. And that's Dottie, next to me.'

Olivia stared at the picture. Vivian had never mentioned this connection. She'd always talked as if she was merely Lady Burley's employee. Then again, there were clearly a lot of things that Vivian had not mentioned. She wanted to ask Lady Burley about the beetles in Vivian's study but Lady Burley started to speak again.

'We were in the Village am dram society together. Dear Dottie, such a treasure. We got on like a house on fire.' She sighed. 'Some things fade as you age, but the guilt doesn't. No one tells you that. The guilt only gets worse.'

'Why do you feel guilty?'

'Well, it was such a shameful business.' Lady Burley blinked. She'd forgotten to take her glasses off and her eyes were huge and viscous.

'What was?' Olivia said, gently. 'Sorry – Vivian hasn't . . .'

'My unfortunate dalliance with Vivi's father, and then Dottie's accident.'

Olivia wondered if she'd heard Lady Burley right. She sounded matter of fact, as if she was talking about her penchant for Tunnock's, rather than for Vivian's father. 'You and Vivian's father were . . . lovers?' she said, tentatively.

'Not lovers, really, there was nothing romantic about it. Vivian's father was the estate manager for my first husband. I think of it as my Lady Chatterley moment.'

Olivia could imagine the aristocratic Lady Burley in her twenties, frivolous and bored, with all that long blonde hair.

'The problem was we were married off so young in those days. Dottie was only twenty when she had Vivian and I was twenty-one when I married Ronnie. I moved into his ghastly big house. Dottie was my helper. We were both terribly unhappy. Ronnie was a rotter, but the irony was I didn't even like Victor. Dottie was terribly cut up when she found us. It was a filthy night, she just took off.' Lady Burley pronounced 'off' as 'orf'.

'She found you with her husband, then ran away?'

'Yes. And poor Vivi, so traumatic for her, she was only five or six years old. I suspect she still blames herself even now for it.'

'For what?'

'Well, you see, she remembers howling in the back seat. Dottie turned to tell her to be quiet and lost control of the car. It hit a tree.'

'Vivian was *in the car* that night?'

'Oh yes. Physically unharmed, but terribly traumatised when they got her out. I don't think she spoke for a year afterwards. Then of course she had a sort of nervous breakdown in her teens. I've always told her she must see a psychotherapist but she won't. I did try to support her, you know. Vic wasn't a kind father, he didn't know what to do with a little girl. He drank. He was rather brutal to her, I suspect. I'd have her to stay with me, sometimes, in the school holidays. I don't have children of my own and I always felt a great responsibility to Dottie.' Lady Burley's blue eyes were inflated and watery, her voice wavered. 'So silly of me, but you know, I almost feel worse about it now than I did at the time.'

'But this is awful. How long was Vivian trapped in the car?'

'Overnight, I'm afraid. The postman found her.'

'She was stuck in a car *all night* with her dying mother?'

'They think Dottie probably died on impact, or soon after.'

It was a horrifying thought. It was impossible to imagine the effect that sort of trauma would have on a child, or the scars it might leave on you as an adult. Vivian's brittleness, her formality, her prickliness and rigidity suddenly made more sense. Her personality was underpinned by this gruesome childhood experience. She might or might not be on some spectrum or other, but that wasn't her real problem. It was her family history that made her vulnerable, and although she'd clearly evolved a protective shell, it wasn't working because the true threat was inside her. It was this damage that made her unpredictable and unreadable.

'She had her little dog with her, at least,' Lady Burley said, in a brighter voice. 'He kept her company that night, and afterwards, too.'

Olivia imagined a little girl clinging to her dog in the back seat with her dead mother slumped over the steering wheel.

'He went on for a long time, died of old age, dear old Thoby. The doctors said that his death probably led to her breakdown in her teens. She went up to Beachy Head, but fortunately a rambler stopped her.'

'Wait – what name did you just say?' Olivia felt as if the walls of the room had inched closer.

'Beachy Head?'

'No. Not the place. The dog, Vivian's childhood dog – his name.'

'Thoby?' Lady Burley looked surprised. 'Darling little thing. Just a mutt, but he kept her going for a good ten years after the accident. She adored him. He was her best friend in the world.' Lady Burley nodded and smiled. 'Dear Vivi, she does love her dogs.'

Olivia

East Sussex, a lay-by

The chaos in her head was overwhelming as she hung up the phone and drove away from Three Elms. She'd left a message on Vivian's phone but she knew she wouldn't respond. She couldn't make the facts line up. Could it be a coincidence that Vivian's childhood dog had the same name as Annabel's terrier? Surely not. It couldn't be.

Then there was Lady Burley's insistence that there was no diary. But Lady Burley was a bit confused, elderly and unwell. She'd muddled Violet's name with her own mother's. She couldn't be relied on, surely.

She felt shaky, chilly and sick, as if she were coming down with the flu. She felt as if she might have to pull over and throw up. She had to calm down. Lady Burley was on heavy medication, possibly suffering from mild dementia. This confusion didn't mean anything. The diary had been tested and verified by a leading expert in Victorian documents.

But she knew that these tests were not definitive. History was littered with hoaxes. The Hitler diaries had been examined by manuscript specialists who'd all believed them to be authentic before they were proven to be forged. The Ripper diary, too, had confounded the experts; complex forensic testing of the hand-writing, ink and paper had all proved contradictory and inconclusive. When it came to verifying historical sources, even the experts could disintegrate in confusion and argument.

And she'd only taken it to one person. She'd been so com-pletely convinced that it was real; it looked, sounded, felt and smelled authentic. She'd never really questioned it properly. Somehow, perhaps because she could see what a great book she could write, she'd convinced herself that a hoax was not a possibility.

But a forgery made no sense. Vivian had no reason to invent a Victorian diary. Nor did she have the skills to fake something so convincingly. She was just a housekeeper, an extraordinarily bright, fanatical, detail-orientated housekeeper, but one with absolutely no training in historical documents.

She said she'd found the diary among Uncle Quentin's papers. Was it possible that Uncle Quentin had made it up? Could Quen-tin have met Vivian, known Vivian's childhood dog? Olivia racked her memory for dates. Quentin Burley had died in the early sixties. If Vivian was visiting Lady Burley in the school holi-days as a child, then she could have been taken to visit Quentin at Ileford in the sixties. He might have met Thoby the dog on one of those visits too. And he might therefore have used its name if he was inventing a diary.

Everyone said Uncle Quentin was an eccentric prankster. And he'd had every motivation to smear the reputation of the step-mother he hated.

But if it was Quentin Burley who'd faked the diary, then

Vivian must surely have known. She'd have recognized the name of her childhood dog and realized that it couldn't be a coincidence. But why would Vivian not have told her? Why would Vivian allow her to write a book if she suspected the diary wasn't real?

She wanted to scream. Her hands, on the wheel, were shaking violently as she pulled over onto a grass verge, redialled Vivian's number and left a hysterical message. 'CALL ME BACK!' she yelled at the end, and hung up. Then she emailed her too.

She had to calm down. She had to think rationally. It was possible that Lady Burley had simply forgotten about the diary. Or maybe she had never looked through Uncle Quentin's papers. She'd been about to go into the care home when Vivian found the document. That must have been a difficult time for her. Maybe Vivian had never told her about the diary. But that too would be odd. Then again, Vivian was odd. Unhinged. She withheld things. She told lies.

But she knew in her gut that this explanation was wrong. Lady Burley might be fragile, but she really did seem compos mentis and she'd have known about the diary, unless Vivian had concealed it from her, and Vivian would only do that if she knew it to be a fake.

She'd started to drive again and was nearing the M23 when her phone rang. Her first thought was Vivian. She grabbed it from the passenger seat but Chloe's name was flashing up.

She couldn't talk to Chloe right now. She threw it back on the passenger seat and let it go to voicemail. She saw that there were previous missed calls from Chloe on the screen and unread texts. It rang again, almost immediately. She slammed her foot on the brake, jerked the wheel and bumped up onto a verge, plunging the wheels into the coarse, overgrown grass, almost hitting a hedgerow.

She picked up just before it went to voicemail.

'Liv?'

'Hi, Chlo. Look, I'm driving . . . I'm a bit—'

'I've got to talk to you. I've been trying to get hold of you all day – I have to see you. Could I come over? Where are you? Are you at home?'

'No, I'm driving. I'm in Sussex.'

'But it's the launch tomorrow.'

'I know – I'm on my way back now, Chlo. I can't really talk.'

'When will you be back?'

'In about an hour. What is it? What's wrong? What's happened?'

'Can we meet tonight?'

'I can't really. I've got to write my speech and get ready.'

'I don't want to do this over the phone.'

'Do what? Look, you have no idea what sort of a day I've just had. Whatever it is, just tell me!'

There was a pause. 'I'm so sorry, Liv. I'm so sorry.' Chloe's voice sounded very odd suddenly, shaky and ominous.

'What it is? Has something happened? Is it the children?'

'No! No. The children are fine. It's David.'

'Oh my God.' She felt her stomach drop.

'No – he's OK. But I think he's having an affair.'

She gripped the phone. '*What*?'

'Oh, Liv, darling, I'm so sorry, but I think David's sleeping with your au pair.'

Olivia sat very still. The drizzle ran down the windscreen. Everything felt curiously far away.

'Liv? Are you there? Did you hear me?'

'He's not sleeping with Marta.'

'I've seen them together. Twice.'

'But that's ridiculous . . .'

'Wait, just listen to me, OK? The first time was about a week before we went to France. I was out running and they were in Ravenscourt Park. David saw me and he came after me, he said it wasn't what I thought. You know what he's like, how persuasive he is, he talked me out of it.'

'This was *three months ago*?'

'No. Yes. Listen, he persuaded me it was nothing, but I was going to tell you anyway because it felt wrong not to say something about it and I tried to get you to meet me before we went to France, but you were too busy. When we were in France, I tried to talk to you. We were on the sun loungers, remember? But you started telling me what he'd done with the money and I just couldn't do it to you . . . You were so stressed and upset, trying to deal with all that, I didn't want to make things worse and I wasn't even that sure what I'd seen. And then the boys interrupted us. Remember? Ben's foot? The scorpion that was a splinter? Then there was the thing with Jess's hair and we all left.'

'OK. I don't understand. What did you see in the park? What were they doing?'

'It's hard to describe. Not that much. It was . . . I think he was touching her face. It just felt wrong, you know. But the thing is, this morning was different.'

'You saw them together *today*?' There was suddenly too little oxygen in the car.

She opened the door and out of nowhere a racing bike appeared, swerving to avoid her door. The cyclist let out a bark of protest that faded with him down the road.

The air was damp, she could hear rumbling lorries and smell the exhaust fumes from the M23.

Chloe's voice sounded curiously distant. 'I was dropping off the Harlequin vase to a client in Brackenbury Road and I walked past them. They were in his car and they were definitely together. He didn't see me. I rang him afterwards and told him if he didn't tell you then I would. He says he doesn't want you tell you because of the book launch but I just . . . I didn't know what to do. I thought about waiting, I really did, but I just can't come and stand at your party tomorrow knowing this, Liv, I can't do that to you.' Her voice broke. 'It would feel like a betrayal. I can't lie to you like that. I'm so sorry, my love. The timing is so, so shit. I'm really sorry . . .'

Olivia put her free hand on the wheel, elbow straight. She felt very formal suddenly. 'What exactly did you see today?'

'They were kissing. I was right next to the car, I saw them very clearly.'

She felt as if something was pressing so hard on her chest that it might cave in.

'Liv? Are you OK?' Chloe's voice wavered. 'Do you want me to drive down there and get you?'

'No. No. I'm almost at the M23.'

She leaned on her knees, then, and threw up into the ditch.

She wiped her mouth with the back of her hand and stared into the prickly hedgerow at the clumps of blood-red black bryony berries and tangled grey trails of old man's beard. She could hear all the cars on the motorway and it seemed improbable that people were still driving, still going about their business, travelling up and down the roads, keeping appointments, running errands, going to work, when this was happening.

She spat a few times, acrid spittle burning her throat. She could hear Chloe's tinny voice coming from the passenger seat where she'd tossed the phone. 'Liv? Liv?'

Marta was up there now, in her house, with her children, right now. That revolting snake. Rage seized her. How could he do this? With Marta? It was such a sad, pathetic, midlife crisis thing to do. It was repulsive. He was old enough to be Marta's father.

The crushing in her chest intensified and then she felt as if something was covering her mouth and nose, pressing itself over her body, screwing her into a ball. She struggled to stand up but couldn't; she tried to breathe but couldn't get any air into her lungs. She felt her diaphragm sucking up and down, help-lessly. She was going to suffocate in fury on a grass verge, with hundreds of cars passing below. She was going to die because she couldn't breathe.

It felt like a long time before she managed to get any oxygen into her body, a few thin gasps of air.

Chloe was wrong. This had to be a mistake.

But she knew it wasn't. David was sleeping with Marta. He'd been doing so for a while. It was obvious now. She was there, in their home, day after day, standing in the kitchen in the morning, braless, in shorts, or coming out of the shower wrapped in a towel. Marta was young enough to be impressed by David. Her attention would have convinced him that he was still spectacular.

And Dom knew – of course – he must have known for months. He could not look at or speak to David because of it and this was, of course, why he despised and avoided Marta. Poor Dom had been living with this hideous secret, hating his father for it but still somehow too loyal to tell. Or perhaps he was too fearful of what it would do to her to know the truth. It must have been going on for months, right under her nose, in their house. Maybe even in her bed.

She thought about David touching Marta's body and leaned over to throw up again. Tears streamed from her eyes as she gagged.

The lies he must have told. All the occasions when he and Marta had been away at the same time – she could think of so many now. She'd been so naive. He was even taking a trip the day after the launch to Copenhagen when Marta, too, would be away, supposedly in Bristol visiting friends.

They'd made a fool of her. The humiliation and betrayal felt physically crushing. Things had been bad between them but he wasn't supposed to do this to her. He was supposed to love her. They were supposed to work this out.

They would never be able to work this out now. Their marriage was over. There was no way she would ever be able to forgive him for sleeping with the au pair. She would never respect him again.

Chloe's voice sounded deranged coming from the seat of the car. She reached over and picked up the phone again. 'I'm OK. It's OK. I'm coming back now. I'll see you in an hour. I'll call you. I'm glad you told me. Don't worry. I'm OK.' She hung up.

But she wasn't OK. Everything was collapsing. She couldn't breathe properly, or think. The room full of beetles, Thoby the dog, Lady Burley's denial, Uncle Quentin's pranks and now this – David and the au pair, seventeen years of marriage betrayed for a Danish *child*. Everything she'd believed in – her marriage, the diary, the beautiful, powerful book she'd written – was fake. Her entire life had just revealed itself to be a towering, toppling lie.

Vivian

The Hunterian Museum, Royal College of Surgeons, London

I did it – not that – but I went. I went to the party this evening.

It is past midnight but I find that I cannot go up to bed. It is partly the thought of the stairs but it is also because I feel certain that I shall be awake all night after the excitement of this evening. This is a good thing as it means that I will not have to face my visitor. She has become so ferocious lately, so full of anger and recriminations, that I fear I shall die at her hands even though they are a product of my own mind.

The library is very cold but I am too tired to light a fire. I have a blanket over my shoulders and I have raised my knee on a stool, but it is painful still. I expect I need to see a doctor.

I thought about not going up to London tonight but in the end I just couldn't stay away. I did not know if I could step forward in front of the crowd, but I felt I had to witness her brief and teetering moment of glory.

It was a virtuoso performance. Given what she had discovered from Lady Burley yesterday it was a miracle that she could stand up there at all, let alone remain so cool and dignified. But she did it. Her ability to dissemble is extraordinary.

I kept my overcoat on. I wanted to remain anonymous and I did not want to stand out because of my clothes. I do not own any formal eveningwear; I would look ridiculous in a dress. I slipped into the museum just as the speeches were about to begin.

It was a lavish and glittering affair. The Royal College of Surgeons is quite a venue and its Hunterian Museum was jammed full – there must have been at least two hundred and fifty guests. As I watched all the beautiful people rubbing noses with the grisly exhibits, I could not help but feel awed by the number of friends she has. I moved around the side of the room until I found myself a spot in Curiosities, behind the skeleton of an Irish giant.

Nobody paid me the slightest attention of course. Why would they notice a plain and faceless person hiding in the shadow of a giant?

I could see Olivia trying to get up the stairs and I felt a little sorry for her then. Behind that smile she must be feeling terribly overwhelmed. People kept stopping her to kiss her, take photos and praise her. She just kept smiling, holding her glass of champagne high so that it wouldn't spill. Only those who knew to look for it would see the fear behind the smile and the pallor beneath that make-up.

The speeches were to take place on the balcony, the next floor up. It was far too high. People had to crane to see. She was wearing the eye-catching sulphur dress. I recognized it from the magazine shoot.

A waiter passed with a tray of test tubes that contained a viscous blood-red cocktail. I asked what it was and he said 'Bloody

Mary', with a note of contempt, as if that was surely obvious. I looked at, but did not sample, the witty doctor-themed canapés as they passed by: quail's eggs made to look like eyeballs, each on its own little medicine spoon; cupcakes with red cross designs.

Olivia did look spectacular. Her hair was pulled up in some kind of elaborate knot and her lips were painted dark red. Her shoes were very high and I was worried that she might trip on the stairs, but I suppose she is used to teetering on high heels.

Her editor came onto the balcony, tapping her glass. She introduced herself as Joy. I had always imagined Joy to be a tall, skinny and blonde, social X-ray type, but in fact she is Joy Sekibo, a short and powerful-looking black woman around my age, with cropped grey hair and large red and gold earrings.

The room settled down and everyone listened while Joy gave an enthusiastic rundown of Olivia's talents as a writer, academic, TV star and human being. She then announced that *Annabel* was number two on the bestseller list already and there was a cheer. I could see Olivia's dress, a yellow stain behind the specimen jars in the floor-to-ceiling display case that acted as a screen. I could only imagine what might be going through her mind as she stepped forward and thanked Joy. Then she thanked us all for coming to support her. She looked radiant and sounded gracious and witty, effortlessly holding the crowd's attention. She was used to performing, with all the lectures and talks she has to give. She was used to attention. But beneath the mask, I knew she must be in turmoil.

If the truth came out, she would have such a long way to fall. I imagined that slavering pack turning on her and for a moment I felt weak, as if I might need to sit down. I was forced to lean against the giant's display case and take a few deep breaths.

Perhaps it was the associations that this thought had

brought into my mind but I knew then that I could not do it to her, not here. The memory of my own public shaming sickens me even now, five years on. Sometimes, though I want to forget it, I find myself reliving the moment when I first realized what was happening to me on social media, an invisible world of which I had only, until that day, been hazily aware.

I was sitting at my desk, having just faced the disciplinary board, and a young DPhil student put his head round the door. He told me that I was 'trending' on Twitter. I hardly knew what Twitter was, let alone what 'trending' meant.

Keen to enlighten me, he brought in his open laptop. Somebody I didn't know had 'tweeted' about my transgressions. They called it 'dung gate'. A lot of other people had already weighed in. It is impressive how vicious people can be in 140 characters. The original 'dung gate' comment was 'retweeted' 847 times and 568 people had 'liked' it. Many had also offered brutal personal comments.

'You've gone viral,' the young man smirked. I think, perhaps, this handsome young DPhil student was rather enjoying introducing me to Twitter. He wanted me to know how ashamed I should be of what I'd done. It felt like a physical assault. I was breathless, shaking and had to sit down.

Anonymity, I've learned, brings out the worst in people.

I focused my attention back on Olivia. She was talking about how she had discovered the diary in a 'tiny Sussex museum' and then she described the hard but rewarding work of bringing Annabel to life. I saw her scan the room as she talked and I wondered if she might be looking for me, but I was on the margins at the back, well concealed by the giant.

She spoke movingly about the strictures on Victorian women's lives, about marital cruelty and the exclusively male institution of medicine. The Royal College of Surgeons, she reminded the audience, did not have its first female member until 1910 and even today only 11 per cent of surgical consultants are female. She even mentioned me at the end, though not by name. She at least honoured that part of our agreement. She called me her 'research help'.

She was dazzling. Nobody would ever guess that she was anything other than entitled to be standing up there, looking down at her admirers.

She got what she wanted. *Annabel* is a bestseller. All her hard work publicizing the book has paid off. I have cut extracts out of *The Sunday Times* and the *Mail*, and the interviews with Olivia that have run in several women's magazines and Sunday supplements. I particularly enjoyed her telling one reporter how the diary *'just fell into my hands, as if Annabel had chosen me rather than the other way round'*, how the process of writing was *'freeing'* and *'creative'*; how she'd modelled her style on fiction, consciously playing with suspense, clues and riddles, but how, ultimately, of course, it's not fiction at all, it's fact. Her readers, she said, *'Don't want to feel tricked or lied to, they want the truth'*.

This week she has been on BBC *Breakfast* and GMTV, where she, with great wit and dignity, tried on a Victorian corset and revealed that a Hollywood film company has bought the option to make *Annabel* into a movie.

There have no doubt been intensive social media campaigns but I have not followed those. I will never go onto social media again, not even for this.

Everything she longed for, in other words, has transpired. I feel quite proud of her.

I do wonder if there was any nagging doubt at the back of her mind as the book unfolded. There must have been, but

presumably she ignored it and carried on, like the rolling dung
beetle that always pushes its dung ball in a straight line, regard-
less of what lies in its path; going over obstacles rather than
around them.

   When her speech was over, everyone was whooping and clap-
ping. She looked slightly stunned, and very alone, suddenly, up
there on the balcony. I buttoned my overcoat and slipped round
the back of the room. To my delight, as I was leaving, I noticed a
small case of beetles that had something to do with Darwin, but
sadly I couldn't stop to examine them as I had to get out before
she came downstairs.

   She phoned me twice after she'd been to Three Elms yesterday. She sounded positively deranged. She has emailed me
too – all exclamation marks.

*Where are you?! I have been to see Lady Burley. She told me about
you – your mother and your childhood dog, THOBY!! This can't be
a coincidence, can it? She didn't know about the diary. She said
there was no diary! What is this, Vivian? Why doesn't she know
about the diary? Is it a hoax? What is this?*

   *I have to go back to London for the book launch now but if you
don't call me back I'm going to come back down the day after the
launch and I'm going to wait for you until you agree to talk to me.
This ends here, Vivian! I need the truth!!*

I sent her a text. Just one line.

Come to tea at Ileford the day after your book launch party, 3.30 p.m.

Olivia

The Farmhouse

Her memory of the hours after the launch was somewhat hazy. David had taken the children home – he'd sent Dom over to tell her this – and she went on to a bar in Lincoln's Inn. Chloe came, she hadn't left the party after all, and Joy and Carol and some other people from the publishing house. Emma and Khalil went home, saying they had to get back for the babysitter.

There was heat and hubbub, more champagne, and although she was in agony, overwrought, nerves flayed, she stayed drinking in the bar because she couldn't go home, she couldn't face David. She couldn't deal with the truth. She didn't have the stamina for that after all the people, all the lying and posturing and pretending.

She'd wanted to obliterate everything and for a while she managed that quite well. Chloe eventually pulled the glass from her hand at about 1 a.m. and led her out to a taxi. She had wept in Chloe's arms in the back seat and Chloe had patted her back and told her not to do anything silly, that it would all be OK, that she'd call her first thing in the morning.

She vaguely remembered watching David sleeping on the study pull-out bed, and thinking to herself 'this is the last time I will ever watch him sleep'. His carry-on luggage sat by the door ready for his trip to Copenhagen. She didn't know how long she stood there for; she was drunk, numb with exhaustion. And then she was in Marta's room. Marta had already gone. No doubt she was waiting in a boutique hotel in Copenhagen wearing new lingerie. She pulled a suitcase from under Marta's bed and hurled all the younger woman's belongings into it, including her dirty underwear and boxes of tampons. She remembered zipping it and hauling it to the window, watching it bounce onto the street below and marvelling that it did not burst.

Then she was back in the study. David was on his front, snoring, oblivious. She scribbled a note and put it on his case:

I have gone to Sussex. You are not going to Copenhagen because you have to look after the children. Marta is not to set foot in this house ever again. When I get back – when I am ready – we will talk about this and you will move out.

She remembered taking ibuprofen and drinking glass after glass of water. She must have changed her clothes at some point because she was in jeans and a jumper. She'd sat in the kitchen for the rest of the night, drinking strong coffee, waiting to sober up, with a dangerous, toxic headache blooming at the base of her skull. As the sky through the kitchen window lightened to pigeon grey, before her family woke, she drove away from London.

By mid-morning at the Farmhouse she was feeling very sick indeed. She slept, face down on the sofa, for four hours and when she woke she was hungry. There were ten missed calls from David, six from Chloe. She showered and changed and stared at herself in the mirror. She had aged ten years in twenty-four hours. She was alone now. Her marriage was over. It had been over for a long time, but she had been too afraid to admit it. Instead, she had lied to herself. She had pretended that this gnawing doubt, this lack of trust in David, was fixable. She had told herself that if she worked harder, paid off their debts, achieved more, then eventually everything would get better, everything would be perfect. But while she was busy polishing the outside, the inside had rotted away. She put make-up on, covering her feverish skin with foundation and lining her already darkened eyes.

At ten past three she got into the car again and drove through the lanes to Ileford.

Vivian

Ileford Manor

At 3.28 p.m. exactly I hear her car coming down the drive, under the elms. It stops outside the front of the house, her boots crunch on the gravel, the door slams.

I go to my bedroom window and look down. She is wearing dark grey jeans and a drapey black leather jacket, her favourite high-heeled boots and a voluminous grey scarf. She has smoothed her hair back into a ponytail. The crown of her head reminds me of the elytra of a beautiful black scarab. She must have had the colour done for the party. Looking down on her, like this, she appears smooth and indestructible. Except, of course, she isn't. Beneath her elytra the wings are gossamer and fragile, so easily torn.

She looks up, as if sensing me, and I step back from the window. She always does this. It is as if there is an invisible energy between us that she feels, without realizing it. Olivia always knows when she is being watched.

As I come down the stairs I hear her rap on the front door.

There is righteous hostility behind the knock and my heart hardens a little as I cross the great hall. I will not welcome her through the front door. I will not allow her to take the upper hand again.

I move towards the kitchen, then down the back passage to the scullery door and out into the rear courtyard. The sight of the well further hardens my resolve. Rooks circle the treetops beyond the outhouses, cawing and croaking. I walk round the side. She is standing with her back to me, raising her hand to knock again.

'Olivia,' I say, but not too loud. She startles and turns. I am quite shocked by her appearance. She is very pale despite the make-up. Her eyes look hollow and bruised. I can see the strain that recent events have had on her: she looks thinner and older; her face is very drawn. I can see the fear playing out beneath her skin.

'Oh, Vivian! There you are.'

'Yes, here I am.' I stop at the foot of the front stairs and watch her come down to me. 'I thought we could go for a short walk before we have tea,' I say. 'I haven't been out all day.'

She looks down at herself, frowning. 'I'm not really dressed for a walk.'

'It's still half an hour till teatime and it won't get dark till then. I have wellingtons you can borrow and a coat if you need one.' I see her grit her teeth. 'Come along.' I march back round to the scullery door.

After a second's hesitation, I hear her follow.

In the gunroom I get her to sit on the bench and then watch her try a few pairs of wellington boots until she finds a fit. 'You should borrow a coat too.' Her leather jacket looks thin and she is only wearing a flimsy grey sweater underneath it. It looks like a rag, but probably cost hundreds of pounds. She will be far too cold in the woods.

'I'm fine.' She gets up.

I hear my father's voice in my head: 'I didn't ask if you're fine, I asked if you need a coat.' But I don't say the words out loud, I simply say, 'Well, it's up to you.'

'It'll be getting dark soon so we won't be going far anyway, will we?' She zips up her jacket. Her scarf is large, though that, too, is made of gauzy material. Does she not realize it is October and cold, with rain threatening?

'Will we, Vivian?'

'Will we what?'

'Be going far.'

'Sunset is at 4.11,' I say. 'We have half an hour, so no, not far.'

My Barbour isn't on its hook, I must have left it in the kitchen, so I have to take the overcoat I wore the night before, my city overcoat. I slide off my shoes, then lever my own wellingtons on. I wince as I do this and wish that my knee were less sore. I lead her out of the gunroom then and lock the door. We cross the courtyard side by side. The clouds are lowering, darkening, presaging a night of wind and rain.

I make sure that we walk right by the well. She looks away as we pass it and says nothing.

We go into the woods by the muddy path behind the outhouses. The bleak light fades further as we enter the blotting canopy of oak and ash, our footsteps muffled by layers of dead leaves over clay. It takes a moment for my eyes to adjust to the dimness. Somewhere above us rookeries are filling with returning foragers; their croaks and caws echo round the otherwise still woodland.

I find that I still can't come here without keeping my ears

pricked for Bertie, even though I know that he is not trapped and never was. It is as if, over the past eight months, I have internalized Olivia's lie and a part of my mind cannot stop believing that he is still here somewhere, still needing to be saved.

It is, I've realized, entirely possible to hold two realities in one's mind simultaneously, and to believe them both at a visceral level.

Olivia walks with her shoulders back and her hands shoved into her jacket pockets. 'Well,' she says in a clipped, efficient voice. 'I'm glad we could meet at last. You've been avoiding me.'

'Yes, I have.'

She glances at me, perhaps surprised by my honesty. 'I'm guessing you're still upset with me?'

I say nothing.

'It's just, you didn't come to the launch so I assume you are upset still,' she continues, 'though I wish you weren't.'

'Yes, I expect you do.'

She slows down. 'OK, look,' she says. 'We could go round and round in circles again, I could say sorry again, but can we shelve all that, just for now? There are some really important things that I need to discuss with you.'

'More important than Bertie?'

'Would you like me to apologize again?' She gives a brittle smile. 'I will if you want me to.'

'I don't need you to say sorry again.'

'OK then.'

The track narrows as we go deeper into the woods. We are still side by side and scratchy hazel branches claw at our bodies but she just shoves them out of the way.

'So Vivian,' she says, 'I was wondering. Why did you tell me Lady Burley had dementia? I've been to see her, you know.'

'I know you have. I never told you she has dementia.'

'Yes, you did!'

'When?'

'Well . . . I don't know exactly when but you definitely . . . If you didn't say it *outright*, you certainly very much implied it.'

'I can't control what you think I'm implying, Olivia.'

'Oh my God, Vivian, you know what I mean!'

'I'm not sure I do, Olivia. I've always given you the facts. Lady Burley has occasional memory lapses, probably as a result of the medication she's on. She can get a bit confused about timescales and names. She also gets very anxious and fatigued.'

'Can we stop playing games now, Vivian, please?'

She sounds exasperated, but I don't understand why. 'I don't play games. I've never lied to you about Lady Burley. She's eighty-six, she has cancer for which she has to take a lot of medication. The doctor says she hasn't got long to live. These are the facts, how you choose to interpret them has nothing to do with me.'

'But – it's . . . You're . . . For God's sake, Vivian, you know exactly what I mean. You've been obstructive!'

'Have I? I've just been doing the right thing. If I'd let you bother Lady Burley for the past eighteen months you would have dominated what's left of her life and I couldn't possibly allow that. It wouldn't be fair to her. She's probably only lasted this long because she's been so happy and comfortable at Three Elms. She loves it there. I just want to make sure that whatever time she has left is peaceful. I had no idea that she'd survive until publication, of course. Over a year ago the doctor said she might not even make it to Christmas. It's a miracle that she's still alive now. I've done what I believed was right, maybe not for me or for you, but for Lady Burley.'

Olivia stops walking. 'Whether or not you lied specifically to me about Lady Burley, you've put me in a very difficult position, Vivian. If I'd have known she was compos mentis I'd have—'

'What? Demanded interviews, begged for materials and stories, required access to this, that and the other, pressurized her into letting you poke around her private things, revealed to her that one of her relatives was an alcoholic brute and the other a murderer?'

'No! I'd have been open and honest with her!'

'Oh,' I say, darkly. 'Yes. I forgot. You're big on that aren't you? Honesty. *Integrity.*'

'What on earth's that supposed to mean?'

'*I* acted with integrity,' I say.

'OK. Whatever. I've given her a copy of *Annabel* now.' Olivia starts walking again, pulling ahead of me and shoving her hands back into her pockets.

I interrupt. 'She won't read it. She hasn't read anything other than a Georgette Heyer in decades. Her eyes aren't good enough to read a book now, even if she wanted to, which she won't.'

She snaps – 'That's really not the point!' – and I feel how fragile she is beneath this outrage, how close she is to crumbling.

And who can blame her? Her marriage is obviously in trouble – she isn't wearing her wedding ring – her children are out of control and her career could well implode. Even though she is behaving as if she has the moral high ground, I suddenly feel sorry for her. She looks so shaken. I'm not sure I can do this. I'm not sure I want to do this.

'Lady Burley has two photos of Annabel. You know how badly we needed those,' she says crossly.

I had no idea she had photos of Annabel. Lady Burley always did have a devious streak and I rather admire her for it. I imagine she wanted to save that little piece of glory for when Olivia eventually came to see her. She'd probably planned to whip the photos out and watch Olivia's face light up, then soak in all the gratitude.

'I don't know why you're smiling, Vivian. She had all sorts of other things too, she remembers Uncle Quentin talking about Annabel's wolfhound. She had a story – an actual direct *memory* from Uncle Quentin – of Annabel performing an autopsy on the dog on the croquet lawn. That's a gold-dust story. But anyway, none of this is what I'm most bothered about. This isn't why I had to speak to you. What I'm really, really bothered about is the dog.'

'The dog?' I have to hand it to her, she does have an eye for detail.

We are deep in the woods, now, crossing the creek where Bertie loved to splash. The light is thick and muted, as if an old military blanket has been dropped over the treetops.

'You must know what dog!' Her voice is hard. 'Thoby. The terrier in Annabel's diary.' She stops and stares at me. The tip of her nose is red and despite the gloom her irises are bright. '*Thoby*, Vivian?'

I try to make my face impassive. I can smell the rotting leaves beneath our feet. A squirrel undulates across our path, clutching a nut, scoots up the tree trunk and vanishes into the tangle of branches above us. I move off. She follows.

'Annabel's dog, in 1898, was a wolfhound called Filcher. He's in the photograph. Lady Burley says the Burleys only ever had wolfhounds. And this is where it gets really unsettling: she told me your childhood dog was called Thoby.'

So, they talked about that, too. She really must have worked it out now.

Her skin looks translucent in this half-light, as if she is

beginning to dissolve from the inside out. There is something about her face that makes me think of my mother and I feel a familiar jolt of longing mixed with fear. Of course, my perception of my mother's physical state is very muddied because when she visits me at night she is always so mutilated and frightening. My mother's face is the colour of parchment, her eyes are ink smears; you cannot see her irises and the gash on her forehead seeps.

Olivia is talking again. 'What I can't get my head around is how expert the diary is, if it's a hoax. It's been authenticated.' She sounds as if she's talking to herself, trying to lay it all out in order to persuade herself that her fears are misguided. 'The ink shows the right compounds for the kind used in the late 1800s. The paper's definitely from the period and the handwriting, the phrasing, it's all completely authentic too.'

'Of course,' I say. The path has become muddy; clay sucks at our boots. Ahead, I can see my hollow oak and the little mound at its feet, and I remember how, in summertime, I used to happily sit in its shade and watch Bertie on his frantic search for rabbits.

'Is it a fake, Vivian?' She half-whispers it, as if we might be overheard in the middle of a Sussex wood. 'Was it Uncle Quentin? Is that what this is? Was he trying to destroy his stepmother's reputation?'

It is interesting to see Olivia struggle with the facts like this. It must take quite an effort for her not to articulate what, deep down, she must know. I can see her fear tenting, inflating, threatening to take off. 'I know you know,' she hisses. 'Tell me!'

I bring her to a halt by the neat mound of earth, but she doesn't even notice it. She is too busy being frightened of the truth.

'She shoved Quentin in a boarding school aged three; he hated her. He could have had a Victorian notebook lying around

Ileford, he could have had some Victorian ink too. He was a story-teller, wasn't he? Did he fake the diary, then change his mind about going public with it?' Her skin has shrunk around her eyes, making them bulge. Suddenly, her voice rises, sharply. 'Vivian! You have to tell me the truth. Have we lied? Have we duped the public – *my public*?'

It is almost a child-like cry and it startles the rooks; they fling themselves into the sky, panicking, their rasping caws echoing across the tree canopy that stretches above us.

She hasn't even noticed where we're standing. I suppose the headstone is quite small, but it was the biggest I could carry to this spot with my bad knee. I carved the words into it myself using a screwdriver, so perhaps they are a little hard to make out. But she doesn't so much as glance down. Her eyes are fixed on me.

I look away. It is too much to meet her gaze. I suddenly remember my teenage obsession with collective nouns. I used to make lists of them: a watch of nightingales, a stare of owls, a mutation of thrushes, a murder of crows. I look at my hollow oak and I think of all the life teeming inside her, unseen, concealed, unappreciated but vital.

When I manage to look at Olivia again her face has screwed itself up like a crushed ball of paper. 'Jesus Christ, Vivian! Talk to me!'

'Do you know,' I say. 'Some people maintain that the collective noun for beetles should be a "fondness"? It came from a famous saying that God, if he existed, must have had a distinct fondness for beetles because he made so many of them – about four hundred thousand known species and goodness knows how many that have not yet been discovered. It's a rather pleasant collective noun, isn't it? Unlike that for crows.'

'Why are you talking about this now?' she cries. 'Are you mad?'

'Mad? I don't think so. I just think people should know that one in four species on this planet is a beetle. It's staggering when you think about it. They're everywhere, they make our planet function, but we rarely even notice them.'

Two puce spots have appeared on Olivia's cheekbones. 'I'm not going to start talking to you about beetles, Vivian! I can't even go there with you right now. That's a whole other conversation we need to have, but not now. Definitely not now.'

I consider telling her that the collective noun for historians is an argumentation, but instead I say, 'Uncle Quentin didn't do this, Olivia.'

Her face drains of any remaining colour. She stares at me with dark eyes.

I look down at Bertie's mound. I almost feel that I should give her some privacy, now, let her get there on her own, which she will, because a part of her has been there for eighteen months.

Olivia is astoundingly good at lying to herself. It is perhaps her greatest talent.

I notice a dead branch next to Bertie's stone. Clumps of black-fingered, white-tipped candlesnuff fungus have pushed through the pores of the wood. They look both sinister and beautiful.

Her voice is low and shaky. 'What are you saying, Vivian? What do you know?'

'What do I know?' I shove my hands in the deep overcoat pockets. Here we go. 'What do I know? Well, quite a lot, as it happens. I know that it is possible, though not easy, to source a Victorian notebook – some auctions or antiquarian bookshops, including one in Lewes, have them. Finding an unused one is tricky, but you can always tear a few pages out. I know that it's relatively simple to source ink from the 1890s in auction too. You can even get it on eBay, believe it or not, though I wouldn't have relied on that. I know that the writing of that era can be close to a modern hand and that it is actually quite hard to disguise your own handwriting, even with a lot of effort, using an unfamiliar dip pen. You have to think carefully about the construction, spacing, pressure and size of each letter, and to keep it consistent. But, like most things in life, if you are dogged, if you really put your mind to it, focus, stick at it and master the detail, then it is perfectly possible to develop great skill in calligraphy and expertise in forgery.'

Her hands are covering her mouth now; her long white fingers, punctuated by dark nail polish, press against her lips.

'I also know that if you read enough Victorian letters in the British Library archives, then you will find that eventually the idiom of a spirited lady of the period comes quite naturally, though it is always best to double check phrases and words in the *Oxford English Dictionary* to be sure that the citation comes before the date from which you are composing.'

High above us the disturbed rooks wheel and caw, reluctant to return to their rookeries.

'I also know, Olivia, that narcissism, egotism, the desire for glory, trumps good sense. Privileged people, I've found, are particularly prone to this failing. The more superior a person considers themselves to be, the less trouble they have believing that wonderful things will just drop into their laps. They call it "fate", or "kismet", "destiny", "karma". They say things like, "The universe just wants me to do this." They accept an improbable gift horse because have an unshakable belief that they're special and therefore special things will happen to them.'

She is rooted to the spot, ghoulishly white.

'I also know that *integrity* seems ever so black or white until it's tested, at which point it quickly turns very grey indeed.'

She cannot speak. I really do feel sorry for her now. I always thought that when I taught her this lesson, showed her my proof, I would feel triumphant. I do not. I actually feel very uncomfortable. Her eyes are huge and horrified. I want to stop but I can't because all this has been stacked inside me for a long time and the truth needs to come out, even though the telling is unpleasant for both of us.

'It suited you not to question the diary too deeply,' I continue, 'just as it was convenient for you that I did most of the legwork. It suited you to ignore certain facts and to invent things and leave things to me. I'm the only person who knows the truth about all this. That probably makes you very nervous. You're wondering if I'm going to go public.'

I can see my revelations darting over the surface of her mind like whirligig beetles, chaotic, uncatchable, too fast to pin down. She has been holding it all together, but now it is all coming down around her. Suddenly, her posture collapses. She looks hunched and battered. I don't want to see her this way. She looks damaged. I don't really want to hurt her like this. I'm fond of her. I realize that, in fact, I want to help her.

And all at once I know how to do that. I can see a way out – for both of us. There is a way forward that would suit us both perfectly. It would mean putting the past aside. It would mean forgiveness. A challenge, but perhaps we are capable of it.

She drops her hands and then I see that her mouth has twisted into an ugly, queer shape. 'You're *demented*, Vivian.'

I feel as if she has reached out and slapped my face.

'Jesus Christ! How could you *do* this to me?'

'You did this to yourself, Olivia.'

'How could you turn on me like this?'

I stiffen. 'I'm not your disciple. I don't owe you anything.'

'I always knew you were unstable. Lady Burley told me about your mother's accident, you being trapped in the car. I know you're damaged by that, Vivian, I understand, but this! Jesus Christ. This is just deranged. It's vindictive! Why would you *do* this to me?'

I was not prepared for her to mention my mother. That feels like a second blow. I turn away, lurch a few paces, but then my foot catches on the fallen branch and I topple sideways onto Bertie's grave, going down on my bad knee. I feel my patella grind into the headstone; a vicious, sharp white sound travels up my leg. Everything goes black for a second.

I grasp my knee and cry out, but she has spun away from me; she is half running already, in too-big wellingtons, jumping over tree stumps, pushing through hazel branches, sticks snapping beneath her, fleeing from me like a startled animal. Her grey scarf floats and flutters behind her as the trees swallow her up.

I lean down and hold my knee in both hands. The pain is very great. I am not even sure that I can get up unaided. Perhaps it is broken. But she has gone.

After a bit, I'm not sure how long, I manage to roll slowly onto my hands and somehow haul my body off the ground, using the tree trunk for leverage. I brush myself down, then, and try to put some weight on the leg. It is very painful indeed, but I don't think it is broken. I find a stout stick and begin to hop after her, leaning all my weight on the stick instead of on my leg. I am very slow, the pain is distracting; it makes me feel quite detached.

As I trace her footsteps back through the curious trees I wonder how long it will take Olivia to realize that she has nowhere to run to.

Olivia

Ileford Woods

It was the snapshot that did it, the instant when Vivian lurched to one side and stumbled a few paces towards the oak tree. It was suddenly clear. Vivian's shape slotted perfectly into the other shape that, for four years now, had lived in the frightened part of her brain.

It was the way the overcoat hung off Vivian's shoulders, seen from behind and slightly sideways; the way she held herself a little off kilter, her head lowered, the back of her cropped hair and the edge of an ear visible above the overcoat collar. It was the light too, perhaps, the shadows of the darkening wood. She knew then with complete certainty that Vivian was the person who'd followed her in London all those times. Vivian was her stalker. She hadn't been hallucinating. She hadn't invented it. It wasn't stress-related paranoia or imaginings, it was Vivian. Vivian in her man's overcoat.

It was Vivian she'd seen in the alley near her office as she went into the cafe each day for her cappuccino; Vivian in the archway at the end of a tube platform and in the street by her house. And then last night, standing at the back of the room by the Irish giant. It wasn't a man; it wasn't a stranger. Or maybe it had been, once. Because Vivian had been following her before she even knew who Vivian was.

This moment of realization made Olivia turn away, electric with fear. Instinct took over then, the overwhelming need to get out of the woods to a place of safety. But even as she ran, wildly, trying to find the path through the trees, weighed down by the wellingtons on the end of her legs, stumbling over roots and stumps, her knees weak, gasping for air, her heart straining and branches whipping at her body, she knew there was no path out of here, that nowhere would ever be safe now. She would never get away from Vivian.

Vivian

Ileford Manor

It is getting dark as I hobble through the gate into the courtyard. We are late for tea, now, it is past four o'clock and the sky has faded so that everything looks gloomy and monochrome. The kitchen and gunroom lights cast a yellowish stain on the gravel. The house looks down as I hobble past the well. I can feel its curiosity. What will I do now?

It has taken me a while to get back and I cannot see Olivia. I wonder if she has taken her car and returned to London. Even if she has, she will be back.

Then I see movement in the shadow by the gunroom door and I realize she is standing on the step, waiting for me. As I get closer, I see that the front of her jacket and her thighs are smeared with clay. She must have fallen whilst running away from me. There is a rub of dirt across her cheek. I see that she is smiling, weakly, pathetically. She holds out a hand to me. It is trembling.

'Vivian,' she says. 'I'm sorry you fell. I'm sorry I ran. I

panicked. We really need to talk about this, don't we? Could we just talk? This is a huge muddle, but we can sort this out, I know we can.'

I ignore her outstretched hand. I pull out the key and unlock the gunroom door.

She levers off her muddy wellingtons on the boot scraper and carries them over the threshold. I hobble in and sit on the bench.

I hold up a foot and gesture at it. She bends like servant and pulls off my boot. The pain makes me wince. 'Is it very bad? Do you need to see a doctor? Should I drive you to the doctor's?'

I don't reply. I look at the ceiling. I feel her looking at me. The patch where the leak was still needs plastering and painting. It has been on my list since the early summer.

'Shall we warm up and see? We need to warm up, don't we? I'm freezing. You must be too.' She is desperately trying to work out how to behave, what she needs to say in order to make this go away. It is quite awkward.

I limp ahead of her down to the kitchen. She walks slowly, keeping her distance, a few paces behind. I fill the kettle and keep my weight on my left leg. She tries to get me to sit down, but I ignore her, so she makes small talk and hugs herself. She is remarkably good at this. Her voice sounds almost normal. She talks about the chilly weather and advises me to clear out Ileford's drains as she, herself, has just had a terrible bill at the Farmhouse from a damp expert, in part because of a blocked drainpipe. Is she trying to win me round with banalities?

As I wait for the kettle to boil I try to distract myself from the pain by listing to myself the household beetles by their common names, which always rather delight me: the larder beetle, bacon beetle, cigarette beetle, drugstore beetle, biscuit beetle, furniture beetle, carpet beetle . . .

I give her the mugs of tea to carry to the kitchen table and we sit on opposite sides, facing one another. I try to stretch my leg out, but the knee does not want to straighten. I think it may be swelling badly now, pressing against my trouser. Olivia's make-up has smudged beneath her eyes, her hair has come half loose and her lipstick has almost vanished. She no longer cares. She puts both hands around her mug. She has taken my pheasant mug. I reach for it and she flinches. I ignore this and prise it out of her hands, then push the one with flowers towards her.

'Oh, sorry,' she says. 'Is that your pheasant mug? It's pretty.'

'Yes,' I say. 'I like pheasants.'

'Well . . .' She offers a weak smile. 'What a muddle, Vivian. What a muddle we've got ourselves into here.' Perhaps she thinks that if she keeps using childish words, this problem will shrink and vanish. It is rather touching.

I take the knife that I left on the table and slice through a chunk of the Battenberg that I'd got out in preparation for her visit. The marzipan has gone a bit crusty but it can't be helped. I put a piece on a plate and hand it to her, then cut one for myself. I look at the cake and for a second I forget about my knee as I admire the artifice of it, the garish colours, the pleasing geometry. I bite into it and feel the extravagant over-sweetness fill my mouth.

She looks at the Battenberg but doesn't touch it. I am disappointed as I want to feed her. She looks so wan and fragile.

She lifts her tea and blows on it and her eyelids close. I see that she is exhausted. Her eyes open again and behind the carefully crafted calm I see what must be panic. I finish the rest of my Battenberg in two bites and dust my hands off.

'One thing that's bothered me, Vivian . . .' She puts the mug down, '. . . is that I feel like you've never really been properly paid for your work. I mean, I know I tried, I tried quite hard actually, to get you to agree to more money, a share of the royalties, but maybe I should have tried even harder? I know you didn't want a share of the profits but that was before we got onto the bestseller lists, wasn't it? We've sold the film rights now, too. I was going to tell you about that, but it's been so . . . so . . . you've been . . . But look, Vivian, what I'm saying is I want you to accept more money. I want you to be paid properly for your work. You earned it.'

If money is the only way she can think of to get rid of me, then she really is floundering. Does she actually believe that she can pay me to go away? I sip my tea and feel it flush the sweet, sticky cake from my tooth enamel. I am not sure how low she has to go before she comes back up to meet me.

'I don't need any money,' I say. 'I have a place to live and plenty to live on. Lady Burley is leaving Ileford to me. I don't want it, as it happens, but it would be cruel to refuse her, as I'm the closest thing she has to family. On the current property market Ileford is worth up to £3 million. Not that I'll be able to sell it. It would be wrong to sell because she doesn't want it inhabited by hedge fund managers. The point is, this is not about money, Olivia.'

'Then what *is* it about?' She presses her hands on the table, flat. 'I don't understand. I don't know why you've done this to me.' The dark clots of her nail polish have chipped, perhaps from where she fell in the woods. She is trying so hard to control her tone. She looks wispy and deranged now, but also cross. I can see the difficult old lady inside her filing a claim for that beautiful face. 'What have I ever done to you?'

I drum my fingers next to her untouched square of cake. 'Other than kill Bertie?'

'Other than the horrible accident with Bertie, for which I am profoundly, profoundly, sorry and always will be. But this can't be about Bertie, can it? I mean, you must have planned this long before Bertie died. It was you, wasn't it, I saw you, near my office . . . and . . . other places?' She definitely looks a little afraid.

'You're right. This was nothing to do with Bertie. It first occurred to me to do this about four and a half years ago. It took quite a while to master the relevant skills, I'm not a historian like you. It took me two years to create a diary to a sufficiently high standard to fool a Victorian documents expert, but I knew it could be done, hoaxes have been done before, and by people far less clever than me.'

'But . . . Oh *God*, Vivian. *Why?*'

I sit back. My knee throbs demonically. 'It's a long story.'

'You have to tell me. Tell me what this is about. Then maybe we can straighten this out?'

'Right then!' The force of my voice makes her jump and sit up straight. 'I need you to go up to my office. My knee is painful and I don't think I can manage the stairs. Can you do that?'

'Your office?'

'Don't pretend you don't know where my office is.' I smile at her. 'I watched you climb in the gunroom window the day before yesterday. I heard you come upstairs.'

She blinks. 'Jesus. You were *here*?'

'I've actually been waiting for you to ask me about my office.'

'Your beetles?'

Now it's my turn to blink in disbelief. 'Of course, my beetles. What else?'

'I . . . You . . .' She can't formulate a coherent sentence so I give her directions on where to find the file on my desk. 'Just bring it down.'

Obediently, she gets up and leaves the room. I hear her trot up the staircase and along the corridor above me. I try again to straighten my knee. The pain has subsided, just a little, and it is very numb and tight. I want it to be a bad bruise, but I know, deep down, that it's more than that and I should probably be at the doctor's. It is dark outside. She's right, the kitchen is freezing. I reach out and touch the radiator. It is icy. The central heating must have misfired again. There is a faint, mournful wind coming down the chimneys. I do not want to have to go down to the cellars with my knee like this to deal with the boilers, but I will probably have to or we'll freeze to death.

After a few moments I hear her coming back with the correct file. Her eyes are wide as she steps back into the kitchen so I know she's looked at it. She hands it to me and slips back into her seat. I can see that she is confused and not a little disturbed as to what I am doing with copies of her correspondence with the Oxford University Museum of Natural History. Her brows are knotted. She is breathing fast.

I decide it's best to read it out before I try to explain, so she'll remember exactly what she wrote. I find the letter I want and begin to read.

> Dear Darren,
>
> I am writing to thank you for what you have done to protect my father's precious legacy and for sending back his original Archeocopris olivia *photographs.*

I look up. She is really alarmed, now, very pale indeed. She opens her mouth, but I silence her with a shake of my head.

I am so glad they enabled you to expose this awful attempt to sabotage my father's life's work. I knew, when I read Ballard's Nature *paper, that my father would never have made a mistake of that magnitude. Of course, I didn't have the skills to find out what was going on, but you did, and I will be forever grateful to you and your team at the Museum of Natural History for taking my objection seriously. By comparing Professor Ballard's images of the faked fossil with the original photographs I sent, you have uncovered this terrible fraud and restored my father's reputation.*

I am of course concerned – and very shocked – that it was possible to steal the original specimen, switch it for a fake and dupe the scientific community in this way. However, I am glad that our original amber fossil has now been recovered and is safe again with you. It takes a particularly warped personality to do something like this, and I am glad to hear that Ballard's career as a coleopterist is now over – forever.

I look up at her again. She is rigid and unblinking. I can't help but smile as I read the next bit.

I'd like to reiterate that I have no desire for any further contact with the department or the university on this matter, and certainly not with Ballard. This has been very distressing for me and since I'm now being considered for a professorship myself I can't allow any more distractions at this point.

As I read out the next sentences I barely need to look at the words. They wounded me so deeply in the past but, interestingly, they seem to have lost their power.

Integrity is everything in academia. Without it, we might as well not exist, so I am very glad that this unscrupulous individual has been publicly exposed.

'You are righteous,' I say, 'when it comes to other peoples' mistakes, aren't you?'

For a while, she doesn't reply. I am sure that her brain is working insanely hard to understand how I am connected to all this. Eventually, she says, 'Were you a friend of Professor Ballard? Is that what this is? You weren't . . . Were you his wife, Vivian?'

I make a tutting sound. 'You assumed Professor Ballard was a man? You should know better than that, Olivia.'

'What do you mean?'

'You still don't know? Really?' I do smile then. 'Oh, for goodness' sake! If you hadn't interfered, my life would be entirely different. Science isn't as rigorous as you'd think. Nobody checked my fake fossil or examined it against the original photographs until you made them. This isn't the first time data has been fabricated or manipulated, or images falsified in a big scientific paper, and it won't be the last.'

'You're . . . Are you saying . . .?'

'Yes.' I nod encouragingly. 'That's right, Olivia. I'm Professor Ballard. Or I was before you had me erased.'

Olivia

Ileford Manor

The words Vivian had just spoken didn't line up. She was having problems even thinking now. Her throat felt parched, her head hurt. Her limbs felt weak.

Vivian was plainly – frighteningly – mad.

She needed to calm down. She had to think about this rationally. But she hadn't had enough sleep to think rationally; everything felt chaotic, as if she were living in a speeded up, out of control film. Everything was moving so fast that bits of her mind were coming loose and flying off.

And now, sitting at Vivian's table, listening to this bizarre revelation, the pressure inside her skull felt immense. She felt as if her brow might explode and spray her exhausted brains across the table.

She looked at Vivian's square, blank face, the little, alert eyes, fixed on something just to one side of her, that strange, encouraging smile.

She leaned on her elbows to steady herself, steepling her fingers against her temples. 'What in God's name,' she said, 'are you talking about?'

Vivian

Ileford Manor

She blinks rapidly and whispers it again. 'What *in God's name* are you talking about, Vivian?'

'Well I did mention, the day we first met, that I was a retired Oxford professor. Sadly, you didn't believe me. It does seem rather ironic that you, with your professional interest in women, should assume that D.V.P. Ballard was a man. The 'D' is for Dorothy, that's my Christian name, after my mother, though I've always been called Vivian, which is my middle name. I've used initials professionally ever since I submitted an early paper as Dr Dorothy Ballard, had it rejected, then submitted the exact same paper two years later as D.V. P. Ballard and had it published.' Olivia seems flabbergasted. 'I know,' I nod. 'You wouldn't believe what we had to put up with in those days. The 'P' is for Penelope, in case you wondered, dreadful name. But since D.V.P. Ballard is now synonymous with scientific misconduct and public disgrace, it seemed prudent not to call myself Ballard any more. Tester was my mother's maiden name. I don't like it much, but there you are. You erased D.V. P. Ballard five years ago.'

Olivia's neck and chest have turned blotchy. If she'd Googled me as Ballard, at the time, which she must have, she would have found academic papers in which I am cited as D.V. P. My zoology department profile picture was a grainy shot of me squatting in a hat, field jacket and khakis next to a Land Rover, entirely genderless. I have always hated being photographed and avoided it whenever possible, so there are probably few images of me out there. My university profile was written in the first person, I have never been on social media and I certainly do not have a website. If Olivia had spotted conference pictures it would have been very easy to mistake my gender. I possibly do look a little bit masculine.

I wear slacks, always have, and I've kept my hair like this since the seventies, when Sweetman was asking me to babysit and make the tea. I remember exactly what triggered me to cut it off. Her father was leading a visiting American scientist through the lab and I heard him apologize for 'all the women', adding, 'at least they're decorative'. The only women at the time were me and my lab assistant. I went into Brighton and had my hair cropped that afternoon. I don't think I look like a man, as such, but people see what they expect to see. So if you're looking for a male scientist you'll probably see one.

She is gaping at me, white-faced and visibly shaken. I honestly cannot fathom why she has not worked this out before, particularly when she went into my office. But she always was too preoccupied to notice what was right beneath her nose. It is possible that in all this time she has never really looked at me properly.

When she walked into the museum that day, I was braced for

recognition. It was always a gamble. I knew that our first meeting would be the make-or-break test. If she hadn't cut off from the whole sorry business, as she said she would in that letter – which I stole from Darren's in-tray – she would have recognized me that day and my endeavour would have failed before it even began. Two years of hard work would have come to nothing.

But she did what she said she would in her letter, she cut off. She focused wholly on her own life instead. She was awarded her UCL professorship and she built up the media career that was just beginning to take off at that time. I suppose she was too busy to further look into, or obsess on, the sad and twisted professor who had tried but failed to ruin her father's name.

There was not the slightest glimmer of recognition on her face in the museum that first day. She had absolutely no idea who I was.

I prod at the yellow crumbs along the knife blade. 'By insisting your father could not have been wrong, by sending in his original photo of the fossil and urging them to investigate, you had a devastating impact on my life, you know. I lost absolutely everything.'

'*I* had a devastating impact?' Her cheeks have gone a greenish hue beneath the make-up. I'm actually slightly worried that she might collapse. 'You did this to *yourself*, Vivian.'

She has her fingers pressed against her temples and every so often she shivers, quite violently. It is very cold without the heating and I'm getting worried about her. She looks really odd. 'Are you all right, Olivia? Are you cold? Why don't you put that blanket over your shoulders?'

'You're insane,' she whispers.

I harden then, and wave her letter at her. 'I particularly like "*Integrity is everything*".'

'This is *revenge*?'

'Actually, no, this was an experiment. I set out to prove, to myself as much as to you, that you'd do the same if the tables were turned. You'd be prepared to lie and defraud the public if everything you'd worked for all your life – your home, your life-style, your career, your identity, your status – was at stake. Most of us would, wouldn't we?'

She hugs herself with both arms and shakes her head, whether in disbelief or denial I do not know.

'It did get rather out of hand,' I concede. 'I mean, I had no idea you'd have ambitions to write a biography. I thought you'd publish a paper about the diary and then I'd tell you the truth. You'd beg me not to expose you, thereby demonstrating that all your talk of integrity is nonsense. You'd see you were no better than me. I was angry, I admit it. It's possible that I wasn't very well at the time.'

'You aren't well now, Vivian!'

I wave this away; it is too easy, too dull, for her to dismiss me as mad. 'You never once asked yourself why someone like me, who'd produced impeccable research for decades, would go to such lengths to fabricate data and publish it in *Nature*.'

'You hated my father? You were jealous of him?'

'Hate is a strong word and I certainly wasn't jealous. Your father was my mentor, he was my teacher.'

She stares at me with round eyes.

'I was his graduate student in the eighties, didn't you realize that? I do have a few reasons to be upset with him, in fact.'

I find that I do not have the heart, even now, to tell her the full truth about her father. She is so enamoured with his memory, and his massive status matters so deeply to her, it would destroy her to know the truth. So, instead, I share some of my more minor gripes. 'Your father was a sexist man. He gave me less space than the male graduates in the lab and fewer resources. He once told me he didn't want to give me as much time as the men because I'd only leave to get married.'

'Now I know this is rubbish! He was *never* sexist!' Her eyes flash, always ready to defend the Goliath.

'Well, they were different times of course, the early eighties, but I'm afraid you're wrong about that. He even had me babysit you once. Don't look so appalled. You Sweetmans have rather a habit of getting me to look after your children, don't you? I remember it very clearly, I wonder if you do? You must have been ten or eleven, I suppose. Your school was closed for a day, I think. There were five male scientists in the lab – and me. Your father walked up to my desk with you and told me to take you to the Palace Pier for an ice cream.'

Her eyelids flicker and I wonder whether she is dredging up a wispy memory of that day. She was a nervy, whiny child, used to getting her way, I suppose. She wanted to go on the helter-skelter but I wouldn't let her. I was livid that I'd been put in this situation and I was never good with children. I seem to remember she cried a bit towards the end and demanded to be taken home.

I'm not sure whether it is the memory of Brighton Pier, or the idea that I once babysat her, or perhaps the realization that her sainted father was a male chauvinist pig, but she looks very distressed indeed now and I find that I don't want to upset her any further.

I just want her to understand. I want her to know that while I may have allowed my compulsive tendencies to get the better of me, that while I may have got in over my head trying to prove a point, I am not a malevolent person. I just need her to understand why I did what I did.

'Let's go back to the question of why I fabricated that *Nature* paper in the first place,' I say.

'Yes, let's. Why?'

'Well, I was almost sixty and the department wanted to get rid of me. You can't be the lone scientist in the lab nowadays. It's all about income generation and public profile. There was enormous pressure on us to secure millions in research grants. We were meant to form international networks, accept plenaries and visiting lectureships. I really don't have the patience or aptitude for any of those things. International travel upsets me and I'm a very poor collaborator. They wanted us all to be "media friendly" too – can you imagine? I can't pretend to be something I'm not. I didn't have the time or energy for it; I just wanted to get on with my research.

'Which, by the way, was superlative. I always scored extremely highly on all their "impact factors" charts. I was internationally respected, doing very important ecological work, but that wasn't enough for them. They started talking about early retirement. They began to make my life difficult, and I did think about going. Then I discovered that when I retired I'd get my pension, but everything else would be taken away from me: my college life, my space in the lab and, worst of all, my house. Apparently an Edwardian house in north Oxford is now worth a great deal of money. The college owned my house and they were going to take it back. My only hope of keeping it was to become a "name". If I went out in a blaze of glory then they'd give me an emeritus professorship, they'd let me stay in my house and continue with my work and keep all my college privileges. I realized I was going to have to produce a piece of research with huge international repercussions, and as you know, that kind of thing – those moments of real career impact – only happen once in a lifetime, if at all.'

She is frowning deeply. 'What? So you wrote a fraudulent paper debunking my father's evolutionary theory in order to *keep your house*?'

When she puts it like that it does sound petty, if not a little insane. But she doesn't understand what I'm trying to tell her, not really. 'My routines – home, work, college life,' I say. 'Those things were vital to me. I'm not good at transitions and I'd lived in my house for over thirty years. It was my home, my place of safety, my refuge. It was a part of me. And college life – dining in Formal Hall, the cycles of the academic year – those things were my stabilizers. They protected me, they were my elytra—'

'Your *what*?'

'Never mind. My shelter, my security. They imposed order on what otherwise feels to me like dangerous chaos. It's hard to overstate how important these things were to me. My home mattered as much to me as your children matter to you.'

'Oh, I very much doubt that!' She balls her fists on the table and her eyeballs strain in her head. 'You did a really heinous thing, Vivian. You must have spent God knows how many months creating a faked amber specimen to photograph so you could "debunk" my father's life work and legacy. You didn't care what that would do to me or anyone else who loved him. And now you're trying to destroy me too!'

'But I'm not.' I tighten my grip on the knife. 'I told you. This – you, the diary – I just wanted to show you that you aren't as morally impeccable as you think you are. You and I are the same, really.'

'We *so* aren't, Vivian!' Her laugh is harsh.

For a moment we sit in silence. She is thinking, I assume.

'How long did it take you to create the diary?' she says. 'You seriously perfected the art. I mean, to dupe my friend at the

British Museum, a world-leading expert, you must have worked obsessively on this, *forensically*. And for what? To trick me? To pay me back for some imagined crime – or crime by association?'

This is all going wrong. I just want her to understand me but I can see that she never will. Someone like her can't possibly understand someone like me. She is a different species. She is staring at me as if I am a repulsive to her. In her eyes I am a dark, destructive nobody.

I want her to know that I was brilliant, too, but that being brilliant isn't enough these days. To succeed today you need to be brightly coloured, noticed, admired, validated by grants and keynote speeches, bestselling books, media appearances and honours. You have to show an impressive face to the world. You have to love the attention, smile for the cameras. You have to be like her.

'I got what I deserved,' I say. 'When my fraudulent *Nature* paper was rescinded, they turned on me: I was dismissed, I lost my professorship, my college privileges and my home almost immediately. I also lost my dignity and my name. For a while the scientific community couldn't talk about anything else. Shame isn't just a word, Olivia, it's a powerful, visceral reaction. It's physical. Even just saying the word out loud makes you feel it, physically, in your guts. The response was positively medieval. I was publicly destroyed – shunned by almost everyone I knew.'

Olivia lifts her chin. 'This won't work on me. I won't feel sorry for you, I never will. I know plenty of older female academics who don't feel the need to falsify research for glory. They just produce spectacular work.'

I have been trying to avoid telling her the full truth about her father but this is just too much for me. 'I did produce spectacu-lar work!' I bellow. 'And your father claimed it was his!'

'Oh, come on. We're talking about his great discovery, I assume?'

'His great discovery was actually *my* great discovery. It was I who first noticed that the speck in the *olivia* fossil wasn't an arte-fact, a contaminant, as your father lazily believed, but a minute fossilized dung ball. My discovery of that dung ball proved that dung-rolling beetles were alive millions of years earlier than we previously thought; my attention to detail led to the game-changing evolutionary paper that made your father's name. I even helped him write it. I fully expected to see my name on it and I remember how shocked I was when it wasn't there. Your father was my mentor, my senior, my superior; perhaps it didn't occur to him to credit me. But without me, your ancient scarab and its dung ball would still be sitting unnoticed in their amber bubble and no one would remember your father's name.'

'This is just not true!' she shouts. 'My God, Vivian! How could you say all this?'

I do stop then, even though I could go on. I could remind her that my story is nothing new. Generations of female scientists have had their ground-breaking discoveries credited to male col-leagues. They have been written out of the textbooks, ignored by Nobel committees, erased from history. I could describe to Olivia how her father spotted my potential as an undergraduate and nurtured and guided me; how he supervised my PhD, then turned me into his acolyte; how for a while I was his faithful helper, there to serve, enable and admire his genius. I could tell her how he turned against me when I was offered the prestigious Oxford college position; how he raged, then accused me of ingratitude and arrogance, of biting the hand that fed me.

I could also tell her that he behaved like this because he was threatened by me. It had taken him decades to secure his reputation, which he only did thanks to me, whereas I, at the age of twenty-four, was being wooed by one of the finest institutions in the world. I had 'the promise of excellence' and his ego could not take that. Ron Sweetman's approach to a threat was attack. I could tell Olivia that her father made a point of dismissing my work in public after that; he humiliated me at conferences, sabotaged my talks, bad-mouthed me to colleagues. He was fixated on destroying my career because he was deeply afraid that one day I would find a way to prove that the discovery of the *Archeocopris olivia* dung ball was mine. I would expose him as the fraud he was.

He was right to be frightened of me. I would have done it, but I couldn't, because I had no proof. Naively, I'd given all the data to him at the time. It had simply never occurred to me that he'd take all the credit. When I heard about his heart attack I was glad he was dead, but I was also disappointed that I would never get the chance to right the wrong he did me.

I could tell her all this about her sainted father, but I don't, I stay silent because I know that telling her would only have two outcomes, neither of them particularly helpful. Either she would refuse to believe me, in which case I would only alienate her further, or she would believe me, and that would destroy her. I have, I realize, lost the desire to destroy Olivia. In fact, I am beginning to feel quite protective of her.

She is wringing her hands. Her lips are edged with pale blue. She is either very angry, or very cold, or both.

'What did you think you'd achieve by hurting me like this?' she croaks. 'You know that if Joy finds out about the diary, she'll have to have *Annabel* pulped? My career will be over, all those people who mutter to each other that I'm "not a serious historian" will have a field day. This will be all over social media and the national papers. This is going to destroy me. I could even lose my professorship. Is that what you really want? Will you feel better when I'm crushed? Will you feel better if you take away everything I've worked my whole life for?'

'It never occurred to me that we'd get to this point,' I say, honestly.

'I can't do this.' She suddenly pushes back her chair, gets up and walks towards the door.

I wasn't expecting this.

I struggle off my seat and pain sears through my knee. I limp after her into the corridor. She hears me behind her and stops, spinning round to face me. I support myself with one hand on the scullery doorframe. She has the look of an untamed animal, smudge-eyed, ready to bare her teeth and bite. She is breathing very rapidly and I see her glance at my hand in case I still have the knife, which, oddly, I do. She is, I realize, furious, but also afraid of me.

'I'm going now.' She lifts her chin. 'I can't stay here. You should just do what you want.'

But she is not the one who gets to decide how this ends. Not this time. 'Really?' I say. 'We haven't discussed our options.'

I know the sort of thoughts that must be racing through her head right now. She wants to run to the gunroom, shove on her boots, flee to her car and drive back up to London and her family. But she also knows that she can't do that. She can't really let me do what I want, because I might want to ruin her.

'Do you know,' I say, resting my shoulder on the doorjamb, taking the weight off my knee, 'all this drama has given me quite an appetite. I don't usually eat supper until seven but I have two lovely fresh wood pigeons in the scullery. An estate manager I know – his father was a colleague of my father's – dropped them over this morning. They're so fresh their eyes are still gleaming. Do you fancy a nice bit of pigeon breast? We could have a bite to eat and talk about what to do next.'

She stares at me, speechless.

I turn and walk towards the kitchen. I am not sure what she'll do, but I do know, from the early days with Bertie, that I must not look as if I care.

After a moment, I hear her socks on the parquet, soft as a puppy, following me back to the kitchen.

Olivia

Ileford Manor

As she watched Vivian's bulky form limp off down the corridor to the kitchen, with the knife still dangling from her hand, it took every particle in Olivia's body not to turn and flee. But she couldn't run away. She had to stay and see this through. She had to contain and control Vivian, once and for all.

She felt as if there was a huge weight sitting on her chest. It was a struggle even to breathe. She was profoundly cold, too. She couldn't stop shaking.

She might, somehow, survive David's betrayal and the collapse of her marriage but she didn't think she could survive if Vivian destroyed her reputation and career too. There were decades of bitterness and resentment inside Vivian waiting to come out. She'd been planning this for years before they even met. This delusion about *Archeocopris olivia* being her great discovery, perhaps it was that, rather than Bertie, that had made her visit the tower with sharp scissors.

She was completely certain, now, that Vivian had attacked

Jess that night. It could only have been Vivian, angry, twisted and tormented by grief, lashing out to hurt her.

Whatever was fuelling this madness – professional bitterness, loneliness, a personality disorder, the childhood trauma – it added up to one thing: Vivian now had power. And Olivia had to stop her from using it.

The claustrophobic fury rose up in her again, layered on top of the fear of what Vivian might do to her. Two urges coexisted inside her, both equally potent: the urge to get away from Vivian, and the need to see this through, to go to the kitchen and scream in Vivian's face, to do whatever it took make this stop once and for all. She imagined what it would feel like to smash her fists into that square, impassive jaw. Or even to grab that knife.

She followed the limping form back to the kitchen without a word. She had no idea what Vivian was planning, but she had no option other than to stay and find out.

Vivian

Ileford Manor

I fetch the pigeons from the scullery shelf. The routine of cooking is oddly calming and despite being unable to rest any weight on my knee I feel a sense of control returning.

I lie the first bird on its back on the chopping board so that its downy chest is exposed. I get out the heavy-bottomed frying pan. I open the fridge, ignoring the smell – I haven't had much energy for cleaning lately – and take out the pat of butter. Out of the corner of my eye I see Olivia enter the kitchen and sit, heavily, at the table. Her body looks very upright and stiff. I cannot imagine what is going through her mind.

I don't want her to suffer, but I know I must be quiet for a while to let her settle. Resting my weight on one leg, I begin to rip feathers from the marshmallow dome of the bird's breast. As I tear upwards, towards its throat, its fragile craw opens and gapes at me like a little red mouth. I can see its last meal, dull coins of corn and oval sunflower seeds filched from a garden bird feeder. The collective noun for pigeons is a 'passel', an indefinite quantity, uncountable, impossible to pin down.

I consider sharing this snippet with Olivia, but then I decide that she might not find an observation about collective nouns very interesting right now.

I take the paring knife from the rack and make a quick incision in the goose-pimpled breast, then I open up its dark, internal blush. I follow the ribcage down, severing sinews until my blade meets a rib. Then I tug out the breast, separating it from the skin, sloughing off the oyster-coloured tendrils of fat. It is all swiftly done. I put the limp carcass aside and do the same to the next bird.

'They're pests, you know,' I say, as I peel and slice a clove of garlic. 'Completely out of control as a species. They do terrible damage to the crops.'

But she is silent. She does not want to make small talk. I hear her swallow as I drop a knob of butter into the pan and switch on the flame, watching the golden dollop melt away. I hope she can get past whatever violent emotions she is trying to control right now and enjoy the meal. I don't just want to feed her, I want her to relish the eating. She needs fattening up too. She is beginning to look scrawny, presumably from the stress and uncertainty.

'Butter, garlic and Middle Farm cider,' I say. 'Wood pigeon used to be Bertie's favourite.' I sprinkle slices of garlic into the bubbling butter, followed by the breasts, one at a time. They sizzle. They smell very good. 'Though of course he always had his raw.'

'Is this somehow about Bertie, Vivian?' Her voice is hoarse.

'No. I do know that was an accident. You did lie about it which

was very wrong and hurtful, but that's in the past now. I'll probably be able to forgive you for it, eventually.'

Her voice is almost a whisper. 'This is just brutal.'

I push the pigeon meat around the fizzing pan, then limp to
the cupboard for the plastic jug of cider. I don't want to be brutal.
In fact, I feel rather the opposite about her, now that she seems
so fragile. The biggest problem is my knee, which is in quite serious pain. Perhaps this makes me sound less tolerant than I feel.

'Brutal is casting someone aside when they no longer serve
your needs,' I say. 'Brutal is refusing to introduce a person to your
friends because they are unattractive and socially embarrassing.'

'What are you talking about? I invited you to the launch! I
practically begged you to come. And you came, didn't you? You
were there?'

I say nothing.

'OK. Are you talking about France then? You would never
have wanted to come up to the house for dinner, would you? You
hate socializing.'

'I'm rather fond of lobster.' I grab a metal spatula and slap the
pigeon steaks. The butter spits, hisses and clicks. I clear my
throat. 'One thing I would say to you is that you should think
carefully about how you treat people who you consider to be
your inferiors.'

She says nothing. She is thinking about this, perhaps, going
back over that moment in France when her small, strawberry-
blonde friend wanted to ask me up and she cut her off and
walked away from me. She is also no doubt trying to work out
what she can say to make me vanish from her life forever. And
she is perhaps trying to control her panic, too, trying to find a
way to bring back the persuasiveness, the spin, the Sweetman
charisma. Only she can't quite manage it.

There are about fifty species of dung beetle in the UK and I can identify thirty of them by their behaviour when threatened. Some attack, some scuttle to safety, others spin in bewildered, panicky circles; some play dead, sticking their legs out as if in rigor mortis; some squeak in fear and others bury themselves deeper into their pile of dung. People aren't so different, really. We all have different ways of coping when under attack. I have not yet worked out what Olivia's method is but I strongly suspect it is the latter.

'I need you to understand something, Vivian.' She sounds tense. 'This is very important. I didn't invite you up to the house in France that day because I was freaked out when you appeared in the village like that. I just couldn't understand what you were doing there. Don't forget I've had a bad experience of being stalked before – you know all about that, of course, but let's not get into that now. The point is, it was very odd of you to appear like that in France. I don't know if you appreciate how disturbing that was for me. I didn't walk away because I felt superior, or embarrassed by you, I walked away because I felt threatened. Rightly, as it turns out.'

I laugh because I was right: she's a digger. I pour cider onto the breasts and watch the golden liquid bubble, fizz and embrace the butter. I can smell the sweetness of apples mixed with the butter musk. I watch it darken and begin to caramelize. The confusing thing about Olivia is that, in with all the spin, there is always a dash of truth. It can be hard to separate the two.

I remember her comment, when we had the argument about integrity, that all historians are storytellers. She is definitely a fabricator. I think she tells herself stories, lies to herself so brilliantly that sometimes she has no idea what the truth is.

She is waiting for me to answer. She hates to feel powerless.

I can't really think of anything to say because she is right, I have observed her in the past, on occasion. I thought she hadn't noticed me. It was important to know who she was in order to be sure that I would produce the right bait. And, I suppose, I was curious. Perhaps I became a little obsessed. She is an interesting person to watch. She has her little routines too, behaviour patterns that are peculiar to her.

'When I got back to England,' she says, slowly, 'I should have come to see you, but I was too upset about Jess's hair.'

'What happened to Jess's hair?'

'What happened? I think you know, Vivian! Someone broke into the tower in the middle of the night and cut it off. They took it.'

I look over my shoulder at her then. She is staring right at me and I catch what I think might be a look of hatred in her eyes before she looks down at her hands again. She is not yet tamed, then.

'Why on earth would someone do that?' I say.

'You tell me, Vivian.'

I feel ill, suddenly. The pigeon fat smells too sweet. My knee radiates nasty pain. I know she will never believe me if I tell her that it certainly was not me who cut the child's hair off. There is no point in protesting my innocence of this nonsensical crime. She has obviously made up her mind that I am the sort of person who would visit a tower with sharp scissors in the middle of the night. This is disappointing, but it can't be helped.

She is picking at the nail polish on her left thumb with the ring finger of the same hand. There is a pale, indented circle in the flesh. I wonder if it has ever occurred to her how like her father David is, an arrogant charmer who thoroughly believes in his own brilliance, despite evidence to the contrary.

But her marriage is not my concern. I turn my attention back to the pigeon breasts. I don't want them to burn.

The hair is certainly shocking: a bizarre thing to happen to a child. I am sure Olivia was very upset about it. It was extremely long hair. Golden and wavy. I can't think of an appropriate comment, so I reach for two plates.

'That night . . .' She really won't let it go. 'You were extremely angry, remember? It was the night I told you about Bertie. It happened that same night.'

I think about our horrible conversation in the Café de Paris. I was more distraught, I think, than angry. Though there was anger, definitely. It is an uncomfortable memory. I would rather not think about it. Not now that I have decided to move on.

Perhaps she thinks that if she forces me to confess to cutting her daughter's hair then she will be able to paint me as a madwoman, a deranged fantasist. She will be able to threaten me with the police, perhaps. Our threats will balance each other out.

I consider telling her that I was, in fact, at the tower that night. I watched the two boys, hers and that other slightly heftier one, just before dawn, stumbling around in the trees and undergrowth, hissing at each other. But of course if I mention this then I will have to enter into a complicated discussion about what I was doing there. Olivia would, I am sure, find it hard to believe that, wakeful and feverish, reeling from the information about Bertie's death, I found myself driving, somewhat blindly, up the hillside. I do not believe that I had malevolent intentions when I parked just below the gates. The whole episode is a little hazy, but I do remember walking up the stony road, through the open gate and into the courtyard. I remember thinking how eerily quiet it was in the pause of the night, the suspended moment just before the birds awake, that tipping point when stars begin to fade.

I was, I suppose, in deep despair; a night wanderer, a lost soul, a shadowy visitor leaning on the ancient olive tree outside that solitary tower. I could tell her that I watched the two boys flit back through its velvet mouth before I limped down to my car. But, of course, I cannot tell her any of this.

She is still staring at me, waiting for me to confess, I suppose, to stealing her child's hair.

'Do you really believe I would do a thing like that?'

'Honestly?' She sounds frustrated. 'Yes, Vivian! After what you've told me today, I think yes, you probably did attack her. You probably did.'

I know that she probably doesn't mean to be so accusatory. I have always found it hard to put myself in other people's shoes, but I can only assume that some kind of maternal feeling is preventing her from blaming her own son. She is wrong about me, though. I am not a violent person. But we must move on from the hair now. The truth would set neither of us free.

I think about Olivia on the podium at her book launch, in her full-skirted yellow silk dress, *Cteniopus sulphureus* teetering on her flower tip, thronged by admirers. The room was packed with cognoscenti, the London literati, all that knowledge and power and pretention focused on one object, her. Now look at her. She is bedraggled and fearful, sitting at my table, stripped of her authority, desperately digging, still looking for a way out. Still furious. She is tough, that's for sure. She is not broken after all. It is going to take a while to win her trust. But I can be very patient.

The pigeon is done. I slide it onto the plates with the spatula. She is shifting around in her seat. She reminds me of a helpless beetle wriggling furiously in a specimen jar. It is alright because I am about to show her that there is a way out. But first I will feed her. Nobody – not even Olivia – can think constructively when hungry.

I pour the caramelized juices over the meat, which is tender and fragrant. I look at the plates, side by side. A pigeon pair. That's what they used to call boy and girl siblings born close together. Not the same, but inseparable, tied together forever.

I grit my teeth and limp to the table with the plates. She doesn't move to help me.

'We've both done regrettable things.' I put the plates down on the table. 'We've both duped and pretended, we've both lied, but I don't think we're bad people, do you? Neither of us is cruel or evil.' I ease myself onto the chair opposite her and stick out my leg. 'So I'd say it's time to move on, wouldn't you?'

She peers at me through narrowed eyes. 'What do you mean?'

'I have no intention of talking to Joy or Carol or anyone else about the diary.'

'Really? You don't?' She sounds breathless.

'All history is storytelling, Olivia, you said that yourself. The spirit in which *Annabel* was written is what matters. What was it you said? "It's perfectly possible to lie with integrity." Well, I think the intention behind the book is honourable. Women like Annabel need to be remembered. They paved the way for every female doctor practising today and for female scientists too. I wouldn't have had my career were it not for the women like Annabel, who shoved aside their embroidery and picked up science books. We should all be reminded of that, shouldn't we? In a way, the existence of an actual diary isn't the point, is it? You yourself said that readers accept invention. They want colour. They want something to pin their imagination to.'

She is staring at me. I can see that she is breathing fast.

'The essence of our story is true,' I continue. 'Annabel was real, she really did live here in Ileford a hundred years ago and she really was one of the first women to go to medical school in England. Whether or not she pushed her husband off the minstrel's gallery is neither here nor there. There's no evidence that she did, of course, the death certificate records it as accidental, and contemporary sources confirm that he was a drunkard. But, equally, there's no evidence that she didn't. I rather like the idea that she shoved him, don't you? After all, she had everything to gain. With Burley gone, she was free to use his money however she wished and the facts do speak for themselves: she enrolled at medical school almost the moment he died. Historians and scientists actually have a lot in common, when you think about it. We both make imaginative leaps and inspired guesses from time to time. And what was it you said about historians and the truth? "We have to invent the stories that get us there." So, yes, Olivia, I think we should put all this behind us once and for all. Don't you?'

The relief on her face is almost comical. 'Yes.' She nods, vigorously. 'God, Vivian. Yes.'

'Good.'

I realize then that I should have made peas to go with the meat. The two plum-coloured breasts sitting on each plate look small and stark without peas. The sight of them brings a wave of anxiety. They just look wrong. I look up at her, but she doesn't seem to notice my distress. She has splayed her hands on the table, as if supporting her torso. 'I should have done peas. I always do peas.'

'No, no,' she says. 'It's fine like this.' She is lying. Everyone knows there must be peas with pigeon.

'I have a packet of frozen peas in the freezer.'

'Really, Vivian. There's no need. Please – your knee. We really don't need peas.'

'I always have peas with pigeon.'

'It's OK this time. It really is. No peas is fine. Special circumstances.' She even tries to smile.

I think about this. 'Cutlery!' I shout. Her shoulders jerk. I get up again and hop across the kitchen to find knives and forks.

She takes the cutlery from me and I watch, keenly, as she slices into the first pigeon breast. I tell myself that I must not worry any more about the peas. I must not obsess about it. I am probably a little overwrought. I have to let the peas go.

Pink and caramel juices ooze from the breast onto the plate. I wait for her to pop a piece into her mouth, but she just pushes it around. Her eyes bulge. I can see a little vein pulsing between her brows. She is still thinking this through, looking for the catch.

She is also, perhaps, recognizing that I have won. My hypothesis was correct. By agreeing with me about *Annabel* she has just proved it. I don't blame her. I would – did – do the same myself.

I pick up my own knife and fork and slice into the flesh in order to encourage her to eat. I am beginning to feel slightly less agitated. Special circumstances indeed.

I swallow the meat. 'After we've eaten, perhaps you could go up to the study for me and bring down the Chocolate Cream Poisoner file?'

She stops playing with her food. 'What?'

'The preliminary research I've done. I mentioned it to you in France. The Venus of Broadmoor? Christiana Edmunds? Obviously France wasn't the right time to talk about it but now that everything's settled and *Annabel's* such a hit, it's surely time start our next book.'

She gulps. Perhaps a piece of pigeon is stuck in her throat, though I didn't see her put anything into her mouth. She puts a hand to her neck.

I get up and hobble to the sink to get her a glass of water, trying to ignore the pain in my knee. 'I'm assuming Joy wants a follow-up as fast as possible, to capitalize on the success of *Annabel*,' I say as I turn the tap on. 'Number two on the bestseller chart in its first week. That's very good indeed, isn't it? I expect people are already asking about your next book?'

She is still struggling. Her eyes have gone watery, her cheeks very red. I wonder if I should hop across the kitchen and slap her between the shoulder blades. I try not to spill any water as I come back to the table, but it sloshes on the floor. I don't look at the plates. It is too late to think about peas.

She grabs the glass from me and gulps at it, staring at me over the rim.

I sit down, sticking my leg out, and pick up my knife and fork again. 'When we've finished eating, I'll make a pot of coffee and we can take it to the library. Are you still very cold? It is cold in here, isn't it? I think the heating's on the blink but I can try to fix it. I can always light a fire in the library too. We can take our coffee in there and put our heads together about the Chocolate Cream Poisoner.' I look up at a spot on the wall just above her head, a little stain. 'It'll be quite cosy in there.'

I can feel that her eyes are fixed on my face.

'Of course, if you're too tired to talk about it tonight you could always stay over – there's plenty of room, as you know. You could sleep in Lady Burley's room. You must be exhausted after the party last night. I know things have been difficult for you lately at home too . . .' I nod at her ring finger. 'But you can stay as long as you like. You could have a nice rest here.' I do look at her then. Her eyelids flutter. 'Eat up now.' I point at her half-eaten pigeon breast. 'You've lost weight. It's important to eat.'

Slowly, she lifts a morsel to her lips. Her eyes are still fixed, blackly, on me. I look down at my empty plate. 'There.' I nod, encouragingly. 'That's right. Good girl. Eat up. '

She stares back at me. She doesn't put the pigeon piece into her mouth.

Olivia

Ileford Manor

There was no way Olivia could stomach anything that Vivian had cooked. Even if she'd wanted to force it down she would have choked. Vivian hauled herself up and limped to the sink carrying the plates. Olivia watched her but did not move. It was bitterly cold in the room. She felt sick. Her head hurt. Everything hurt.

She watched Vivian's cropped, grey-flecked head bend over the washing-up basin, watched as she tipped the uneaten pigeon into the compost bin and washed, rinsed and stacked each plate on the drainer, then the knives and then the forks. She refilled the basin with clean, soapy water and washed the glasses separately, rinsing each one methodically under the tap. Then she wiped her hands on the royal wedding tea towel and turned around.

'It really is terribly cold in here.' Vivian's voice was deep and too loud. 'Why don't you make the coffee while I go down and see to the heating? The boiler's old and rather temperamental, but I can generally fix it myself. The real coffee's in the blue china pot above the kettle and there's one of those cafetière things on the shelf above it. I won't be a moment.'

Olivia nodded, but didn't move.

Vivian limped past her and out of the kitchen.

For a moment or two she just stared at the empty space by the sink where Vivian had been. This was her future. If she ever tried to get away, Vivian would expose her and take her down. She had the power to ruin what was left of her life. And she knew that dogged, fixated mind so well. This was it, forever. Vivian would never let her go.

She didn't go and turn the kettle on. The pressure inside her head felt overwhelming. After a minute or two she got up and went into the corridor. The air was icy. She could hear the wind bumping against the windows in the great hall. The door down to the cellars where Uncle Quentin once kept a savage bear was open. She could hear Vivian's uneven step coming back along the stone floor down below.

She peered down the steep concrete stairs. There was a banister on one side only, a sheer drop to flagstones on the other. The colourless strip lights flickered. She could make out vaulted ceilings. This would have been where the kitchens were originally, stretching along the bowels of the house. She could smell cloying dampness, a sinister, neglected stench. The top of Vivian's head came into view. The overhead light picked out each coarse, cropped, silvery strand.

Vivian looked up, startled. 'Oh, Olivia, there you are! Good news. I think I've fixed it. It works most of the time, but I must get a heating engineer out. Did you make the coffee already?'

Olivia said nothing. She could not speak.

Vivian grasped the banister with her left hand and began to

climb the steps. Her knee was clearly badly damaged. She had to swing her whole leg sideways from the hip onto each step because she couldn't bend it. This lurching made her very unstable. Olivia stood motionless at the top of the stairs, watching her.

Vivian was almost at the top now; just a few more steps and they would be level again. Her square face still had a confused look – her eyes were bright and anxious. 'Olivia?' she said. 'What's the matter? Is everything all right?'

Everything went very quiet and still inside Olivia's head.

Vivian's foot slipped as it swung up to the next step – perhaps her slipper caught the edge – and her free arm flew up in an attempt to rebalance her body. Her hand grasped at the air and for a second it was right there, right in front of Olivia's nose, patting at the space between them, desperately looking for something to hold on to, some kind of help as the hand on the banister started to slip. Olivia stepped forwards. She felt Vivian's rough wool cardigan under her fingertips and then there was a sort of chaotic toppling as Vivian's body went sideways, her free arm swung and her other hand was ripped off the banister. That, too, briefly opened and closed in front of Olivia's face, clasping at air.

The noise Vivian's body made as she hit the flagstones was surprisingly muted. Her head bounced off them a few times and then went still.

Perhaps it was the padding of her cardigan and slacks, or perhaps Olivia's senses were so detached that she couldn't absorb sounds, couldn't process the reality of this dense object hitting a stone floor.

After what could have been moments or minutes she walked down the stairs to where Vivian was lying. Her body looked all wrong.

Olivia's legs were shaking so much that she couldn't hold herself up. She fell to her knees by Vivian's head. The small round eyes stared up at the ceiling. One sclera held a little blood-shot map, the other a pool, perhaps a tear. There was a mess beneath her head, too, something sticky and oozing, and an odd, sickening, ferrous smell.

'Vivian?' Her voice echoed off the vaulted cellar ceilings. 'Vivian, can you hear me?' She bent down so that her face was right next to Vivian's mouth. 'Vivian!' She waited to feel a breath on her cheek. But there was no breath.

Olivia

Ileford Manor

Olivia sat at the kitchen table. Her hands were still trembling but she couldn't feel them. It was as if they belonged to someone else. Her body felt entirely numb. She'd tried to tell the detective sergeant everything in as logical a way as possible. She wondered if her self-control might seem odd. She thought perhaps it would be better if she cried. But she couldn't seem to summon any tears.

The two detectives sat side by side, opposite her, at the kitchen table. The younger man, the detective constable, maintained a pleasant and non-committal look, while the more senior officer, a woman about her own age with prominent eye-bags and a faint Birmingham accent, asked the same questions that the uniformed officer had asked just a few minutes before. She wasn't sure why she had to repeat things. Maybe they always did this, checking answers off against each other. But she couldn't sit here and answer repetitive questions all night. She needed to leave Ileford. She had to get out of this house and never come back.

They were both friendly, clearly trying to reassure her or calm her down. The detective sergeant said she recognized Olivia from the TV. She'd seen her on *Would I Lie to You?* and heard her on the radio. It felt ludicrous to be making small talk at a time like this, but Olivia assumed that she was only trying to get her past the horror of what had just happened.

The constable didn't look much older than Dom. Poor Dom. She had to talk to Dom. She couldn't just sit here. She needed to get back to London to the children. David wouldn't have told them what he'd done. She needed to be there for them. And she needed to look David in the eye and tell him that their marriage was over. Everything was such a mess. She shouldn't be here, she should be there, with the children. She felt tears coming. Then she started shaking.

'It's OK, it's a shock, here . . .' The more senior detective pushed a packet of tissues across the table and the constable asked if he could get her another blanket. She shook her head.

She didn't even know why the detectives were here. The ambulance had been the first to arrive, lights flashing on the driveway, and two paramedics had rushed down to Vivian and started doing things to her body – she hadn't watched – and then she'd heard another car in the driveway. Two uniformed patrol officers came through the open front door, giants in bulky black stab vests with radios crackling at their shoulders. One had gone straight down to the basement, where the paramedics were still doing things, while the other had asked her name, what had happened and whether there was anyone else in the house.

She'd tried to explain to him about Vivian's knee, that she slipped and fell. As she was talking she'd heard a paramedic at the bottom of the cellar steps say, 'Life extinct 6.23 p.m.' That word, extinct, felt brutal. She'd heard herself let out an odd, strangled noise. The police officer asked, then, if she'd moved

Vivian at all – she said no – and then another car drew up outside the house and moments later this detective sergeant and her constable had come through the front door.

She didn't know whether all this was normal procedure. Maybe this many people always arrived after a 999 call if someone died. The paramedic had said to the detectives, 'The main injury's a head trauma.'

She wondered if she'd heard a note of suspicion in his tone, a question mark in there somewhere. She wasn't sure. Perhaps she'd somehow given the ambulance dispatcher the sense that this was something other than an accident. When the voice on the other end of the line had asked what happened, Olivia remembered a stabbing guilt, a paralysis, when she had been unable to answer. Eventually she said, 'My friend slipped and she's not moving. I think she's not breathing. She has a bad knee – she couldn't bend her leg and she just . . . she fell.' She wondered whether that pause was why the dispatcher became suspicious and sent not just an ambulance, but a patrol car, and then two detectives.

'So . . .' The detective sergeant looked down at her notebook. 'Miss Tester, Vivian, she was your friend?'

Olivia tried to think. 'No. Not really. It was a professional relationship. She'd been – we'd – she'd given me some background materials when I was writing my book. My subject, Annabel Burley, lived in this house. Annabel's diary – the Victorian diary that my book is based on – was found here, among the Burley family papers.' She swallowed again. She felt as if there was something lodged in her throat.

'I see. So Vivian gave you permission to write about Annabel's diary?'

'Yes. Well, she got permission from Lady Burley for me to study it and other Burley family archive materials.'

'And you said Lady Burley's in a care home?'

Olivia nodded. 'Three Elms House.' She gave the name of the village but the detectives didn't write it down, they obviously knew where it was.

'All right, Professor Sweetman, if you can bear with me, I know this is hard, but I just want to be really clear about what happened tonight. You said the two of you went for a walk in the woods and then Vivian cooked you pigeon breasts at about . . .' She glanced at her notes. 'Five thirty – which you both ate – and then she went down to fix the central heating and she fell coming back up?'

'Yes. She had a bad knee. She twisted it, I think, when we went for our walk, she stumbled in the woods, she was limping a lot, but it had been stiff for a while, I think. I think she probably needed a knee replacement . . . I went to see if she needed help and I heard her falling as . . . as she came back up the cellar steps.'

'You heard her fall? A moment ago you said you saw her fall. Did you see or hear the fall?'

'I don't know.' Olivia felt tears coming again. 'Both? I think. I'm sorry.' She wiped her eyes with the heels of her hands and swallowed. 'I just . . . It's quite hard to take in. I can't believe this has happened.'

'I know. You just take your time, you're doing really well. A shock like this is hard to handle. Now, did you actually see her fall?'

'I don't know, I sort of did. It's difficult to . . . the lighting isn't great. She'd asked me to make the coffee and I was just coming to the top of the stairs as she was coming up. She slipped – her foot definitely slipped – and she sort of fell sideways and backwards.'

'So you did see her foot slip?'

'Yes, maybe, but it all happened incredibly fast. I . . . I think I reached out for her . . .' She felt her throat constrict. She took a deep breath. 'I'm sorry. I'm not being very clear, am I?'

'Don't worry. You're doing just fine.' The detective nodded and wrote something down.

'So you didn't go down to help her with the boiler?' the constable asked.

'Well, no. I was making the coffee. She asked me to make coffee. I didn't know the basement steps were so dangerous. She's never shown me the basement steps. I haven't been in this house very much. I . . . We had a professional relationship. She was a very private person.'

The senior detective nodded and handed her another tissue.

She wiped under her eyes, leaving black smears on it. She knew she must look a mess. 'I was just popping in today to thank her really. It was my book launch party last night. I'm sorry. I'm really tired, I'm a bit . . .'

Olivia suddenly couldn't stop crying. She felt snot pouring out of her nose and heard herself making strangulated noises.

'It's all right.' The detective sergeant sounded quite maternal. 'You have a good cry. Take your time now. It's OK. No rush. Let's get you a cup of tea.' She looked at the constable. After a beat, he got up and went over to the kettle.

Olivia wiped at her eyes and nose again. 'I should have gone down to fix the boiler myself.'

'Do you know how to fix the heating in this house?'

'No.'

'Well then.'

'But I should have gone with her at least, you're right, she was limping quite badly.'

The woman glanced around the kitchen. Her eyes rested on the wall calendar for a moment. 'Why is Lady Burley in a home?'

'She's elderly and she has cancer, maybe dementia too, I'm not sure. This will be awful for her . . . Oh God. She's very fond of Vivian.'

'Don't worry. We'll go and see her next. You have a house near here, you said?'

Olivia wiped her nose and eyes and shook her head. 'Yes, but I live in London. I need to go home now, back to London. I need to see my children.'

The detective nodded. 'Of course you do. We'll just need you to come in and make a statement though.'

'A statement?' She looked from one detective to the other.

'It's just routine,' the young man said, plugging the kettle in. Olivia nodded.

'It might not be a good idea to drive yourself, you've had quite a shock,' the senior detective said. 'Is there anyone you want with you?'

She couldn't think of anyone who could come down from London. Clearly not David. And Chloe was away today, it was her mother's birthday. She thought of Emma. Her anxious, panicky response to this wouldn't be good, but her legal expertise might be reassuring. 'Maybe I could call my friend . . .'

'Yes, good idea. Go ahead.'

Olivia pulled out her mobile, ignoring the missed calls from David, and called Emma's number. Emma didn't pick up. She left a message and then tried Khalil, but he didn't pick up either.

'Not in?'

She shook her head. She couldn't think of anyone else she could ask to drive all the way down to Sussex to get her. She could probably try Joy or Carol but she wouldn't want either of them to see her like this. She straightened her spine. 'Honestly, I'll be fine in a minute, I really will. I just need to get back to London as soon as . . . as this is . . . My children are there and I really need to get back to them.'

'Is your husband around?'

'Yes, he's there – he's with them now, but he has to go away.'

She saw the detective glance at her ring finger.

'I really need to get back to London.'

'Of course you do. But don't worry about your children. If your husband has to go, then we can arrange for someone to go to your house in London and look after them while you come with us.' Her voice was reassuring but there was a hint of rigidity behind her words. Olivia felt as if invisible doors were slamming shut around her.

She needed to get away from this table, from these two detectives and their intent eyes. 'Do you mind if I just . . . I need to go to the loo,' she said.

'Of course,' they said, in unison.

She got up, unsteadily, and walked out of the kitchen. She could feel them both there, watching her. As she turned into the corridor she heard the younger detective say something in a low voice, though she couldn't hear what. She paused in the hallway, pressed her back against the wall, and listened. The female detective said, 'There's no sign of anyone making coffee in here, is there? You know, I've got a funny feeling about this one. That's not just shock. Something's definitely off. I'm going to call in the circus. I'll go and have a word with the paramedics, then take a quick look around. You stay here with her. Make her drink that tea, we don't want her collapsing on us.'

Olivia hurried into the scullery loo, her socks slipping on the cold flagstones. She bolted the door. She was shaking again, despite the blanket round her shoulders. She didn't know why she'd told them she was making coffee when she wasn't. She'd just said it because she didn't want them to think badly of her for letting Vivian go down to the cellars alone. And it was true that Vivian had asked her to make coffee. But if she went back in and said something about misremembering, and not having actually made the coffee, then all this would start to sound suspicious. She had to leave it. She didn't know what the detective meant by the 'circus', but presumably it meant more people.

She thought of Vivian lying down there in the basement, with her sticky skull, strangers prodding her and the two immense patrol officers staring down the basement steps. She felt tears pressing against her eyes. Poor Vivian. She wanted to go home. She sat on the loo even though she didn't need to go. Her teeth were chattering. She felt as if she was sitting in a bath of ice.

After a while, she flushed and went back to the kitchen, holding the blanket tight around her body. The young constable was standing by the table. The detective sergeant had gone.

'My D.S. says I need to get you to drink the tea.' He gave her a kind smile, 'And eat a few biscuits if you can manage it. You've had a pretty big shock.' His voice was deep, surprisingly firm and quite posh. She wondered if he might be a keen graduate trainee, older and smarter than he looked.

She sat down, picked up the mug and sipped the lukewarm liquid. It tasted disgustingly sweet and strong. She put the mug down again. 'Look, I wonder if I might be able to come in later and do the statement. I really need to see my children.'

She noticed then that it was the pheasant mug, Vivian's favourite. Vivian would hate her to be drinking from it. Her eyes filled with tears again. It was inconceivable that Vivian was gone.

'It's best to just come in and do it now, while it's all fresh in your mind.' The young detective watched her closely as he spoke. 'It shouldn't take too long.' He'd emptied Vivian's tin of digestives onto a dinner plate and put it on the table. The sweet smell of them, and the tea, made her feel sick again. She tried to breathe. She pressed her back against the radiator, which was warming up now. This was going to be OK. This was just normal police procedure.

She hadn't done anything wrong. Had she?

She wasn't sure exactly what had happened, not really. It was all a bit of a blur. She remembered stepping towards Vivian and the feel of rough wool, Vivian's cardigan, beneath her fingertips – and the broad, open hand patting the air between them. But Vivian was already slipping then, wasn't she, because her foot caught on the step? She'd surely reached out to stop her from falling and that's when she'd touched the cardigan.

It all felt so confusing, so tangled and surreal. The difference between pushing and pulling was fractional, a sliver of grey. She couldn't really think about what had happened.

It didn't matter. It was over now – for both of them. Vivian couldn't do or say anything to harm her any more. An autopsy would reveal her poor, twisted, damaged knee. The stairs were definitely perilous down to the cellar – anyone could see that. There was only a rail on one side. The heating system would prove faulty. This was dreadful, a truly dreadful accident, but there was no reason for the police to believe that it was anything other than that, a tragic, unfortunate accident.

She was going to have to be clear with them. She must talk about Vivian's knee and nothing else. She must allow no glimmer of ambiguity, no shiver of doubt to enter her voice because she could feel them waiting for that. No matter how understanding they seemed, they were not on her side. It was their job to pretend.

If they tried to pin the blame on her she could go to prison.

She felt a cold wave of sickness roll through her body. What would happen to the children? But they couldn't arrest her, surely. Not without evidence. They had nothing. They would never be able to prove that she had pushed Vivian.

She needed to calm down. There would be no reason for the police to suspect anything untoward. There was very little to link the two of them. Nobody else knew the true extent of Vivian's involvement in *Annabel*. She'd never admitted the truth about Vivian's role to Joy or Carol, and even David didn't know how much Vivian had contributed. Her name wasn't in the acknowledgements pages. There was no trace of her on the book. Nobody would ever find out what Vivian had done.

She squeezed her eyes shut and felt the room spin. She wondered if she might actually be sick.

'Are you OK? You're not going to faint, are you?' the young detective said, suddenly close and concerned. 'Here, put your head down if you feel faint.'

She opened her eyes and tried to smile up at him. He had nice brown eyes. 'No,' she said. 'I don't think so. I'm just really, really tired . . .'

Before he could answer she heard footsteps in the corridor and the female detective came back into the kitchen holding a white notebook. She was still smiling, but there was something else behind her eyes, something more shrewd and perhaps less accommodating.

'I was just having a quick look around and I found this.' She laid it on the table. The cover was pale and plain, with a brown border and the image of a glorious green beetle, jewelled and iridescent, right in the middle, a gold pin stuck through its body. Olivia had never seen this notebook before but she knew immediately whose it was.

'I've had a quick flick through.' The detective's Birmingham accent seemed stronger than before. 'It's a bit confusing, to be honest, so I thought I'd bring it through for you to have a little look. Maybe you've seen this before?'

'What is it?' Olivia didn't touch it. She felt as if there was a dangerous dog breathing inches from her and that if she moved, spoke, gave anything away, it would snap and savage her.

'Well, I don't know. It seems to be a diary of sorts – or maybe some kind of confession?' The detective sat down next to Olivia and she caught a sweet whiff of perfume. Her mouth felt very dry.

'It seems to be mainly about you, Professor Sweetman. It's actually quite intense. Something about . . .' The detective flicked the pages to and fro. 'An amber fossil? Your father, Ron Sweetman? Some kind of scientific hoax? Or a personal betrayal? And someone called Bertie, who died. There seems to be a lot about Bertie. Does any of this make any sense to you, Professor?'

Olivia felt a cold, sharp pain in the middle of her chest as if something metallic was lodged in there. It was difficult to breathe.

The detective read out a line. '"*Olivia is a cryptic species.*"'

'Bertie was a dog. Vivian's dog.' Olivia picked up her mug and looked at the tea. She couldn't bring herself to drink it, but she pretended to, anyway.

'A dog?'

She put the pheasant mug back down on the table. 'Yes. He sadly died a few months ago. She was upset about that, I think.'

'She certainly sounds upset. But the things she's saying here, she sounds as if she was more than a colleague, would that be right? More like a friend?' She laid the notebook, open at its first page, in front of Olivia. 'It all sounds a bit complicated, to be honest.'

Olivia stared down at it. She recognized Vivian's orderly grammar school cursive. She scanned the first page. It was crammed with words.

I have taken to writing things down . . . I need to make sense of how I come to be in this uncertain position. Writing things down seems to ease the chaos in my mind a little . . . I cannot just sit here and wait for her. Not again.

She reached out, slowly, and turned the page. She saw her own name, over and over. Surely – surely – Vivian hadn't written everything down. Surely she hadn't produced some sort of confession.

The cold, sharp feeling in her chest intensified.

It didn't matter what this book contained because Vivian wasn't here to defend it. She had to be very careful now. She had to make them believe that she was just an acquaintance of Vivian's, a work colleague who'd popped in to say thank you and share a quick bite to eat. Nothing more. She had to make it clear that this notebook contained nothing but the rantings of an unhinged and lonely housekeeper.

She made herself look up, then, into the detective's pale grey eyes. She forced herself not to falter or look away. She shook her head. 'I'm really sorry, but I have no idea what this is.'

She looked from one detective to the other and gave what she hoped was a rueful shrug. 'The thing is, people do get obsessed with you sometimes when you're on TV. They pursue you and write to you, they latch on and project all sorts of things onto you. It can be quite odd – in fact, really unsettling at times. I've actually been stalked in the past.'

The female detective smiled steadily across the table at her without blinking. Then her mobile phone began to vibrate. She got up, held up a finger, and moved towards the kitchen door. 'Ma'am,' she said, in a low voice as she stepped out into the corridor, 'that's right, yes. I think we do have enough to . . . Yes . . . I'm bringing her in right now.'

Olivia took a breath and looked into the young male detective's eyes. She tried to smile, though she could feel the panic rising inside her. She heard a uniformed officer's radio crackle. One of them must be standing right outside the kitchen door now. 'Listen, I don't know what's in this notebook, but to answer your first question, we were definitely never friends.'

'Never?' The young man raised his eyebrows.

'Definitely not. Never. No.' Olivia shook her head. 'I hardly knew her.'

She realized, then, that they would find Vivian's papers. They would see all the work she'd done, the months of meticulous, painstaking research. 'I mean . . . We worked together. She was . . . sort of . . . my research assistant. My helper.'

'Your *helper*?' The female detective stepped back into the room. Something about her posture had changed. She looked larger. Her face was still neutral, but her grey eyes seemed flinty as she walked towards the table. Behind her, the shadow of a uniformed officer blocked the doorway.

'Yes. Kind of. But honestly . . .' Olivia gazed up at her. 'You have to believe me. I hardly knew Vivian Tester.'

ACKNOWLEDGEMENTS

My deepest thanks to Professor Helen Roy for your beetle expertise, patience and kindness, and also to Dr Suzannah Lipscomb, Keith Skinner, Darren Mann of Oxford University Museum of Natural History, Dr Sarah Beynon and Professor Naomi Chayen. Without your generous help I could not have begun to write about history professors, TV presenters, Victorian diaries, female scientists or beetles. Thank you to my brother, Paul Atkins, for all the Sussex nature tips. Thank you also to Hannah Beckerman, Liz Woolley, Helen Parker, Miranda Charlton, Madeleine MacPhail, Noelle Buchan, Mark Butcher, Lucy Billen and Fi Jamieson-Folland for your time, honesty, ideas and insights. Stef Bierwerth, without your superb editing and support I don't know where I'd be. Also Jon Butler, Cassie Brown, Kathryn Taussig, Hannah Robinson, Bethan Ferguson, Rachel Neely, Julie Fergusson and all the Quercus team, I know how fortunate I am to have you fighting my corner. And of course, thank you, Judith Murray, none of this would have happened without you. Finally, thank you, Izzie Shaw, for your keen editorial eye; my mum, Sue Atkins, for answering all my grammatical queries; John who read this too many times to count and Sam and Ted who put up with me always being in the shed. As Olivia says at her book launch: 'You're my world'.

Note:
Unlikely as it may sound, I fell in love with dung beetles whilst writing this novel. For those who share my curiosity, this is a great place to start: www.drbeynonsbugfarm.com